D1800079

The Liberty Bell Files:
J. Edgar's Demons

Also from John D. Beatty
Fiction
Sergeant's Business and Other Stories
Crop Duster: A Novel of World War II

The Stella's Game Trilogy
Stella's Game: A Story of Friendships
Tideline: Friendship Abides
The Safe Tree: Friendship Triumphs

Non-Fiction
The Devil's Own Day: Shiloh and the American Civil War
Why the Samurai Lost Japan: A Study in Miscalculation and Folly (with Lee Rochwerger)

A Sun Tzu Companion

The Liberty Bell Files:
J. Edgar's Demons

John D. Beatty

•JDB• COMMUNICATIONS,•LLC•

West Allis, Wisconsin

Copyright © 2021 by John D. Beatty and
JDB Communications, LLC
All rights reserved, including the right to reproduce this book or any portion thereof in any
form or by any means, electronic or mechanical, including photocopying, recording, or by any
information retrieval system without permission in writing from the publisher. All inquiries
should be directed to JDB Communications, LLC at jdbcom@gmail.com.

First Paperback Edition ISBN 978-1-7347952-6-4
First E-Book Edition ISBN 978-1-7347952-7-1

Love the One You're With
Lyrics and performance by Steven Stills
Copyright © 1971 Atlantic Records

The Sun is Burning
Lyrics by Ian Campbell
Performance by Simon and Garfunkel
Copyright © 1964 Columbia Records

Out in the Country
Lyrics by Paul Williams and Roger Nichols
Performance by Three Dog Night
Copyright © 1969 ABC/Dunhill

And When I Die
Lyrics by Laura Nyro
Performance by Blood, Sweat, and Tears
Copyright © 1968 Columbia Records

I Came for You
Lyrics by Bruce Springsteen
Performance by Manfred Mann's Earth Band
Copyright © 1980 Warner Brothers

For Julie,

My first date...

Foreword

Or, What This Book Is NOT About

There's a saying in the Bureau: If you're gonna write a memoir, make sure it's *not* about anything *real*.

Why anyone says *that*…I dunno. So, I wrote *this* book.

After retirement, my wife convinced me that parts of my 30-year FBI career are *interesting*…and she wanted me out from underfoot.

Truth be told, I didn't need much encouragement. I figured that *someone* really *should* write about the Special Projects Division and the Liberty Bell Files that we worked on there….

But, of course, there *is* no such thing; there never *was*. There *can't* be a law enforcement entity like it, not in the United States. *Don't* start looking for it; you *won't* find it. Law enforcement the world over will deny it exists. I was never *in* such a thing.

And Liberty Bell Files? *What* a crock. Who would ever *imagine* such things with a hokey name like *that*? *Who's* kidding *who* here? There *can't* be a collection of such files. That would be illegal, a violation of a *basketful* of federal statutes, the Constitution, the Declaration of Independence, and even the Articles of Confederation, the Boy Scout Oath, *and* the Prime Directive.

I made both the Division *and* the Files up whole cloth.

So *help* me *Hanna*…

How We Got Together

Or, Building A Team From Scratch

The note slipped under my door read:

Report to Room 12B in Building 62 at 1800 hours. Tell no one.

Huh, I thought; *more bullshit of the cloak-and-dagger variety.* But what else was I to do?

So, I *went*…and my life changed utterly.

I arrived two minutes early—5:58 PM. I did *not* expect to see two of my classmates—Julia Parkinson and Ellen Drew—in the basement corridor outside 12B. But there we *were* that early May evening; three soon-to-be graduates from the first FBI Academy class of 1980.

"Should we *knock*," Ellen (nicknamed *Nancy*, of course) asked, hand poised. Ellen usually wore business attire with shoulder pads that hid a pretty figure (but *nothing* like the girl-detective) when not in uniform. She had permed brown hair that barely moved and blue-green eyes that *seemed* dull. So did *Ellen*, for that matter, seem dull. She had evinced no sense of humor at *all* in the weeks we'd trained together.

"Well," I said, "they said to *report*. To me, *that* means…."

Julia pushed the door open. Room 12B was just a 10x10 room with better-than-average GSA furniture along the walls and a little table in a corner with a warm coffee pot (so someone *had* been there). A small refrigerator sat in another corner. Windows high on the wall let in diffused sunlight to add to the fluorescent lights in the acoustic ceiling.

But, there was no one to report *to* when Ellen checked her watch. "1801," she sighed.

"A *joke*," Julia grinned. She had an *infectious* grin, blue eyes, titian hair, and *always gorgeous* figure. She and Ellen were the only women in our class.

"A *test*," I mused, "to see if we *follow* orders...."

"You don't think the past seventeen weeks have shown *that*," Ellen snapped. "No: *this* is something else."

Did I *say* that Ellen lacked a sense of humor?

At that moment, a woman and a *very* big man we'd never seen before came through the door. "You're *early*," the man frowned. He was about six-eight, with a ruddy complexion, enormous hands, and teeth like bathroom tiles.

"No," Ellen declared, "*we* were here at 1757."

She *also* had a tendency to do *that*.

"No matter," the woman said. She looked like a grade-school teacher: prim and proper and about five-five. "We're all here now. Please, be seated." We sat on separate chairs—the three of us on one side and the two of them on the other. Each chair was a different shade of green or yellow—the General Services Administration's color palate is as limited in their choice of materials. Nearly all GSA cushioned chairs are Naugahyde, chosen for their *lack* of durability and the fact that, unlike cows, Naugas shed their skin with factory-like regularity.

"I'm Gwen Forsman, Deputy Director for Personnel," the woman said. "*I* decide *where* you go after graduation." This week, we would be told where our first assignments *would be*, so we were on tenterhooks, *vibrating* with anticipation...

"Senior Special Agent* Ernest Packard," the man declared, "Special Projects Division.** *You* have been *selected* to work for *me*."

And we were *stunned*.

---

* Abbreviated SSA.
** Abbreviated SPD.

Ellen frowned. "Special Projects?" She was an FBI Brat—born to it like a military brat—so *she knew* the Bureau. We got classes on FBI organization during Week 1 at the Academy. That Friday, the instructor said... "*And* there's the Special Projects Division. *Mandatory* tour of the Smithsonian tomorrow; bus leaves at 0900 from the front of the building. *Be* there..."

"What does the Special Projects Division *do*," Julia asked.

"I can only tell you *that after* you change your Desired Assignments Form," Ernest said.

"*I* wanted New York," Ellen said, rather loudly, "and I was given to *understand* that I could *choose* my detail because of *my* class ranking."

"That's *true*," Gwen smiled, "but the requirements of the Bureau are such that you are being *asked* to *change* your Desired Assignments."

If *you* were among the top 5% in the class, *you* got the *first* of the three postings/details you *selected* on what's called the *Desired Assignments Form* known as *Your Dream Sheet*. Like most dreams, *they don't* often come true.

"*I'd* wanted Detroit," Julia declared, "and as the *top* graduate, I believe...."

"Once *again*," Gwen smiled, "we are *requesting* that you *change* that."

"And me," I asked meekly. "I'm nowhere near *their* rankings." I had no illusions about *my* (lack of) class standing. I *expected* to be sent wherever they needed me.

"*You'd* come to me regardless," Ernest said.

"But *why* are Julia and Ellen..." Julia and Ellen were Numbers One and Two in the class: they posted the class rankings every week

"Be*cause*," Gwen sighed, *not* unlike a frustrated mom.

"Well," Ellen declared, "I *wanted* New York and New York I *shall*...."

"*Not* get," Gwen interrupted. "*Choose* Special Projects, or you'll *get* Anchorage or Omaha." For weeks our instructors had been telling us, *screw this up, and you'll spend your career in Anchorage–or–yep, it's Omaha for you*—both said to be the depths of FBI Hell.

"So *changing* preferences for *us* is...." Julia pursed her lips.

"Still *optional*, but," Ernest said, "SPD, Anchorage, or Omaha. If it *helps*, I *got to* Special Projects *from* Omaha. I arrested Salvatore Guarani there in 1964."

"*You*," I said, rather loudly. "We *saw* that movie on you and Sal the Snake...Number Five on the Most Wanted list then."

"I'd been in the Bureau less than a year, and I saw him in line at the Post Office right next to his wanted poster. Put the cuffs on him right after he'd mailed the box tops for his kid's Space Cadet uniform."

Which was *not* what the training film depicted...at *all*.

"*Spectacular* arrest," Gwen said. "Made Ernie's reputation as a fast-thinking agent."

"*And* as a non-game player," Ernest/Ernie groused. "My Special Agent in Charge* wanted to give it to somebody *other* than his greenest rookie. I said I wouldn't fill out the reports like *that*. He filled 'em out the way *he* wanted; I griped to *his* boss, and next thing *I* know, *I'm* in the SPD."

"For the betterment of the *Bureau*, Ernie," Gwen replied. "You *know* what kind of man J. Edgar was looking for then."

"Yep," Ernie agreed. "*Yes*-men...*except* for those he drew into the SPD."

And so...Julia, Ellen, and I changed our *Desired Assignments* and repaired to our barracks/dorm rooms to contemplate what had transpired.

And to wonder just *what* was *so special* about the Special Projects Division. We just didn't *know* each other well enough to talk about what we'd volunteered for/been roped into...

Yet.

✳✳✳

After graduation the next week, we had *three* weeks before we had to report to our details. Getting stuff packed up and saying goodbye to everyone at home took me two weeks. I waved my *stuff* goodbye on

---

* Abbreviated SAIC.

the moving truck on Friday, and on Saturday, I drove my Buick out of Hell.

Hell is a *neighborhood* in Pickney, southwest of Detroit—only it's not really *there*. Hell got its name in the 1800s from a local mill operator on Hell Creek—extinct since—who paid his vendors in the whiskey he made. Wives would complain, *'Father's gone to Hell again'* when they came home roaring drunk. We got *that* story growing up, and it makes more sense than the others, which are legion.

Hell became famous in the 1940s when the dam holding back the last vestiges of the creek failed, flooding Pickney's Regency Avenue on a sub-zero January night. Newspapers printed *Hell Freezes Over* headlines and "reports" of bread landing butter-side-up and other rare happenings all week. No "investigative journalists" were going to refute the nonsense then; everyone knew it was a joke, but the Chamber of Commerce has taken it seriously ever since.

Without fixed boundaries, it's hard to tell precisely just how many people live *in* Hell. Traditionally, it was the *ten* blocks of Regency Avenue between 4th Street and 16th Street (don't *ask* about the math) that the Chamber of Commerce calls Tartarus[*] Road. On Tartarus is Gunga Din's Bar, Grille and Gift Shoppe (from the poem: *I'll get a swig in Hell from Gunga Din*); Beelzebub Press, where the souvenirs come from; and Inferno Motors, my dad's used-car lot/brokerage on the eastern end. Other businesses with *related* names—like the Gate of Salvation Baptist Church at the *west* end of Tartarus—and unrelated, like the Piggly-Wiggly in the middle, and several homes rounds out what Mahoun[**] Realtors calls *Hell's Hundred Acres*.

It took me two days to drive to my *new* home in Dumfries, Virginia, where I had wrangled a one-bedroom apartment. Ellen and Julia had apartments in the same building two floors *above* me—fittingly *and* depressingly. We met our stuff there Monday morning: Ellen's from Albany, New York; Julia's from Southfield, Michigan.

---

[*] A Greek name for the underworld. Mail *was* delivered to either Tartarus *or* Regency Avenue.
[**] The guy's name *was* Mahoun, a Scottish word for the Devil.

I furnished my 15x12 living room with a pre-Columbian corner sectional sofa that had been in our basement. To this, I added a worn chair with a leg that cracked in the move, a 13" color TV that had been in the garage, a couple of beat-up little shelves, and a scuffed sofa table. My parents' old queen bed and my childhood bedroom furniture *sans* twin beds populated my bedroom. Some pots and pans, utensils, odd crockery, a used toaster, and mismatched tableware Mom was about to take to Goodwill adorned my kitchen. I satisfied myself that my brother Steve got *less* when *he* moved out in '67. My brother Dean bolted in '66, so *he* got nothing at all. When it came to be *her* turn, little sis Bridgit would get to haul off what's left that the folks want to unload.

I had books on nearly every horizontal surface and in boxes stacked on the floor of my new digs. And upon *one* of those stacks of boxes rested my *only* lamp—with a three-way bulb—under which I had to do *everything* requiring light.

I needed furniture…and *so* much more…

Until the first time you've *had* to do it yourself, you have no *idea* what it takes to put a household together. In retrospect, you feel like an idiot for having assumed that dish drainers, toilet-bowl brushes, shower curtains—with rings—and coat hangers would be *included* in the lease. I went out Monday night…*and* Tuesday morning…*and* Wednesday afternoon…and got a *few* essentials. I was even mildly—stupidly—surprised the apartment did not *include* a vacuum cleaner *or* a broom…. *those* I got Thursday.

After my phone was connected Friday, I called my family. I scribbled my number on my little whiteboard in the kitchen, *and* I wrote it down on a slip of paper and stuffed it in my wallet. I hoped that *someone* would ask for it…someday.

Late Friday afternoon, I was making a list of *still*-needed stuff *and* a grocery list. The knock on my door sounded somewhere between a retiring *could I borrow some sugar* and an insistent *turn that damn stereo down* …which I *didn't* have. Something *told* me it was…

"*Hey*, Julia, Ellen," I said while opening the door. Julia was in cutoffs and loose tank-top over a flouncy camisole, her hair in a ponytail over her shoulder. Ellen, behind her in a *short* skirt and a crop top, *sort of* smiled. I'd seen them in business suits, *training* uniforms, athletic uniforms, athletic uniforms in the *pool* during drown-proofing, and in *some* more leisurely attire in the cafeteria and sightseeing tours around Washington. But I had *never* seen *that much* of Ellen's or Julia's arms…*nor* legs, *nor* abdomens…before *that* evening. Nor had *they* of *me* as I greeted them in my ragged, holey cutoffs *sans* drawers.

There are two kinds of people who spend their weekends studying: those at the *top* of their class and those at the *bottom*. The three of us *kinda* got to know each other because we spent *many* of our eighteen weekends studying in the dorms.

Fair warning: I had not *had* sex—or even made out—since '78. And *I* thought *both* my classmates were attractive.

"*Hi*, Dave," Julia grinned brightly. "Can *we* come *in*?"

"If you *don't* mind my *slight* disaster," I sighed. *I'll be working with them. They may as well get used to MY version of domesticity.*

"You should see *my* place," Julia said, glancing but not *looking* around.

"*Just* like ours," Ellen sighed as they turned right—as if instinctively—toward my tiny kitchen, with its 3x4 *island* counter that was more like an *ait*—an Olde English term for a mud flat.

"*We're* going to dinner, and *you're* coming with us," Julia declared, scanning my books. She would have done *any* centerfold proud, and I'd have bought every issue I could find.

"Get *something* decent on, Dave," Ellen sighed. "A&W tonight. And *before* I forget, give us your phone number. Here's *ours*." She handed me a note with *their* numbers in tidy block-letter copperplate.

On that humidly-balmy evening, we walked two blocks to the A&W drive-in. We talked about *ourselves* because we had *no idea* what was ahead of us. "*My* dad's an engineer," Julia sighed. "Home every night. *Mom*, though, she's been in law enforcement since I started school. First

Pontiac PD, now Oakland County Sherriff's Department. Between shift work and overtime, I didn't see *her* for months at a time." She grinned brightly. "Didn't keep me from wanting the FBI: have since high school. How about *you*, Dave?"

"My father is a used car dealer and broker, home nearly every night except Thursdays when he goes bowling with his high-school buddies. Mom *was* a legal secretary, but she's been a temp with Bridgit still at home. You have brothers and sisters?"

"Nope: only child. You?"

"Two older brothers, younger sister. Ellen, *you*…"

"FBI all my life. Two older brothers; two younger sisters. My family has lived in Albany for the last ten years. Now I'm *here*; Ben owns a boat brokerage on Long Island; Harry's still at Princeton…."

"What did your *dad* say about the Special Projects Division," I asked.

"He said he'd never worked *with* them, or *for* them, or had much *contact* with them."

We were in a new town, quaffing root beer and foot-long hot dogs in Friday-night-hang-out rags with the only *other* people we knew well enough *there* to do *that* with. It was *nice*; it was *chatty*; it felt *intimate*… until *then*.

We were quiet as we walked home, but not the cold, eerie quiet of the end of a bad date. This was a *silence of mystery*, as in *what have we got ourselves into?*

✳✳✳

Saturday noon, I got back from the store with two armloads of groceries, planning a tenderloin filet for dinner. Of course, I had *no* thought whatsoever of *opening* the door…

And Freddie held it open, smiling cheerfully. Freddie was a blonde moppet with a wide grin for everyone and everything, like all Down's children. I'd met her while I was moving in and knew she lived with her little brother and her parents somewhere in the building. "Thanks, Freddie," I said.

"You're welcome," she said, following me to my door. "*I* can open *that*," she smiled, grabbing for my keys. She stuck the *right* key in the deadbolt, *then* in the knob…picking *just* the right…

"You've done *this* before," I said, slightly alarmed.

"I watched you," she said, opening the door and following me in. "You're friends with the new girls."

"I *work* with them." I put my groceries away while she scanned around the kitchen and living room. I had interacted with some *special* kids in school—*mainstreamed*, they called it—but never with a Down's kid. I wondered what she was interested in, how literate she may have been.

She lit on my little workboard with airplane subassemblies on it. "You're good," she said.

"Thanks," I smiled, "do you build models?"

"I make pictures," she answered. She'd snatched my kitchen phone pad and my phone pencil and was sitting on the end of my sectional by the porch door. "Daddy makes kites. Mommy makes food. Jimmy makes poop and pee." She wore a t-shirt and jean jumper that her free hand absently fiddled with, crossing and uncrossing her bare legs as she drew.

"Ah," I said. "How *old* is Jimmy?"

"Five," she said, dropping my pencil and getting up. "Bye," she waved and went out of my open door. She left a *most* detailed sketch of the view out my porch door, including the leaves on the trees around the parking lot, the signs on the little strip mall across the street, and the rust chips on my railing.

That evening, the knock on my door was my building super, a beefy black man, and Freddie with a large basket. "Welcome from building management," he said.

"Well, thanks," I said, "and *thanks*, Freddie."

"Welcome," she smiled, handed me the basket, and ran off.

"She's a good girl," I said. "Where does she live?"

"At the end of the hall," the super answered. "I'm George Mackenzie, her step-father."

"Pleased to meet you," I said, trying to hide my surprise. "Freddie draws well."

"She *does*," George agreed, "whenever she can. She drew your view from the living room?"

"I take it she's done it before."

"*Every* apartment she gets into, and that's nearly all of 'em. If you need anything, leave a message on my machine or a note on my board. I do minor maintenance, but if there's an emergency or something big, call *this* number." He handed me a card. "They do *major* services in an hour or so, 24 hours a day. You know where your shutoffs and your circuit breakers are?"

"Right here," I pointed at the closet by the door. "The salesman showed me when I signed the lease."

"Good. They *don't* always. Be seeing you." He started to leave, then stopped. "Freddie's not...."

"A typical kid, yeah."

"No, not what I meant. She's twelve; what they call *mosaic*. She has a very high IQ—higher than *mine*, even. Don't talk down to her; it can upset her."

"I'll remember that."

***

Sunday morning...quiet. No *good* idea why, but Sundays are often quiet.

Screaming, roaring quiet.

It struck me that first Sunday, *truly* on my own—college dorms hardly counted—how *that* particular day drove home just what *living alone* meant. It meant that the rest of your life is out in front of you...*alone.*

And on Sunday...*everything* was on hold...except perhaps your upstairs neighbors having boisterous wake-up sex *right above you...*

Church-goers can content themselves in a haven of group solitude. Mom took us sometimes. I had my baptismal certificate from the Gate of Salvation Church. I'd read the Bible, but I'd also read the Koran and

Bhagavat-Gita, Mein Kampf, and *The Communist Manifesto.* In high school, there was *Lord of the Rings, The Hobbit,* and *The Silmarillion.* I'd *had* to study *The Wealth of Nations* and *Das Kapital* in college. I'd also read *The Book of Mormon* and *Atlas Shrugged; Fear and Loathing in Las Vegas* and *Dianetics; The Book of Five Rings* and *Siddhartha,* Voltaire, Einstein, and *lots* in between. *What* people believe, *how* they believe it, and what they *do* about it *interests* me.

To paraphrase Jethro Tull, *my* God was *not* the kind you had to wind up on Sundays. *This* meant that getting out of bed on Sunday mornings was optional.

Then, *someone had* to knock on my door at 9:06 *that* Sunday morning.

"*Coffee,* Dave," Julia grinned, pushing a box of doughnuts into my hands. "Need *coffee.*"

"*Knife* for the *rolls,* Dave," Ellen demanded, striding by me with an armful of groceries that smelled deliciously like fresh bread and warm baked ham. "Some *mayo,* some *mustard?*"

"Coffee," I stammered, "sure. Haven't *made* it yet…bread knife? Drawer left of the sink. And *mustard…*"

"No *coffee* yet, Dave," Julia accused, fists on hips. "And *where's* your sweetener? Do *we* have to do *everything,* Dave?"

"Not *everything,* no," I answered. Remember here that I'd *just* crawled out of bed, and there was a hint of a grin on *those* faces as I stood in *my own apartment* in my sleep-skivvies, complete with holes in *revealing* places. "But, I'll just go back to *bed,* and you guys can do what*ever* you *want….*"

"*Don't* you dare," Ellen declared, "*we're* going to the matinee of *The Empire Strikes Back.* I haven't seen it yet, so *don't* spoil it…*why* aren't you *dressed* yet, Dave?" She wielded my bread knife with the rattling handle as if it were a scepter. "Get a *little* more decent, Dave. Breakfast will be ready by the time you've at *least* got a shirt and some *decent* pants on."

My partners *smiled* at me *despite* my disheveled appearance. My favorite lyric is from Manfred Mann:

To her Cheshire smile, I'll stand on file
She's all I ever wanted.

I never had high socio-sexual expectations. I was told I was *good-enough* looking, but I was *socially* awkward and sexually inexperienced. The one thing I liked from *any female* was a smile.

I hadn't seen the movie—it came out just a month before. Seeing the second *Star Wars* saga with them—surrounded by kids and teenagers *wowing* every explosion and twist of the plot—was fun.

Since my partners were in culottes and tube tops* and I was no *more* formal, we went to The Crab Shack for dinner, a strip mall seafood joint that *didn't* serve crab *at all*.

By 6 that evening, we agreed that we should take our own cars the next day because we had *no* idea what we would be doing for our first day.

I understood why Yoda said, "*Do*. Or *do* not—there is no *try*." We would be working together; we *had* to be *doing* together. We *needed* to be a team. We *knew* that even if my partners had taken *most* of the initiative so far. And we seemed to be getting along just fine. They even smiled indulgently as they rolled their eyes whenever they spotted me *admiring* their legs.

And my partner's *legs* were *breathtaking* works of God's art, and I did believe enough of Him to have *that* power.

I thank *Him* profusely for sharing those lovely visions with me.

---

* It *must* have been a uniform code for that day. Women and girls all over *town* wore *exactly* the same thing, regardless of what they looked like *in* them.

The Special Projects Division

Or, The Outfit that Doesn't Exist

Quantico is one of those quaint suburbs of Washington DC where practically nobody lives permanently. Still, *thousands* of people pass through, reside and work briefly, and leave. In Quantico, there's the Marine Corps Museum and a score of motels. There's also the Naval Investigative Service HQ and gun shops on every corner. Too, there's the FBI Academy and used car lots everywhere. Besides that, there's the Marine Corps Base Quantico and more than a few pawn shops. Finally, there's the isolated two-story concrete-and-glass warehouse-like building in the middle of an otherwise vacant block that houses the Special Projects Division of the FBI.

We walked into the glass-enclosed lobby from the parking lot. There was no big sign out front like was there was for everything *else* the government owned in Northern Virginia, DC, and eastern Maryland. There was just an FBI seal on the lobby's outer door with *Special Projects Division* under it in white peel-on letters. Julia and Ellen were in fashionable business suits with tasteful skirts and sensible, high-neck blouses. I, of course, was in my best blue pinstripe with a tie but *no* snap-brim fedora. They told us that those were discarded when J. Edgar died, but some older agents still had them hanging on their hat racks. One of our instructors wore one to show how to be *spotted* as an FBI agent.

A uniformed GSA guard stood at a podium just inside the door, standing next to a pass-thru metal detector. He glared at the three of us in turn. "Help *yuou*?" He was as friendly as an annoyed skunk.

"We've been assigned here," Ellen explained.

The guard looked at my classmates suspiciously. "Nu *vimmee-a*issigned *here-a*. *Yuo* ire-a *meesteken*." He sounded *just like* the Swedish Chef, making him hard to understand quickly.

"*They're* assigned here just like I am," I said.

"Und *yuo* ire-a *vrung*," the Swedish guard declared. "Now *go*."

"May I speak with your supervisor, please," Julia asked *so* nicely, unbuttoning her jacket. She had a *way* of convincing people; she would have made a *great* cult leader, serial killer, or both.

"*One*-a-man *poost*," the Swedish guard snapped—hard to do when sounding like a Muppet. "I *answer* to *noboody*. Now yust *turn around* and...."

"Everyone answers to *somebody* in this town," I interrupted. "Now, get whoever *you* answer to on the phone, or let us talk to Senior Special Agent Packard...."

"*No* such *per*son *here*-a," the Swedish guard declared, a little more like English.

There was something *not right* about the guard's uniform. "When did GSA start issuing Sam Browne belts? And, *why* are you wearing it over the wrong shoulder?"

"Oh, a *smart* guy, eh," the Swedish guard snarled, his accent suddenly devolved into something incoherent. "What shoulder am I *supposed* to...."

"The *right*: it was designed to help hold up the sword on the *left* hip...."

"I'm left-handed, *smart* guy," the suddenly-American guard grinned. "So, just pack up your *girlfriends*...."

"It doesn't *matter* with a Sam Browne," I explained, carefully weighing my gun-pulling options. I could get my weapon out fast *enough* to graduate, but not as fast as *all* my classmates.

I *just* started to brush my coat back, hoping I'd give Julia and Ellen a chance to brace this guy *after* he shot me when... "*That's* good, Fred," a tinny voice sounded from somewhere in the room. "Don't want you to get *shot again*."

"OK, Dusty," the guard smiled, extending his hand. "Fred Macon. You'd be *Ernie's* rookies?"

"We *would*," I sighed. "Hazing?"

"Hazing," Fred smiled, revealing two gold teeth. "There *will* be *more*. Good catch on the Sam Browne: you're the *first*. Go on through."

✳✳✳

"*Welcome* to the *Special Projects Division*," declared a little man with a big mustache just inside the double doors off the lobby. "I'm your Special Agent In Charge, Dewitt Harris. *They* call me *Dusty*, but *you'll* just call me *sir* for now. Come on in."

We'd had a class in Week 18 called *Welcome Aboard!* It was all about our in-briefings and our introductions to our fellow agents and administrative staff. They even talked about how we'd be told who to answer to…

But…

"This is *us*," Dusty swept his arm widely as we walked into a room the size of two basketball courts with a high acoustic ceiling. Several people lifted their heads or turned to look at us idly. "Fifty-five agents for now; four administrative staff." The big space was divided into untidy, unequal areas by baby-puke-green, fiberglass-and-steel movable walls, filing cabinets, banker's file boxes, tables, whiteboards, tall steel carts, and shelves laden with boxes and binders. A basketball hoop—*sans* backboard or net—hung on the wall, forlornly crooked, at the far end from the entrance. "Some wiseguy hung that thing up there, and we just never took it down. Down *here*," Dusty led us along one side of the big, relatively quiet room that smelled of dust and, vaguely, mold, "is where *Ernie* hangs out."

Ernie looked up from a long steel-leg table scattered with files in a room twenty feet long and about ten feet wide, with shoulder-high windows that let in soft, even light. Ernie grunted, "thanks, Dusty." He got up, extending his hand. We shook it; it seemed uncharacteristically flabby. *Maybe he knows his own strength.* "Grab a seat." We wheeled office chairs up to his table.

"Now: what they fed you in the Academy about your on-boarding? Yeah, everywhere *but* here. Except for the occasional wrong number, we *don't* answer phones with civilians on the other end. We *now answer* to just *two* voices: the Attorney-General and the Director. Even the *President* doesn't give us orders directly."

Ernie made a sweeping gesture. "What *we* do here *most* of the time is clean up what *one guy* feared in the dark of night, what kept him awake for decades: the *Liberty Bell Files*."

"Impossible," Ellen pronounced loudly. "Helen Gandy *destroyed* all those files. They no longer *exist*."

Ernie smiled slowly, spread his hands on his table. "Stop…right… there, Special Agent* Drew. Miss Gandy destroyed only what she *knew* of J. Edgar's *personal* files. She *didn't* know about," he swept his arm, "… *these*. We've *been* working on *them* since 1972, and *their* number was *orders of magnitude* greater than Miss Gandy even dreamed. Your self-assuredness is admirable, but do *not* presume to know more about your *new* job than the detail that's been doing it for *eight years*. Are we *clear*?"

"Crystal, sir."

"Good. These *had* been stored at field offices all over the country. They're *still* being located from time to time. Files on organizations, individuals, UFO sightings, *supposed* subversive activities couched in TV shows, radio commercials, newspaper cartoons, and even circus performances." He grabbed a file. "Here…" he pushed it to Ellen. "Read the first-page summary." She opened an old brown cardstock folder; an aged piece of thin paper was stapled to the inside, which she read:

---

* Abbreviated SA, what most FBI agents are. There are also Senior Supervisory Special Agents (SSSA) who get more money, responsibility, and paperwork.

File Number Ending 067265-LIB
File Created 6/7/42
File Name: Edward Steven Copenicium
DOB 6/25/1901, Evans County, Texas.
Subject expressed disloyal opinions June 1942 in Dallas, TX. Stated "if this war needs us, they're really hard up," while not expressing mirth.

"*This* poor guy had a file on him because he *didn't* laugh at his own joke. *So now* we have to look all these people up, see what they're up to, see how subversive they are *now*—*if* they're still alive—close the files and send them to Central Records for microfilming. Here…" He pushed one at me. "Read for the class." *This* file folder was a battered manila; the paper inside yellowing, the type fading. A typed label on the tab bore the letters *LIB* preceded by an overlong, hyphenated file number:

File Number Ending 651925-LIB
File Created 12 Dec 67
File Name: Fauna
DOB unknown (probably 1964). Large feline won biggest cat in Idaho at state fair September 67. Unnaturally large (over 40 pounds) for a domestic feline. Owner is Laurencia Smith Newman *nee* Flannagan (DOB 1932), an outspoken opponent of the Vietnam war and the current military draft who has visited Sweden, Switzerland, and other pacifistic countries. Possible lines of investigation include radiation-enhanced animal breeding.

"The cat's almost certainly dead, the owner's pacifism irrelevant, and the need for the file moot. But we look them up, write *another* report for the file, close it out, and send it to Central Records. *But…*" He read himself…

File Number Ending 239601-LIB
File Created: June 12, 1931
File Name: Church of Idiot Worshippers
Founded by one Salaam Morori, AKA Sam Morris (B. 1881?) ca 1915, Grand Ledge, Wyoming. Organization formed in large storefront. Uses

the term "idiot" in the ancient Greek sense, meaning "one's own," referring to one's unique inner self, or the Russian sense of "holy fool."

1935: Membership hit nearly 1,000 before merging with the Church of the Open Mind and absorbing the Church of Women's Faith in the Eternal Wound.

1942: Moved to large warehouse in Cheyenne.

1950: Membership about 2,000. Members thought to be primarily unmarried men and divorced women. Meetings said to last about 6 hours; initial faith-based discussion leads to propositioning and subsequent orgies. No marriage recognized by this organization.

1957: Dues-paying membership near 5,000; dues $50/meeting; most members meet every other day.

1961: Church does not kick back dues to members per Ft. Collins PD despite claims to the contrary. "Churches" in Wyoming, Montana, Idaho, Nevada, Colorado and California.

1962: Organization renamed Church of the Blessed Climax Sleep.

1971: IRS granted church/nonprofit status. Investigated by Reno PD for prostitution without a license; no charges filed.

"Outfits like this are *seemingly* innocuous, but *I* looked into it, and it's still going strong." He made a face: an odd sort of expression for his big, beefy puss. "It's *these* that we root out; *these* that we have to look into, and in *these* that *maybe* we find something worth anyone's *time*. I *just* made some calls on it," tapping the file with a finger, "and found that the Denver Division has *another* file. You three are on a plane to Denver tonight."

"*What*," Julia gasped. "What are we looking *for*?"

"*Field* experience." Ernie stood up, his full height intimidating. "Your tickets will be waiting at National Airport; your flight's at 23:30. Copy this file and study it; check out this definition of the word *idiot* if you think it's relevant. Take a cab to the Federal building from the airport, pick up a car from the motor pool *and* the file, and investigate. For *future* reference, my children*, keep a bag packed at all times. You'll spend *at*

---

* As hard as some SAs tried to be irritated at being called *children* in this way, it was just too *Ernie* to be an issue. Ernie was a *lot* of things, but an *ism-ist* was *not* among them, and he let you *know* it.

least a week every month on the road. While you're out there, *solicit* cooperation from the locals, don't *command* it."

Rookies fantasize that they'd be off chasing spies or terrorists or—hope against *hope*—both. But we *knew*—because the Academy *told* us—that the *most* we could hope for, for *at least* a year, was filling out paperwork for someone more senior.

Yeah ...

***

"Why in *hell* are we flying to Denver in the middle of the night," Ellen groaned, loading her bags into my trunk. We met in the apartment parking lot at about 9. A quick round of paper/scissors/rock had established *who* would drive to the airport.

"Budget," I declared, doing the same. "Carter's not willing to pay for rookies to jet across the country during business hours."

Ellen looked at me with curiosity. "How would *you* know…?"

"I know how the government's organizational mind works. I half-thought they'd send us back *tomorrow*, but day-*after*-tomorrow at the ass-crack of dawn makes sense." I shrugged. "They're *also* testing our resilience."

Ellen knew the Bureau better than any of us. But, this simple reasoning seemed, for *her*, a revelation.

"You *changed*?" Julia squinted at me, loading her luggage. "Hadn't *thought* of that."

"Yeah," I said, closing my trunk. *They* were still in their reporting suits and high-neck blouses and brought suitcases. *I* wore jeans and running shoes, had rolled and packed everything I'd need into a backpack and a suit carry-on. In ROTC and the Army Reserves, I learned to take *only* what you can sling over your shoulder when in the field. "Not *reporting* to anyone…."

"I had *half* a mind to change out of this suit," Ellen interrupted, "but…I had *no idea* we were going to be…."

"Somehow, *I* didn't think of changing at *all*," Julia sighed, climbing into my back seat. "*So* surprised…"

"We *should* run up…" Ellen started, hesitating.

"No *time* now," Julia replied.

And there wasn't. By the time we got to National, parked, got our tickets, and made our way to the gate, they were making their final boarding call.

"*Middle* of the night," Ellen complained, pulling her seat belt around her before she opened her *Time* magazine. Julia opened *Portnoy's Complaint.* I opened my *Lucifer's Hammer* and read until the snack came an hour after wheels-up: cold cuts, rolls, carrot and celery sticks, a flat chunk of cheese, and a bottle of Mateus. I stowed my wine; my companions drank theirs and slept until we landed two hours later.

✳✳✳

"Sunup in *Washington*; one-thirty in the morning *here*," Julia yawned widely as we unloaded the cab in downtown Denver. The entrance to the Federal Building was off Stout Street, a practically deserted parking lot edging a concrete palisade in front of a wall of glass doors.

"Let's just go see who *might* be in the office," Ellen said, picking up her two suitcases.

"Check," I agreed, shouldering my luggage.

The guard, a youngish Hispanic woman, glanced at our IDs and called up to the 5th Floor. "Three of *your* guys from…?"

"Washington," I blurted, hoping to *sound* important.

"He'll be right down," she sighed. "Something big in the works?"

"Not that we can talk about," Ellen offered officiously.

The young man who came out of the elevator took *one* look at us, and his face fell like a stunned falcon: he hadn't *expected* three *young* SAs. "Wyatt," he mumbled, "we got *the call* yesterday afternoon." He straightened his tie absently as he glanced at Julia and Ellen—ignoring me—and came to something like an attentive pose. "*You* guys…"

We introduced ourselves and flashed our credentials, hoping that their newness didn't stick out like a neon sign. "We *just* got in," I announced loudly. "Is there a crib in this building?"

Wyatt shook his head. "No, sorry. The Metropole at 20th and California's what we use. What…*why* are you here *now?*"

"We're looking into…." I started.

"Budget cuts," Ellen smiled. "*You* know; Carter's got his fist on the purse strings."

"Yeah, I get it. Emilia," he called to the guard, "can they use that trash can cart? LOT easier to get their luggage over there on *that.*"

The cart was a four-wheeled wood contraption equipped with a pipe handle on two ends and four wheels, only *three* of which touched the ground at any one time. We stacked our bags on it unevenly and rolled outside. Three rooms were waiting for us when we got to the hotel. I was on the 2nd Floor; my workmates were on the 4th, of course.

And I briefly wondered as I nodded off: *Was this the deep end?*

The Idiot Worshippers

Or, The Church of the Blessed Climax Sleep

"Hullo," I answered the jangling phone: the clock said 5:32.

"Rise and *shine*, Davie," Julia's *too*-cheery voice came. "*Big* day ahead of us." For reasons known only to her, Julia took to calling me *Davie* in private.

"And how in the hell would *you* know *how* big our day shall be," I mumbled.

"Our first day as *real* FBI agents, doing real FBI-agent stuff, Davie."

"Just let me get a shower," I sighed. "You down at breakfast?" I pictured *those* eyes, *that* smile…

"*Hell*, no. You're mistaking *me* for Nancy Drew. I'm lying here starkers in my bed, with the A/C blowing over me."

"She called *you* already?" I tried *not* to imagine Julia *starkers* in bed… with the A/C blowing…*chilling her…ho-boy…*

"She said *she* didn't want to be disturbed before 6."

I told myself *professionalism, professionalism, professionalism* as I involuntarily envisioned her *naughty bits* that I saw *glimpses* of during our drownproofing training in that *icy* pool…*ho-boy.* "*That* means…?"

"…that I'm calling her as *soon* as I hang up with you. See you soon, *Davie*-boy." Julia also had a *racy* sense of humor.

And NOW I need a COLD shower.

I got down to the dining room just after 6, taking a table near the windows and facing the entrance. Julia came just after I ordered, bright and cheery like she always seemed to be. Ellen came not long after my breakfast arrived, looking somewhat straggly. "Could not sleep at *all*," she complained. "Bed feels like a sack of rocks."

"Not *that* great," I agreed, cutting my hash browns. "Better than sleeping on cold concrete; done *that*, too."

"*When*," Ellen frowned tersely.

"ROTC summer camp at Fort Bragg," I said, loading my fork with eggs. "The bugs were so bad we had to get away from them; found a concrete pad and crowded onto it—the whole platoon, girls *and* guys."

"My *uncle* is at Fort Bragg now," Julia declared.

"Uncle?" I sipped some coffee to wash down my eggs.

"He's my age, an Army Ranger."

"You *track* this uncle of yours," Ellen asked, sipping her *entire* breakfast— grapefruit juice—disdainfully glancing at us. Ellen seemed to expect everyone to be like *her* and was consistently surprised to discover that we *weren't*.

"JJ's my *step*-uncle, technically," Julia answered with a small smile. "His mother married my grandfather. Six weeks older than I am."

"Sounds complicated," I said, finishing my toast and glancing at my watch. "We should get going."

We took turns pushing the hard-to-manage, tottering cart through morning downtown sidewalk traffic. I shouldered my briefcase/backpack, but my partners had to lug their FBI Bookstore valises *and* purses. We rolled the cart to a somewhat surprised day-shift guard, who smirked, "wondered where *that* went," before we took the elevator up to the 5th Floor.

For a moment, approaching that big, imposing door that said *Federal Bureau of Investigation—Denver Division*[*], my partners looked puzzled.

---

[*] Each state has a *Division* office that oversees the *Resident Agencies* and other offices in that state.

I briefly panicked because we didn't have a contact name or instructions beyond '*get ye to Denver.*'

But we strode through the door like we knew what we were doing.

"One moment," the pretty, young-ish receptionist smiled when she saw our credentials. "Agent Grafton: the three from *Washington* are here." She looked up. "He'll be right out."

About a minute later, a smallish, graying man with brown eyes and a ruddy face wearing a department store suit emerged from a door alongside the reception desk. "Tony Grafton, ladies, sir," he held out his hand. "Special Agent in Charge. Come on back. When Wyatt *called* me last night…." He went on in a similar, apologetic vein for some moments while he led us to his conference room. It was a typical GSA-furnished space that smelled and *looked* like it had recently been sanitized and vacuumed. "*What* can I do for you?"

"We're working on the Church of the Blessed Climax Sleep," I cleared my throat. Even though everything he *owned* likely pre-dated *our* time in the Bureau, Tony treated us like *superiors*.

"*One* moment, sir." Tony stepped out the door and shouted, "*Nenning!*" While he did *that*, we glanced at each other in minor amazement, still not quite believing. Tony returned in a few minutes, adjusting his tie. "Agent Nenning is on her way. Can I *get* anyone anything? Coffee? Water? Tea?"

"Not for *me*, thanks," I replied; "*no*, thank you," "no, thanks," said my partners.

A dark young woman carrying a file box entered the conference room. "Special Agent Corinne Nenning," she introduced herself. "I've been inventorying *these files*…."

"Files," Julia asked, flashing her curious face.

"These *Liberty Bell* Files. They put me on them after my maternity leave," Corinne explained, setting the box down.

Tony explained. "We *knew* of the directive that said that all of these had to go back to Washington *years* ago, but we *just* found *these* in storage and had Agent Nenning *inventory* them."

"And *this* one stuck out," Corinne said. She handed me a slightly bulging file folder. "Church of Idiot Worshippers/Blessed Climax Sleep. We haven't done *any* fieldwork on it since '72."

"*What* stuck out," I asked, all innocent-like. I could tell that Corinne had been hefty recently but was taking the pounds off. I'd watched Mom do that often enough with her diets, so I knew the signs, especially the saggy face.

"I had some neighbors who were into *that*, and it's the biggest of the lot."

"I see," I smiled, trying *not* to look *too* interested in a married woman. *Baby* meant *married* in the Bureau: no two ways about it.

"*This* box contains all the Liberty Bell Files I *found* here: twenty-three."

"OK," Ellen declared. "If you'll just give us a *few* moments, we'll get back with you." As Tony and Corinne left, we glanced at each other quizzically. "They have *no idea* who *we* are."

"Nope...nor *what*, either," I agreed, flipping the Climax Sleep file open.

"Think they're clear of the door," Julia whispered.

I looked at the glass panel next to the door. "Looks like."

And we burst out giggling as *quietly* as we could.

This was our introduction to the mysterious *power* of the mere mention of *The Almighty Washington*. Anyone who came from *there* flashing credentials was automatically *assumed* to have *much* more important business than *whatever* the local office was working on. They were *also* believed to be of higher rank and position *and* possessing higher bowling averages and lower golf handicaps.

And if anyone had told us *that* before *that* morning, we'd have thought *they* were nuts...or at *least* that they were off their meds.

*****

"How many of these churches *are* there in Denver," Ellen asked absently, looking out the van window. The five of us were in a GSA pool van: Tony and Corinne were in front, Julia and Ellen in the middle seat, I was in the back.

"Just the one," Tony answered, turning onto a quiet residential street lined with cars. I looked at the sprawling ranch houses on large lots without sidewalks—that *usually* meant higher-income neighborhoods. "They *said* to bring you out here, so I'm *bringing*. Right…down…here." We parked in a cul-de-sac with four houses on it, with cars and trucks parked on both sides of the street…more than you'd expect for residents unless they all had parties going on mid-morning on a weekday. One house was an immense three-story Colonial Revival mansion with an attached, four-car garage. A sign on the mansion's lawn read *Church of the Holy Rest* in big gold letters, and underneath was a legend in letters a third of the size: *formerly, Church of the Blessed C-Sleep.*

As we approached the house's double-front door, I dimly wondered if they were open: there were no cars in the driveway. A sign next to the double front doors read: "Open 8 AM-9 PM, Seven Days a Week: Sessions begin every half-hour. *Please come in.*"

I wondered what a *session* might include: perhaps a few minutes of small talk followed by satyriatic sessions lasting hours, followed by sleep. I glanced at my watch: 10:30. *They may just be ready to go…?* Suddenly, my upbringing and chivalric instincts regarding the fair sex kicked in. I thought *briefly* about suggesting: "ladies, *you* should stay out *here*," thinking that my female companions should be *protected* from seeing *that.* Having seen *too many* adult films in my quarter-century on Earth, I imagined that we'd be meeting people in various stages of undress, come-hither smiles and half-full wine glasses in hand, mingling with half- or *completely*-naked people doing what comes naturally in that scenario[*] accompanied by Barry White-like music emanating from everywhere.

Then Ellen opened the door, and the distinct scent of lavender and sandalwood wafted out. Just inside, Corinne and Tony flashed their credentials at a young woman and a young man dressed in smart business

---

[*] *Not* sunbathing.

attire, sitting at a wide table, literature racks at their elbows, small stacks of forms in front of them.

"How may I *help* you," the young woman smiled genuinely. "I'm Barbara; this is James. We're the residents."

"We're doing a follow-up investigation, miss," Tony began, hanging his badge* around his neck. My partners and I hastily followed. "Our files are quite dated...."

"They *would* be," James grinned sagely. "FBI"s never *been* here."

"Here," Corinne asked.

"*This* building," James answered. "We moved here in '75. We're a church to the IRS, but it's more a *club*, frankly."

"No religious overtones," Corinne asked, poised to take notes.

"Oh, there *are*," Barbara declared, handing us brochures. "Not in any *conventional*, Judeo-Christian sense, but certainly overtones of *peace*."

I glanced at the four-page, glossy, quality-workmanship brochure. The main themes that caught my eye were *rest* and *sleep*. I didn't see *anything* about climaxes. I admit to being a *little* disappointed before Julia elbowed me. "Come on."

We followed Barbara and James down a short hall to a wooden door marked *A*. James opened it a crack, peered in, then stuck his head in. "Rest," he smiled. We went further down the hall to Door B. James repeated his inspection, but he opened the door wide this time.

Once again, my instinct was to *protect* my female companions...but Ellen led us in. Inside...

While your imagination, gentle reader, might be conjuring all manner of salacious carnality, you will either be *relieved* or *disappointed* at what we saw. Wide, upholstered structural ledges along the walls of the big, barely-lit, windowless room were dotted with big, soft pillows an adult could wrap their arms around. All the ledges were populated; *several* had persons embracing, holding hands, or sitting very close together, all

---

* Also called credentials. They'll get you in almost anywhere, but *doesn't* get you a better table at *any* restaurant.

of whom gazed at us sleepily. Most had their upper garments open or removed; all had their shoes off. No one was naked or even *half*-naked, though women with exposed brassieres *could* count as half-naked per the creed of J. Edgar.

There was neither hanky *nor* panky. I couldn't decide if I was disappointed or relieved.

A woman in a short tank top, leggings, and bare feet stood at a lit podium. "We have visitors," she said quietly.

"*Don't* let us interrupt," Barbara said. "The FBI wants a look around."

Julia stepped up, looked at what was on the podium, made a surprised face, and then came to me. "Kahlil Gibran," she whispered and led us out.

For the next half hour, we inspected several more rooms on the first and second floors. We found nothing but different readings in any other room. Then, we started catching people coming out of Room H with *no good idea of what we were supposed to ask*.

Tony and Corinne seemed to be watching *us* as to what *they* should be doing, as though *they* were looking for clues from *us*…

And *we* didn't have a single one…so we faked it…poorly.

Tony stood next to me as I spoke to a 30-something woman in a business suit with shoulder pads that would have been big on a football center. "How long have you been a member of this organization," I asked, trying to *sound* more confident than I *felt*. *I didn't ask her name… what am I doing?*

"All my life," she answered, brushing away an errant wisp of dark hair. "My parents *met* in the old Union Hall downtown. *I* went there before the club moved out *here* and changed its name."

"And you worship here…*how* often?" *Interview 101: NAME FIRST…*

"No," she smiled. "I come here for stress relief maybe three times a month."

Ah-HAH! "Stress relief," I smirked. "Just how does this *stress-relief* work?" My young, non-agent, male mind saw this attractive woman in a pile of arms and legs, relieving *her* stress with some glistening man while *still* thinking *um…name?*

"Well, as you might *imagine*," she sighed. "We sit down in a room, say *hi* to the reader and everyone else, get as *comfortable* as we want within *decorum*, *listen* to the reading, and just *relax*. Today, I snoozed a bit." She smiled, a wise, knowing smile. "You *believe* those stories about orgies?"

"Well," I replied, "it *is* what we have in the files.…" *I'm missing something…LIKE HER NAME!*

She smiled beatifically. "Yeah. Dad says *some* of 'em were true before the old man died."

"Which *old man* was that?" *What did I forget…?*

"The founder of the Idiot Church. He'd lost control of the practices *years* before he died sometime in the '50s. What the Church was interested in by *then* wasn't *sex*. It was that *blissful rest* you get *after*…you know?"

"Ah, yes," I lied. I really didn't know *what* that was, always having to get dressed and leave *after*…

"*The Book of Rest* should put you straight," she smiled again, straightening her collar while gazing in a nearby mirror. "It's got everything about the club and our philosophy…or *church* if you prefer."

"One more thing," I said before she turned away, "does the church, or *club*, recognize marriage?" *Is this an interview or…what?*

"Why *wouldn't* they?" She sauntered off nonchalantly.

Or…what. That was it: my *first* interview as a real FBI agent…and I had no *idea* who she was. We spent another hour asking the same questions—we could *hardly* call them *interviews* because none of us got names *or* took notes—and collecting literature.

James and Barbara—the *only* names we got—were the local *managers* of the club/church and lived in the upper story with their two children— they had a separate entrance. There were 600-odd members, age 16 to 84, including twenty families…and as many as three generations. Unaccompanied minors were *not* allowed in sessions. *Real* sex was heartily discouraged, though *allowed* if all in the session agreed…and the couple (only) went behind a screen and were *quiet. Discrete self*-pleasuring wasn't in-policy but *happened.*

Our *pseudo*-work complete, we piled into the van and headed back to the office. Not one of the people we spoke to was at all reticent; none said they knew of orgies, though one suggested that we talk to his grandmother. Several *non*-interviewees had been married *in* the church—James was a justice-of-the-peace, and several clergymen and a judge were *associated* with the church. Other members had gotten legally married elsewhere *and* in the Church of the Blessed Climax Sleep.

Was this subversive?

∗∗∗

"*This* file and the one in Washington are both *way* out of date," I sighed over my beer. The three of us got in at the end of the hotel's happy hour, sitting in one of two booths in the tiny bar area just off the restaurant. There were only four stools at the bar itself, and four little tables. There was a *lot* of take-out booze. I had discarded my suit for my traveling jeans and t-shirt with a short denim jacket that covered my weapon neatly.

"That, *and,*" Ellen smirked into her club soda, "the *contents* are questionable." She had left her jacket in her room; her *blouse* bulged uncomfortably with her weapon under it.

"And, *our* way was paved with a phone call," Julia grinned into her gin-and-tonic. "They treated us like the pros from Dover." She had changed into a loose sweatsuit that drooped on her right side, where *her* weapon was. "And *I* need more costume changes on the road."

"Yeah," I agreed. "You two brought *all* that luggage and *nothing* comfortable?"

"How was *I* supposed to know," Ellen answered indignantly. "I brought what I thought I might need for *business*, not pleasure."

"They didn't *give* us a lot of preparatory information," Julia agreed. "Could go and *get* some more clothes, but we're headed back to DC in twelve hours."

"*I* need some sleep," Ellen declared, "We'll catch the shuttle at six; get to the airport by seven for our 8:10 flight." She smiled authoritatively and left.

Julia and I didn't have time *or* opportunity to say "good night" or "say *what*," let alone "who put *you* in charge?"

"Wow," Julia shook her head and grinned. "Take-charge girl."

"Yep," I agreed, finishing my beer. "Want another?"

"I'm taking *mine* to my *room*," she declared. "Come *with* me, Davie."

I followed her up to her room, identical to mine, except it was two stories higher. She set her plastic cup down on the little table by the loveseat across from the queen bed and the little TV. She reached under her sweatshirt, pulled off her gun, tossed it on the desk six feet away, and sat. "*Have* a seat," she said absently, patting the loveseat next to her.

HOO-boy…

I sat gingerly, hands on my knees, staring at the bed dead ahead of us as she tapped the TV remote, stopping on a *M*A*S*H* rerun. In 1980, this *kind* of situation was *supposed* to lead to erotic activities accompanied by pulsing *do-de-DUNK* music portrayed in poorly lit films shot in rooms like this.

It was nearly five minutes before she sipped her drink. "We're *not going* to, Davie," she breathed. "*Too* complicated. We *have* to *work* together."

"*That's* true," I agreed, shifting my weight uncomfortably in my tight jeans. "So, we'll just watch TV…."

Then, she took her bra off under her sweatshirt. I'd *seen* Mom do it, but I found it to be somewhat like the guy taking off his vest without taking off his jacket: an exercise in limber limbs…and fascinating. "You do *that* with skill," I said as she pulled the garment out from a sleeve.

"I do it without *thinking*," she grinned. "Sorry. *That* was cruel to *you*." She *not*-looked at my *naughty bits*. "Davie, I *like* you." She put a gentle hand on my thigh, "but getting *involved? Not* good. Maybe you *should* go."

I *softly* put *my* hand on *hers* and murmured. "I haven't *had* sex since my law school finals." To those readers who *didn't* attend law school, the last night in the dorms often becomes a soul-wrenching orgy *so* exhausting even twenty-somethings get worn out.

I suddenly regretted that blurt, hoping she didn't take it as pathetic pleading *please, just once*. But, she grabbed my face, laughing. "*Ho-boy, Davie*," she managed at length, her sweatshirt bouncing lustily. "*All* right, *changed* my mind: let's take the edge off us *both*." She stood up as she whipped her sweatshirt off. "But *Davie*: we're *not* getting romantically *involved*, OK?"

Just sex? Better than the shower. "But," I gulped as she pushed her sweatpants off swiftly, "can we at least *snooze* together?"

She looked curious as she peeled her underwear off. "Why?"

"I've never done *that*." As *she* was disrobing—ten seconds tops—I sat frozen on the loveseat, unable to move.

"*Sure*," she smiled, crawling into bed. "You *coming?*"

I breathed deep, mumbled "*workin'* on it," and got naked in record time—for *me*, anyway.

"No *kissing*, Davie," she breathed. "*Too* intimate, OK?"

"Sure." Right *then*, I'd have agreed to *anything*.

Though I'd *seen* more sex in movies than I'd *had*, I still preferred a live woman: the *3D* ones respond better than the *2D* ones.

If there hadn't already been a church for *climax sleep*, I would have had to *start* one.

✳✳✳

"Sleep OK," I smiled at Ellen as she arrived in the lobby.

"As OK as could be *expected*," she grunted, squinting. "And good morning to *you*, too."

"Morning." Julia came out of the elevator at about that moment, and it was all I could do *not* to burst into a wide smile when I saw her. But she looked at me with her infectious grin and bright eyes…and a *barely* noticeable *tic* of her eye as we went out to wait for the shuttle.

Now, everyone knows that there are *two* kinds of winks:

- Those meant for *everyone*;
- Those meant for *you*.

Her wink said, *me, too,* as she declared aloud, "morning, guys. We *got* everything? Ellen, did *you* look at those files at *all* last night?"

"I did, some," Ellen sighed. "Some *bizarre* stuff in there." She frowned slightly, her eyes shifting back and forth between us before she mumbled, "just keep it *quiet*. Nothing worse for a *woman* in the Bureau than to get caught being *involved* with an agent in her detail."

That obvious? "*What* are you…?" I started.

"Just *fun*, Nancy," Julia sighed, "just *fun*."

"Then why didn't you call *me*," Ellen frowned slightly. "*I* could *use* some *fun*." She glanced at me. "What? You think *I* don't *like fun*?"

"*No*, but," I stepped forward as the shuttle van pulled up to the doors, "you left so *early*…."

"Yeah," Julia added, "you *said* you were *tired*…."

"*And* you think I'm an old stick," Ellen grunted, hoisting her bags into the back of the van.

"You *did* give us morning marching orders when you *left*," I said.

"Yeah." She seemed…contrite. "Look, I *know* what you guys *thought* about me at the Academy. 'Thinks she *knows* it all; thinks her *shit* don't stink.' Well, as a woman *and* a legacy, I was under a microscope the whole time I was *there*. Jules, as the only *other* woman in the class, you were their *only* distraction. I couldn't look twice at *anyone* for fear of…ah, *shit*." She sat in the back row of the van, between Julia and me. "School's *out*, you guys, and *I* need a night out *and* some of *that*. How about Friday? What do *you* think?"

I shrugged. "I've got a Reserve drill this weekend, but Friday…?" Because my family couldn't have afforded my education without help, I won an ROTC scholarship that helped pay my way. Because of *that*, the US Army *also* owned a piece of me for the next decade.

"*My* place," Julia smiled. "I've got some ribs in my freezer."

"*Perfect*," Ellen declared, slapping both our thighs before she leaned over and whispered in my ear, "no *kissing*, Davie. Too personal." She whispered in Julia's ear a moment later; Jules smiled and winked *for* me.

Good thing *we* were the only passengers *in* the shuttle.

✳✳✳

"Where's…there's no *security* here?" Ellen thought it odd that the podium and metal detector were gone from the entryway/lobby. "I thought *all* Federal buildings had a guard."

"Maybe not," I sighed, lugging the file box. "Monday was hazing, so *maybe*…."

We walked through the cavernous lobby, our footfalls loud on the slate floor. A solid *click* signaled the inner door being unlocked. Good thing because we hadn't been issued access codes. "Huh," Ellen shouted. "They've probably been watching us since we got to the parking lot."

At three in the afternoon on a Wednesday, we expected everyone to be hard at work. But, there was *nothing*, not a soul anywhere. *So who let us in?* Ernie's room…nada. We looked at each other quizzically before I asked, "We haven't *been* upstairs, have we?"

"Nope," Julia agreed. "Let's have a look."

Thinking ambush, we decided against the one small elevator…we *had been* buzzed in, after all. Instead, we took the *least* obvious of the two staircases—the one closest to Ernie's room—as stealthily as possible…

…And were indeed *ambushed* by a dozen people just inside another double-basketball-court-sized room. "Glad you figured it out so fast," Ernie boomed. "We had bets on how fast you were gonna get up here. Tony *said* you guys were pretty smart."

"Tony…"

"Grafton. We worked together on the Manson mess."

"*Charlie* Manson," Ellen gasped. "You worked the Manson case out of *here*?"

"We were pulling records together from *everywhere,* vetting the stuff, and taking it to LA. Tony was a courier. J. Edgar was terrified by the *idea* of *helter-skelter.*"

The upstairs room, unlike the downstairs, was filled and subdivided only by filing cabinets of all descriptions. However, there had been *some* attempts to keep the *types* of cabinets together. I was marveling at this display of the humble filing cabinet's evolution when I spotted an enormous carnival wheel at the far end of the room. "What's *that* for," I asked.

"You'll find out Monday," Ernie said.

"Why Monday?"

"Because that's *the* day. Now, come on: you brought some files back."

We followed Ernie back downstairs as he whistled tunelessly. "You did *OK* in Denver," he declared, "and you *probably* figured out why we sent you."

"Sink or swim," I blurted.

"You *got* it. If you couldn't handle *that* little errand on short notice and with minimal information, you *ain't* gonna work here." He looked at each of us in turn. "Our *main* output here is SSAs. That's what the behavioral science eggheads say, anyway. For now, *they're* in fashion in the Bureau."

"We got lectures from them at the Academy," Julia offered. "The guy who profiled Ted Bundy…."

"*That* blowhard," Ernie sniffed. "Can't hold either his tongue *or* his liquor."

✳✳✳

"Goodnight, guys," Ellen sighed, trailing her bags into our building. "Need sleep."

"Me, too," Julia declared. "See you tomorrow. I'll drive."

"OK," I said, following them into the elevator. I was just unpacking, looking through my small stack of mail: junk and instructions for annual training in August from my Reserve unit, the 511th MI Company. I was just about to figure out what to do about dinner when the phone rang. "Hello…"

"Da*vie*," I could *hear* Julia grinning into the phone. "You interested in dinner?"

"Well," I replied, thinking of my larder: two TV dinners, pork chops, a frozen pizza, chicken thighs, and a steak in the freezer; a sack of potatoes, two cans of soup in the cupboard; three hot dogs, a bottle of mustard, a jar of mayo, some Mexican takeout in the fridge; one bun on the counter. "Was *just* thinking…."

"Meet me downstairs in ten minutes."

So I was downstairs in eight minutes. We decided on a Chinese joint called the Yellow Horse, a storefront in another strip mall down the street. Julia hadn't said a great deal since we got in my car, but she spoke first when we sat down. "Davie," she smiled, "we can't do *that* too often because we…."

"Might twitch the needle, yeah." Annually at least—on demand at worst—we were hooked up to a polygraph* and asked questions just to make sure we were on the straight and narrow. Twitching *that* needle was *not* A Good Thing. Most of their questions were about subversive and criminal activities. Still, *some* were about our relations with fellow FBI agents. "So, a *one-time* thing?"

"*Hope* not," she shrugged, "because you're *pretty terrific* in bed." *Any* guy likes to know that *he's* gratifying…*especially* without practice. "Just not on *any* kind of a schedule, or more than once or twice a month." She smiled, a secret kind of smile. "Besides, I want to *find* a guy I can kiss *without* twitching the needle."

I nodded sagely. Part of me was relieved because, ultimately, I wanted someone *I* could introduce at an office party. "Thanks. *You're* pretty good, too." She smiled at that…like I knew *good sex* from *bad* after fewer than none-of-*your*-beeswax encounters. "And Ellen…on Friday…?"

---

* Called "The Box" in slang. Even though they could *never* work on a politician, reporter, or any *other* pathological liars, they are *still* in use by federal law enforcement.

"Dinner and wine. She *won't* want a threesome."

We talked about other things, drove back to our building, and said a *professional for public consumption* good-night with a wink that said, *see ya, lover.*

And I *didn't* need a cold shower that night.

✳✳✳

"So, OK. I'll consolidate the *old* file with the Denver file, make a new inventory and summary. Do your reports based on your notes," Ernie said the following day. That day we *finally* got walked around the office, introduced to the other agents, and were issued key codes to get in the front door.

"Notes," I asked tentatively. "*Sure, we…*"

"Took notes," Ellen smiled. She was a *convincing* fibber.

"And scan all that literature you grabbed," Ernie continued. "I've already inventoried it." He shrugged. "Neither dangerous nor subversive."

"*They* seized on the promiscuity, I'm guessing," Julia suggested. "From J. Edgar's day…."

"Huh," Ernie grunted. Ernie had a vast repertoire of inflections for saying *huh*, covering the full spectrum of emotions. *This one* spoke volumes about Julia's suggestion: *very good, kid; keep it up.* "While true, that's not necessarily *all* the truth. Sex in public—even if *approved of* by bystanders—can point to more liberal mores." He looked around at us—younger than he by a generation— and grinned. "*That's* the way it *is*, kids. This *is* the *Bureau*. J. Edgar's shade still stalks these halls. *These* people may be libertines, but they're *not* preaching sedition and none of them are approachable…."

"Approachable," I said before I blurted, "*mice.*"

"*Exactly*," Ernie smiled. Ellen and Julia looked puzzled. "The four main motives for turncoats and spies, my children: Money, Ideology, Compromise, and Ego—*MICE* in the spy and blackmail trade. Nearly anyone can be turned into a source or a *problem* if approached with the *right* one of those four."

"Offer a big spender money," I said, "or a tell a disaffected employee that there's a better way of life he could work for." I'd learned *that* in Human Intelligence Officer Basic.

"Yes. Or, what we *might* be looking at here—public exposure of illicit behavior," Ernie nodded, "or appeals to a passed-over bureaucrat for promotion...*if* they do what the bad guy wants. *That's* what a lot of these files were for: to determine *who* or *what* might employ MICE to compromise security or commit crimes. Wrap this one up and send it to Central Records. But first, do your Expense and Time Reports."

"Our *what*," I blurted. At the Academy, we were pelted with a gazillion different kinds of reports. But, no one *ever* mentioned either expenses *or* time reporting.

"Yeah," Ernie declared, pulling forms out of his drawer. "Expense and Time. When you *travel*, you fill *these* out. You got receipts for everything?"

"Of course," Ellen announced. Julia and I just looked guilty.

"Just remember to receipt *everything* in the future. Just check the *Standard* boxes this time. And be as precise as *possible* with your time on the road. You *don't* punch a clock—strictly speaking—but the head shed wants to know how long we're out there and on what."[*]

We had table spaces in Ernie's room and were assigned desks with our own phones in The Pit—the area outside Ernie's door. *My* desk was between Morgan Towne—a spindly brunette with a lovely smile and dulcet voice—and Frank Hitchcock, a bulky, older guy with odd brown eyes and big hands. Julia and Ellen were on the other side of the cubicle wall. "*Where* you work is up to you," Ernie told us, "as long as you *do* it. We don't make that many *arrests* because of the nature of our work...."

"Um," Ellen asked—timidly for her, "how are we to be evaluated if we don't make arrests?"

---

[*] *Most* FBI agents *work* (office, home and elsewhere) about fifty hours a week, continuing education, update courses, and range time included. If *SPD* did that *little*, we'd have been considered *lazy*.

"*Excellent* question," Ernie smiled. "Remember, when you're talking to other law enforcement at *any* level, *solicit* cooperation, don't *demand* it; that's *not* how *we* work. Now get two new Rolodexes and a ledger each out of the supply cabinet and get to work"…then turned and walked away.

We blinked after him, gazed at each other, and scattered to our desks.

I started to read, scratching out notes. *Usually,* I would have had different colored sticky-note pads scattered all over my desk. While there *were* stacks of 'em in the cabinet, *this* was Rolodex land. Ernie had a dozen in his workroom—steel and plastic—in all the colors they *ever* made. He also had a computer terminal tucked away in a seldom-used corner, next to a microfilm reader/printer.

In 1980, getting data into a computer was a laborious process, and *retrieving* it could be even *more* challenging. Computers then were better at number-crunching than intuition. *We* needed *text data retrieval*, which is more intuitive than analytical. Computer programs of the intuitive type were not available to us *if* they existed at all. Hence the Rolodexes.

I made my first Rolodex entries and soon discovered *why* we needed *two*: one was a master directory to everything else. And *that* led to discovering why the supply closet had so *many* 8x10 ledgers, both indexed and plain. And *so* many pencils and erasers for entries that needed to *change*. And *so* many stick pens and felt-tip pens for *permanent* entries. Thus, a *master* Rolodex would point to a *different* Rolodex or ledger. In a day, I was using *three* Rolodexes—which would point to a *ledger*…or *two*…or *more*.

And *this* was how our personal dataset was built. And I managed to figure all *this* out before lunch on Thursday. I could *not* have been more proud.

I was so excited to tell my partners that it must have been stamped on my forehead, and I could see it on theirs when we met at lunch at Bell's Cafeteria two blocks from the SPD. "Oh, this stuff is *easy*," Julia declared. "Making a *paper* computer work like those *fake* computers on TV...."

"Yeah," Ellen agreed. "Once you realize the *genius* of the system...."

"Which system," Morgan asked from across the table, "the *Packard* System?"

"You call it the *Packard* System," I asked. "Named for Ernie?"

"Yeah: *everyone* here uses it. I've been here for two years and haven't found *any better way* for the esoteric stuff *we* work on." She smiled. "Ladies: you're too *dressy*. Wear stuff you *don't* have to dry-clean if someone throws up on you. And *pockets*: get rid of your *purses* as *fast* as you can. Just glad you guys joined us. Now we can get our own rest room.* All three of you need to come to my party this weekend. New SAs in the area are invited."

"There's a DC office?" Julia seemed surprised.

"Yeah: on 4th Street. Biggest in the country. My dad worked there '69 to '75."

"Oh, *you're* a legacy, *too*," Ellen brightened. "*My* father's in the Albany office…" And off *they* went, recounting family moves, long weeks when Dad wasn't around; the missed concerts, games, plays, proms.

Just worked *out* that way, I guess…

***

"Closing meeting," Ernie stood and stretched his full height behind his desk Friday afternoon. We were in his room, hammering away on typewriters or, in my case, trying to dream up something *not* snarky to say under *Threat Assessment*. There was nothing we didn't know about the Church of the Blessed Climax Sleep by then, and there had *never* been

---

* Julia and Ellen raised the number of women assigned to Special Projects to thirteen—nine sworn and four administrative staff. GSA building management policy insisted on a minimum of 10% male/female ratio before a "ladies only" restroom would be authorized. There was no corresponding female/male ratio, which was a concern in the word processing pools at the time.

anything subversive about it. Still, I had to admit…*some members may be vulnerable to approaches by foreign powers or criminal elements*…so I said *that.*

"Where," Ellen asked, looking up from her typewriter.

"Gaston's," Ernie answered, "down Evansville Avenue about a half-mile, on the north side. Be there by three."

"Two-thirty now," I glanced at Julia. "Does *that* mean…?"

"It *means* that unless you've got some life-and-death job to finish—and you *don't*—you're leaving the building until Monday." Ernie shrugged on his coat. He looked out-of-place without his snap-brim fedora that was parked on a top shelf. "Let's go."

Gaston's was a faux-French cocktail lounge that catered to the government contractors in the neighborhood. There weren't many patrons: a half-dozen at a long bar, a few at tables and booths. Just beyond a group of pool tables, a set of double doors opened onto a large room where I saw Dusty talking to Fred while twizzling a drink. We got ours at the bar and ventured in.

The tables were arranged in a large U. Dusty sat at a small table at the top of the arc. As we arrived, several others came in behind us, filling the room rapidly. The room *seemed* drafty, hot, and wet, and everyone took off their coats.

"*All* right," Dusty shouted, "let's get started. *Seats,* everyone." Ellen and Julia flanked Ernie; I sat beside Ellen. "So, today, we welcome three new SAs: Clawson, Drew, and Parkinson. Please rise."

We stood up; I felt like I was on display.

"Ernie: will they suit?" Dusty sounded as if he were pronouncing sentence.

"I believe so," Ernie answered, his face not moving. "They show initiative, daring, good analytic skills. They're team players: they'll do."

"Very well." Dusty stood up. "Raise your right hands and repeat after me. I—state your name—do solemnly swear that I will never divulge the activities of the Special Projects Division and that they will be my *only* concern during working hours, except in situations most dire, so *help* me, *Hanna*."

What struck me as odd is that no one snickered at this *oath*—I thought it *had* to be more hazing. Everyone else in the room—nearly fifty people—took this as something serious.

So did we.

"Thank you and be seated. Down to files. SSA Brock."

"*Three* files closed this week." Edwin Brock was a lumpy man with wisps of gray hair and a strained voice. He seemed to be older than an FBI agent *should* be. "SA Gruber?

"File number 34-56421-3498-LIB," Christian Gruber began, reading from a paper. "Thomas Ahern, AKA Fabulous Adam, born 1936. A professional wrestler, Ahern made public statements in 1955 and 1956 that were detrimental to the wrestling sport and construed as unpatriotic. Thomas Ahern was killed in a barroom brawl in Houston in 1973 and thus no longer poses a threat. File sent to Central Records as closed."

"Good. Next?"

This went on for some time. Each presenter read about stuff that *sounded* maybe subversive or compromising…once, or people who *could* have been…once. Finally, he called on Ernie. "SSA Packard."

"SA *Clawson* has a report."

I DO? I felt like I'd been selected to report on what I did on my summer vacation. I cleared my throat loudly, my mouth dry. "My, um, my…we've been working on, um, the Church of the Blessed Climax Sleep. There's nothing particularly…."

"*File* number," Dusty declared, visibly annoyed. "Come *on*: we don't *have* all night."

"I, um…"

"File number 35-26945-239601-LIB," Ellen offered. "Originally the Church of Idiot Worshippers. Long story short: they're not *quite* a church, but the IRS treats them as one. It's a *club* that *once* threw orgies. Nothing subversive about it *now*, and there probably *never* was. File updated and sent to Central Records as closed."

The room was silent, waiting, until it burst into applause. "*Great* save, Drew," Dusty announced. "*A round* on the Division. Clawson: a *great* partner you've got there."

You don't know the half of it. I nudged Ellen with an elbow as I sat down. "Thanks."

"You'll thank *me* later," she smiled, nudging me back.

Will I? "You remembered the file number?"

"No, but how would *they* know? Like I *said...later.*"

If you can't *dazzle* 'em with brilliance, *baffle* 'em with bullshit...or a convincing bluff.

The Weekend We REALLY Bonded

Or, The Greatest Party Ever

"**G**reat ribs," I declared that evening, sitting at the islet in Julia's kitchen. Her kitchen, like *mine*, was *maybe* six feet wide by ten long, with a sink, dishwasher, and cupboards on one side; cabinets, refrigerator, and stove on the other, with a microwave above the stove. It was big enough for one person to cook in, but *not* two without injury. Julia sat on the inside; Ellen on the outside; me on the end. The only furniture the building provided was the islet's *four* stools. How *four* adults could sit there was a mystery.

"Yes, indeed," Ellen added. "Family recipe?" Both she and Julia had changed into *matching* shorts and sleeveless yokes.

"*Sort* of," Julia answered. "My Dad's the cook around the house: Mom *can*, but she's out a lot. Dad got this rub from his college roommate."

"So, roommate to father to daughter," I sighed. "At least it stays alive."

"Yeah. *I'm* going into the living room," Julia declared, hefting her wine glass and the bottle.

I sat in an old red wing-back chair; Ellen and Julia shared what looked like its companion sofa. Between us sat a slightly scratched coffee table adorned with coasters in several patterns, most labeled *GM*. Julia's furniture, like mine, was *probably* family cast-offs. "Hosting my *first* dinner party," Julia smiled. "How'd I do?"

"Fine," I nodded. "Couldn't *ask* for better."

"As good as any dinner party *I've* been to," Ellen added, "and *I've* been to *way* too many. I'll have to start doing it, too. You, too, Dave."

"*Have* to," I asked, puzzled.

"*Expected* to," Ellen nodded. "Bureau tradition."

"So, this afternoon," I asked, "what was *that* all about?"

"Half-*real*, half-*fake* is *my* guess," Ellen declared. "Since they—*we*—don't *have* any more than a handful of prosecutions, they do *that* regularly to feel like they're doing something." She shrugged oddly, cocking up her left shoulder and tilting her head. "*Feels* that way, anyway."

"*We* need to be better prepared," I said. "Why did Ernie throw me in the deep end like that?"

"See what you would do," Julia said.

"See what *we* would do," Ellen nodded sagely. "We had to *show them we're* a *team*." She leaned back into the sofa, stretching and crossing her legs. "*Good* wine, Jules."

"Yeah," Julia said, leaning back, stretching, and smiling.

"Uh-huh," I said. What I *know* about wine would fill a postage stamp. A law school classmate tried to teach several of us *wine appreciation*. She could *afford* to teach us to *appreciate* the difference between Ripple and Boone's Farm.

I gave in to the urge to lean back and enjoy the *company* and the *stillness*. We sat silent, unmoving except our heads and eyes, for 21 minutes: there was a clock right in front of me on a shelf by the TV. I felt calm, relaxed, *happy*, gazing at my partner's legs *without* their eyes rolling.

"How *is* he," Ellen asked Julia; then Ellen winked at me…that little *tic*.

"He's fine; *just* fine," Julia answered…then *she* winked.

"Dave," Ellen sighed, standing up, "*c'mon*." I followed her out the door and across the hall to her apartment. Ellen was a more *focused* and *determined* version of *very* athletic Julia. We slept soundly until I kissed her cheek as I left; she stirred, smiled, and rolled over.

And, *do-de-DUNK* never occurred to me.

✳✳✳

Morgan's building was in the middle of a block of nearly-identical three-story red-brick townhouses with different colored trim. It was nearly 8 o'clock Saturday night when I got there, still 80 humid degrees without a *breath* of fresh air.

Morgan's front door was open: I half-expected curb-to-curb cars parked on the quiet suburban street. There were *some*, but not *that* many. I spotted Julia's Chevy, but not Ellen's BMW—so they carpooled it.

Morgan was in the kitchen just inside the door; she waved me in, said, "go mingle," and went back to her guests. I looked around until I saw the beer keg. Sal Kell, one of our classmates, pumped for me. My partners, Sal and I were the *only* ones there from the just-graduated class. "So, Sal," I drawled, "where did *you* end up?"

"I asked for LA, San Francisco, or Sacramento, and I *got* Baltimore," Sal answered, gulping his beer. "You?"

"SPD."

"*Yeah*," Sal blinked furiously. "Huh."

"What have *you* heard about it," I asked, curious.

"Nothing. What have they got you doing?"

"They've kept us busy…."

"Getting coffee and filing dead reports?"

"Yeah, sure." We chatted about classmate assignments we knew of for a few minutes and *another* abysmal Washington Senators season. There were ten other people on the first floor that I could see. There was no traffic up the stairs to, presumably, bedrooms where raucous party-*do-de-DUNK* would be ongoing. I was weary from my first drill with the 511th, still in fatigues *sans* shirt, so I stuck out like a preacher at a stag party. Predictably, no one was paying a great deal of attention to an unfashionable Army 1st Lieutenant.

"Sal, I've gotta *find* someone," I said. He'd already been distracted by another guy who knew more about baseball—hell, *dogs* knew more about baseball than *I* did by *then*.

The second floor had a bathroom, bedroom, and small sitting/TV space just inside a balcony. One of three chatting women glanced up at me and went back to the conversation.

So I went up *another* flight of stairs...

And I spotted Ellen out on the balcony, Julia in a chair, and *another* woman sitting with Julia. The other woman looked up at me with what *looked* like genuine *interest, smiled...*

To her Cheshire smile, I'll stand on file

She's all I ever wanted...

...And said, "Hi!"

"Dave Clawson, *this* is Beth Ritter; Beth, Dave," Julia declared. "Beth and I were neighbors in college, hails from Ohio."

"*Another* Great Lakes refugee," I said, lamely.

Ya know those scenes in the movies where the heroine looks up and sees *that* stranger and immediately falls head-over-heels in *lust*? *Real* guys *can't* make *that* happen.* I ambled *just* fast enough to get there before the pretty mirage vanished, hopefully *not* so fast as to come off as an over-eager lounge-lizard. Beth was a short-haired dishwater blonde with hazel eyes and a small, lithe body...and *nice* legs emerging from the *shortest* skorts I'd *ever* seen. "Move for work or school?"

"Work," her *lovely* voice answered. "I'm in accounting at the IRS."

"Oh," I gasped in mock terror, "we need to be careful, Jules."

"*Nothing* to do with fieldwork," Beth smiled. "You are *all* FBI?"

"Feeble Bureaucrats Incorporated," Ellen called in loudly from the balcony, leaning back against the railing. "We have the honor of having been in the same class and assigned to the same detail." She stepped out of the damp air and closed the glass door behind her. "And we're *great* buddies, ain't we?"

"Sure," I answered, glancing at Julia.

"We are *so* honored," Julia smiled. "*Dave* is our *shining studly*-light."

---

* Except that loudmouth in the corner saloon who brags about it happening to him *every* night. But, if he's *there* from sundown to last call *every night...when?*

Studly-light? "Well, I try...."

"And because *he's* our *good* buddy," Ellen declared, "*Julia* and I are off seeking more *appropriate* company." With that, Ellen and Julia went down the stairs, arm-in-arm, giggling like co-eds out for milkshakes. And, they *both* winked at me...a little tic that said *good luck, buddy.*

"Mind if I sit down," I asked politely.

"I think *that* was the idea," Beth giggled.

"How...I mean, *what's* your...*who* do you *know* here...?"

"Morgan," she said, leaning back in the chair and crossing her legs. "Coincidence running into Jules, though."

"Ah," I nodded sagely. "And *you* live...?"

"About ten minutes from here," she answered, lowering her eyes and voice demurely, "but *we* just met, Dave, and I don't do *casual.*" We *knew* what *do casual* meant. It was important in 1980 to get everything out in the open, right up front, especially for young working women.[*]

Defining relationships in the '80s was important. In the popular vernacular, *seeing someone* meant going out occasionally and perhaps getting as far as second base...sometimes. *Dating* included *do-de-DUNK* less often than the more committed *going steady, shacking up/ living together,* or *engaged* and *married. Casual* was just one *do-de-DUNK,* sometimes with real names exchanged.

"I was *just* asking about where you lived," I smiled my most— *hopefully*—disarming smile as I leaned back and crossed my legs. *That* casual move was painfully short-lived in combat boots. "Just making conversation."

"You don't *have* to do that," she sighed, arching her back. Beth wasn't *well*-endowed, but *that* little move produced a *most* alluring *profile.* "My evil twin can hold up *her* end."

Evil...twin? "Is she *here?*" I quickly eyeballed the exits, wondering how hard jumping over the balcony rail would be. *I went to jump school...good landing on concrete from three stories up, and I might limp away...*

---

[*] That made it easier to ambush guys on the third date with '*you never TRY anything.*'

"She's *inside* me, *ever* watching me. The *witch* wants to drag you by your belt into this *empty* bedroom and *have* her *way* with you."

Ho-boy. "Ah…you…um…." *Run! Now!*

"I wouldn't *mind* if she *could* leave my body and ravish you. But she *can't*, so I *do* mind. There's a *lot* more to a *serious* relationship that could lead to *something* more than just *hunchy-punchy. We'd* need to get to know each other, Dave."

"*I* believe you're right." I decided—despite my brief panic over the "evil twin" bit— that I wanted *more* from Beth. And I *wanted* to wait for it *if* she started to sound *sane* in the next few moments.

"*I* need *respect*, and *like*, and mutuality of understanding just in case one of *your* little guys reaches his goal."

She wants to agree on how to raise the kids before we swap phone numbers? Sane, if a little premature. "*Admirable* thinking. But I gotta ask: Do you treat all the guys you just met to a description of your evil twin's desires and your reasons for denying those desires?"

"*Only* those I decide I'm *going* to give my number to. *I'll* show you *mine* if *you* show me *yours.* She reached into a shirt pocket and pulled out a business card, scrawling a number on the back.

Approaching rationality... "I don't *have* real ones yet." I scribbled the main office number on one of the generic cards they gave us at graduation. "Call the office, and you *might* get the last occupant's voice mail—*I* haven't set mine up yet. Call me at *home*," I wrote *my* number on the back, "and you *might* get a machine as soon as I *get* one. But call after…say…seven, and I *should* be there any night."

She took mine; gave me hers. "No machine, but a housemate, Cindy. She's there *most* mornings, works *most* nights. Introduce yourself before next Wednesday, and we'll *see* about *later.*" She stood up, pushing her skorts down *maybe* a millimeter. "*Let's* rejoin the party."

I stood up, and she burst out laughing. "Dave: I *like* you. Not many guys sit through my evil twin schtick. But…" she winked *slowly*, "*call.* C'mon…" Then she stopped at the top of the stairs, her face serious.

"*She's still* down there." She looked up at me. "There's a *woman* on the next floor…" She undid the top button of her blouse plus the two closest to her waistband and then smeared some lipstick around her mouth. "Now, *you*." She pulled my t-shirt out and mussed my short hair. "Unconvincing," she declared, and before I knew what was happening, she was grinding her lips into mine. Not a *kiss*: more a *grinding attack* that dimly hurt. "There. *C'mon*," she grinned, hooking my arm and heading down the stairs, "be a *real guy* for a minute."

"*Hey*, Melanie," Beth said when she saw one of the women who ignored me on the 2nd Floor. "What's doing," as she *conspicuously* straightened her blouse.

"Not…much," the dark-haired woman looked at me sideways. "You?"

"Just…oh, *go* clean yourself up, Dave," she pushed me into the bathroom, whispering, "Meet you downstairs."

I made myself presentable, knowing what just happened. As I stepped out again, Melanie glared at me as if I'd killed her cat. I was a *beard*, all right. I'd been worse things. *That*, at least, was *reasonable*.

When we met a short time later, she brought me a fresh beer. "Melanie tried to hit on me as soon as I got here; *her* kind doesn't take *no* for an answer." She bumped my thigh with her hip. "*Thanks* for playing along."

"*Any*thing for a lady," I sighed, confused but amused and intrigued at the same time. I wished I'd had enough experience to *know* if Beth *was* crazy or just had one of *those* nights.

And I *loved* her smile.

Beth drifted away; I drifted towards Ellen and Julia, who were chatting up a couple of guys and a gal, party-fashion. At about 9:30, I had to go because I had to be back in Anacostia early in the morning. I found Morgan, bade her goodnight, and headed for the door when someone grabbed my belt.

"Hey," Beth smiled. "Taking off?"

"Yeah: got drill tomorrow."

"Well, *call* me," she said, following me out the door. I was halfway down the short driveway with her behind me when she reached for my elbow. "I really *am* sorry," she *sounded* sincere. "I just didn't want to wedge my way past her again without sending a message she *couldn't* misunderstand."

"I'm not used to the *knight in shining armor* bit."

"Well," she reached up and kissed me again. "*Call* me, and I'll make it up to you."

Sometimes, the moment just *seizes* you, so I leaned down and kissed her…for a *while*…and she *didn't* run away. "OK, I'll call."

"My evil twin can't *wait*, and *she's* really sorry, too."

✳✳✳

I stopped for gas at an all-night station and put air in my often-soft left-front tire. I got my mail out of the box (more junk and an electric bill… to the previous occupant) and climbed the stairs. I found my apartment as I had left it that morning: odds and ends of furniture, bare walls, books stacked on every surface, porch door open…

What? SHIT!

My first thought was for my weapon and credentials, which I found in the safe bolted to the closet floor. After that…I wasn't sure, as I hadn't found places for all my stuff yet. *Did I leave it open?*

And the phone rang. "Yeah?"

"Davie, is *your* porch door open?"

"Yeah."

"Mine too. So is Ellen's."

"OK. Anything…?"

"No." Silence. "We're on our way to you."

I opened my door a crack and tried to make sense of my shambles.

"Hello," I heard a few minutes later as they made a beeline into my kitchen. Ellen wore a zipper-front shift, wine glass in hand; Julia wore a loosely-belted robe. She sloshed more wine into two glasses and handed one to me as I sat on my end stool. "How did you get on with Beth?"

"I got her out of a jam with Melanie…." I shifted on my stool and ventured a look behind the island: *nothing* on Julia's legs; *no* shoes; *nothing* else.

"Yeah, *Mel's* pretty aggressive," Ellen sniffed. "I've known *her* since Atlanta."

"How did *you* know *her*?"

"Another FBI brat. She followed some gal here."

"So," Ellen declared. "What about our intruder?"

"Well, the police *aren't* here," I sighed, "so *I'm* guessing more hazing. So, broomstick in the porch door track?"

"*Good* idea," Ellen said, finishing her wine. "*I'm* for bed. *C'mon*, guys," she sighed, turning towards *my* bedroom.

"*Right* there," Julia said, downing her wine as she stood up. "*C'mon*, Davie."

No *do-de-DUNK*; just sleeping-with-buddies companionship.

It felt safe.

✳✳✳

Julia opened an eye at me as I got dressed Sunday morning. She winked when I kissed her cheek as I left. Ellen had *already* left.

When I got home after drill, it was hot and sunny, with a dull miasma hanging over us. Sunday night's laundry pile was good-sized but not titanic.

There's something Godawful about weekend evenings when living alone, without the *immediate* prospect of companionship. Though Julia, Ellen, and I had scratched each other's itches, there could *never* be any long-term intimacy unless one of us left the Bureau.

That's what I was thinking about—*and* dinner—when the phone rang. "Hi, Dave," the bright voice asked, "Beth: from the party."

There was a theory about how *soon* people should contact each other after the first exchange of phone numbers: no *less* than two days, nor *more* than seven. Beth was *not* a believer in *that…thank God.*

"Sure," I said, suddenly feeling better about laundry *and* the rest. Strange how your mood can change in an instant with the sound of a *particular* voice. "How *you* doing today?"

"Fine. Bored with laundry and puzzles. You? You had some *Army* thing today?"

"Reserve drill. You do puzzles?"

"Yeah, a lot of number-heads do. If you hadn't been doing *that*, what *would* you have been doing?"

"Trying to make sense of my new apartment, looking for furniture, doing laundry, and thinking about calling *you.*"

"I *know* some people in the furniture business."

"Really? Well, maybe *we* should…."

"I'll meet you at Hale Brothers Furniture in Georgetown Saturday. It's *good* furniture, but it's not *that* expensive."

"OK: say 0900…."

"They open at 10."

"Ten, then."

"Don't be late."

I sat and blinked at the phone when I hung up. *Two minutes and I'm looking forward to next weekend.*

The extraordinary plainness of furniture-shopping as a first-date activity suddenly smacked me upside the head. It *hinted* at domesticity. And, there's something about being in public with someone you *like* and *might* even…

Yeah, *some*day…*maybe…*

Founders of the Fourth Reich

Or, Sometimes You Find A Live One

We were told to be in the office by *7 every* morning, but on Mondays we first met up on the 2nd Floor, home of that enormous carnival wheel. Since *on-time* was *late*, we showed up at 6:45.

The end of the room where the wheel lived had a row of steel tables against a solid row of file cabinets. When we got up there, nearly everyone was already sitting on tables, sipping coffee, deep in conversation. Before I got there, I imagined that idle FBI chit-chat would be about criminals and cases. But mostly they talked about sports, especially golf and fishing. Sometimes, home improvement or car repair, gardening, or cooking were bandied about. Occasionally, kids and wives and sweethearts. *Rarely* model-building, to my disappointment.

"OK: everyone ready?" Dusty grabbed a long lever behind the wheel.

"Just *yank* the damn thing, Dusty," Ernie growled, a mouthful of Danish in his mouth.

"*Round* and *round* we *go!*" Dusty pulled down with both hands, and the enormous wheel started to turn, slowly at first but with increasing speed. Some watched in fascination; most ignored it. Ernie watched the *Time* magazine-size flapper that noisily clattered away.

The wheel turned for more than a minute as it began to slow down *ever* so gradually. "Where'd it come from," I asked Ernie.

"Evidence storage was going to pitch it; it came here instead."

We watched in rapt fascination as the wheel slowed for what *felt* like another five minutes before it stopped. "C-17-4," Dusty announced. "Row C; cabinet 17, fourth drawer. Agent Nussbaum; *your* turn." Sam Nussbaum disappeared for a few minutes and came back with an armload of file folders. He was a short, stocky guy who would never have *been* in the FBI if J. Edgar were still around, *especially* not wearing a *kippah*. "Hand 'em out," Dusty intoned.

As Sam passed by, someone from each team grabbed at least two folders; some grabbed three; Ernie grabbed five. When Sam ran out of folders, Dusty clapped his hands together. "OK, let's get to it."

✳✳✳

Ernie set the pile of files down on his blotter, shrugged off his coat, and sat. "OK, *this* is how this works. *After* we get the week's files…."

"Don't we *lose* something when we do that," Ellen interrupted. "Aren't they in some sort of order?"

"Wish they *were*," Ernie replied. "But we *got* them in random batches, boxes, and truckloads. Any *new* files we get, we stuff into empty drawers."

"How were they…I mean, what were the instructions about who or *what* warranted a Liberty Bell File?" Julia, among other admirable traits, could see the obvious that no one else *thought* of.

"Executive Directive 30-001 and its addendums." Ernie reached behind him, pulling a binder out of a row of binders. "Project Liberty Bell." He pushed the binder across his desk. "Read it *all* for a study in ambiguity. Hoover wanted to collect information on any*one* or any *organization* that even *sounded* remotely subversive. *Hell*, there are files on the *Boy Scouts* in there—some wiseguys *said* it *could* have been a den of gays that could be exploited." He shrugged. "By the time I joined the Bureau, few people in the field *cared*. They just chalked the whole project up to J. Edgar's paranoia. Some offices made stuff up out of whole cloth. *Here*." He handed me a file folder. "Read the summary sheet to the class."

File Number Ending 06745-LIB
File Created: November 16ᵗʰ, 1954
Name: Sisters of The Proletarian Revolution
Origin: Based in or around Jersey City, New Jersey. Founded by one Alice May Gibbs (b. 1922), AKA Karla Marx AKA Sapphire (first known 1942), an exotic dancer and pornographic model.
Narrative: The manifesto (photostat enclosed) calls for the overthrow of the US Government "by means foul or fair, employing The Sister's unique talents for influencing men." Members: approx. 50. No known activities beyond handing their manifesto out on street corners in Jersey City.
Updates: 1960: Karla Marx arrested in Jersey City for pandering.

"*Huh*," Ernie grunted, turning to his biggest Rolodex. "*Sisters*...no... *proletarian*...no...OK, under *R-Revolution*." He rolled around to another Rolodex: a green plastic one. "And there's... Revolution, *Proletarian*." He looked up, grabbed a ledger off another shelf. "*And* we have brothers— *two* sets, fathers, mothers...now we have *Sisters* of the Proletarian Revolution." He shrugged. "Wonder if we'll find *cousins* somewhere."

"Don't know," I offered.

"*Huh*," Ernie declared—his *most* authoritative *huh*. He glanced at Ellen. "What do *you* think?"

"About *what*?" Ellen had *issues* with spontaneity.

"Sisters of the Proletarian Revolution, of course. What have we been talking about?"

"Well," she hedged, "sounds like a crypto-Red outfit. We should read the manifesto, see what..."

"I *guarantee* you that the first line is *sisters of the world unite; you have nothing to lose but your chains!* or some such," Ernie declared.

I risked his scorn and read:

> *This shall be our cry, Sisters: People of the world unite! You have nothing to lose but your bonds!*

"*Bonds*, not *chains*," Ernie sighed. "She probably did S&M back in the day. Julia: that's yours. What's next, Ellen?"

File Number Ending: 06746-LIB
File Created: 1ˢᵗ November 1954
Name: The Rescue Moby Organization--West
Origin: Based around Little Rock, Arkansas; founded by George Apple (DOB June 1925) AKA Ahab.
Narrative: Apple wrote short story "Ahab's Return," published in "Galaxy Explorers" magazine May 1951 issue (photostat attached). Short story declares that Ahab was a space-time traveler who was attempting to communicate with whales. Story castigates Japan for their whaling practices, potentially upsetting our Japanese allies. Membership unknown.
Updates: November 1956: The Rescue Moby Organization-West identified by letterhead. Further investigation has not uncovered any other Rescue Moby organizations elsewhere.

"What do you make of *that*?"

"Well…based on the ambiguity of the guidelines as *you* describe them, I'd say that the field created the file thinking that they could upset the Japanese."

"But how many of those agents in '54 were war veterans who wouldn't *care* about pissing off the Japanese," I asked boldly.

"An *excellent* point, Dave," Ernie declared. "Indeed: who *would* care?"

"A rookie," Ellen stated. "Somebody who wasn't *in* the war except as a kid, but who does what he's *told*."

"Brilliant," Ernie said, beaming. "And…?"

"And…" Julia started, glancing at Ernie sideways, "*quota*. Someone *needed* a Liberty Bell File."

"Ah! *You*, my *good* girl, have hit upon the most *pernicious* of Directive 30-001's requirements. Supplement 10, Section 5, Paragraph 21A." Ernie pushed the massive tome at me. "Read same."

I flipped through the thin pages until I found…

> *All field offices and agencies shall produce at least one Liberty Bell case each day.*

"*There* you have it, my children," Ernie sighed, placing his chin on a massive hand, elbow propped on the table. "Nine-*tenths* of these *damn* things were *conjured* out of nothing. *Many* of the rest are like *this* one—desperation. That *one summary* and the old photostat you can barely read is probably more paper than that so-called organization ever generated on its own." He sighed again, a most prodigious sigh. "Another one-man-band of a subversive organization. Ellen: *close* that one. Julia: your next file?"

File Number Ending 6234-LIB
File Created: March 21ˢᵗ, 1944
Name: American Phalangist Party
Origin: Circa 1941. Founded by two Lebanese-American brothers, Daniel (B. 1920) and Max (B. 1922) Eutaw, Toledo, Oh., of 2ⁿᵈ-generation Lebanese immigrants.
Narrative: Political party organized to back a candidate for mayor of Toledo, Oh, in the 1942 elections. After loss, party seemed to vanish. Strong overtones of Lebanese nationalism and (possibly financial) support for Phalangists in Lebanon.
Updates: 1967: American Phalangist Party rallies in Toledo and Detroit drew more than 2,000 persons to hear several anti-war, anti-draft speakers. Anti-Israel messages were also heard.

"I've *heard* of them," I declared, glancing at Julia. "Where I grew up, there's a large Arab/Lebanese population. I remember seeing posters and wondering what a *phalange* was."

"*Might* be worth further study," Ernie declared. "Yours. OK: *three* down, *two* to go. Next, Ellen?"

File Number Ending 2215-LIB
File Created: 22 September 47
Name: World Solipsist Revolutionary Front

Origin: 1 January 1946, by Raymonde Uralian Foust, AKA George Dunn (b. 1921), in Miami, Fla.

Narrative: Upon declaring organization's existence, Foust declared that "since only the individual can be proven to exist, there is no need for governments, states, or any external order whatsoever", refusing to pay sales tax for his breakfast: one cup of coffee in a Miami pharmacy. Arrested and retained until next day, Foust paid a fine and released from custody.

Updates: 1959: As a result of audit, WSRF/Dunn filed for tax number in Fla.

1961: WSRF/Dunn issued proclamation to Ft. Lauderdale newspapers that Bay of Pigs was a hoax perpetrated by "the Washington phantoms."

"Huh," Ernie declared. "Another one-trick pony: I'll take it. Next, Dave."

File Number Ending 1694-LIB
File Created: 25 July 70
Name: Student Freedom of Faith Coalition
Origin: C. 1970, by Stephanie Carroll (b. 1950) and Anna Leigh Juneau (b. 1949), in Berkeley, CA.

Narrative: Coalition formed among college students in the aftermath of the Kent State disturbances May '70. Initial declaration states: "we the free students of America denounce all armed force and all police presence on the campuses of our universities. All armed forces and police are Godless robots of the Satanic One in Washington and should thus be destroyed."

Updates: 1971: SFFC membership is said to be near 20,000 in seven states, from CA to NY.

1972: SFFC takes credit for the shooting of two Air Force recruiters in Chicago; negative result.

1972: Undercover officer Hamady missing after penetrating SFFC meeting at UCLA.

"*Oops*," Ernie grunted, his most *interested* grunt. He looked up at us, hovering in anticipation. "Dave: yours. OK: get to work."

For the most part, our *work* at that stage was to organize a query sheet, listing who we would call first, what we needed to find out *next*, and on and on. We also had to enter our cases in our databases for later retrieval. Some names appeared more than once in Liberty Bell Files, which was *why* we created the paper databases.

The first thing *I* did was call Hamady at the Academy—he'd been an instructor there since he came in from the cold of undercover work. He pointed me in the right direction on the Chicago shootings…which was to the guys who were convicted for them in '74 and had *nothing* to do with the SFFC. That's how *most* of the *potentially* serious files got wrapped up: Already done by the time *we* saw them.

I found Julia and Ellen chatting up Ernie close to noon. "Lunch," I asked.

"With me," Ernie declared. "I prefer The Red Devil, just around the corner."

✳✳✳

Walking to The Red Devil took maybe five minutes longer, but it was a much less frenzied place to dine. Ernie's appetite was minimal for a big guy; he ate the same salads Julia and Ellen ate. We shared small talk for a few minutes before Ellen asked. "So, Ernie: you *married*…?"

"*Three* times," he answered. "Wife Number Three's my *best* attempt."

"Ah," Julia said. "Kids?"

"Three of my own; five step-kids. Number One daughter is in her fourth year at Colgate—business major. Son One in the Philadelphia Police Academy. Number *Two* Daughter is a freshman in high school and lives with Number Two *Wife* on the Eastern Shore. Number Two Wife also had two boys from her first marriage. Number *Three* Wife has a son and two daughters from her first husband. Her oldest daughter is living with her boyfriend in Patuxent; the other two are with us. Dennis is fifteen and puts up with me, but Farrah is thirteen and calls *me* The Fascist." He shrugged. "I've been called worse."

"Did you serve in the Army," Ellen asked. "I saw that picture high up on that shelf...."

"I did a year in Korea," Ernie answered. "Started college in '50, ran out of money and joined the Army in '52. Finished school on the GI Bill, did two years with the KCPD, and joined the Bureau in '62."

"And you got sent to SPD because you got Sal the Snake," I asked.

"That, too," Ernie said. "I wouldn't play ball in Omaha, but SPD was a reward then. SPD now is a *training ground*, among other things you'll find out about *later*." He twisted his neck. "I did a *lot* of traveling when I first got here. I could put my card on any FBI desk anywhere and get anything I wanted. *Just* like you did."

"That *was* surprising," I offered, glancing at Ellen and Julia.

"It was *meant* to be." He looked away briefly before he did that odd shoulder stretch of his. "I'll tell ya how we got to be *what* we *are*. Before J. Edgar was cold in '72, Clyde Tolson—I worked with him a couple of times—told us to get ready to *disband*. The next day Pat Gray issued Directive 72-981 that *stopped* creating the oh-so-*illegal* Liberty Bell Files and had all *existing* files sent to us. We had to figure out what to *do* with them while cleaning up or handing off our open work. *That* took a year. Ruckelshaus had our *current* building cleared and moved us here from downtown."

"How did you hand off your open cases," Julia asked. "Must have been a daunting task...."

"Not really: *most* went to the DC office. Kevin Donegan—God rest his *gentle* soul—was our SAIC at the time. He knew everyone, so it was *easy*. When *he* died a year later, Clarence Kelly gave the eulogy—fellow Irish cop. Mickey Kelley is an odd duck but an *innovator*. When *he* took over as Director, he looked around, said 'find out how many of these *might* have actionable activity.' He sent us an *unnumbered* directive that said *continue to march until I tell you to stop*. Kelley appointed Harry Gowan as our SAIC and left. That was it. Kelley condemned us to research *thousands* of more-or-less cold case files that may or may *not* have *ever* been real, and we've been doing it since he was here in September '73. The current Director appointed Dusty to head the division last year." He gave his most neutral shrug—his arsenal of shrug variations was almost as vast as his repertoire of *huhs*. Ernie had no peers as a non-verbal communicator, combining shrugs and grunts with his most expressive face. He could speak *volumes* without saying a single coherent word. "*And* we developed the Bureau's leadership training program, which *you* are now in."

"*Yeah*," Ellen said, surprised.

"*Really*," Julia and I both said.

"Indeed. Slogging through *this* mass of sheer *bullshit* has trained many SSAs and SAICs. We pick only the *best* material for it: *patient* natural leaders and quick-thinkers. If you can manage Liberty Bell Files away, you can get through *most* of DC's crap. *Here* you learn case management from the trenches, and you learn that you *need* local cooperation to do *this* job. As the Academy told you, FBI agents are *supposed* to play well with local law enforcement, but most in the field get their *authority* confused with their *responsibilities*. *We cooperate with* and *help* local authorities. Our graduates *remember* what they learned here. Some we *looked* good but that we find we *can't* train we *send* elsewhere after a short time."

The gentle reader needs to know that the FBI doesn't *solve* crimes *per se*. They *manage cases to a conclusion*, big and small. *Most* are concluded after an ocean of reports is amassed, the information assimilated, and the perpetrator/s becomes obvious. The mass media has FBI agents waving their guns around like flags in every episode and chapter. In truth, most agents retire having *never* pulled their weapons or *ever* having heard a shot fired in anger.

We were processing Ernie's revelation when he declared, "I think *you* three are *likely* to stick the program out."

Great…I guess. "How long *is* the program," I asked.

"As *long* as it *takes*," Ernie said. "Everybody's different. Once you get made SSA, or you get a grade bump, you've passed. Sometimes you stay with us, but if the Bureau needs you elsewhere, *there* you go."

"Who was in our apartments Saturday night," Ellen asked, trying to act all innocent.

"*Me*," Ernie declared. "If you'll read the fine print in your contract, you'll see that your supervisor can enter and inspect your dwelling with or without your permission *or* presence."

"*Security*," Ellen pressed, "or just nosy?"

"The *former*, I assure you. Dave: *close* your closet so they can't *see* your safe. Julia: your holster on the closet *handle's* a dead giveaway. Ellen: your *shotgun* needs to be secured better than just a trigger lock. *Back* to work."

***

"Dave, I have a *special* file for you," Ernie declared Tuesday morning.

File Number Ending 99402-LIB
Date Created:
Name: Founders of the Fourth Reich
Origin: Ca. 1962, Skokie Ill. Founded by David Scarborough (b 1945) and William Durst (b. 1945). both of Skokie.
Narrative: Tenets include the assertion that Martin Borman is the rightful leader of the national socialist movement. Founders wish to lead the movement in the Midwest. They appear to be more concerned with national socialism in a literal sense than with the racist overtones of original organization. Founders decried anti-Semitism and eugenics in their founding manifesto.
Updates: 1964: Membership over 3,000 in Illinois and Indiana.
1969: Meetings between high-level leadership of this organization and KKK confirmed.
1971: Several members were arrested for synagogue bombing in Arlington Heights, Ill.
1972: Scarborough and Durst found shot in the head in Chicago.

"Ought to have *Active* files on this one," I observed.

"If there *are*, these *contents* become part of that Active Case* file. Hand it off to whichever office is on it now, probably Chicago."

I skimmed their manifesto; it had overtones similar to *Mein Kampf* but less forceful on the social engineering at gunpoint and lacked the *living space* arguments. They were, however, *very* anti-communist.

It took me most of Tuesday to discover who was working on the '71 bombing. At that time, it belonged to the Cook County district of the Illinois State Police. I reported my findings to Ernie, who expressed mild surprise. "OK: get on an airplane and take that file to Chicago."

"Um," I sputtered, "can't we just inter-office it to Chicago and…."

"Lesson Number *Two*," Ernie said loud enough for all to hear: Julia was typing at the other end of the room. "These files *and* their contents *never*—I repeat, *never*—leave our possession until they are in the hands of those who need them. We *always* maintain a strict chain of custody. Can't run the chance that Chicago would just *lose* it." He inhaled deeply. "Liberty Bell probably broke more laws than any other FBI operation, to include those COINTELPRO *gang-bangs*. Remember *that*. *Nobody* outside of law enforcement can *see* this material or even know these files *exist*. Understand?"

"OK. Tomorrow?"

"*Tonight*. I'll have The Skipper cut the tickets. Get thee and thy partners to Chicago." *The Skipper* was Louise Skipper, the matronly secretary who made our travel arrangements.

"Do we tell the Chicago office that we're in town? I was on the *phone* with them…."

Ernie inhaled deeply and assumed a posture—complete with facial expression—as though he was about to address the village idiot. "We go in, we do what we need to do, we get out. The locals don't *need* to know what *we* do unless we need *their* support, or they need *ours*."

---

* About one in a hundred Liberty Bell Files ended up being turned into an Active Case file that could be handed off. Many—like this one—would become part of *other* files *after* the Liberty Bell-specific summary and file IDs had been destroyed.

It was a 10:35 flight out of National to O'Hare, two hours and change, and a time zone. We got in at 11:55 local time. Ellen and Julia had figured out how to travel: one bag each, comfortable traveling outfits, no booze on the plane. Still, Ellen was puzzled as we got our rental car. "Why do *three* of us have to carry this one file? *You* could carry it as well, Dave."

I shrugged. "*Team-building.*" There were times when Ellen could be frustratingly obtuse.

Julia drove us to the Ramada in Des Plains, about a mile from the State Police district headquarters. It was nearly one when we went to our separate rooms, a door apart.

I shouldn't have been surprised when the phone rang. "Rise and shine, Davie," Julia's voice said. "Let's go get some bad guys."

"We're delivering a *file*, Jules. We're not making any arrests." I couldn't help but wonder: *Are you naked in your bed, Jules? I can hear you through the wall…and there's this adjoining door…*

"Details, details. C'mon; *get* going…and no time for *that*. See you at breakfast in a half-hour."

HOW did she know what I was thinking? Was I steaming up her phone?

✳✳✳

"Special Agents Clawson, Drew, and Parkinson," I declared to the receptionist. "Here to see Lieutenant Kowalski." The district headquarters was a busy place at 9 in the morning.

"*One* moment," the red-headed civilian with a severe glare answered. "Lieutenant Kowalski will be right with you. Please sign in." We signed, left our still-generic cards on the counter, then wandered off to gaze at the pictures and posters on the wall. It was typical public building fare: safety posters, memorials to fallen troopers, and photos of incumbent senior officers.

While we were cooling our heels, Julia and I spied a stack of flyers for a place called Wolverine Military Academy. Julia *studied* one and stuffed several into her purse. Curious, I put one in my jacket pocket. I had to nudge her when a sallow, slender man with blue eyes came through a door behind the receptionist. "FBI? Stan Kowalski, senior investigator."

"Agent Clawson; Agent Drew; Agent Parkinson," I replied, shaking his hand. Stan's grip was soft but sure. "We're here to talk about...."

"*Not* out here," Stan frowned. "Come on inside." We followed him into the office, a large space divided by cubicles of different designs and different eras. "Don't want to talk about *this* case in public."

"Why's that," I asked as we entered a small conference room.

"Because Chicago PD has a suspect with dangerous friends in the Cook County jail."

"Ah," I replied, handing Stan the *clean* file. "Then, *this* is *way* out of date."

Stan studied the sanitized file for a few moments. "Might have been helpful when I *started*." He shook his head. "We've been watching these bastards all over, coordinating with Wisconsin, Indiana, and Iowa. They have offshoots as far off as Pennsylvania."

"They're an active group, then," Ellen smiled, glancing at us.

"They're a *pain-in-the-ass* group, then," Stan sniffed. "Bunch of assholes playing dress-up once a week, strutting down the sidewalks in their bad costumes acting like they're brownshirts. *Most* of 'em are harmless, but... as you can *see, some* are trying for the big time."

"The one in Cook County lockup," I asked.

"Yeah. Jefferson Knox Bielefeld calls himself the *Reichsführer* of America. We're holding him on suspicion of the synagogue bombing *and* the killing of Scarborough and Durst. We've got enough on him to...say: you wouldn't want to do me a *favor*, would you?"

"Like what?"

"*Act* like you've got federal charges, so he'll cop to our *state* charges? Chicago FBI isn't interested."

"We'd be *glad* to," Ellen smiled.

That *was* what Ernie said we were *supposed* to do.

"Well, Mr. Bielefeld, we're here to *offer* you…." Julia started after we flashed our credentials. The Academy introduced us to scores of interview/interrogation techniques, called *approaches*. The most *used* and the most *effective* approach is called the *Direct approach*: just *ask* what you want to know. *Most* sources just answer…truth or not. We had done two hours of preparation on this guy, who had a most *colored* background, and knew *that* wouldn't work on him. Julia was offering him something he wanted…or *thought* he needed—called the *Lifeline approach*.

"You will address me as *Reichsführer* if you address me at *all*," the portly, dark-haired man in the orange jumpsuit declared. He glared at us in a most uncongenial fashion. The small interrogation cell was stuffy; we'd removed our coats.

"Very well, *Reichsführer*. We want to *offer* you…."

"Drop dead," Bielefeld snapped. "I make no deals with ZOG."*

"Well, then," Ellen began. "We'll just tell you what we have that will strap you to a gurney with a needle in your arm." She had a most penetrating way of saying *that*.

"You can do to me what you want," Bielefeld growled hesitantly. "I'll be a celebrated martyr."

"But how about your *family*," Julia asked quietly. "Will they…?" He had a wife and three kids…and was 26.

"They'll cope."

"Not when we put it out that you're a race traitor, that you've been *cooperating* with ZOG all along," I shrugged. "Not hard to start *that* rumor."

"No one would believe it," Bielefeld sighed.

"If we snap up Franks and Cannily tonight, let it slip *accidentally* that we did it because *you* ratted them out as the doers back in '71." I added, "what would *they* think?" Bob Franks and Don Cannily were two names

---

* Zionist Occupation Government, a term that neo-, crypto-, and *real* Nazis use for *everything* they don't like.

high in the organization, according to Stan's organizational chart, *and* who they believed *were* responsible for the synagogue.

Bielefeld blinked—the first time we'd got a different response. "They *wouldn't*...."

"Really," Julia smiled. "Want to roll *those* dice?"

"Now *come on*," Ellen added, with a come-hither grin, "we'll show you *ours* if you show us *yours*."

"For instance," I added, "when did you first *hear* about Fourth Reich? You grew up in Ohio."

"I first heard about Fourth Reich at Wolverine Military...."

"*When* was *this*?" Julia pounced. Bielefeld's juvenile record was sealed—no one *needed* it...*yet*.

"I went to Dad's older sister after Mom killed him and my sisters in '69. They wanted *me* for pimping out my sister—*she* made me good money—and Aunt Greta found a brochure for Wolverine. The judge said OK, and I went to Michigan."

"What about..." I started, but Julia cut me off.

"Did you know JJ Elrath at Wolverine," Julia asked, scowling.

"Yeah, *that* asshole rat bastard. We softened *him* up for...."

"He's my *uncle*," Julia interrupted with a twitch of her neck and a most *fierce* frown on her face. *Easy, Jules. We're trying to soften him up, not pound him into pâté.*

And the room fell silent. I've never heard four people *so* quiet *so* fast and for *so* long. "Your...uncle?"

"Yes, *and* my friend. Now, ZOG has enough to strap you to a gurney for your participation in the deaths of Durst and Scarborough.[*] *We* want to know: just *how* did you get involved in Fourth Reich at Wolverine?"

Bielefeld breathed deep, craned his neck slowly. "OK. I was inducted at Wolverine by...."

---

[*] Murder of private citizens is *not* a federal crime. Killing federal officers or crossing state lines to commit any murder or escape prosecution *is*, but this was a bluff.

For the next six hours—in relays, with two different stenographers—we got the low-down on the synagogue and on the shootings of Durst and Scarborough and his weapons trafficking connections.

In the end, Julia glanced at her watch and asked one last question. "*Why* did you join the Founders of the Fourth Reich at, what, age fifteen?"

"Protection," Bielefeld answered. "Once I was initiated, I was immune. As long as I didn't ask questions, I was one of *them*. One of the guys your uncle ratted out was a member, so we *tried* to get him to recant." He shook his head. "Elrath. *Toughest* bastard *I* ever *heard* of—and in a trailer park, you meet a *lot* of tough bastards. But *that* sonofabitch *wouldn't* turn tail no matter *what*. But, somebody said 'he *has* to stay alive,' so *we* left him alone."

"Somebody *who*," Julia asked.

"I just followed orders; never *asked* who *gave* 'em." He giggled slightly. "And *those* stupid bastards, especially Franks and Cannily, *buy* all the bullshit about race war and Aryan supremacy. I just spout it as long as it keeps me in beer and broads."

***

"Well," I declared, stepping outside the Cook County Jail, "We've got *twenty minutes* to be on our airplane back to Washington."

"*Screw* that," Ellen rasped, slinging her coat into the car.

"Yeah," Julia declared. "Let's find some rooms, change our tickets for tomorrow. Flights to DC from O'Hare are about a dozen a day."

We got rooms at a Holiday Inn a mile from the airport and met for dinner in the restaurant. "So, Julia," I asked innocently, "your uncle was in a *reform* school?"

"He wasn't sent to a *reform* school. He was sent to a military-academy-style *boarding* school that turned out to be…not good." She looked frustrated. "He *saw* something, then *told* someone what he saw. They nearly killed him for it." She shook her head gently. "But JJ's such a *sweet* guy. *Hard* as *nails*, but a sweetheart."

"Wish there were more of *them*," Ellen sighed, sipping a vodka martini. "Now *our Davie*, here…."

"*Your* Davie has a date with Beth Saturday."

"*Don't* try to bed her on the first date, Davie," Julia said.

"I *never* do, Jules. What do *you* want, Jules? *Your* future life?"

"*I'm* no politician," Julia declared as dinner arrived. "I want to get as high up as I can within the bounds of my planned home life."

"What's *that* look like?"

"Husband, kids, a house in the suburbs, white picket fence. I never *liked* being an only child: my parents spoiled me."

"Well," Ellen frowned, cutting into her chicken breast, "I want the *guy* but can't *do* the kids." She set her knife down gently. "My family has Huntington's. After watching our *aunt*…it ends with *me*, my brothers, and sisters. I made *sure* of it two years ago."

We were all quiet. I wanted to reach out and hug Ellen, but she was too far away. Julia looked at her with sympathy. "Sorry, Nancy," she mewed.

"That's why I have so many first dates: I come out with *that* before the second drink arrives." Ellen looked amused, mildly.

"That *might* be off-putting," I said softly.

"How about *you*, Davie," Julia asked.

"Never saw *me* as a father figure. One brother has five kids; the other has *one* that we know of. My *sister* wants a platoon of 'em. I want the woman—the companion, the partner. *Kids*…" I shrugged.

Ellen looked at me, amused. "Finding out more about Davie all the time."

I switched gears. "*Different* subject, Jules. That *brochure*…"

"*Later*, Davie."

✳✳✳

We hadn't even got to our cubes Thursday before Ernie pointed at Julia, Ellen, and me, "*You* need to be at 1600 Fifteenth Street tomorrow morning at 0800."

For…what?

"*This* is our secret weapon, children," Ernie declared at 0803 Friday, "*why* we need *airtight* applications on the *rare* occasion when we *make* criminal referrals. Meet Supervisory Special Agent Glenn Harper." Ernie introduced a bespectacled man with unkept hair, in a white lab coat complete with a pocket protector with a slide rule sticking out. "Glenn is in charge of our Telephonic Research Unit—the TRU. *We* call it the Annex."

"Welcome, welcome," Glenn smiled, gesturing to chairs in a paneled conference room in the Bell Central Office for the District of Columbia. "Please, be seated." As we got comfortable, I was dimly aware of subtle vibration, of a background humming-buzzing-rattle. He opened two doors on a wall cabinet that contained a whiteboard; the noise grew. "What we *do* here is research on non-intrusive telephonic monitoring…."

"Wiretaps," Ellen declared, her arms across her chest.

"*Drew*," Ernie interjected with a slow shake of his head. "What *we* call traps. Go *on*, Glenn."

"Simply put, they are *traces*. With electronic switching, we no longer need the laborious and time-consuming work of following relays."

"Like Hollywood: two minutes?" I asked.

"It was *never* that long," Glen grinned. "Local traces could be made in about thirty *seconds*: direct-dial long-distance about a minute or so. *Now*, on a touch-tone line, we know what number's being called as soon as the last digit is entered." He drew two circles on the board, connecting them with a line. "A calls B." He drew a square in the middle of the line. "Central Office connects A to B. Simple." We nodded. "*That's* where *we* come in. We don't *listen* to the line; we just read the connection data."

"That's for *touch-tone*," Julia said. "But not everyone *has* touch-tone dialing."

"*Now* the *tics* of the old dial instruments are translated to *pulses* in the Central Office," Glenn declared. "As of January, the whole *country* is touch-tone *ready*. That analog equipment will still *work* at least until the end of the century. Beyond that…" he shrugged. "*Dialup calls* take a few more *seconds*."

"*Now*, Glenn, the scriptorium," Ernie said.

We were led through a vast and noisy room full of relay racks—the source of the rattling hum we heard in the conference room. Ernie actually covered his ears as we walked. The sound *that* day was a cacophony of the *constant* clacking of *tens* of *thousands* of mechanical relays operating at once. In today's Central Office, you hear the roaring of cooling fans and air conditioners—loud but not *as* loud—while running at *orders of magnitude* greater speeds.

And *this* was the biggest, *busiest* Central Office in the country.

We came to a steel door without a knob that Glenn and Ernie put keys into, and the door opened effortlessly. Ernie threw a switch on the wall inside…

On the far wall were three framed documents under dim lights. The first looked like a bit like a reproduction of the Declaration of Independence. Ernie took it off the wall and handed it to me. "*This*, children, is our get-out-of-jail-free card." I read the iron-gall ink on parchment script with difficulty…

> *In my Capacity as Commander in Chief of the United States, I do hereby Charter the Fourth Department of The Government of the United States. This Department shall have the Authority to, Using Any Means Necessary, Violate the Laws of the United States, including the Constitution, and the Laws and Statues of All of the States in the Union, or to Violate the Sabbaths of the Lord, and to defy the Common Law as The Department Deems Necessary, When Acting in the Defense of the Republic…Signed this First Day of October in the Year of Our Lord, 1789, G. Washington.*

I *should* have had a little trouble breathing—I held an *original* document signed by *George Washington*….

But because it *was* in a glass-covered frame, it was like scoring bare wrist on a *fourth* date.

"Presidents sign *this* the day *after* they're sworn in," Ernie said. "The only one who *didn't* was Carter, but he *finally* saw the light and signed after the hostages were taken in Teheran." He passed the second frame to me; I handed the first to Julia. The *second* document was a printed version of the first, signed by every president from John Adams to US Grant.

I stared at Lincoln's signature for a long time. "But, is it *constitutional*," Ellen asked, gazing at Washington's signature.

"Never been *challenged*," Ernie said. "And here's *why* it falls on us." He handed me the *third* document: a printed copy of the second *with* a change:

...The Special Projects Office of the Justice Department is hereby chartered as the Fourth Department.

"Sam Grant's flourish," Ernie declared. "Until *then*, Special Projects consisted of a dozen or so marshals, on their own, doing what they *needed* to do. Taft brought it over to the Bureau of Investigation." [*]

"Why the *fourth* department," Ellen asked.

"The first *three* departments formed were State, War, and Treasury," I said. "*SPD can break the law?*"

"Yep," Ernie said. "The TRU is our sword; this scriptorium and what's *in* it is our shield. *They* are why we need *solid* criminal referrals: *what* we do and *how* we do it can't *afford* to be *that* carefully scrutinized." He sighed heavily. "This is *also* why *we* get to do the Fed's dirty work; jobs no one else *can* do because we *can* do them. You'll learn about *those* later."

The TRU enabled us to do a great deal more than almost anyone else. This charter was *how* we got away with a *lot* of what we did. Nonetheless, we were *cautious* about *everything*...

Because George Washington and *all* his successors *ordered* the SPD to defend the republic using *any means necessary*. [**]

---

[*] A precursor to the FBI.
[**] Remember: this is a *novel*...a *fictional* story. Don't go off looking all this stuff up.

Another Wild Weekend with Women

Or, My First Date with Beth and the Aftermath

"**S**o, Davie," Ellen said Friday night, stretching and standing up, "where are you *going* with Beth? Someplace *romantic*, no doubt." We were in her kitchen, dining on chicken and shrimp stir-fry, egg rolls, fried rice, and green tea.

"We're meeting for furniture shopping in Georgetown." I said, sipping tea. Ellen stopped; Julia rolled her eyes. "Maybe *lunch*?"

"You're going to *die* a *bachelor*, Davie," Ellen said as she started picking up our plates.

"But not *alone*," Julia declared. "You'll *always* have someone around."

"What makes you say *that*, Jules," I asked.

"Simple," Julia answered. "Your *number one goal* is to please others."

"True," Ellen called as she loaded the dishwasher. I wondered why a one-bedroom apartment with a kitchen too small to change your *mind* in needed a dishwasher…but we *had* one.

"I *aim* to *please*." Julia grabbed her wine glass and headed for Ellen's living room. I picked up my still-half-full wine glass and followed. "But I *might* want Beth for a *life* partner, not just…" I sat on a folding canvas beach chair, Julia, on a sort-of folding canvas love seat.

"Fine," Ellen declared, stretching out next to Julia.

Once again…silence. Julia was in a shorts-and-halter outfit; Ellen in a t-shirt and skirt. I had no clock to gauge how long we sat as the shadows rose on the buildings next door. I hadn't noticed before, but Ellen was about an inch shorter and ten pounds heavier than Julia and struggled with weight. Julia just seemed to be *perfectly* put together; Ellen was less *model*-like but still a *beautiful* woman.

They gazed at me a *lot* more than each other…which was creepy, unnerving, *and* exciting all at once. At dark, I kissed them on the forehead and went home.

The way it *should* have been.

✳✳✳

"Morning, sleepyhead," Ellen smiled, pushing her way into my door the next morning. Julia, following her, smiled.

"Morning," I managed, slightly confused.

"Good *night*," Julia asked brightly. She never seemed dark.

"Was *quiet*," I admitted, following them into my kitchen. "Read a little, got to bed early, sort of…."

They both looked at me, puzzled—Ellen even cocked her head like a puppy hearing a new sound. "*Quiet*," she asked at last. "You weren't *talking* to *Beth* about *today*?"

"No. Was I supposed to?"

"Well," Julia said, "it *is* pretty common. So, breakfast? Eggs; bacon; toast; coffee?"

Stop with the Puzzled Puppy Maneuver. It was *the '80s*. You *had* to have *been* both *single* and *there*.

✳✳✳

"So: what do you *need*," Beth asked as we walked side-by-side into the big furniture store. "They've got *everything*." She drove a Karmann Ghia into the parking lot just as I arrived.

"I need bookshelves," I declared, "at *least* fifty linear feet of 'em. And an end table or two; *lamps* if I can swing it. Maybe a lounge chair. If the budget holds, *maybe* a new bed: mine's been around for a while. I may have been *conceived* on it."

"OK, *maybe* three grand," she declared. "But *don't* concentrate on the price tags—like I said, I *know* someone. Priorities?" She wore a gauzy blouse and diaphanous, flouncy slacks above tiny, sandaled feet.

"*Shelves* and *lamps*. After I get my books organized, maybe I can figure out the rest."

"Décor?"

"I always figure if it *fits* where I put it, it's *decorous*. If *not*, it *isn't*."

She looked at me with a little grin. "*Such* a *guy*. OK; let's look." The store stocked a wide variety of hardwood furniture. We found three white-oak shelving units totaling sixty adjustable linear feet. We found bookcase-end tables that I thought would fit nicely at the end of my sectional *if* I got rid of the corner section—no great loss. And a couple of brass lamps. I decided on a high-back chair and stool combination that almost sorta-kinda went with my sectional.

Beth declared to our salesman, an older gentleman named Harold with a soft Virginia drawl and a twinkle for her, "*we* need a bed. *Ours* is a *little* worn out."

We tried several—Beth plopped down repeatedly and glanced at me expectantly as I played along. We tried a *king* bookcase headboard with built-in reading lamps. "Oh, *honey*," she gushed, "*perfect* for reading poetry to each other at night."

"Sure, dear," I declared, grinning at the spectacular joke we were playing on the world as we picked out a spring and mattress. Beth whispered in Harold's ear, and the price of everything went down by half. "Let's talk about delivery…" *What's THAT in her grin…is she…WHAT did he say?* "Sorry, what was that?"

"I asked if you'd *be* there for delivery," Harold ventured. "Building management or a neighbor…" He looked back and forth at us in anticipation.

"Depends on a *lot* of things," I said. "Work schedules…"

"The *baby's daycare*," Beth added.

"Day of the *week*," I squeaked, surprised again. "What's your availability for Dumfries?"

"Well, everything but the lamps and the end tables are in *stock*, so… Wednesday?"

I wrote the check. We left the store, arm-in-arm, grinning at the world.

We got as far as her car before she gripped my arm and bussed my chin. She was five-five to my five-eleven, so she had to reach to get *that* high. "*That* was *fun*, Dave," she said. "But now, *our work* begins."

"Work…you mean figuring each other out?"

"If anyone figured *me* out, they'd have to fill *me* in. No: *we* have to work to see if we *can* become *really good* friends."

"I have *another* stop to make before I take you to lunch, *if* you don't mind." I nodded to a gun store across the street from the strip mall. "I need an off-duty weapon."

In the '80s, few women of *my* age knew anything about firearms, and *anti*-gun culture was rampant. *This* was make-or-break for *that* part of our lives.

Then, too, there was my offer of a *meal*—our *first* together. But *this* was the *'80s!* The era of the liberated female at its peak! My innocent offer might *not* be seen as a gentleman simply offering to treat a lady to a repast. *Au contraire, mon frere!* Such an offer *could* be taken as an *insult* to a woman's independence, to be *diligently* met by a *harsh* rebuke followed by a harangue of *righteous* indignation and a chorus of "I Am Woman!" joined by every female in the zip code.**

Instead…"*OK.* I haven't been to *this* one. I'll buy my *own* lunch today. *Next* time."

YES! And there would BE a next time!

✳✳✳

---

* French for *fuhgeddaboudit, Jack.*

** This *had* sort of happened to me once or twice in college, *without* the song.

"Your dad told *you* that your mom was pregnant *two weeks* before your sister was born," Beth grinned, sipping her iced tea." "That's *so* funny,"

"They just weren't ready for that *birds-and-bees* discussion with me at *almost ten*, I guess." We were on the veranda of a tony faux-French café, enjoying a light breeze off the Potomac as we dined on salads and polite little sandwiches.

"Did you get it *then*?"

"Dad talked about two people loving each other *so much* they made a baby." I chuckled. "*Then*, it was enough." I reached around for my Sig Sauer P220, the preferred off-duty weapon for federal officers, feeling it snug in its new holster on my hip.

"So when *did* you get The Talk?" I flashed back to our time in the gun shop and the easy way she took an offhand *and* a supported shooting stance. *She knows what she's doing…and she's hanging on my every word.*

"In the summer of '68, I practically *lived* in the finished basement of my best friend, Pete. One day, he and I were rapping about *Lord of the Rings*. His twenty-year-old sister, Kim, had heard us—in *that* basement, you could hear through the ducts—talking about the possibilities of hobbit sex. But we didn't *really* know how *it* was done for humans. She *laughed* from upstairs. Pete asked what was so funny, and *she* said, 'want to *see* how *it really* works?'

"Oh, wow!" She planted her chin in her hand and her elbow on the table, eyes gleaming.

"Yeah. She called her eighteen-year-old friend from down the street— Marilyn. First, they *talked* about the *basics*, *including* the *need* for foreplay. Then *I* paired off with Kim; Pete and Marilyn went around the corner for…ah, *hands-on demonstrations*. Kim was wearing some *tiny* shorts and a *tiny camise-thing,* and I got on top of *her* in *my* underwear. I had an *accident* that she *felt*."

"What did she *do*?" Beth seemed…entranced.

"Smiled *real* big, *giggled* a little, kissed my forehead, said it was good for *her*, too, like I knew what *that* meant."

"You got The Talk *and* your first girl-orgasm at the same time." Beth grinned. "Would that *all* First-Lovers were *that* generous. And you fell in love with Kim."

"*Lust*, anyway. She was my kid-sitter* until I was 12, then a *buddy*; stayed one *after*. I called her in the spring of '76, and her number was disconnected. Her dad said that after Christmas, she fell in love and moved away, all within about six weeks."

"Huh."

"So, how do *girls* get The Talk?"

She made a curious face: part amused, part surprised. "The *timing* is easier: our first period. *I* got an '*it's for the baby*' story from Mom—at twelve, *that* pacifies most girls. But *I* wanted to know how the baby got *started*, so I asked the librarian, and I got a *pamphlet. Then* my Aunt Ruth—my dad's divorced sister—showed me a movie. She was *in* it: twenty years *younger* and forty pounds *lighter*, but it *was* her. I think she wanted to put me *off* sex for good, but *that* effect only lasted another five years."

I imagined one of the many silent stag films I'd seen, with lousy lighting and grainy details. "Some intro."

She smiled sagely. "I've *never* been *sexually active*—whatever *that* means. I dated my *last* guy—Rich, in Zanesville—for *four years*. On January 4th, 1978, he came to my apartment with the stuff that I'd kept at *his* place, threw it on my sofa, and said he was moving on. *I* said, 'what about us?' 'There's no *us*,' he said." She stretched her arms above her head as if grabbing for passing clouds. "That was *that*. I got this IRS job that spring and moved here."

"*That* is *cold*. I *promise* I won't do that." I'll never know what gave me the guts to make *that* promise on our first *day* together...

She smiled, reaching for the scudding clouds. "Both my evil twin and I are pleased."

✳✳✳

---

* She first "sat" for me and her brother when we were 9; not exactly *babies*.

"*So,*" she sighed, standing by her car door after our late, impromptu dinner. It was nearly nine, the bugs were out.

What I *expected* was a couple of hours—maybe—of interior decoration advice from a pretty someone with a better sense of aesthetics than *mine,* who I had kissed at a party.

What I *got* was *ten hours* of pretending to be married with a baby, conversation, shared memories, laughs, smiles, occasional hand-holding…and furniture-and-gun-shopping. A LOT different from any other first date *I ever* had.

"*So,*" I answered, holding her hand loosely and swatting away a mosquito. "We *should…*"

"*Soon,*" she smiled, turning her chin up. So I kissed her; she kissed *me…* a lingering, sweet, *gentle* kiss…*no* grind, *no* probing for tonsils; tender and promising. "Call me when your furniture comes."

It was 9:30 when I got home, so *most* of the building's lights were on. Many of the tenants were young, single professionals. I could hear grown-ups *and* kids in the pools. The weather was temperate—many balconies were occupied.

I'd just spent a delightful day with a *beautiful, very* interested, *very* eligible young woman who *wanted* to hear from me again *soon.* And there was some loud *do-de-DUNK* goin' on above me…

I wanted Beth in *my* lumpy bed, with *her* slender legs around me. *That* was *not* to be…yet. And the idea of a *shower* and its *release* was *not* appealing. I *briefly* thought about calling Julia or Ellen to *take the edge off,* but decided *not* to use them like that.

Oh, SHE'S enjoying it up there…So's HE…

I *felt* Beth's lips on mine, *tasted* her sweetness *again* and *again,* and wondered *if* hoped *that* she felt mine. I hadn't *had* many lasting relationships in my life—none lasted more than six months. *They* didn't make me feel *this…*

I needed advice from that *one friend* who could give me *that* kind of advice. After three rings, *that* long-remembered voice said, "hello?"

"*Hi*, Kimmie," I answered. "This is Dave Clawson…" It had taken me about three hours to find her, living near Pittsburgh, a few months before.*

"*Dave*," she said, surprised. "*WOW! How* did *you*…?"

"I joined the FBI after law school."

"*Oh*," she said, subdued. "So, how are *you*? How's your *family*?"

We talked about each other's families—ironically, she'd married *another* Dave—but there was curiosity in her voice. "What's this *about*, Dave? You didn't just *call* after five years just to catch up."

"First, congratulations on your marriage…."

"Thanks. But we *know* each other better than *that*, buddy. What's *up*?" *We do indeed.* Kim was *always* willing to listen, before and *after* my 'lesson.' One of many *earnest* questions I *had* asked my *kid*-sitter/buddy was: when does a guy know that a girl really likes *him* and she's not just out for what she could get? "I met this girl."

"Oh! Does it *feel* right?"

"I *think* it does. After so *many* others…."

"Trust your *gut*, buddy." She was quiet. "Dave: The *first* time I slept with *my* Dave felt a *lot* like that time with *you and me*."

Huh? "Like…*you and me*?"

"*Yeah*." Silence again. "*You* were my *first*, sweetheart; *he* was my *second*."

"You *didn't*…*you* didn't…uh…." *How do I ASK THAT?*

"I *did!* I felt *fabulous!*"

I *suddenly* remembered her holding my head to a breast with one hand as she brushed *under* her chemise with the other, wearing a serene smile I looked *up* to see.** "Wow. How come we *never*…?"

"We could *never* repeat *that*, and if we'd *talked* about it, it would have *ruined* the *magic*."

---

* It was an Academy *assignment*, I swear!

** She *was* about a foot and a half taller than me then. I didn't catch up until I was 17.

"That's so." *Then again, it WAS safer for her NOT to do either, accident or not.*[*]

"As for *your* girl: it's *not* who you can *get along with*, honey; it's *who you can't live without*. Does it feel *that way* with *this* girl?"

"It's *starting* to."

"There ya go, sweetheart. Listen: give me *your* number and send me a birthday card next month. Yours is in *March*, as I remember. Let's stay in touch; keep me *informed* of your love life…*and* everything else."

"OK; I'll…

"Good *luck*, sweetheart…*gotta* go."

My neighbors upstairs must have drifted off into C-sleep.

Mine was *almost* as good that night.

❋❋❋

Something real with Beth… That thought ran through my head as I did the week's wash, measured, and planned for my new furniture.

Something real. I went down to the pool, still warm from the day's bright sunlight. I stepped into the water, did a few laps, and stretched on a chaise.

Something real. Then Julia took her shirt off and laid it on the next chaise. In a two-piece not-*quite* bikini, she was a sight to see. She smiled vaguely at me—like a workmate-cum-neighbor—and stepped into the pool.

Something real. As Ellen stepped out of her terrycloth skirt on the other side of me, I decided it *couldn't* be real. She was *exquisite* in a tight, low-cut high-hip tank. She smiled and waved before joining Julia in the shallow end of the pool, where they sat *in* the water with their backs against the wall.

Something real. Until our encounter with the *Reichsführer*, very little of what we'd done thus far had been *real*. The Founders of the Fourth

---

[*] The teenager in the *amorous* arms of a *trusted* girl had *no* such thought.

Reich were a *real* organization that *should* have been tracked…but wasn't. The files for nearly everything *else* we'd worked on were either cold as a mackerel or should *never* have been created. Having sex with *two* women with whom there was *no* possibility of a long-term future *seemed* like a bad porn film script.

I stared at my two surreal friends chatting, when I suddenly thought: *my turn to make dinner Friday.* I got up, dropped *casually* into the pool, and joined them. They glanced benignly at me before Julia remarked: "I never *made* drapes before, but drapes for those porch doors would cost a *fortune.*"

"I *know*," Ellen replied, "I'm just gonna stick with the roll-down shade for now. How about you, Dave? Stay with the shade with your new décor?"

"Probably," I boldly declared, contributing to this *real* conversation, having not even *thought* about curtains or shades or anything else other than getting my books off the floor. "I'm getting curtains for my bedroom, though. What's the difference between drapes and curtains?"

"Drapes reach the floor and have heavier lining," Julia said, "and *I* need those, too. I'm making my curtains in two layers: a sheer gold and an opaque blue. Want me to make some for *you*?"

"Yeah, sure, thanks. But I wanted to ask you guys if you had anything you *couldn't* eat Friday: allergies and that. I'm thinking Chinese?"

"Two weeks in a *row*? How *imaginative*, Dave," Ellen teased.

"OK, how about fish and chips? I'm a good hand at frying."

"OK," Julia declared, "*that* sounds good." She pulled herself out of the pool. "*I'm* for the books. You guys signed up for continuing ed[*] yet?"

"*Just* about to," Ellen said, backing out herself, water rippling down her *incredible* front. "Principles of forensic accounting looks good to me. Dave?"

"Um, I don't have a head for numbers."

---

[*] Continuing education was *important* for all FBI agents; *required* of rookies and, as we found later, of *all* the SPD.

"I can *help*," Ellen said. "I was an accounting minor."

Of COURSE, you were. "I'll send my paperwork tomorrow. Your turn to drive tomorrow, Jules."

"Yep," Julia said. "How was your *date*, Dave?"

"Fabulous," I sighed. "Found furniture and an off-duty weapon; had lunch, talked for *hours*; had dinner late." I scanned back and forth. "*Great.*"

"*Terrific*, Dave," Julia smiled, winking *really, babe*. "Gonna do it again sometime?"

"Maybe something less spendy." I winked back; *thanks*.

"That or go *broke*, eh," Ellen giggled, winking, *have fun, babe*.

My workmates/bedmates/buddies donned their coverings and left. We had concluded a *real* conversation about *real* things with nary a *single* sexual inference or innuendo.

Except, of course, those in my *head…maybe* theirs…

The Butterfly Society

Or, Cause and Effect Are Not Always Related

"Well, my children," Ernie smiled after the Monday Wheel Game. "I trust you all had restful weekends."

"Sure." "Yeah." "Absolutely."

"Dave, *you* got a new weapon."

"I *did*," I agreed. "The store called it in?"

"Gun stores in the area call the DC office duty desk when we buy a handgun using our credentials. J. Edgar could *not* understand *why* we didn't want to carry that heavy Smith-Wesson all the time. How does *it* feel?"

"Better than the Smith." I was curious. "You *carry* a Sig-Sauer?"

"No: I was lucky enough to get a Baby Browning before they were made illegal." Ernie gazed at Ellen and Julia. "You?"

"Mom gave me a Walther PP Super for graduation," Julia said.

"Dad handed down his old 9 mm Colt Commander," Ellen sighed.

"As you know, you *must* qualify with it *if* you carry it in lieu of your duty sidearm. So, get thee to the range, children. On to cases. First: Julia."

File Number Ending 94068-LIB
Name: Stewart, James Lablache, AKA Stewart Granger
Date Identified: 16 March 1968
Origin: Born 1913
Narrative: As a performer during the 1940s and 1950s, subject refused to participate in anti-subversive activities or investigations, claiming

that his British citizenship prevented same. Subject shows no interest in taking out US citizenship.

Updates: 1972: subject became a citizen in 1958; said to be retiring from acting; claims he is moving to Spain.

"Huh," Ernie grunted, his *whose idea was THIS, huh.* "Who's the originator?"

"SA Kalinda. Did the update, too."

Ernie's face twisted sideways, as he did when he was deep in disgust. "Kalinda. Yeah. He's naturalized himself. Busted for selling secrets to India last year. Dave: This is *another* one for your cleanup expertise."

"Fine." In the past week, I had *cleaned up* five files that never *should* have been created. I even got an *atta-boy* for it Friday.

"Ellen."

File Number Ending: 06784-LIB
Name: Gelts, Albert Steven
Date Identified: 21 October 1959
Origin: Born 1927, Nogales, Ariz.
Narrative: Beginning in 1954 reports by Nogales PD suggest subject's ranch near MX border was the last stop for several traveling salesmen. Neighbors (nearest was three miles distant) reported seeing subject digging in desert at night. Subject also known to have sold several cars believed to have belonged to salesmen.

Updates: 1959: Initial interview with subject revealed that ranch was a used-car dealership and repair shop. Satisfactory paperwork produced and inspected.

1965: Surveillance and interview does not confirm smuggling allegations made by another neighbor.

1971: Casual, accompanied search of premises revealed no evidence of concealing draft evaders, deserters or other criminals. Car salvage and trading business appear to be thriving.

"What do you think of *that*, Ellen?"

"Neighbors with a grudge, maybe."

"Not to mention good eyesight," I said. "They can see *three miles* in the desert at night? The desert's *mighty* dark at night."

Ernie gazed at me. "You'd *know*; you did Officer Basic down there. This looks like a cleanup, but Dave's already loaded with those, so… Ellen?"

"Fine."

"Dave? Your next file?"

File Number Ending: 44621-LIB
Name: The Butterfly Society
Date Identified: September 26th, 1965
Origin: Organization origins unclear. Los Angeles office based on informant Holly Mossfield's information on Long Beach and Malibu chapters of organization.
Narrative: Edward Lorenz, popularizer of so-called chaos theory, announced his "butterfly theory" in 1963. "A butterfly flaps its wings in the Amazon rainforest, causing an air disturbance that triggers a tornado in Texas." Quasi-poetic slogan implies small changes in equilibrium can trigger much larger and much more energetic disturbances half a world away. Idea seems not only to defy Newtonian physics but common sense. Butterfly Society encouraged "unconventional thinking as to how to bring about social change," in itself a subversive idea.
Updates: 1968: membership said to top 10,000 in twelve chapters in CA and OR.
1970: Holly Mossfield interviewed by Dayton, OH office in connection with an associated organization—Solarians—and individuals connected. No actionable result.
1971: membership said to reach 15,000; said to have participated in anti-war, anti-draft marches; no direct evidence found.

"Sufficiently subversive for J. Edgar," Ernie said, glancing at Julia. "Yours. Next, Ellen."

We went on for the other two: uninteresting, bizarre, and almost certainly dead-ends.

*** ✳✳✳ ***

"Hello," the voice said Wednesday night.

Pleasant, deeper than Beth. Must be... "*You're* Cindy. Dave Clawson."

"*Beth*," Cindy called, "*Dave's* calling, *finally. There* or *here?*"

"*There*," I heard, barely, followed by Cindy taking a breath and, "she'll be here in a minute: she's down in the basement, but we have a couple of long cords. So, you're with the Bureau? What office?"

"Special Pro..."

"SPD? I *dated* a guy at the SPD for a while, but *he* moved on. I date a *lot* of FBI guys because I work for the Justice Department—secretary, legal assistant, now word processor—so I know more than a few guys in law enforcement. But, see, you guys put your pants on one leg at a time—I've *seen* you do it—so you're not *that* much different, but before I came to Washington, I didn't think so: I'm from Duluth originally. Most of you guys are OK, but *some* are assholes. I just want to make sure you *know* that you're Beth's *first* since Rich." She *finally* took another breath and dropped her voice an octave. "She's a sweet kid; don't hurt her like that last asshole did in Zanesville. I know *you* probably won't—Rich was unique—but...*here* she is. Bye, Dave!"

"*Hi*," I heard Beth, at last, a little breathless. "Your *furniture came?*"

"*Hi*," I answered. "Yup, they brought one of the lamps, too. Maybe they'll send two *more* when the rest of the stuff comes."

"Yeah, maybe. Does it all *fit?* Does it *look* right?"

"Well, it looks fine to *me*, and it *seems* to fit."

"I'll have to see it. I'll be there in twenty minutes. Bye!" *Click.*

You'll...O-kay. I looked around my slightly disarrayed living room, with the boxes on shelves, floors, and books everywhere *except* put away. Twenty minutes...*move your ass, Clawson.*

I tried: oh, did I *try* to make my living room look more *lived-in* than *dumped into* for those precious minutes. I wrestled boxes off the floor and onto shelves...but they overhung, making them *look* haphazardly stuffed...which they *were*. I had to face it: the *only* room fit for company was the bedroom, with its cowboy motif dresser, desk, and nightstands. *Um, no. Not at ALL OK.*

Then, there was *entertaining*, for which *few* bachelors are prepared on short notice. I set out my two matching wine glasses and the bottle of wine that came with the building's welcoming basket. The fruit was gone, but I set what remained of the basket's cheese and crackers on the islet. I shoved my mail up into the little lockable coop where the islet met the wall, which was *supposed* to pass for a desk.

And after *these* extensive preparations came a buzzing at the intercom-thing. "Yo," I called into the intercom.

"Hi," Beth answered.

"Come on up to 221," I answered, hitting the lock switch. *This won't take…oh, shit!* There I was in my underwear: I'd called her before I'd *changed* completely…*and she's got about ninety seconds before she's…*

Knock, knock, knock!

DAMN, she's fast… "*Just* a minute," I yelled, rushing into my bedroom, grabbing my pants that I'd taken off just *minutes* before. I came back out, opened the door, and… "*Hi*," I smiled, all nonchalant. "*So* glad you could…."

"I'll *bet*," she grinned in a gauzy shirt/shorts combo and sandals, clutching a grocery bag with a big purse over her shoulder. "I *just* brought…*where's* your kitchen?"

"*Just* around here, to the right." The entry hall was a good ten feet long and pointed straight at the sliding double doors of the living room, another four feet over to the kitchen, twenty to the bedroom *or* bathroom door.

"*Nice*," she said, setting her contributions on the islet. "Now, if you'll *just* pull your zipper up, I'll kiss you *hello* and have a look around."

"Ah," I grinned, probably turning a *very* amusing shade of red. We touched lips briefly; hers were *softer* than I expected.

She looked around the living room for a few moments, turned, and smiled. "They look *OK*. You haven't done much *to* the place?"

"Just no *time*...."

"Uh-huh. Where's the *bed*?" I pointed her to the bedroom, which I *swear* I wasn't gonna show her—or even talk about because we just weren't *there* yet. "Nice: *very* nice. And the bathroom's right *here? Excuse me*."

Now, this just *might* have led to a *do-de-DUNK* scene...but somehow, I wasn't sure I *wanted* it to. "Can I change my pants while you're in there?"

"Sure. And *please* change your *t-shirt*: it stinks. Let me know *when*..."

I obliged...swiftly. I had some cutoff sweats that were moderately comfortable in my cool/cold/muggy apartment. The AC/heater units struggled to keep an equilibrium; the one in the hall made the living room *reasonably* nice most of the time and the kitchen *OK* unless you were cooking. The bedroom unit could turn *that* room into either a meat locker or an oven, and *anything* in between. "I'm..."

"Hi," she stepped out of the bathroom...*shirt* off, revealing a *crop top*, sandals in hand. "*Warm* in here," she declared, "*hope* you don't mind," her midriff rippling in the late afternoon sun.

"No, *I* don't mind. It *can* be dank in here," I agreed. "Wine on the divan?"

"You've *got* a *divan*?"

"No, but I've got a sofa."

"Let's try the *stools* first, pal. Hang this for me?" She looked amusingly severe as she handed me her shirt. "Just because I *show you* some *skin* doesn't mean I want *you* to *handle* it, as much as that *brazen hussy* of an evil twin might *want* you to." She looked past me into the bedroom. "*Lovely* bed. Evil twin...*now*," she stepped towards the bed. "Now, Dave's a *nice* guy...he *may* be *the one*, evil twin...now *don't*..." and she flopped face down on the bed. The quilt I was using for a bedspread inched up; *she* wiggled up the bed, dragging it with her towards the pillows. "Dave," I heard, muffled, "in all seriousness, I have *had* a *miserable* day." She rolled to her side and frowned, head on pillows. She regarded me carefully, propping her head up with a hand. "My evil twin schtick: does it *bother* you?"

"It confuses me, frankly. We barely know each other, and your evil twin keeps *saying*...."

"Yeah." She stretched and sighed. "*Come* on: *no* games; have a lie-down."

So, I did, and she rolled on her back. "*Story* time. My *mother* is *completely* uninhibited," she said. "My sister and I took our cues from *her*; our brothers were *constantly* embarrassed. I developed my evil twin schtick *after* Aunt Ruth showed me her movie. It excited me *and* informed me...*and* it scared me a bit. In church, they said *that* was bad; in school, my *friends* said *that* was *good*." She glanced away. "*Maybe I should*...."

"Did you have any *other* boys...?"

"Rich was my only *long-term* one." She regarded me with her Cheshire smile. "Now *you*, if *that's* OK."

"You mean you *want* to...."

"I..." She stared, blinked. "If I *just now* changed my mind, Dave, would *that* be OK?"

"It's *your* decision, my dear."

"*My dear*, huh," she grinned broadly. "It *should* be *mutual, my dear*. I can *see you'd* be *agreeable*."* She slid up next to me, her nose inches from mine. "If we just *make out*...no; *too* tempting...and I'm *thirsty*, evil twin!"

And she rolled off the bed.

We shared my wine and cheese, her bread and salt, and more details of our lives and what our work week had been like so far. *She* didn't care for westerns; *I* didn't care for slapstick comedy—most of it, anyway. We both liked rare beef, old rock-and-roll, and chocolate. We didn't *like* politics nor politicians a great deal—and, brother, were *we* in the wrong town for *that*.

---

* *Impossible* to hide *that* in *those* cutoffs.

After two hours, she got solemn, quiet. "Before we go any *farther*, Dave, I want to *tell* you…I wasn't *candid* when I told you *why* Rich ditched me."

"OK."

"I *had* to have an abortion two days *before* that." I *didn't* react; she stared. "Did you *hear* me?"

"Yeah. Nothing to do with me; we hadn't *met*."

"But, I had an *abortion*…."

"You said '*had* to have,' so *that* was between you and your doctor."

"Rich didn't *see* it that way. I told him the doctor said it *couldn't* come to term and *had* to be aborted. I didn't *get* as far as *ectopic pregnancy* before he walked out. Came back the next day, dumped my stuff, and… you know the rest. I never told anyone *that* part."

"About the…?"

"Yeah."

"Sorry," I sighed, reaching for her hand; she took it. We sat there for I don't know *how* long. I felt sad, but *that* didn't have *anything* to do with *me*…and I *meant* it.

"Guess my *bra* size," she grinned as the sun dipped behind my balcony rail.

"What do I get if I *win*?" I was mildly surprised at her mood swing. She could *do* that, just to *stop* feeling sad.

"I'll take this itchy crop-top off in *front* of you." She *had* been fussing with it.

"OK." I stared at her chest briefly, having been given permission. "30B."

She blinked. "*How* would a *guy* know a bra size without looking at a label?

"You're *about* my little sister's size, and I *did* laundry."

She looked blank. "Where's my *shirt*?"

"Bedroom closet."

She left and returned, shirt in hand. "And *now*, your *prize*." She turned around, slipped her crop top over her head, and pulled her shirt on, buttoning as she turned. "What, you thought I was going to *show you my boobs*? *They're* not much to look at. Anything more than a mouthful's a *waste*, right?"

"They're *yours*," I answered. "I *try* not to objectify women."

I could see her evil twin wanted to flash me—and she *could have* in *that* shirt, even if the gauzy material didn't *hide* much. "*Hold* me, Dave." She stepped forward while I sat, and I wrapped my arms around her—the first time we really hugged. "I really *have* had a rotten day, and I'm *so* tired." She pitched her head back, resting her chin on the top of my head. "The *truth* is, I'd fall asleep before *you* finished. I've been debating telling you *that* for the past…" she glanced at her watch, "…hour." She kissed my forehead. "Want to go to a party Saturday?"

"A…party?" She could shift gears *so* fast….

"My cousin Flo got engaged. There's a *big* to-do at the Arlington Country Club."

"Arlington…sure, OK." The Arlington Country Club was at the pinnacle of the D.C. social scene—where the posh met to nosh. At *The Arlington*, the *highest* of the *high* entertained their *highest*-level friends and brokered their *highest*-level deals. Occasionally they deigned to *welcome* the great unwashed—by *invitation only*—to put their affluence on display while they feigned bonhomie befitting the event. If you *lived* inside the Beltway, you *knew*. "What time?"

"Pick me up at two. It's summer lawn party casual with a jacket."

"OK," I said, *not* understanding what *summer lawn party* or *any* of the rest meant. "1400 at your place."

"Oh, *you'll* fit right in." She stepped back and grinned widely, her hands on my shoulders. "You're a *great* guy, Dave. I *really like* you *a lot*."

"Well," I smiled, "I *really* like *you* a *lot*."

Then she REALLY kissed me good-night…and a *sweeter* kiss I'd *never* experienced with *any* girl *ever* before.

✳✳✳

"Whaddaya *want*, goober?" *That's* what my *fashion-dumb* ears *heard* Thursday evening at The Bond Street Gentlemen's Apparel *Boutique*. With those *syllables, sales associate* Rubin—a dusky guy about my age wearing a jacket and silk tie—managed to convey just how *fashion-dumb* I was.

What Rubin *actually* said was… "May I *help* you, sir?"

"The *gentleman* has a casual summer lawn party *with* a jacket at the *Arlington*," Ellen declared, pushing me forward. "*Prepare* him."

"Of *course*," Rubin smiled, a somewhat odd smile. "*When?*"

"Saturday afternoon."

"*Hmm*," Rubin frowned. "Not a *great* deal of time, but *The Bond Street* can do it." He sized me up swiftly and glanced at Ellen. "The *shoes* to the *hat*, then?"

"The *works*," Ellen stated. Both she *and* Julia had condemned my wardrobe as *hopeless* when I told them about the party.

So, *here* we *were*…

"*Come* with *me*, sir," Rubin intoned. Behind a curtain, I stood on a low platform while he did the measuring. "Your friend is definite in *her* requirements," Rubin smiled.

"She knows how helpless I am at this kind of thing," I agreed. Everything I saw on the wicker mannequins around us looked *familiar* but somehow *different*.

"New to the neighborhood?"

"Still passing Michigan water."

He chuckled. "Briefs or boxers or bikini?"

"I need *underwear*, too?"

"I need to know *how* to *fit* your trousers."

"Oh. Never *tried* a bikini…" I'd seen them in locker rooms and barracks, in ads. They looked too much like jockstraps to be comfortable for long.

"They *might* be more comfortable when standing around in the sun. Polypropylene *never* stays wet." He glanced conspiratorially. "I'll throw in two pairs. 34 waist; 36 chest; 32 inseam; 14 neck; 30 sleeve; small-frame automatic. Magazines?"

"*Yes* to the auto, *no* to the mags. How much is this gonna *cost* me?"

"Law enforcement discount, and *another* for first-time customers, but *fashion* isn't cheap."

"How about just *clothes*?"

"*This* is *The Bond Street*, sir; *we* don't do *just clothes*."

We left with my purchases just after the store was supposed to close. I had trousers, jacket, and shirt in soft spun cotton, socks of some lightweight fiber, a not-*bad* Panama hat, and outrageously light shoes… with the bikini underwear thrown in. The total was shy of two months' pay at retail, but Rubin had knocked it down to just over three weeks' salary. Without my Reserve pay, I'd have been short on the rent *or* groceries in July. "So, I need a new costume every time I *go* anywhere," I lamented.

"Socially, yes," Ellen declared. "You *know* this place exists on money and image. But, the *Arlington*…buddy, you get invited there, you *have* arrived."

"*How* did Beth get invited, again," Julia asked.

"Her cousin's engagement party."

"Ah," Ellen mused. "Did you get a *name*?"

"Cousin Flo."

"*Hmm*," Ellen mumbled, turning into our parking lot. "*Florida* Ellington, daughter of Senator Maxwell Ellington of Ohio. But *maybe Florence* MacNeil, daughter of Assistant Secretary of State for the Americas Harry MacNeil, but I thought she *was* engaged last year. Either/or. Get yourself ready to breathe air *way* above your pay grade, Dave."

"How the hell would you know *that*, Nancy?"

"*Society columns*, Dave…"

In three hours, I had learned that my wardrobe was shabby and—the *gravest* of DC sins—cheap. Before then, I *did not* know I was *utterly* fashion-hopeless…

I thought maybe I should pick up a copy of *GQ* once in a while…*and* read the society columns.

✳✳✳

"Hello. You have reached the Solarians. Please leave your name and number, and we will return your call if we see fit. Goodbye."

By Friday morning, I'd closed out *five more* files. *This* one looked easy. I made some calls, got a phone number on the only name *in* the file. "That's the *most*…huh." I stretched my arms above my head stiffly. I'd started swimming laps in our building's pool two or three mornings a week before work—before sunup if I *could*—but I'd forgotten how hard *that* can be on the body.

"*What's* the most *what*," Morgan asked, looking over. She was friendly enough, helpful when asked but *could* be kind of pushy.

"That *answering* machine. It said, '*we'll return your call if we see fit.*' First time I've heard *that* one."

"*What's* the case," she asked, suddenly more than casually interested.

File Number Ending 53479-LIB
Name: The Solarians
File Identified: 5 Nov 68
Origin: Ca. 1967, Oakland, CA, by George Neitelsmidt, AKA Romulan Prime, AKA David Gorniak (b. 1941).
Narrative: Appears to be partly based on the Norman Spinrad novel of the same name and on the Isaac Asimov characters of the same name (AKA Spacers in Asimov's Foundation series). Tenets seem to be that certain people are destined to become actual Solarians in future lives, that their life-forces are such that they will survive their Earthly shells. With religious overtones, members seem to be convinced of the imminent end of human civilization and encourage others to believe the same.
Updates: 1969: No tax returns filed by Neitelsmidt; Gorniak works as a janitor at Oakland School District.

1970: IRS audit yielded no organization tax return; membership of Solarians said to exceed 2,000 in five states, though no member list available.

"*Huh*," she shrugged, perching her glasses on her nose and reading. "That's…*interesting*." She shuffled through a stand of files, pulling out a thicker one. "Read *this*."

File Number Ending: 00698-LIB
Name: Subarian Society of America
Date Identified: March 14th, 1937
Origin: Ca. 1875, Chicago, IL, founder said to be George Neitelsmidt (b. 1841), AKA Akkadioso, AKA Miles Deupree. Modern organization ca. 1941, Denver, IL, also by George Neitelsmidt, AKA Simon Encanto (b. 1920).
Narrative: Subaria or Subartu originates in Bronze Age (3rd-2nd millennium BC) Mesopotamia, also thought to be Assyrians or Hurrians. Contemporary organizations seem to believe that their founder is of these peoples, has survived using "soul-flying" techniques taught for a fee. Concern for the record is that the individual most associated may be hiding his identity.
Updates: 1955: Society has chapters in Co, Wi, Mi, Oh, and In, with as many as 3,000 members.
1961: IRS records show Society has paid taxes as required.
1966: Obituary for George Neitelsmidt appeared in Indianapolis papers.
1970: G. Neitelsmidt, AKA Wilson Pinero, interviewed in connection with bombing of Army Math building in Wisconsin.

"Same name," I mused. "Coincidence?"

"Well," she smiled, "listen to *this*:" She played a recording[*] on her phone:

---

[*] Our phones had recording capability that *often* worked. Frequently, the recordings were garbled or had "ghost" recordings with them, making them unintelligible. The Annex said they were *working on it* when we asked.

"This is the Subarian Society of America. Please leave your name and number, and we will return your call if we see fit. Goodbye."

"*Too* coincidental…" I started.

"…To *be* a coincidence," she finished. "We *need* to look into *these*…."

"And I was *just* going to *close* this," I groaned.

"So was *I,*" she sighed.

Morgan worked for Harry Benz, an unassuming man…for an FBI agent, anyway. In the SPD, the concepts of *case-poaching* or *turf* were *verboten*; no SSA minded *their* SAs working with *other* teams. We brought our teams together in a conference room. "*This* is what we're seeing," Morgan stated to the group, reading the summaries of both cases. "Dave was working the Solarians; *I* was working the Subarians…."

"And *Neitelsmidt* popped up," Harry nodded. "*Again.*"

"*Shit,*" Ernie grunted, genuinely unhappy. "Thought we got rid of *that* plague."

"What," I asked, mystified. Julia and Ellen were simply puzzled. Frank and Tom—Morgan's teammates—looked interested.

"That *name*—Neitelsmidt—was used by a clan of grifters when the ink was still wet on the Declaration of Independence," Ernie declared. "Harry, let's call for the microfilms and run them down again. *You guys,*" he pointed at the six of us, "connect the dots, find *who* to contact, and start an Active Case file consolidating these files."

It took a couple of hours to make a list of names in seven states we could call on…and a correlation with The Butterfly Society file. I called the Dayton office, and I got switched to Special Agent Bob Bruits. "Hey," I said, "Dave Clawson, SPD. Have *you* got anything *recent* on a Holly Mossfield…?"

"Yessir, I *sure* do. Got Mossfield in my sights now, just writing up an application for a warrant."

"For *what,*" I asked, glancing at the clock that was edging 3 in the afternoon.

"Interstate fraud; blackmail by mails. Goes by the name of…."

"Neitelsmidt," I blurted, not *sure* just why.

"*Yeah*. How'd *you* know?"

"Part of *another* investigation. When are you planning to pull the trigger?"

"Tomorrow, if I can get the warrant tonight." There was a pause. "You guys gonna swoop in and take it from me? I've got *three months* invested in this."

"No, but we *might* come to visit next week. Can you send us a telex if and when you make an arrest?"

"*Promise* you won't take her from me?"

"I promise *I* won't, but I can't *speak* for my bosses."

"Well, *that's* good enough for me."

I told both teams what I'd found out. Ernie was uncharacteristically expressionless. "OK," he sighed. "We'll wait for developments." He glanced at the clock. "Closing meeting."

✳✳✳

"Fish and chips, Dave," Julia grinned, swilling her beer. "*Fabulous*." She wore an open-weave tank top/shorts combination that concealed *nothing*. The temperature out on my porch was edging 100, but it was a noticeably *dryer* 75 in my kitchen.

"Dad told us not to expect a wife who could cook like Mom, who is *exceptional*." I was in a pair of canvas pants and a loose t-shirt.

"Huh," Ellen sniffed. "I kinda *like* this English beer…Guinness, is it?" She wore a shapeless sleeveless shift with a distracting floral pattern.

"Irish, *not* English. It's hard to get."

"I suppose," Ellen said. "Gonna try *your* sofa, Dave."

"It's time," Julia agreed, following her.

We laid back, watching the shadows lengthen, watching each other digest. From the room's only chair opposite the sectional, I had to look sideways to see Ellen…who started to drift off after a few minutes; so did

Julia. I just went to bed since it was getting dark, and I thought it would be a long day tomorrow.

I was awakened by Julia crawling into my bed, listening to my noisy neighbors. Without *effort*, we were able to go into that blissful Climax Sleep.

I don't know *what* time it was when she kissed on my forehead, whispered, "have fun tomorrow," and left. I'd barely fallen asleep again when Ellen gently woke me. It took *no* effort to get to C-Sleep with her—maybe because we were only half-awake. By sunrise, she was gone.

And *that*, I felt, was *that*...

Only...I woke up at about 3 AM, in my *chair*, alone.

My bed had *not* been slept in.

I'd had some erotic dreams before, but *that* one...

The Arlington Country Club

Or, How I Found Our Secret

"Hi, there," the frazzled-looking brunette at the door said, "you *must* be Dave."

"And *you* must be Cindy," I offered my hand.

"I *am*. She'll be down in a minute, just making last-minute touches on her hair, poor dear. She doesn't like it *long* but can't make it do what she wants *short*, either. Can I offer you something? *Any*thing? Beth said *Arlington Country Club,* and I just went *bonkers!* I mean, *who* gets invited to *there* without knowing *someone* or at least someone who *was* someone once. I've driven *by* it, but I've never been *in* it or knew anyone who *has* or worked there. No, I can't say that. I knew a lobbyist once who was a member, but we were just friends, so I never *got* there. That was the closest I ever got. His name was Steve-something; he was in real estate or taxes or real estate taxes or something. I take it you've never actually *been* there, but Beth's *uncle* is a senator…."

As she prattled on, I began to wonder why she wasn't turning blue. Amidst that stream-of-consciousness rambling, I swear she never took a breath. But I just nodded, smiled, and prayed that Beth wouldn't be *too* long.

I endured two minutes of Cindy's babbling before Beth rescued me, her hair tidily pulled back. She wore a diaphanous white-and-yellow dress and *impossibly* high-heeled sandals that brought the top of her head up to my nose. She smiled brightly, declared, "you look *fabulous*, Dave," patted

Cindy on the arm, and went out the door. Once out, she whispered, "*lose the hat, Dave: it looks silly.*"

"Julia thought it looked *dapper.*"

"*Ju-Ju* was being kind."

"Ju-Ju? Never *heard* that. Didn't know you *knew* her that well."

"College neighbors. *She* called *me* Mighty Mouse because she said I always managed to *save the day.*" She gave my Buick a quick once-over and declared, "there's a car wash on the way. Get the *full* treatment: I'll cover it."

After our car-washing-and-waxing, it did *look* better. It was no *younger*—a 1970 LeSabre with bubbling paint and some rust around the wheel wells—but at least more *presentable*, considering where we were headed.

I pulled into a long line of cars *much* better-looking than mine…most driven by chauffeurs. Beth showed her invitation to a guy in a suit with an earpiece and a bulge under his armpit. This *allowed* us to enter the arching driveway that *started* a quarter-mile from the clubhouse.

We *finally* got to the front door of the main building—a five-story, hundred-yard-long Colonial Revival structure that looked like a movie set. A liveried valet drove the Buick away, and we went to stand in a line with metal detectors. I got to the front, flashed my badge at a guy with a Secret Service badge around his neck, who nodded and said, "over *there* if you *would.*"

Beth went through the metal detector while I just tried *not* to look either too sheepish or menacing, not knowing *why* I was segregated. It flashed through my head that I was violating some *secret* dress code. An older Secret Service guy standing by a table glanced at my credentials and asked, "are you *armed?*"

"Yes."

"Here," he put a red star lapel pin on me. "It's to let *us* know that *we* know you're armed."

"Ah," I was relieved the Fashion Police hadn't busted me. "Big deal here today?"

"Half the *Congress* is here."

"I'm the guest of the senator's niece. We just met a couple weeks ago…" I had no *idea* why I felt compelled to reveal *that* much detail…

And to my relief… "I *get* it," he smiled. "If there's an emergency, you'll hear a claxon sound *twice*. Just keep those around you down and stay put until someone with a *badge* gives *you specific* instructions. 'Get out' or 'run for your life' are *not* specific instructions. Our standard procedure for these affairs. Enjoy yourself and keep the pin."

"Security," I mumbled when I caught up with Beth, sweltering in the sun in *another* line. Rubin *was* correct; the bikini *was* dryer.

At the end of *this* line, a young woman in a tux-like outfit with a severe pencil skirt flashed a black light at the back of the invitation. "*Family*," she said and pointed to a velvet-roped aisle with a red carpet, where *another* young woman opened a velvet gate.

"Aunt Hy was *this* thoughtful," Beth smiled as we passed through the gate.

"You know her well?"

"We spent summers at their place on Lake Erie. Uncle Max got me my job at the IRS."

"Ah," I answered, walking along a red-roped but empty lane to the clubhouse. This bypassed the great unwashed *non*-family in the *other* lane, who glared at us as *they* crept slowly and sweatily towards the building.

The portico was cooler than outside—and had *no* line. *This* guardian— an older gentleman in a tux—opened one of a pair of doors with a sign that read *Family* in a fancy script. Just inside *those* doors was a stair corridor, where two Secret Service agents glanced at my lapel, nodded slightly, and *convincingly* continued their statue act. At the top of the white marble stairway was a small room arrayed with tables laden with enough appetizers, beverages, and flowers to satisfy a hungry, thirsty, and sensually appreciative infantry company.

"*There's* Aunt Hy," Beth nodded, heading in the direction of a matronly woman sitting in an armchair five yards from the top of the stairs, chatting with a man our age. "Aunt Hy, *this* is David Clawson. He's in the FBI."

"Ah," Aunt Hy smiled, offering her hand. "*So* glad to meet you." Then to Beth, "This is *Bill*, Florida's fiancée. Have you two *known* each other long?" Bill was about 6 foot, maybe 180 pounds, with brownish, short hair and a cowlick.

"Couple of weeks," Beth answered, grinning in my direction. "Just getting-to-know."

"Splendid!" Aunt Hy stood up. "*Max*," she called out as she waved. "Max! *Bessie's* here."

A large man with close-cropped, *perfect* hair and a substantial razor burn broke off a conversation with two other men in a doorway and started towards us. "Bessie," he boomed, "*so* glad you could come!" He hugged Beth briefly, then held her with one hand while I shook the other. I concluded that he shook so *many* hands he'd learned to do it without looking *or* thinking…or actually grasping. "Brought an *escort*, Bessie?"

"This is Dave Clawson, Uncle Max. He's in the FBI."

"Yes," Max answered. "I can *see* he's armed. What *detail* are you in, young man?"

"Special Projects Division, sir."

"Special Projects? Thought we defunded them. Well, *no* matter." Uncle/Senator Max's demeanor changed slightly. "*Pleased* to meet you, Dave. *Glad* you could come."

"Happy to be invited, sir," I answered, still *sort of* shaking his hand. "I'm from Michigan, so I *never* voted for you."

I never saw a human face transform *so* quickly in all my life. Suddenly Uncle/Senator Max was a bundle of mirth, now *gripping* my hand… *hard.* I thought about becoming alarmed but decided instead on smiling/wincing—Beth practically doubled over laughing. Aunt Hy fell into the chair, laughing and rocking back hard enough to lift her feet—and the front legs of her chair—off the floor. Fiancée Bill tried to suppress *his* giggles, unsuccessfully.

"Son," Uncle/Senator Max finally managed, *finally* releasing his *iron* grip, "*that* was the most *honest* introduction I've *ever* heard! Bessie, dear: he's a *keeper!*"

"Go find Florida, dear," Aunt Hy finally giggled, *sort of* composed. "she's out *there* somewhere." And as we left, we heard Aunt Hy let out another *whoop* and Max a *guffaw*.

If nothing else, I was *entertaining*.

✳✳✳

"I haven't *seen* Flo in a while," Beth said, "so I'm not sure *I'll* know her. She's about Aunt Hy's height, redhead last I knew." We wandered around the ample space, rarely making eye contact with the other revelers but bumping into some. The reception lobby was a fifty-foot-round, crowded space with a bubbling fountain in the middle, surrounded by a balustraded balcony. It was punctuated by winding staircases and tables for bars and appetizer trays.

"What's *Hy* short for," I asked.

"Hyacinth. My mom's Rose and I have an Aunt Honeysuckle and an Aunt Lily. Grandma Daisy was big on flowers." Waiters and waitresses with trays of champagne flutes dodged in and out; part of me dreaded the thought of getting anything on my *lovely* new outfit. I took note of politicians who I could recognize, not lingering in one place long enough to attract attention. She grabbed my hand. "There's *Georgia*," Beth finally said, pulling me in a different direction.

Holding a girl's hand in a crowd says you're a *couple*, that where *one* goes, the other *wants* to go…usually. I don't know if girls feel the same way, but I would *hope* so. Holding Beth's hand as we navigated the reception was, for me, a first. I'd never *had* that kind of friendship with a girl long enough to be considered a couple. And I *hoped* that today it meant *we came together, we're leaving together.*

I smiled and introduced myself to Florida's younger sister, Georgia, a titian-haired younger woman taller than Beth but probably no heavier. "*Hi*, Dave," she smiled. "Glad to meet you. FBI? I work at the Hoover Building. What detail?" I told her. "Oh, *wow*," Georgia exclaimed. "I'm *impressed*. Dusty Harris is still in charge over there? *You'll* want to chat with Mike Sweeny, the SAIC at the DC Division. He's over...there." She pointed towards the fountain, where a small, grey-haired man was being bored by a fashionably dressed woman, carrying on without respite. *One of Cindy's family, no doubt.* "Let's interrupt Congressman Sondermann's wife." Georgia led us across the crowded space, dodging two champagne-bearers on the way. "*Mrs.* Sondermann," Georgia cooed loudly, "Mrs. *Abadan* was looking for you over by the portico."

"Oh, *thank you*, dear," Mrs. Sondermann smiled, suddenly forgetting all about Mike and scurrying away.

"Mike," Georgia smiled, "*this* is my cousin, Beth Ritter, and Dave Clawson; he's over at SPD."

"*Ah*," Mike smiled, visibly relieved. "Someone who *doesn't* want to blab about law enforcement all night."

"We can talk about anything you *want*, sir," I answered, still clutching Beth's hand.

"How about the *utter* banality of Washington must-go-to parties? And call me Mike if we're not working. So, where are you *from*, Dave," he asked, looking around vaguely.

"Michigan," I started, "I *just* got...."

Beth kissed my chin and whispered, "*I'll* be around."

I kissed her forehead and she drifted off. "I *just* got assigned to SPD..." I continued. We chatted about people (Mike knew most of our SSAs), assignments, and places, while in the back of my mind, I realized that it was the first time *that* had happened to me. Not my *first* party with a girl, but my *first* where I had *any* confidence that I'd *leave* with her.

Then I realized the tempo of our conversation had changed. "*Where* in Michigan," Mike asked again, handing me another champagne flute and taking my half-full one.

"Oh: Hell," I said. I took the booze to be polite; I *sipped* it because I don't drink a lot, but I *was* thirsty. Getting blasted to keep up with the crowd doesn't make sense to me. Getting hammered to celebrate or commiserate makes even *less*. I *sensed* that Mike felt the same way, *not* swilling *his* either.

"*Really*," Mike grinned. "When I *got* to the Detroit Division, someone had a newspaper framed above his desk…."

"Hell Freezes Over? Yeah," I grinned. "You get those in town."

"Well, where *I'm* from—Goerke's Corners, Wisconsin—*nobody's* going to make *that* town so famous, especially now it's becoming a glorified bus stop. What made you pick the Bureau?"

"A recruiter. I *barely* got good enough grades to graduate law school, as much as I *loved* it, but I knew passing the bar would be unlikely. So, I applied, and here I am." *Not that far from the truth, either.*

"Sounds like *my* story. But how'd *you* get SPD?"

"They picked two classmates and me out of the Academy last month."

Mike blinked several times. "Huh." He looked embarrassed, shuffled his well-shod feet. "*Hoping* I'd meet one of *you* someday."

"You…?" …*who?*

"Understand that the Academy's one of the *most peculiar* schools in the world. They generate *so much* data on *everyone*, much of it they *never* use."

"You *worked* there?"

"Before I got the DC office. Academically, the *top* graduate and *bottom* graduate are usually no more than ten whole *percentage* points apart. Physically, *maybe* five or six. It's the *psychological* grades…those they *don't* post on the board…that determine *so* much of your future, and those are *so subjective*." He sipped more champagne. "*Three* of you made the CAQ charts stand on end."

"CAQ?" *WHAT the…?*

"Cooperative Action Quotient. It's what it says: aptitude for cooperative action, teamwork, and ultimately, leadership. It's the score that the faculty gives to candidates on a scale of one to twenty, one being the *absolute best* team-worker. They passed *your* scores around to the SAICs a month ago—no names attached—and asked if the evaluation method was flawed because *three* of you got *ones*…and no class *ever* had seen *that*. What's more, you three got lower scores *together* than you did with *anyone* else."

Huh. "Well, I wasn't at the *top*…."

"Don't matter. *I'd* have wanted *one* of you if Dusty didn't already have dibs on all three. Who's your SSA?"

"Ernie…"

"*Yeah? I* worked with him…" And we chatted for a while longer until Mike had to excuse himself, slipping me his card with his home number scribbled on the back.

I got a sense of how a prize cow might feel after having a ribbon hung around her neck.

✳✳✳

"So, do you *have* family in Michigan, Dave," Florida asked. She was practically her sister's clone, except she probably had twenty pounds on Georgia, *all* in her chest and hips. I'd never really *seen* a wasp-waisted woman before, but Florida *was* one, and her hair *was* still red. The private dinner after the party felt a *little* like a mad tea party,, where nine people talked about nine different things simultaneously, though *most* decorously.

I'd had a great-if-occasionally-*tedious* time that afternoon. I met *way* more members of the DC elite than I could recall. Most of them were *primarily* interested in what they could get out of a party thrown for someone they barely knew *if* they knew Florida *or* her fiancée at *all*. Beth and I had held hands, bumped shoulders, laughed, smiled for at least *part* of the evening.

"I *do* have some family," I said, telling about my parents and little sister. I named nieces and nephews I'd seen maybe three times and one

I'd *never* seen—I didn't even know a *name*. There were uncles and aunts and cousins I saw only around Christmas and every other Thanksgiving. My mom's mom was in a home— she hadn't uttered a rational word in a decade—with the rest of Mom's family in Utah. I'd met them *four* times in my life.

"*You* want to meet your *congressman*," Uncle Max declared, less a *question* than a *statement*. "I'll *arrange* it." I was surprised at how *little* he actually ate *or* drank, though I'd seen him holding drinks and canapes off and on for nearly six hours. It struck me that he never ate all of *anything* nor drank a *full* glass …and he barely broke a sweat or *looked* like he'd spent hours on his feet.

"Yessir," I said, "*Thank* you, sir."

✳✳✳

It was close to midnight before we headed home. Beth didn't sit *too close* on my bench seat…which was OK because it *was* still in the 80s, soggy-humid, and my A/C needed a Freon charge.

I escorted her to her door, expecting…I wasn't *sure* what. She put her key in the deadbolt, turned the knob, and pushed the door open. "Cindy's bunking out," she declared. "*Come* on in."

"You know *that* by the *door?*"

"When we're coming *back,* we lock the *knob.* When we're *not,* we *don't.*"

I followed her into a cool, dark room, with a living room off to the left and a kitchen/dining room to the right, both about 15x20. Dead ahead were the stairs. She closed the door behind us, then took my hand again, staring up the stairs.

Two shining yellow eyes looked at us from up the stairs. "Hannibal," she said, "meet Dave."

The eyes moved slowly down. They belonged to an orange cat that stopped and sat about halfway down, staring at me passively.

"Yours," I asked.

"Brought her from Ohio."

"Why is a female cat named Hannibal?"

"Her name *was* Puffy, but Cindy called her *Hannibal* for some reason. She *answers* to Hannibal; she *ignored* Puffy."

We'd had cats, dogs, hamsters, gerbils, and a parakeet at home, so pets weren't a problem…but Hannibal just *stared* at me. "Is she trying to *tell* me something?"

"She's just interested." She squeezed my hand. "As much as I *want* to go up those stairs with *you tonight*…bad *timing*. Too *messy*."

Oh. THAT. "That's OK."

"*That*, and…we haven't decided on baby names yet."

"*Peter* or *Kimmarie*," I said.

"*Justin* or *Amy. Rain*check?"

"I'll *collect* on it."

"Soon."

I didn't need a cold shower after yet another *memorable* goodnight kiss, nor did I *think* of calling Ellen or Julia to *take my edge off*.

This just kept getting better. And for *that*, I was *happy*.

✳✳✳

I was somewhat disappointed that my Sunday morning was *not* invaded by my partners bearing hot ham and rolls. The solitude did give me a chance to do laundry and finish the P-40 model I'd been working on since graduation. I stood my Tomahawk—a P-40 in British desert livery—on her wheels, changed laundry loads, and called the folks at home. Then I went down to the pool.

"Hi, guys," I said, slipping into the pool. Julia and Ellen were once again sitting in the shallow end of the pool. The temperature had *blazed* past 90 even without the sun; scudding clouds dominated the sky on light breezes.

"Hey," "Hi," replied my fellow cattle. I'd debated filling them in on Mike's revelation about our CAQ but hadn't figured out just *how*. It *did* explain why we worked so well together both on *and* off duty; maybe *that* was the approach to take. But it *still* felt like we were some sort of experimental *beasts* that the Bureau wanted to control, keeping us together to see what happened.

"Tony Addison, this is our *work* partner, Dave Clawson: Dave; Tony." Julia introduced a dark-skinned guy with odd grey eyes who was sitting with them. "Tony and his boys moved into the building this weekend."

"Ah," I said, shaking Tony's hand. "Where *are* you?"

"531," Tony said, sort of smiling. He had an odd gash on his cheek. "Julia says you're from Michigan. About the only state I *haven't* been to."

"Oh," I said, glancing at Julia, who had a glint in her eye. "What do you *do?*"

"I *used* to deliver airplanes, but now I work for the FAA."

"I see," I said, catching Ellen's microscopic shake of the head that said *stop now, Dave.* "Sounds exciting. What did *you* guys do this weekend?"

Ellen sighed, "nothing as exciting as *you* at The Arlington. How *was* the party?" We talked about not much more, agreed it was my turn to drive in the morning. Julia—in a modest tank suit showing *no* cleavage *or* butt cheek—pulled herself out. Tony followed, chatting about the building and the neighborhood as they went.

And I wondered what *just* happened.

"He's a *widower*, long-term," Ellen mumbled. "Two boys, eight and ten. They ran in Jules' apartment while the movers were hauling furniture; we entertained *them* all day." She shrugged. "Right down the hall from us." She gave a meaningful glance. "Dinner at A&W. There's something *there* with Jules."

"*Ah,*" I added to the air. "Where are the boys *now?*"

"Grandparents. They watch them a *lot*, but *not* yesterday." She stretched her arms. "How was it with *Beth* yesterday?"

"She said the hat looked silly."

"That's what *I* thought, too, but Jules was adamant." She arched her back, forcing her chest out. "Other than *that…?*"

"Fabulous."

"Great, Davie." She patted my knee underwater. "Future *there?*"

"I *hope*." I glanced at her, grabbing her hand. "You OK with that?"

"Just like *we* have to be OK with the *possibilities* of Tony and Julia." She squeezed my hand. "I'm *glad* for you *and* Beth, Davie."

Me, too. "Sorry, Nancy."

"*Don't* be, Davie." She scowled, stroked my hand—then my thigh— gently. "I've *enjoyed* our intimacy more than I can say. But, *I* have a possibility myself."

"Yeah? Anyone *I* know?"

"Nobody *I* know yet, but I know *of* him."

"Ah, a *mystery* man." I told her what Mike had said.

It was as if she expected it, smiling slightly. "It *felt* something like that, like we were *meant* to work together." She sighed. "Sex *never* felt like *that* with anyone else…ever." She smiled sadly. "I *like* Beth. *That* part of our partnership's *over*, Davie."

"Yeah."

And it *had* to be because we *were* such a great team.

Road Trip With Another Team

Or, We Work Together Because We're Meant To

"**S**o, *which* case are we actually working *on*," Ellen sighed on the jetway in Dayton. It was nearly midnight Monday when the six of us landed.

"Butterfly Society's the primary," Tom said, dragging one of those new wheeled bags behind him. His traveling mufti seemed out-of-place in the late June heat—a Navy sweatshirt.

"But the others associated with that name—George Neitelsmidt— will be fair game," Morgan finished. She wore pegged jeans and a stadium shirt.

"Did we *see* the arrest report yet," Frank asked. He was the only one dressed for the Midwestern humidity: shorts and a t-shirt.

"I *need* to eat," Julia declared, shifting her backpack on her shoulder. "I'll hail my *own* cab."

"*I'll* go with you," I said. We got to the cab stand, where Julia said, "nearest open restaurant," as we got in. The others got in another cab as Morgan declared, "nearest hotel to the FBI office on Cleo Road."

Julia and I stopped at the Denny's just across the parking lot from the airport, paid the cabbie too much for a five-minute ride, and went in. Other than ordering eggs and toast, we didn't say much until I said, "So, Tony...."

"*Nice* guy," she smiled. "*Nice* kids. Tony said they're shy with *most* people," she shrugged. "But *I* opened my door, and Freddie *led* them in."

"Their father didn't mind?"

"I flashed my badge— offered to watch them—the movers were dollying a mattress as we talked—and he looked *relieved*. Ellen came, and we ended up making lunch and taking them to the park."

"Sounds like serendipity," I said, sipping my coffee. "Ellen says he's a widower?"

"Yeah. Didn't get the *full* story, but his wife died suddenly when the youngest was a baby." She sighed. "Hard to *get* more without *sounding* like an interrogation."

"We *could* look it up...."

"We *could*," she snapped, "but we *won't*," she added, patting my hand.

We finished our meals and got another cab to the Holiday Inn without much more discussion...but she squeezed my hand gently and winked when we parted.

That wink meant *we're on our way, lover.*

✳✳✳

"Morning, Davie," Ellen grinned when we met in the dining room at about 8, better rested than the night before.

"Morning, Nancy," I sighed, sitting next to her. Frank sat on her other side, Tom in front of her. Frank's age was indeterminant, though I knew he'd been in the Army.

"Don't *say* anything, Dave," Morgan, in front of me, chided mildly. Morgan was maybe three years older.

"*Yeah*, Dave," Julia added, on the other side of Tom. "Just *ignore* the rest of us."

"OK, *OK*: good morning, *everyone*," I declared. "Happy now?"

Tom and Frank looked up in mild amusement; Ellen looked blank. "You *said* something?"

"OK, I'm *late*," I sighed, ordering the eggs Benedict. "*I* get the ribbing."

"You *do*," Frank said. "The last one at breakfast gets the *worst* of it."

"Habit if yours?"

"On *our* team, yeah," Tom grinned. "*Had* to break Morgan in."

"*They* did *that*," Morgan agreed. "Our first road trip, they pulled *this* on *me*."

"And you passed," Frank mumbled into his coffee cup.

So, we *were* a team…but we had work to do.

***

"Special Agent Towne, SPD," Morgan flashed her badge at the Dayton office receptionist—an African-American woman with big hands but tiny wrists.

"Six people from *Washington* are here," the receptionist said into the phone with some distress. Once again, *The Almighty Washington* walked into an FBI office and was instantly viewed as either the pros from Dover or something more ominous.

"We're *really* after Bob Bruits," I said. "Want to talk to *him* about…."

"Gary Fellini," a tall, thin man with brown eyes and a bald pate said, walking through the side door. "Wasn't *expecting*…."

"We want to talk to one of your detainees: Holly Mossfield," Julia said. "You arrested her Saturday, according to the Telex you sent us."

"*We* sent you," Gary looked surprised. "When?"

I showed him the flimsy piece of paper. He sighed, "Bruits; OK. What's *Washington's* interest?"

"Related to a Liberty Bell File," Ed declared…

"*Liberty…Bell*…oh, *shit*," Gary whispered—and suddenly looked like a wet noodle trying to stand up: we'd *just* become the *something more ominous*. He took a deep breath, steadied himself on the receptionist's counter, and shook his head. "I *knew someone* would come looking."

"Come *looking*," Morgan asked solicitously, "for *what*?"

"*Come* on," he said, leading us out of the reception area. The Dayton Resident Agency was in a newer industrial park building with an open floor plan. "Since I've *been* here, they've *haunted* me," Gary grimaced. "I *know* the head shed *asked* for them *all* years ago, but," he shrugged. He opened the door to an unfinished, un-air-conditioned space—a wave of heat floated out at us—with concrete floors and bare concrete walls. "We were in the *old* office on Albemarle Street until '74." Along two walls, sitting on the bare concrete, were columns of boxes with *LBF* scrawled on them. "When I got here last year, Steve Tucker showed me *this*." He swept his arms at thirty-odd pillars of five or six file boxes each. "Tuck retired in January and dropped dead in March."

"Why didn't you just let us know they were *here*," Tom asked quietly. "We find 'em all the time."

"It was the *volume*," Morgan whispered, gently touching Gary's arm. "*This can't* have been an accident."

"It *wasn't*," Gary agreed. "Tuck thought the Liberty Bell order was J. Edgar's private joke on Tolson—Tuck and Tolson worked together before we carried guns. I spent my first *year* as a rookie making a file a week."

"*You* probably filled *two* boxes," Ellen declared, walking towards the stash. "Huh." She squatted down, then went on hands-and-knees, audibly sniffing. "The bottom tier, and *maybe* the second, have got moldy...*may be* too bad to use." She stood up again. "But *this* is *not* why we're here. *We* need to see your prisoner and what you've got on The Butterfly Society."

Relief visibly washed over Gary's body. "What do I do with *these*," he asked dreamily as if he were on the edge of Climax Sleep.

"*We'll* get them where they belong." I calmly declared. However, I had no idea *how*...

That's how we became the *Saviors* from *The Almighty Washington*.

✳✳✳

"Holly, these are Special Agents Parkinson and Clawson," Bob Bruits said to the thirty-something woman handcuffed to the table. "They want a word." Bob was a swarthy man with light brown eyes and a broken nose.

"OK," Holly sighed, seemingly resigned. She was well-groomed despite two nights in the county jail, but her teeth were suffering from neglect. Though her voice sounded tired and sincere, her brown eyes darting between us betrayed an always-scheming grifter looking for an angle.

We'd spent part of our morning looking at Holly's file. Fingerprint hits coming in revealed two *different* identities for Holly; one from Florida and another from Indiana. Her file was getting more interesting by the moment…especially since the Indiana card was for Holly *Neitelsmidt*.

"Holly: tell us about your association with The Butterfly Society," I started. "When did *you* become part of it?" On sources like Holly, who lie to stay ahead and *sometimes* to stay *alive*, you use a *combination* of approaches.

Holly looked puzzled for a moment. "*Never* heard of it."

"Not *so*, Holly…or should I call you Mrs. George Neitelsmidt?" Julia's soothing tone and genuine smile often put people at ease…

But not Holly, who maintained her puzzlement. "No, I never *heard* of…."

"You can't stall forever, Holly," I said. "You were an informant in California. We have you on file…" *That's* the *We Know All* approach.

"Never *been* to California," Holly declared. "Sorry, can't help you."

"*Again*, not so, Holly," Julia said, holding up her booking photo from ten years before. "See there? Oakland, California PD. So, when did you…?"

"*That's* not me," Holly declared. "Doesn't even *look* like me. I tell you I've never *been*…" Lifelong grifters have two talents: chameleon-like adaptability to changing situations and the capacity to *convincingly* stick to one story or identity *just* long enough to wiggle into another. And, they are *masters* of that timing.

"Holly: do your *teeth* hurt?" I interrupted, hoping to get her off her stride long enough to get a straight answer to a seemingly incongruous, out-of-the-blue query that had nothing to do with the investigation.

"Yeah," Holly frowned with a double-take. "You a dentist?"

"No, but I can get you dental care if you want it."

There was a long silence…and Holly blinked at me with astonishment. "Well, I…"

"All *you* have to *do*," Julia smiled, "is tell us about some of the stuff we already *know* about you. Nothing *much*, *nothing* important. Ancient history. *Nothing* to do with your *current* charges, but...."

"We *know* people who *know* people," I said. "The state's attorney will be *happy* to...."

"*Indiana's* the key," Holly mumbled, not looking at any of us. "Look *there*. You want anything *more*, I want a walk; *complete* immunity. And I want this bad tooth fixed *today*." She pointed to the right side of her face.

"*Can* be arranged." There came a knock on the observation window. "*That* means yes. A *deal...that'll* take some doing, but you gave us *something*." I smiled widely. "We'll show *our* good faith now and get you looked at, then tomorrow *we'll* talk. Just hang tight here, and I'll come to take you to a dentist."

Outside, Bob and Gary shook our hands earnestly. "Could *not* get a *single* straight answer out of her Saturday *or* yesterday," Bob gushed.

"The marshals are waiting to take her to the dental clinic," Gary declared. "She was going there this afternoon anyway. Surprising that she rolled up on *that* so fast...."

"Yeah," I sighed as if it were an everyday occurrence, "but it's all in *how* you *say* it."

Of all the interview techniques I *ever* used in my career, *I'll Take Care of Your Toothache* was *always* the most effective. And they *still* don't teach it.

✳✳✳

"Then she folded like a gas station map," Julia declared that evening at dinner. The hotel restaurant had one table big enough for eight people— Bob and Gary joined us—and we had *commandeered* it that night.

"Not *quite*, Julia," I said, maintaining my modest demeanor as much as I could. Any law enforcement pro has a certain admiration for interviewers who can crack—even if for a *moment*—a grifter like Holly in a short time. We hear stories about interrogations—even in the old days of bright lights, sandbags, and day-and-night sessions—when con men and con women dissembled over and over again until no one could remember their *first* lie. "I just used what we were going to do in another couple of hours anyway."

"That's *so*," Gary admitted. "We *had* to: the doctors told us that infection was dangerous."

"We *saw* what they took out," Bob said. "Didn't think that molar was *human*."

"But, will she be able to dissemble better *without* that distraction," Frank asked. "I'd have thought you *could* have gotten *more* out of her."

"*True*," Tom said, "but the doctor's statement's in the record, and if something *was* dangerous, we'd have had a *tit* in the *ringer* if we *hadn't* taken care of it."

"*Real* decorous, Tommy," Morgan shook her head. "There are *women* in the Bureau now, remember."

"And we don't *use* ringers anymore," Ellen declared, "so *my tit's* never been *close* to one."

"Mine, neither," Julia said, sticking her chest out.

"Or *mine*," Morgan said, doing the same. "Yeah: *you're* at more *risk*." Morgan's bust wasn't *near* Julia's 36C.

"Or *mine*," I said, sticking my chest out.

"*You've* had too many beers," Bob sighed, "and *I* have to get home to the wife. See you guys in the morning."

"Yeah, *I* should get," Gary said. "Office opens at 7."

"Expect us before noon," Morgan declared.

✳✳✳

"*So*," Ernie said on the phone, "we took a vote here, and Clawson and Towne *lost. You two* get to drive those files back here."

Of course… "*Thanks*, Ernie," I said. "We'll wrap up here today…."

"Not likely," Harry interrupted. "Mossfield's prints hit at the scene of a bank robbery that cost the lives of a teller and a guard in Texas. A facsimile copy's on the way. Leverage *that* and find out *how* she got the Neitelsmidt identity."

We had Holly in again by late morning. The Texas robbery was in '74, a bang-up year for bank robberies when Patty Hearst got caught on camera doing it. Morgan joined me for a chat about the bank jobs…and about both Indiana *and* George Neitelsmidt.

"Holly, how are you *feeling*," Morgan began. Holly had a bruise on the side of her face.

Holly answered slowly. "Taking pain pills." Her eyes were somewhat dull and not as *twitchy* as they were the day before. "Hurts to talk. You here about my immunity?"

"Well, we *would* have been, Holly," Morgan began quietly, "but Agent Clawson's got a problem that *he* can't seem to *solve*. We were hoping *you'd* be able to help."

"I want my deal," Holly repeated flatly. She didn't move her mouth much, so she was a little hard to understand.

"Well, *let's* talk about the Permian Bank and Trust in Odessa, Texas," I said, "15 November 1974."

Holly winced, twitched an eye. "What…?"

"Your *fingerprints*, Holly," Morgan added smoothly, softly. "They were *there*. Two people *died*. Texas wants to talk to you about *that*." She sounded as if to a lover about their future—rich, deep, passionate. *This* is called *Sympathy/Empathy*.

"My…" Holly sighed, staring Morgan in the face. "*Can't* be…."

"*Can* be, sweetheart," Morgan continued. "Full left palm on a teller's counter." In *some* interview techniques, words like *sweetheart* can be used, but *never* like *that*, even in *Sympathy/Empathy*. What Morgan was doing wasn't in *any* books…

"We…no one was *supposed* to get hurt," Holly sighed, as if in relief. While an interviewer *should* get into a source's *head*, Morgan got into Holly's *heart* and *soul*…dangerous stuff, yet she did it with *casual* ease.

"Neitelsmidt, Holly," I asked softly. "Where's the name from?"

"I started using it in about '68," Holly sighed, staring at Morgan. "I was working the Butterfly con in Indiana…" Holly looked as if something inside her just got…*released* is the only way I can describe it.

"Butterfly con," I asked.

"The Butterfly Society. We *said* we raised money to support food banks and job agencies, but really we were just scamming. Worked pretty good. Neitelsmidt was easy to use, they said…."

"Who *told* you to use it, Holly," Morgan smiled, touching Holly's hand gently. The *Temptation* approach, discussed by the instructors, *isn't* in the manuals. Professionals advise *against* it because it can produce an uncontrollable response the same way physical torture can—yielding whatever answer the source *thinks* the interviewer wants. But *this* wasn't *Temptation*. *This* was following up on whatever Morgan did before.

"*Lots* of us used it," Holly smiled. "I wasn't the only one."

"Why, Holly? Why the name *Neitelsmidt?*" Morgan leaned forward invitingly. She was wearing a button-down shirt. I hadn't noticed until that moment that it was *un*buttoned *lower* than decorum suggested… certainly lower than J. Edgar's dress code allowed.

"No origin. The name has no origin." Morgan wasn't *that* well-endowed, but *I* could see—and *Holly* could see—*enough*.

"I *see*," I smiled. "Tell us about that bank."

"I was there two days before," Holly said, not taking her eyes off Morgan. "I *wasn't* there when they *hit* it."

"And the Solarians, Holly," I asked. "What was your association with them?"

"Like I told those cops, I was paid ten bucks to hand out flyers for them in San Francisco." She pulled her hand back. "Listen; this dope's wearing me out, and talking hurts. Can we save this for a while?" Whatever that *effect* was didn't last long for Holly. I wondered—seriously—*what* I'd just seen. Interrogation? Seduction? Hypnosis? All three?

"Sure, Holly," Morgan purred. "Anything *you* want."

We left the intimate atmosphere of the interview room, joining the rest of the team in the observation hall. "Frank," Morgan declared as

Holly was removed, "*your* turn." I was surprised as Morgan embraced Frank warmly. Tom acted as if *this* were routine; the rest of us looked at each other in mild surprise. "How's Joanne, Frankie," Morgan smiled before she let him go. "Talk to her last night?"

"Yeah; *good*, Morg," Frank answered casually. "She says hi."

"We'll get together on the Fourth of July." She casually buttoned up her shirt.

"*Policy* says that *being* gay…." Gary began in an authoritative tone.

"Don't go *there*, sir," Morgan answered. "I play *roles*, and I *have* a fiancée."

"Yeah," Tom added, "and Jerry's…where?"

"Not *sure*," Morgan sighed. "I *thought* Afghanistan, but I got a message last week that said Pakistan."

"What's he doing *there*," Ellen asked.

"He's with CIA and speaks Pashto and Urdu. He took off Christmas night—*after* the Russians invaded Afghanistan. He gave me a ring, and I haven't *seen* him or *heard* his voice since."

There are just some situations you can't account for…not entirely. And there are some interviews that, for whatever reason, stay with you for a while.

***

"Well, at *least* it's an automatic transmission," I sighed. The loading dock in the back of Dayton's office made it easier to load the two-hundred-odd file boxes into the rental box truck. Gary put a railroad seal on the door latch when the last box was loaded.

"Good that *you* know how to back one of these things up," Morgan agreed, sitting on the other side of the truck when we rolled away. We shared the wide front bench seat with our luggage in case we had to stop.

"*Piece* of cake," I sighed, having driven enough trucks of *that* size for my dad and for the Army. The truck's *un*-air-conditioned cab boasted an

AM-only radio to help more-or-less strangers to fill eight to twelve *hours* of sunbaked monotony. By the time we hit I-70, Morgan was already yawning and flapping her shirt. "So, where are you from, Morgan, other than the FBI?"

"Born in Houston, grew up in Atlanta," she sighed. "How about you?" We chatted for a few hours about our backgrounds and families before she finished with, "then Jerry packed up and left. He still pays half the rent, but I was lonely, so I got Greta to room with. The 2nd Floor would be empty if I didn't." She sounded lonesome when she finished.

"If you want, I can see if I can find out about Jerry through the 511th." It was likely that one of the many *attached specialists* to my Reserve unit had *some* knowledge.

She glanced over at me. "*That* would be nice, but *don't* do it because you want to get into my pants because it *won't* work." She was quiet, suddenly. "Sorry, *that* wasn't fair."

We passed a sign that read *Zanesville Next 5 Exits*. "*Beth* is from Zanesville."

"Yeah." There was a pause. "Women in the Bureau have to be *so* careful."

"That's what Julia and Ellen tell me."

"Yet, *you're* sleeping together."

I inhaled deeply. "We're *not* anymore. *I've* got a *friend* now…."

"And Beth's *great*; happy for *both* of you."

"Julia's interested in a neighbor; *nice* enough guy."

"Huh." Then the radio played…

> And if you can't be, with the one you love
> Honey, love the one you're with!

"We *want* someone we can bring to the Christmas party."

"Me, too." She went quiet again. "We're children of the '60s stuck in a '30s institution."

"Not *that* bad, is it?"

"No. *Then* the woman would have been terminated if she got caught. Now, *both* parties might…*if* it gets in the way of work." She wedged herself into the corner by the door. "I can't blame *you guys* since *I* did the same when *I* got here."

"You *can*, but you'd be a hypocrite." I cleared my throat. "And, with Holly…"

"I play for *both* sides, sometimes." She shifted again. "Takes *the edge* off."

"Uh-huh." I looked ahead and saw an exit with a McDonald's. "Want a break?"

She looked over, surprised. "Sure." We got burgers, fries, and coffee to go. The strip map I studied marked all the Federal facilities where we could secure the truck if we *had* to—we were never more than two hours from any of them.

"Want to *drive*," I asked. We were just west of Columbus at about 7 at night.

"Never drove anything *this* big," she said as we adjusted the mirrors; she was about three inches shorter than me.

"Just remember we're longer than a car, and the back end's lighter than the front, so be careful braking." We managed to get back on the Interstate without mishap, moving quietly east, having run out of things to say for the moment. I watched the traffic on the westbound for a while, then the eastbound…and my companion.

Morgan was thin and wiry with long arms and deep brown eyes, and *long* legs. She wasn't *well-endowed*, but her figure was OK. I must have been doing something *too* obvious because she clucked her tongue and sighed, "I'll take it *all* off for a *better* look if you want."

"No, I…"

"Oh, stop *apologizing* for *everything*, Dave," she smiled in the gathering dusk. "Women aren't that *delicate*. Besides, *you're* not *that bad* yourself."

"Do *all* women do that? Check guys out without really looking?" I had to admit that the female tribe was something of a mystery to me. There

were only a small number of girls in the Hell area—about a third of my high school and all claimed by the jocks—so the competition was fierce.*
I can honestly say that I didn't have a real *date*—meal, entertainment, transportation—until college.

"*Most*, I think," she said. "Most do it after a *while*; some do it out of boredom. *I* do it…habit. I do it to *women*, too. Occupational hazard. Dave: you didn't blink when I said I was *bi*."

"Nothing to do with *me*, Morgan." She looked puzzled; I decided to change the subject. "Ever wonder why *we* got picked out of the Academy for the SPD?"

She was quiet, staring straight ahead into the gathering night, gripping the steering wheel so hard I heard knuckles crack. "I asked Poppy. He said 'better you *didn't* know.'"

I told her what I'd heard at the party; she stared into the looming darkness for a while, then she smiled. "Uncle Mike's in DC? Huh."

"He's your uncle?"

"Family friend. He was in the Atlanta office with Dad when his wife passed away and spent a lot of time with *our* family. I haven't seen or heard from *him* since I was 12. I should reach out."

"I *got* his number."

"Yeah?" She was quiet again; I figured she'd just drop it…but "it makes sense. The last *twenty* of us assigned to SPD right out of the Academy in the past decade…*about* when they seriously started the psychometrics. Also explains why we all work *so* well together."

We drove for another hour or so before she said anything else. "Where's the next Federal facility we can secure the truck in?"

I used my little penlight to look. "Pittsburgh Federal motor pool."

"Let's stop."

"We *can* make Quantico."

"Yeah, but if we keep going, we'll be at the office at about three in the morning. Nobody's gonna be there until six at the earliest, and we

---

* Kim was more a *buddy* than a *girl*…except when she *was* a girl.

can't get *at* the keys to the back door. Want to sleep in this truck until someone shows up?"

"OK: Pittsburgh."

✳✳✳

"*Come on*; I'm *decent*," Morgan declared outside my motel door. "*Open the door*." We'd put the truck in the underground garage downtown and walked three blocks to this not-bad little motel just before midnight.

"OK," I sighed, opening the door in my sleep-skivvies.

"Just had a *nightcap*," she grinned as she walked in. She came in from the *steamy* heat and sat at my two-foot diameter table, weaving slightly. The only light in the room was above the mirror over the sink. "But it was *too much*."

You have something to say. "How *much*?" *NO do-de-DUNK, Clawson...*

"Couple *shots*, *no* more," she said, seemingly drowsy. "What you *said* got me thinking."

"What about?"

"Stuff." She pushed her shoes and socks off, then took her bra off under her t-shirt. "*Please* tell me you're *not* embarrassed."

"I've seen your tribe do it often enough."

"My *tribe*," She sniffed, swaying as she stood up. "*I'm* going to *lie down*." The *other* queen bed that I *hadn't* been on was only about two steps away. "Problem?"

"Nope."

"*Good*." She whipped the bedspread back and laid down. I turned my chair, wondering just *what* was going on. "My *tribe*. *You* have *no idea* what it is to be a member of *my tribe* in *your tribe's* world; *no* idea." She sat up suddenly and unbundled her hair, which came down to about mid-back after she shook it loose.

"You're *right*. How *could* I?"

"And *now*...and I *frankly* don't know *what* it is to be in *your tribe*, either, so *that's* pretty dumb, come down *to* it."

136

"Uh-huh."

"Dave: I *like* you." She started lifting her shirt. *Uh-oh…* "And I'm going to level with you because we're alone in a little motel room and *I'm* stoned, and I *shouldn't* be, and it's *so hot,* and I want to take what *little* I have on *off* and lie in the blast of an *air conditioner* with a *guy* because it's one of my *favorite* things to do, but I haven't been *naked* with a *guy* since Christmas and…." She stood up again, silhouetted in the light from the bathroom, forgetting about her shirt. "I'm going to *take* these *shorts* off, but I *have* underwear on." She slid her waistband down a bit, stopped, then looked sheepish before she grinned, "Oh, *shit,* I *don't.*" She plopped down on the bed, her feet on the floor, and started snoring.

I swung her feet up on the bed and threw the bedspread over her… the *least* I could do.

✳✳✳

"*UGH,*" was the *first* sound I heard in the morning. "I was *here* all night?"

"Uh, yeah," I groaned, blinking as the crack of sunlight came through the inevitable gap between the curtains. "*You* passed out."

"*SHIT,*" she breathed, wrapping herself in the bedspread as she looked around and spotted her bra on the table. She did *something* swiftly, looking down. "Dave: *tell me we didn't…*because I *had underwear.*"

"We *didn't*; you *said* you *didn't.*"

She dropped the bedspread, swung over, and sat down on *my* bed, sighed deeply, then laid down next to me. "Dave: if you *promise never* to *divulge* a *word* of *what happened* to *anyone,* I'll give you a *blow job* every *week* for a *year.*"

"I *won't,* but Morg; if you've *got a problem*…."

"*Not* what you think. Not at *all* what you think."

"OK. Just *what's* the problem?"

"*Follow* me," she said, going into the bathroom. "Sit *there,*" she pointed to the toilet as she stepped into the tub, drawing the curtain. Soon, the water was running, and her shorts and t-shirt flew over the curtain rod. "*Oooh*," she sighed.

And I waited…

"I take a medication that I'm not *supposed* to mix with alcohol. I *thought* I could handle it because I took the meds *late* and wanted a drink *later*; it *seemed* OK the night before *last*. Sorry."

"It's OK." I heard some splashing, some sluicing, and the water turned off.

"Makes my skin *crawl* after."

"Uh-huh. What's it *for?*"

"I got stung by a scorpion when I was a kid. It turned out I'm allergic to the venom, and it screwed up my nerves." I saw a hand reach out. "Hand me a washcloth?" I tossed one over the rod. "Thanks." I waited, heard some splashing. "It's important that the Bureau *doesn't* know about *that* reaction; they *know* about my condition. My *schedule* got screwed up…woman who can't hold her *liquor*…."

"Know *what* exactly?"

"That when I *misjudge* my *meds,* I act like *that.* I'm going to *give* you my *body* in gratitude-in-advance for your silence."

"Not necessary."

"You *sure?*"

"Yeah."

"Guys *say* I'm hot."

"You *are*, but *that's* not necessary."

I *heard* her stand up behind the curtain. "Hand me a towel? Thanks." She opened the curtain, wrapped in the towel, staring at me. "The *one* advantage is that it screwed up something in my brain, so I don't feel *cold* anymore. We should get going…if you're sure you *don't want*…?" She opened the towel *just* enough…

"I may be a *horny* bastard, Morg, but I *won't* accept sex as a reward for acting like a decent human being."

She smiled, stepped out of the tub, bent over, and pecked my cheek. "*Good*. Beth's a *lucky* girl."

> *Turn your heartache right into joy*
> *She's a girl, and you're a boy…*

NOT this time.

✳✳✳

"Well, *you* guys took your time," Dusty declared as I backed the truck up to the front door. It was nearly two in the afternoon Thursday.

"We got worn out in that truck and stopped in Pittsburgh," I said. "There was a Fourth-of-July parade and construction all over town this morning."

Which was true, but not the *whole* truth. We also had a leisurely breakfast and boiled in the blazing late June sun through the windshield all morning, requiring *several* relief stops.

Everyone turned out to unload the two-hundred-odd boxes before Dusty yelled, "STOP!"

"What," Ernie growled.

"*This* is the Dayton Collection!"

"The…what?" I didn't have to *act* mystified.

"Before *my* time," Ernie sighed, "SPD had one *main* mission: internal investigations. When Bobby Kennedy became Attorney General in '61, J. Edgar *stopped* that function, gathered up all *those* files, and shipped 'em to Dayton labeled *Liberty Bell Files*. Why *Dayton* is *anyone's* guess."

"And *here* they are," Dusty added. "But some of these…maybe a lot… aren't *those* files at *all*." He shook his head. "Bureau politics be *damned*," he declared. "Upstairs with the lot. We'll figure it out in due course."

We were just finishing up with the move—wearing gloves for the moldy boxes—when The Skipper tapped Dusty on the shoulder. "Sir, the Director's on the phone."

Another half an hour later, Dusty came out of his office. "Ernie; Harry," he yelled; Ernie and Harry went.

"*Now* what," I grunted. "Ain't unpacked *this* trip."

"We *may* have another...." Morgan whispered as they emerged again a few minutes later.

"*Come*, children," Ernie called.

"*My* crew; *my* office," Harry called.

We filed in quietly, waiting. Ernie flipped his wall calendar up two months before he turned to us again. "Monday morning 0700, report with bag and baggage to Andrews AFB. The Mounties *may* have a location for *FC* in Alberta. The Duluth and Minneapolis offices are *preparing* to welcome parts of the San Francisco task force. *We're* going to liaise with the Mounties and carry what *they've* got to the task force guys."

We know *now* who *FC* was, but in 1980 he was the most elusive terrorist in North America who had yet to *kill* anyone. All we really *knew* about him was that the bombs he mailed were works of art...and no one had *any* idea *why* he was sending them.

"And *here*," Ernie handed us each a stack of envelopes paperclipped to a flimsy form. "Your expenses for your *first* two weeks."

I studied the form, frowning at the language, then stared at the *amounts* as Ernie explained. "You get $25 per diem when you are more than fifty miles from the office on official business. You an *additional* $25 per diem every day you spend over 12 hours on official business. You get $0.15 a mile for every mile you *travel* over fifty miles on official business. You get $10 for breakfast, $15 for lunch, and $25 for dinners on duty—weekday, weekend, holidays, eaten or *not*—more than fifty miles from the office on official business...unless you have receipts for *more*. You get $15 for every meal consumed *after midnight* while on official business. Your *lodging* allowance starts at $50 a day and goes up to $150 depending on location *in addition to* the lodging *bill*. You get *another*...."

I added up the numbers as Ernie droned on. Six *days* in the field covered not just my *direct* expenses but my new duds, as well.

And SPD teams were *always* going *somewhere.*

Our tax dollars at work.

***

"*That* was great," I smiled at Julia Friday night. "Didn't know you could *poach* bass like that."

"I didn't *either*," Julia agreed, "until I ordered it in Dayton. Figured *someone* has the know-how, so I went over to The Crab Shack and asked the cook."

"Simple," I declared, swigging more wine. "*I'm* for the living room."

"Me, too," Julia grinned.

"I'll *join* you, " Ellen said, bringing the bottle.

And we reclined in our respective places…waiting.

I hadn't *heard* from Beth; I called her *twice* that week but no call-backs.

"*Good* night, guys," Ellen announced after maybe twenty minutes, getting up. "Day at the range tomorrow."

"See ya, Nancy," Julia said. "Call when you're ready." She glanced at her clock. "Go *home*, Davie." She winked *have fun.*

Huh?

So I went home. At 8:01, the intercom buzzed. "Yeah," I answered, puzzled.

"*Hi*," a familiar voice answered…and I buzzed her in.

Moments later, Beth was at my front door in a tank top, *hip-high* skirt, and her *inevitable* sandals, with a bottle of wine sticking out of her shoulder bag and a big smile on her face. "*Ju-Ju* said you'd be here by eight," she said when I kissed her *hello.*

"Ah," I said, leading her into my kitchen. I poured two glasses and sat on the end of the islet.

"*Her* idea was *wine* and *relaxation*."

"What *kind* of relaxation…?"

"*This* kind," she took my hand and placed it on her breast. *No…bra…* "Nipples *hard* as *diamonds*." They *were*, too: the hardest I'd *ever* felt… "They *hurt* when they get this hard." She sipped her wine. "The *thought* of *you* has made me all *hot* and *bothered*." She sipped wine. "I *had* a chat with Ju-Ju last night," she said softly. "About *her* and *you*." Something in me *fell*, hard…but she squeezed my hand, *hard*. "I told her that when *I'm* with you, *you're mine*." She finally looked at me. "OK?"

"Uh-huh," I breathed, squeezing her hand. "You two were neighbors in the dorms?"

"Yeah. *Wild* times. All the *college sex* we could *handle*." *College sex* between relative strangers in the '70s wasn't like *married sex* or *boyfriend-girlfriend sex*. It involved *lots* of fondling and kissing, and *some* of it only *semi*-private. But there wasn't much *full-body contact,* if you *get* me. I spent six *years* in dorms of one kind or another, and I had *some* such encounters—I worked a lot—but *very* few *home runs*. "I only ever had *real* sex behind closed doors."

"My *real sex* was limited."

"And *now…here* I *am* to *save* the *day*." She slid off her stool, whispered "David or Elizabeth," and held out her hand. "Dave: *your* baby names?"

"David or Elizabeth."

"We *agree*, then."

Boy, did we…

✳✳✳

"Julia and Ellen are going to the range," I sighed, watching the dust motes dancing in the A/C breeze and morning sunlight. "*I* should, too."

"Can *I* come?"

"I can sign you in as long as you have safety gear."

"I want to practice with my .45…*and* my .22." She gazed at me. "Do *we* have a *chance* for something serious? I've thought that *sex* was the only

142

thing Rich and I *really had* that *worked.* I want more for *us*, ya know? *I* need *more* than what happens in *bed.*"

In a few years, this would become *I want to discuss our relationship.* "I *hope* we do."

"I want *my* children to be christened and baptized. Do *you* believe in God, Dave?"

"*Not* the way you'd expect." I'd never really articulated my answer to *that* question. "*Mom* says 'God is neither neutral nor benevolent,' but took us to church on Christmas and Easter. *Dad* says, 'Einstein was right about God being the Universe: huge and uncaring,' and says he hasn't been in a church except for weddings, baptisms, and funerals since the war. *He* enlisted after he graduated from college in 1943, said he spent the war patiently waiting—made it sound like fishing. Mom told us the Army drafted him into the Special Engineer Detachment of the Manhattan Engineer District because of his degree: inorganic chemistry." She didn't flinch. "He was stationed at Oak Ridge, Tennessee, supervising the lab techs." *Still* nothing. "Mom was a Calutron Girl, monitoring the dials of the mass spectrometers that extracted enriched uranium isotopes, not knowing *what* it was *for.*" *Still* nothing. "When they were told that they had spent *two years* extracting the fuel for the Hiroshima bomb, they were both glad their weapon *had* worked and *horrified* by it." *Nada.* "They were married five days after VJ Day."

"*God*, sweetie." She had a little *tell-me* frown. "*Your* take."

"Marquez said, 'I don't *believe* in God, but I'm *afraid* of Him.' Like Voltaire, I think if He *didn't* exist, we'd have had to *create* Him for the sake of morality. *I* think they're *all* right: God is what *we* make of Him ourselves." *There! Not bad if I say so myself…*

Time seemed to stand still, gazing into each other's eyes before she smiled, "Robert or Jessica." She swung around on top of me…her training as a gymnast gave her a fantastic range of motion.

"Dean or Rebecca." Why *those* names I never knew…

She *was* as *generous* a lover as Kimmie had been.

***

"*Hey*, Dave," a familiar voice said not far away. I went to the Hobby City shop over in Southbridge Sunday because I had to find a home for my Tomahawk—I didn't have space.

"*Frank*," I exclaimed, returning the *big* model of HMS *Victory* to the shelf. *Not for a month's rent, thanks.* "You building something?"

"Looking for another *gun* to build." I'd noticed that he had a couple of small artillery pieces in his cubicle and a foot-long Roman catapult in the break room that he'd built. "You?"

"Looking for something to strike my fancy."

"You don't have a stock?" Most model builders have a store of unbuilt kits sitting around. *I* did/do have a half-dozen unbuilt kits at a time, but like *all* model builders I wanted/want more.

"Yeah, but...there's always the allure of a new..."

"Yeah. Joanne indulges me." I didn't know a lot about Frank, other than he had a dry sense of humor, and he was maybe a decade older than I. "You don't have *that* issue, though."

"Nope, still batching it." I pulled down a small-scale model of *Yamato*. "Never built one of *these*."

"My buddy was building that *big* one. Wanted to get back to it in the worst way."

"The four-footer?" I gestured to a built version atop the shelves. "*Did* he?"

"*Not* the way he wanted. We were on a battery barge in the Mekong Delta in '66 when he caught a frag in the throat. He bled out before he hit the deck." He reached up for a German self-propelled gun. "*This* looks promising."

"*This* doesn't," I sighed. "Something about most contemporary ships that just turns me off." I glanced up again. "*Hello*," I smiled at a steamboat kit. "*That'll* do."

As we made our way to the register—impulsively snagging paint and sandpaper, glue and brushes, putty and knife blades on the way. "I'll buy you a cup of coffee," he offered.

We sat in a diner across the parking lot from Hobby City. "Work with your hands much," I asked.

"There's an allure to the miniature world, capturing life in time and space. A *story* that models tell. You?"

"I built models as a kid. They made comic books come alive..."

"There's *that*. They were neat to blow up, too."

"Or burn with lighter fluid. I built some structures for Dad's model railway. Then I went to *work* for my dad. In high school, I learned that auto mechanics and restorers got paid *x* dollars, but rebuilders of carburetors and fuel pumps and injectors and turbochargers got paid x *times y* dollars. Doing *the latter* gave me spending money in college and law school. *Death* on my social life, but I had money to pay for school *and* food *and* lodging *and* gas that my fellow students didn't. My Reserve pay and GI Bill *helped* but *couldn't* cover everything. So, yeah, I *like* to work with my hands."

"Huh. Kinda like how I got into law enforcement."

"How's that?"

"Backed into it. My dad was a part-time sheriff in rural Wisconsin. A month after I got back from 'Nam, he hung a badge on me to help corner a gang on a bank-robbing-and-murder spree. We went to a barn where *another* part-time policeman was waiting, and Dad went behind the barn to flush the guy out. A guy comes screaming out of there, waving a gun, and the cop drops him. Then the State Police came, *then* the FBI just walked up and took charge. As soon as the guy said, 'this is the FBI' on the bullhorn, the last guys came out, hands up. I figured *that* was the place to be if I wanted to be in the law enforcement game, and I'd *been* thinking about it. Went to college, worked with Dad for a couple years, applied with the Bureau, and here I am."

"And you've been with SPD for *how* long?"

"Three years. I started out in Phoenix in '74 but got moved here because I did something *foolish*."

"Which was?"

"I tapped a guy on the shoulder in a grocery store, said, 'you dropped something,' and he threw his hands up. He was wanted in three states for bank robbery and made me for a fed as soon as he looked at me." He made a face. "Of course, he had two buddies in the car outside waiting for him. I took them *all* in...on a Sunday. My SAIC was so pissed he could hardly *see*."

"Rookies aren't supposed to *get* that lucky."

"Got *that* right. SPD came calling a month later." He cleared his throat. "You got a girlfriend?"

"Yeah." I *should* have thought of Beth *like that* before, but up to that instant, I *hadn't*. Don't know *why*, babe, but...*thanks, Frank.*

"Good." He was quiet for a moment. "Better than *with* your partners."

I must have blushed. "We, um..."

"Temptation and new place and isolation from family. " He sighed. "There's *that,* and there's *shitting where you eat.*"

"I shall endeavor *not* to." I stared out the window, my sphincter puckering. "*That* obvious?"

"There's been *talk.* Parkinson's got a friend?"

"She *does.*" I thought for a moment. "If *Beth* and I were to ask *you* and your *wife* out for..."

"When and where?"

That's all it took.

FC

Or, Dean

"**S**o, where's this *island?*" We gazed around us as we climbed out of the vans, somewhat mystified. We had come in two vehicles to what the woman in a State Patrol sergeant's uniform driving the lead van declared was Beltran Island, Minnesota. The only body of water was a puddle in the dirt parking lot about the size of my apartment, and there were no *islands* on *it.*

"*There,*" the sergeant pointed to the carved sign on the log-cabin-like structure that read *Trading Post and Post Office.* Below the big sign was a smaller one that read *Beltran Island, MN. Population 36…Or So…In Season.* Unlike other errand-runners of local origin, the clear-eyed and assured sergeant whose name tag read *Elder* didn't chatter nervously.

"Great," Ernie said, stretching his back. "We're to meet *here…*" he glanced at his watch, "in ten minutes."

We'd flown into the Duluth airport on Monday, disembarking by the Air National Guard terminal. We got into these vans and drove to Thief River Falls, meeting the Duluth and Minneapolis teams. The following day, we were back in the vans for *this* five-hour trip. On the way, we saw few signs of civilization except for a few small towns where we could stretch our legs or isolated gas stations where we could top off.

Then we got *here.*

So, I asked, "what makes *this* an *island,* Sergeant Elder?"

"Look *around* you. Sir."[*] The forest around us—primarily old-growth pine trees scattered with oaks and fringes of birch stands—was as high as the tallest buildings in DC.

"*I* get it," Tom said. "An *island* in the *forest*." We'd been driving through this ocean of trees since we picked our guide up two hours before.

"Yessir," Sergeant Elder smiled mildly. "The trading post has refreshments and restrooms. I wouldn't go *too far* into the treeline. After last night's rain, the mosquitos and ticks will be out in force. This time of year, they drive even the *bears* mad." *That* made it clear what clinched *this* gig for her.

The cleared area around the trading post was about fifty yards in diameter. A picnic area under a rough-hewn roof sported a couple of concrete-and-wood tables and benches. It stood between the trading post and a couple of cabins marked PRIVATE on the edge of the clearing. A two-door concrete block garage marked COUNTY PROPERTY stood near the road. Four large propane tanks, a small electrical substation/generator surrounded by tin sheets and a chain-link fence, and a red-painted shack with a sign that said FIRE EQUIPMENT rounded out the island's structures. Several well-worn trucks and a rusty car also shared space.

"Where do the *other* twenty or so people live," Julia asked as she absently brushed a mosquito off her bare arm. We all wore denim or cotton duck pants, sensible shoes, short-sleeved shirts, and exposed weapons. As it *was* sticky-humid and about 90 degrees, we'd left our nylon jackets in the vans.

"There are five homes that make up the *permanent* population," Sergeant Elder said. "Four are a couple miles north, on Gruber Trail. One's three miles south on Satu Road that we passed on our way here. I check on them every few months." She gazed around at us. "If I was to ask what a bunch of out-of-town FBI agents was doing up *here*, *how* would *they* answer?"

---

[*] The way she said *sir* made it synonymous with *dummy*, as NCOs often did with punctilious or ignorant officers.

"The Special Agent In Charge would say that they're meeting the Royal Canadian Mounted Police on a cross-border matter," Harry said mildly. "Good enough?" Harry was one of those enigmatic, inscrutable guys of indeterminate age who you just didn't *ask* about.

"Yessir," Sergeant Elder nodded. "If you'll *excuse* me," she headed for the trading post. Then, I went into the trading post, followed by Julia, Morgan, and Frank. Ellen and Tom checked out the other structures. Ernie and Harry spent their time scanning the perimeter.

All of which took maybe fifteen minutes.

A sign inside the store read: *We have everything from needles to battleships…as long as they're small and you don't need much.*

Right enough, they *did* have a *little* of everything, including house paint and breakfast cereal, bourbon and kerosene, shampoo and car wax. But they had a *lot* of ammunition, hunting, fishing, and camping gear. In the back was a bait shack, where crickets chirped and worms squirmed, oblivious to their imminent doom. We gathered again in front of the trading post.

"Well, they're overdue," Ernie sighed, opening a bottle of water.

"A bit," Harry agreed, lighting a cigarette. If I had to guess, about one in four agents I'd met had the habit. SPD policy forbade smoking around the Liberty Bell Files due to their irreplaceable nature, so no one smoked *in* our building.

"Do they *have* the phone number of the trading post," Ellen asked, sitting on a picnic table, where we had all drifted to get out of the *brutal* clear-day sun. I'd seen the sun like that in the Arizona desert, but *that* sky was more golden than this *relentlessly* bright blue.

"Yep," Ernie answered, "and of the two residences over there, *and* the garage, *and* the fire equipment shed, *and* that power station. They also have the radio call signs of the nearest stations. If they *need* to, they'll *call.*"

We sat quietly. The real test of law enforcement professionals isn't the ability to follow clues, or make brilliant deductions, or get answers out of people. No, the most significant gift a cop can have at any level is the ability to simply wait for *something* to happen. If it's perpetrators committing crimes or lab techs doing their science, or superiors delivering instructions, or subordinates carrying them out, *waiting's* a real skill. Beat cops have it easy; the people around them provide plenty to watch. But at Beltran Island, all we could do that morning was…wait.

The *other* essential cop-skill is filling out paperwork. Some eggheads performing a study on law enforcement in the '70s concluded that most cops spend nearly half their time filling out reports, requests, and reports *on* requests. *That* study was driving the automation of our jobs but hadn't gone *near* where it would later. So a *lot* of our time was filling out reports and requests.

We passed the time with chit-chat and snippets of conversations amounting to not much more than a few syllables. We shared no stories of the old days, no dreams of the future. All we did was wait for the Mounties and watch the trees grow.

"*There*," Tom said, watching the road a couple miles off. This was the first vehicle we'd seen in the half-hour—that *felt* longer—since we stopped. The road we'd come in on—straight as a die for miles—had some *hills* that other states would call *mountains*. The car Tom spotted was exposed on a hill to the north.

We all stood up and started walking towards the road.

And that car…drove *right* on by…

In an air of collective disappointment, we all went back to the picnic benches.

"Not a *lot* of traffic here," Ed observed.

"Not *this* time of year, not *this* time of day," Sergeant Elder said. "Most of the lakes around here are pretty quiet when it gets *this* hot. Before dawn, you'll see some fishermen. During deer and bear seasons, you'll see *some* traffic. But, right *now*…not much. And the rain drove the fish deep."

"You know the area well," Ernie asked.

"I grew up on Gruber Trail," she answered. "Dad was a lineman for Minnesota Power and Light, maintained that auxiliary power station over there. I had my first job *there*," she hitched a thumb at the trading post.

"Huh," I said. "Why out *here*? How did *this place* come to *be* here?"

There was silence; everyone seemed to glance at me as if to say, *why do you think, moron?* But then, their faces said, *how in the hell should I know?* *Then*, their expressions became…*what?*

"I've wondered at *that* myself," Frank said softly. "Why are there so *many* freeway exits with *nothing* and so *few* with *truck stops?* And in *other* places, single gas stations? And in some *others*, abandoned truck stops?"

"Marketing," Harry said. "Ever been to Wall, South Dakota?"

Blank stares. "*Where?*" Morgan looked both puzzled and amused.

"Wall, South Dakota. BIG tourist trap in the middle of nowhere. *Literally.* They've got signs on I-90 advertising it from Lake Michigan to the Pacific."

"Oh, *yeah*," Tom said, "I've *seen* those signs in *Montana*. Never *went*, but, yeah."

"*Yeah*," Frank chimed in. "I spent a month bumming around Europe after law school. I saw a sign at a water-bus stop on an Amsterdam canal with an arrow pointing west that read *Wall Drug, 7,000 Kilometers.*"

"Wall Drug started offering free ice water in the '30s," Harry nodded. "The stop got to be *so* popular, other stores, restaurants, other *stuff* started to come. After the war, they started putting the signs out across the country. Now, that place sells everything from soup to nuts, *including* ice water, and the drug store's still in business. That tourist trap with its connected stores and restaurants is bigger than the *town*."

"*You* got that file," Ernie grunted.

"Yep. The Bismarck office started it in '56. I closed it ten years ago."

That was the most extended conversation we had all that time.

"*Heads* up," Harry said, watching another car drive over the distant hill ten minutes later. Instead of getting up in anticipation, we waited…

Before *another* car rolled over the hill after the first sedan.

"A *stronger* possibility," I observed.

"Sure as hell *hope* so," Ellen groaned. "Getting *splinters* in my *ass*."

A few minutes later, the two cars pulled into the big parking lot next to our two vans, and eight people—five men and three women—clambered out. Two men were in grey and blue RCMP patrol uniforms; the others were dressed like *we* were. The smallest man advanced a hand. "Inspector Alf McGill," he declared, "Division A, Royal Canadian Mounted."

"Supervisory Special Agent Harry Benz," Harry answered, "Special Projects, FBI."

"Well, then, let's get down to what we're *here* for," Alf said, striding towards the picnic benches.

"*Hi*, Neil," Sergeant Elder said to one of the uniforms. "How's the family?"

"*Hi*, Margie," the uniform said back. "They're *good*. Yours?"

"Hanging *in* there."

"You two know each other, I take it," Ellen asked Margie.

"Cooperative policing out here," Neil said. "Blizzard of '77, we patrolled the whole Minnesota border with five Mounties and four US police."

"*We* were the *only* law enforcement for over two hundred miles of US/Canada border for a month," Margie nodded. "Dug ourselves out of *nine feet* of snow, had nothing to eat but beans and canned corn for a week." She glanced at us all. "An hour north of here, the only way you'd *know* where the US ends and Canada begins is if you saw the *sign* behind the trees."

"Ladies, gents," Ernie announced, "we have *business* to discuss." We all gathered around the tables, where the Canadians plopped a large file box on one of them. "We're told you have some actionable FC intelligence?"

"We think it *might* be," Alf said, gesturing to Neil and the other uniform. "Sergeant Hardin and Constable Galinsky: the *floor* is *yours*."

"Sir," Neil nodded, reaching into the file box. "We know pretty much *everyone* out here for a couple hundred square miles on *both* sides of the border. When we first *saw* the bulletins on FC, *we* thought: *Frank Chaffin* is an odd duck who'd moved into an old cabin near the border in '75. He *said* he was Canadian, but something about him said *American*."

Neil and the constable went on for several minutes, detailing their research on Frank Chaffin. We had copies of the San Francisco task force's files on FC—most of us had read *some* of them—and a lot of what our Canadian friends were saying made sense. What got *my* attention was Neil's statement about motivation. "It's *not* clear what this person's motive is, but Frank Chaffin visited the library often, and his reading habits seem *less* than savory."

"You can *see* what he checks out?" Tom seemed startled.

"*In*directly," Russ Galinsky sighed. "My sister works at the library in Olein, the closest town to the Chaffin cabin. I, ah, *persuaded* her to scribble a list."

"What did *that* take," Ellen asked, smirking.

"*Half* my record collection," Russ said; most of us chuckled. "His reading list wouldn't raise any *flags*, except it seems that a couple of chemistry books went missing after he checked them out."

"Interesting. What else?" Julia tried not to sound bored.

"He read a great deal on the Industrial Revolution and Clark Kerr's *Industrialism and Industrial Man*—an anti-capitalist work that the library had to get from Ottawa. There were a few others in that vein…*and* he checked out *On Walden Pond* over and over again."

We all stood around, looking at each other. One of the Canadians near me yawned.

"The last attack—two weeks ago—hit the president of United Airlines," Harry said. "So far, he's hit universities and airlines; that's as close to a pattern as he's come."

"You said *he*," one of the Canadian women said tersely. "You know it's a *man*?"

"We know enough about serial bombers, in general, to say that *FC* is *likely* male," Harry told her. "We're not going to use any *other* term until we get *HIM or HER*."

"Where's this Chaffin now," Ernie asked.

"I did a wellness check on the cabin last week," Russ answered, "I didn't *see* him. *Looks* like he's decamped."

"Can we look at the cabin?" Harry stared north. It was nearly four in the afternoon by then—the Mounties research was *quite* thorough—and we were five hours from Thief River Falls.

"You *can*: it's *about* six hours from here."

Harry glanced at Ernie, then at Alf. "How far to where *you're* staying?"

"*Four* hours. Nutters just *have* to live in the middle of nowhere, don't they?"

***

"I'm too *damn* old to be in a sleeping bag," Harry declared, stretching his back stiffly. When we got back to Thief River Falls around nine that night, the only eatery still open was an all-night doughnut shop. Despite the lateness of the hour, they took pity on us, scrambled a mess of eggs, and fried up a couple of pounds of bacon and potatoes. We had to break into several groups scattered throughout the doughnut shop, joined by four Duluth and two Minneapolis agents. "Did it *enough* in the Marines; *ain't* gonna do it again."

"I *hear* you," Ernie declared. "I had my fill of *fart sacks* in the Army." The discussion at Beltran Island about what to *do next* was brief. The Canadians admitted that *they* were in a full-up rooming house and that the nearest other accommodations on *their* side were *another* two hours off.

Before we left the Island, Harry and Ernie called to secure an Army helicopter from Camp Ripley to get us to where this Chaffin character had been...or at least closer *to* it than Beltran Island. After the chopper was arranged, the decision to return to our luggage in our own *far*-less-buggy rooms was *not* hard to make.

Lest the reader thinks this is typical for the *whole* Bureau, rest assured that your tax dollars are not so easily spent by the FBI. But the *SPD*...

that's *much* different. When assigned to jobs like this one, they spend money like Congress on junkets. It's the enormous budgetary authority that the Special Projects Division has—in addition to the cachet of *The Almighty Washington*—that moves *so* many mountains.

"*I* get to do it again next *month*," I sighed. "Annual training in Arizona."

"You're a Reservist," Tom looked surprised. "Didn't *know* that."

"Hard to accommodate in the Bureau," Frank sucked his teeth. "Not *impossible*, but…" It was said by some that the Federal Government was the absolute *worst* employer for a Reservist or a Guardsman to have. They often make it *so* hard to attend drills or annual training that careers—one or the other—suffered. And *I* was going to need the Advanced Officer Course *if* I got promoted to Captain: I *was* eligible, and the executive officer slot in the 511th was opening up.

"In SPD, it's easier," Ernie said. "Schedules are more flexible." He cracked his knuckles loudly. "OK, folks, let's *wrap* this up here. We need cross-team liaisons in Minneapolis and Duluth to get ready for San Francisco when *they* get here. Dave and Tom; Duluth."

"Right," Harry said. "Morgan and Julia are for Minneapolis tonight. Go back with our hosts from there and check out the task force preparations."

I went to my room to pack my bags, and the message light on the phone was blinking. I called; a personal message was in the office. The pink message paper read: *Call home as soon as you get this; about Dean. Dad.*

No one in the family had *seen* or heard from Dean in *years*. The URGENT box was checked…Dad rarely did *anything* urgently. That the box was checked—he had to *ask* them to—meant *this* was important.

"Shit," I whispered.

"Not *again*," Morgan groaned, studying the vending machine selections: she *also* had a sweet tooth. "Do it in the *bathroom*."

"Not *that* kind," I sighed. "*Family* kind."

It was nearly 11 PM in Thief River Falls—midnight in Hell—when I called. "Hello," Mom answered after the first ring; the phone was on *her* side of my parent's bed.

"Hi, Mom," I answered, as cheerfully curious as I could sound.

"Dave," she sighed, "so *glad* you called. Here's your father." Usually, this order was reversed; I rarely *talked* to Dad when I called.

"David, hi," Dad grunted, probably half-over Mom in bed. They had *something* against long phone cords, and they only *had* one, and it was in the basement. "Dean's in a hospital in Minnesota."

"As it happens, I'm *in* Minnesota on business. Which…?"

"I know; that's what the *Bureau* said." The Bureau had a 24-hour switchboard for family emergencies. "He's in the Hennepin County Hospital in Minnetonka."

"Let me see what I can find out." I cleared my throat. "If, ah, he needs…?"

"Cross *that* bridge when we come to it," Dad said. "Just find out what's up, please." Dad never said *please* to us kids but was never particularly stern. We were always told that we were on our own to make our own mistakes once we moved out…like *they* did.

"OK, Dad. I'll get back to you as soon as I can."

And just how was I going to do that? I was *supposed* to go to Duluth.

"Trouble," Morgan asked, leaning on my open door. I didn't remember *her* being *there*.

"Yeah: *family* trouble in Minneapolis." I sighed.

"Switch with Julia," she said.

As it turned out, it *was* that simple.

✱✱✱

"Roomies *again*, Dave," Morgan declared, throwing her bag on the queen bed closest to the bathroom. The hotel closest to the Minneapolis FBI office had but one room available at 3 in the morning. One would *become* available, the desk said, tomorrow.

"Until *tomorrow*," I added, dropping my bag at the foot of the other queen. "But, *Morg*..."

"*Anna*," she sighed, sitting down. "My *birth* name is Mor*gana*, but I *don't* use it. My *partners* call me Morg; *off-duty friends* call me *Anna*." She glanced over at me. "*Your* bed; *my* bed. Bathroom's *neutral* territory."

"Sure," I sighed, too tired to argue. "I'll strip in the bathroom. Did you *take* your meds?"

"You're my *conscience*, now?"

"I'm *concerned* about my *friend*."

She crossed her eyes and stuck her tongue out at me. "Yeah, I *took* 'em. I *don't have* any *booze* with me." She started to pull her stadium shirt off over her head as I switched off the only light left in the room. "Go ahead and strip, Dave. We're *not* gonna get crazy, and *I've* got nothin' *I* need to hide."

"Fine," I sighed, slipping out of my duds. "Let's get some sleep."

It was quiet after the kerfuffles of sheets and bedspreads.

I didn't think I was *that* tired...

The *next* thing I knew, it was morning, and I saw Morgan, wrapped in towels, standing in the bright sunlight streaming through our window, which she'd just opened. "Morning, Dave," she said quietly, not looking at me. "Sleep OK?"

"I *think* so," I answered.

"*Really*?" She sat on *her* bed, crossing her legs and leaning back with a slight grin. "You *sounded* restless." Her bust wasn't *much* bigger than Beth's, though Morgan *was* half a foot taller and probably thirty pounds heavier.

"Don't *remember* anything."

"You said *no* a lot. Care to *comment*?"

"No."

She was quiet for a moment. I looked at the clock; I'd probably slept for four hours. "Get a shower, and we'll get some breakfast before we head for the office."

✳✳✳

"Heard *anything* from the Great White North," Morgan asked George Trapani, the SAIC of the Minneapolis office.

"Not *yet*," George answered, glancing at the clock: it was nearly 10, and we were *just then* strolling in. "They weren't *supposed* to land until 10:30 or so, weather permitting." He was a rather large guy, out-of-shape enough for me to wonder how he passed the bi-annual physical fitness test.

"OK, *where* are *we* supposed to...." I started, but George cut me off.

"One floor down," George gestured back out the way we came. "A suite we share with the Commerce Department. They use it for foreign trade missions when they're in town."

The suite looked out over Minneapolis, with a view of the Mississippi in the eastern distance. It had five single-desk offices, two larger, more open spaces, two conference rooms, and fifteen phone lines. It was furnished entirely in typical GSA Naugahyde fashion, but the walls were barren; pictures had obviously been removed. "Commerce took out *all* the artwork," George explained, "so as not to harm the cultural sensitivities of visitors."

"Uh-huh," Morgan grunted with a wink at me. "*This* will do fine. What's *your* impression of this Chaffin fella?" The tone of voice she used would have been considered insubordinate if we *weren't* from SPD...but we *were*.

"Well," George drew himself up surreptitiously, "I read the San Francisco files, perused the Mountie's material, but I'm not sure there's *any* connection. *This* guy, whoever he is, mails the bombs from San Francisco; we *know* that. Would *this* guy out *here*, what, fly to 'Frisco every time he got the urge to blow something up?"

"*Good* point," Morgan agreed, sauntering along a window wall. "But what if he was to take a *bus*...or *drive*?"

"That's a *week* one-way on a bus; three *days* driving," George sniffed. "Who'd do *that*?"

"Who *wouldn't* do that would be someone with unlimited resources *or* someone with a job," I offered. "But the *bigger* question *should* be *who would* mail four bombs to seemingly random targets without making *any* demands. What strikes *us* about this individual is *that*: *he's making no demands*. No threats of more attacks, no *do THIS or more will be hurt*, no *this REALLY pisses me off* manifestos, and no real pattern that could *lead* somewhere."

"Right," Morgan agreed, still looking out the window. "First university targets, now airlines. We've seen the initials *FC* and *RV* in the bomb guts. He uses a *lot* of wood—either as a countermeasure or out of poverty since it's cheaper than metal. Maybe he's a *nature* lover, wants to make the *trees* get back at us. He uses Eugene O'Neil stamps; maybe he's big on O'Neil's brand of existentialism and realism, communism and addiction." She shrugged and turned around, leaning against the window, her arms across her chest. "But he's a *craftsman*; he takes great *care* and *time* with his devices—like he enjoys the *work*, not the *result*; the *journey*, not the *destination*. The psych profiles out of Behavioral Science are probably *half-right*, but we'll have a *third* set of *teeth* before we figure out *which* half is *which*." She smiled and shrugged authoritatively… with a little *trace* of a smile like I'd seen her give Holly. "But *maybe*… just *maybe*…this university/airline bomber—this *Unabomber*—is just *one smart misdirecting son-of-a-bitch* making us look in *one* place instead of somewhere *else*, working for *God*-knows-*who* doing *God*-knows-*what God*-knows-*when*." She shrugged again, a bare movement of her shoulders. "George: what do *you* think of all *that*?" Addressing a SAIC by his first name would doom any other SA…but not *us*.

George pushed out his chest—a not inconsiderable feat: *The Almighty Washington* had asked *his* opinion of *their* surmise about the most wanted person in America. For a SAIC in the hustings, *this* was a *Dear Diary* moment…but *this* was *more*. "The task force believes that he's young, a loner, and some sort of a craftsman, that's true," George muttered as if a *floodgate* had opened. But…*your* idea of misdirecting…that *may* have some merit. And what if he *does* commute? *That* might open the net considerably."

"So it *might*," Morgan smiled *again*: a *Mona Lisa-like* curling of the lips. "But, maybe we'll know *more* when we hear from that cabin in the woods—if this guy's even *related. Now*," she glanced at me, "do you know anyone at the Hennepin County Hospital? There's someone there we need to talk to on a *related* matter."

***

"Special Agent Towne, FBI. We need to *see*...."

"Dean Clawson," I declared. "I'm his brother, David." I flashed *my* credentials. We weren't *supposed* to use our credentials for personal matters, but sometimes it was just a lot less trouble.

The desk clerk, an inattentive redhead whose body conformed *disturbingly* well with her chair, tapped her keyboard. "Clawson... Hospice room 612-West." She looked up. "Don't know how *conscious* he might be."

"Let's find out," I growled, hopefully not with *too* much apprehension. A medical technician led us through a maze of doors and corridors. We could smell the bleach-funk of clean sheets and the pungent aroma of disinfectant.

There's a great deal of confusion about the term *hospice*, but it's really quite simple: it's where *many* people go to die. However, not *everyone* who goes to a hospice *dies* there. It's often just a slower-paced hospital. Just as often, a *pre*-funeral home.

A sign above a heavy steel door said *HOSPICE*. Another just beneath it quoted Dante in Latin that I read aloud in English: "abandon all hope, ye who enter here. Kinda morbid." *I* only recognized it because I took four *semesters* of Latin.

"When we bring *them* here, they aren't *aware* enough to read it," the orderly smirked.

I need to explain about Dean as well as I can. I'm not sure *why*, but Dean was not *really* close to *anyone* in my family—with the *early* exception of me. The only communications Dean had with us after Christmas '66 was a letter in '70, saying he was married. There was another in '73 that said his wife was expecting. That he *called me* when I graduated high school that year was remarkable…but he had *no interest* in talking to our parents. He visited Hell in '75, but I was in college in Ypsilanti; he didn't stay long enough to say much more than *hi* and *bye* to Mom. On the plus side, he didn't try to borrow any money. So, his absence for a decade and a half was just…*that*. I *got* closer to Steve—a year older than Dean—after Dean left. But he was *still* my brother, who taught me to throw a Frisbee, and I thought about him once in a while.[*]

The *tragedy* was that we never *talked* about Dean, either.

Each "room" was a 6x8 space defined by two dummy walls with a curtain in front. Each had a chair and a bed, a nightstand, a lamp, and hangers for IVs and monitors. Every other "room" had a window above the bed. The whole ward was blue with a white acoustic ceiling.

The technician stopped, pointed. I barely recognized Dean. His hair was ragged, skin flaccid and yellow; lips chapped and bleeding; a cannula in his nose that had been broken; IVs in both arms; tubes under the sheet led to bags. He was sort of awake, mumbling. "He's been here *four* days…" the tech said.

"How did he *get* here," I asked, trying to sound more *cop* than a *brother*.

"Police found him in a shooting gallery in Minneapolis. He had his Michigan driver's license."

"What's his prognosis," I asked.

"*Multiple* organ failure; pleural pneumonia; hepatitis B; anemia; malnutrition; untreated fractured ribs, nose and right knee; sepsis; some *other* things we…"

---

[*] Why I chose Kim and not Dean for my Academy people-search project, I *never* knew.

"*Thank* you," Morgan nodded at the orderly dismissively, pulling the chair up to the bed. She glanced at me furtively; I stared at the wretch that was my brother and sat on the bed.

Dean's eyes darted around for a while before they settled on me. "*Who* the hell are you," he rasped, then coughed wetly.

"Dave; your little punk brother."

His face seemed to light up. "How'd you *find* me?"

"They called the *folks*. I just happened to be in the neighborhood."

Dean's eyes were dull for a moment, then he turned to look at Morgan. "Who's your *friend?*"

"My name's Morgan," she answered. "Pleased to meet you."

"Uh." He coughed again. "So, you *found* me." He looked up. "Not much left, is there?"

"You had a wife and kid last *we* heard."

"Long time ago."

"What happened?"

"She got sick of *me*." He sighed. "*You* know *that* song-and-dance."

"So…"

"She *split*," Dean sighed. He seemed to shrink in the bed. "Then… *then.*"

"She divorced you?"

"I dunno."

"You OK?"

"*No.*" He shook his head swiftly as if trying to get something out. "I'm done for pretty soon."

"You in pain?"

"*All* the time." He coughed. "With the dope, I don't *give* a shit. Not *long* now." He broke off into a deep coughing fit. "I *gotta…*"

"Rest," Morgan said softly.

He faded fast. "Yeah," his eyes fluttered, "yeah."

✳✳✳

There were two messages on my phone when we got back to *my* hotel room with Chinese takeout. One said that the cabin in the woods hadn't been occupied for a while. No evidence of bomb-building. The Mounties would keep looking for Frank Chaffin—so would the FBI—*just* in case. Small task force adjuncts would remain in place for a while.

The *other* message….

We ate our dinner in silence at the tiny table in my room. Morgan's room was on the 4th Floor, but she hadn't moved her luggage. I glanced out the window from time to time…"There's *family stuff* I need to talk about, Anna. *You* don't *have* to be here."

She'd changed into big shorts that floated above her thighs stiffly, like tents, but came almost to her knees. "There's a *lot* of things that I *do* that I don't *have* to. Just *here* for my *friend*."

"Just *don't*…."

"Wouldn't *dream* of it. Just think of me as part of the furniture."

I reached for the phone between the beds and dialed. "Hi, Mom. Get *Dad*."

"*Just* a minute," she said. Holding her hand over the phone, I heard a muffled "pick up the extension."

"Hello, David." Dad was formal most of the time.

"Hi, Dad," I answered. "Dean passed away a couple hours ago."

"*Oh*," Mom gasped. "How?"

I glanced at Morgan, wanting to run away from *this*. "He was *very* sick." I closed my eyes tight as I recited the litany of my brother's conditions. I *wasn't* going to say that he'd been living rough. *Dad will figure it out.*

"What about his wife, his child?"

Mom wants good news. "Your granddaughter Marjorie was born in Minneapolis on 15 September '73." The paltry collection of personal effects they gave me when we left included a picture of an infant with a date and a name. Morgan smiled, uncrossed her legs, then crossed them the other way.

"His *wife?*" Dad choked, like when his father died when I was eleven.

"We're *looking* for her." Morgan leaned back in the chair and gazed out the window, shorts still hovering above her thighs. *HOW do they do that? WHY do they do that?* "How's Bridgit these days?"

"She's fine," Mom answered. "She's starting high school in the fall." At fifteen, Bridge was a *developing* girl, but I'm not sure that *beauty* came into it. Mostly…cute.

"She *has* a *boyfriend*," Dad mumbled. Morgan stretched and stood up, reaching under her sleeveless top to scratch a mid-back itch. I hoped that my sister would become the kind of *handsome-cute* that Beth and Morgan were. It kept me from thinking about…*this.*

"She has a *boy* who is a *friend*, Father," Mom corrected. "They're just library buddies." Morgan bent over at the waist, placing her palms on the floor *without* bending her knees. I always admired people who could do that; *Beth* could do that. *I want to watch her and NOT do THIS.*

"They were *holding hands* yesterday," Dad declared, "out on the porch swing." Our porch swing was where Steve courted his future wife. Allison went with him to college, then to Arizona, and *they* had five kids. Morgan stood up straight and sat on the end of my bed.

"So *what*," Mom declared. There followed a silence…one that meant a change of subject. That's how our family communicated. "What *now*," Mom mewed before she started crying.

"The county cremated him already," I said. "They'll send him to Charon* Brothers." They wouldn't have wanted to see him like *that*. Morgan slid closer.

There are ways that silence can communicate volumes. I could *see* Mom in the kitchen, on her aluminum-tube-and-vinyl folding-step-chair at the counter next to the wall phone, burying the receiver in her lap. Dad had been in the basement with his trains and was now sitting on

---

* Charon was the ferryman across the River Styx in Greek mythology. The brothers-in-law McGillicuddy and Strathearn chose *Charon* because theirs were too long for a sign, and it *was* catchy for the only funeral home in Hell.

the basement steps, holding his hand over the receiver on *the extension*—what we always called the phone in the basement—so no one couldn't *hear* him cry. I started to cry, holding that phone in that sterile hotel room in that strange city while telling my parents their second-born child was dead because he just gave up. Morgan put an arm around me. "Mom, Dad? You there?" I struggled to speak beyond my tears.

"Yes, David," Dad said, deeply rasping. "Thanks for calling."

"OK, Dad. Mom?" Nothing. "I'll call later. *So* sorry." And I hung up, remembering Dean's lunatic laughter.

I never figured out *why* his death was *so* upsetting. A wasted life? An abandoned wife and child? A family ignored for many years?

I didn't *know* why, and I was in the *knowing* trade.

But it *was THAT upsetting*.

✳✳✳

"What," I startled awake. Sunbeams streamed through the window.

"Huh," someone grunted behind me.

I waited. My shirt and pants were off; my shoes and socks were off; I had the sheet over me; I could feel someone's warm *something* against my underweared backside. I reached behind me under the sheet, felt something loose and satiny over something substantial and warm.

A hand grabbed mine. "Morning," Morgan murmured, squeezing my hand. "Before you *ask*, I *wouldn't* take advantage like *that*."

"But *how* did I…?"

"I gave you a dose of my meds; they can have *that* effect if you're not used to them. *We* needed sleep. Yes, *I* stripped you; you *didn't* argue."

I brushed her behind with my thumb. "*You* changed."

"*I* wanted to sleep."

"In *my* bed?"

"You were vibrating like a tuning fork, sobbing like a little kid." I felt her roll onto her back. "*You* OK now?"

"Tired." I felt like a wet rag. "Time is it?"

"5:01."

I rolled onto my back, turning to look at her. She had an oddly-shaped chin, like Kirk Douglas without the dimple. She held my hand softly, but I could *NOT* pull away. She smiled her odd little smile. She rolled on her side, her eyes *locked* to mine. "Am I *taking* advantage *now*, Dave?"

I'd slept for hours without dreams or stirring, as far as I could recall, but still, I felt weary, despite full bladder. "No."

"Good," she smiled, leaning forward. "You had a *good* cry last night for at *least* three hours. I've never been hugged *that* hard before, though. Felt like you were adjusting my *back*."

"Don't really remember," I said honestly. Sights and sounds of my childhood got mixed up in my head. I remembered a stormy shouting match between Dean and Mom one day not long after Christmas. Hours later, the argument started up again, this time between Mom and Dad *and* Dean. And a day after that, Dean stormed off.

And *something in me* went…*sproing!* I *felt* like I woke up *again*, with this pretty woman in my bed, enigmatically smiling. I was *spent* but neither of us had removed a *single article* of clothing. *We HAD done something….*

I *thought* I had cheated on Beth. As I grieved for a brother I barely knew, I felt *worse* about cheating on Beth.

✳✳✳

"Hello," Cindy's voice was bubbly. They had pulled our team out Thursday after one of the San Francisco teams arrived. Their FC experience was *far* greater than ours, leaving little for us to do.

We had flown back to DC Thursday afternoon, my teammates making appropriate noises about Dean. It was hard to express such things in that environment. Before we left Minneapolis, Morgan and I discussed the case with the first of the 'Frisco team. They thought *Unabomber* was a much better case name than FC, considered by some to be a blind alley or countermeasure. We spent the rest of Thursday making notes for the record, adding to what was becoming a *mountain* of Unabomber paperwork.

"*Hi*, Cindy," I sighed. "Is *Beth* there?"

"Yeah, *hi*, Dave," Cindy burbled. "She's been wondering where you *were* since you *didn't* call after *last* weekend…" And I let her rattle on, too weary to argue.

"Can I *talk* to her," I asked. The Bureau was very generous about bereavement leave, but as of then, my folks hadn't planned a memorial or anything else.

"Sure, Dave. Bessie! It's *Lover-boy!*" I'd have to tell Beth that I'd cheated on her, too…soon, before the guilt ate me up. And I needed to mention that my brother had died, and I had another sister-in-law-and another niece someplace who I'd never meet. Yeah, *this* was gonna be easy.

"Hi, *Lover-boy*," Beth said moments later. Yeah, we'd been together for about five minutes, but I was falling pretty hard for Beth, and I thought *she* was falling pretty hard for *me*. I debated bringing up the whole *death in the family* routine in a new relationship. I wondered just how it would *sit* compared to that *other* bombshell I had to drop. It might sound like *the-dog-ate-my-homework-then-the-flying-saucer-came* does to a teacher.

"*Hi*, Beth," I said, trying *not* to sound guilty on the phone. *This* girl was different; *this* girl felt right. "You *busy* Saturday night?"

"Nope. Thought you had a *drill?*"

"I *do*. But, after the staff meeting, maybe I can drop by…?" I would tell my company commander, and she would murmur *all* the right things and probably tell me to go home.

"How about *tomorrow*? It's the holiday."

Oh, yeah; forgot. "Um…I've got to clean up around here: the *rest* of my furniture came while I was out…" I was *really* pretty worn out, and the place *was* a disaster.

"I'll come over *tonight*; bring corn-on-the-cob." She sounded *insistent*. *Maybe guilt-dumping on my turf would feel better.* "Sure."

Two hours later, she was grinning at my door. "*Hi,*" she swept in bearing two large paper bags, pecked my cheek softly, and made for my kitchen. "Looks like your *building's* got something planned." She wore a *short* summer dress and her inevitable sandals. I thought she must have had a closet *full* of them.

"Yeah," I sighed, following her. "Big cookout tomorrow afternoon; *they* supply the dogs and burgers. W*e* supply everything else." I sat on the end stool at my islet while she put her groceries away, including American cheese that *wasn't* Velveeta. I raised my hands as though to plead my case. "Beth, I *want* to…."

"So, was it *Julia*?" She stacked a dozen ears of corn on the counter, then leaned sideways against the stove a few feet away, her arms across her chest.

Huh? "Was…*what?*" I sat, stunned, sort of. *How would she KNOW?*

"Was it *Ju-Ju* you had sex with?" She stepped closer. I had to look up a bit to see her smile that reminded me of Bela Lugosi greeting his guests in *Dracula*. "Even after I asked her *not* to?" *Or a Cheshire cat…*

"No, Morgan." I hesitated; her face didn't change. "My *brother* passed away yesterday afternoon." I decided *that* wasn't the way to break *this* news…

She *instantly* took my head to her chest and let me cry as I held her *tight* while she murmured, "*so* sorry; so, *so* sorry. It's OK, sweetie; it's OK…" I felt and heard her heart rhythmically beating against the side of my head. It was as soothing as I imagined a clock sounded to a newly-separated puppy as I babbled about Dean, who gave me a Detroit Tigers shirt for my sixth birthday that I wore until the logo looked like white speckles on a light blue field and was more a *hole* than a shirt…and about playing checkers with him *every* Friday afternoon until he left…and I hadn't followed baseball or played checkers since.

She held me for a *very* long time before I let go. She held my face in front of hers. "Are you calling her *Anna*?"

"Yeah." I felt like asking if she knew how much cash I had in my wallet, as in, *what don't you know?* "You know her *that* well?"

She gently wiped my tears with her thumb. "Don't think she's *had* guy-sex since Jerry went overseas," she sighed.

"You *know* she…."

"…swings *both* ways, yeah."

She kissed my head softly. "Where's your booze?"

"Just what you see here," pointing to my liquor *cabinet*—a cubby on the islet wall. The wall was *all* cubby holes from counter to ceiling. My inebriant stock was one sealed bottle of warm wine and one *un*sealed; the only booze I had…and I'd *bought* none of it. "There's some beer in the fridge."

She turned the glasses over and poured from the unsealed bottle. "I met Morgan and Jerry at a party after I first moved here. We talked for I don't know *how* long." We swigged wine as she leaned against the islet. "They knew I was miserable because I told them all about Rich— couldn't *help* myself." She stared at her wine. "We went swimming in the Potomac the next day. Only *Jerry* didn't make it, but Morgan and I had a *blast*, the best time I'd had in *months*. We really seemed to *click,* if you know what I *mean*."

"Yeah, I think so." I tried to imagine *both* women in bathing suits, having seen Beth in less *and* more. Morgan was easier to imagine than Beth, for some reason.

"It got dark; she had a sort-of tent." She looked serious. "I hadn't *done* it with a woman; I didn't know I was going to *then*; haven't *since*. But it was *so* smooth, *so* fast, *so* satisfying, so *exhilarating* that I didn't even know *it* had happened until *it* was over. We didn't even take our *suits* off!" She inhaled deeply. "Dave: don't take this wrong, but I'll *never* have an experience like *that* again. I *couldn't*."

"OK," I said, trying to be nonchalant while I vibrated my wine glass to my lips. "So, you had...."

"It *wasn't* sex," she declared, "it was *nirvana*." She looked around briefly. "Morgan looked into my soul and knew *how* to release what I *needed* to release." She shrugged. "*That's* what she *does*." She looked at me, her eyes boring into mine. "She did *that* for *you*, too?"

"Yes," I blurted...startled because come to think of it, that's *exactly* what it felt like. I *couldn't* have put it better.

"Uh-huh." She stroked my hair, still sort of towering over me.

"So, *we*...?" I wasn't sure where to *go* from wherever we *were*.

"So, *you and I* have a chance at a lasting and fulfilling relationship, sweetie. We've had two and a *half* dates; we spent a *great* night *and* morning together. *Since then*, you had soul-healing *nirvana* with *our* friend Anna." She smiled, looking into my heart. "*You* needed it. *She* knew that; *I* know that; I *would have* tried had *I* been there. I *love you* for telling me. *That* confirms the possibilities of *us*."

"Then," I gulped, "having...with...."

"My pal Ju-Ju?" She smiled prettily. "I told her that when *I'm* with *you*, you're *mine*. It doesn't mean that I *own* you, but I don't want *her* to interfere with you and me; she *won't*. *Anna* certainly won't." She made a curious face. "*Sex* is sharing pleasure and sometimes *relief; making love* is *much more*."

"*You and I were* making love...for *me*, anyway."

She smiled with her whole face. "*Me*, too." We stared at each other for a few moments; she nodded, like a sage whose pupil made a good point. "Are you going to Michigan *soon*?"

"My folks haven't figured *anything* out yet. Steve said he couldn't make it until *late* July. Ernie said he can track down Dean's ex-wife."

We just looked at each other, sipped more warm wine. "You look tired, sweetie. Want to lie down?"

"I *am* tired, but I don't want to screw up my sleep cycle." It wasn't quite 9 in the evening; it was still light outside.

"Come *on*, babe," she said, reaching out her hand. "Let's make some *more* sense of your apartment. Start with the books on the couch, hey? *You* read a *lot* of history…a ship model, huh? Ju-Ju said your curtains won't be ready until next week…."

And hours before *that,* I thought I'd screwed Beth and me up. Just goes to show what too much thinking does to ya.

✳✳✳

I would *never* have *thought*…three women I'd…laughing together…

But, Saturday night, the 5th of July, there we *were.* We'd watched three different fireworks displays from the roof of the building the previous night. Freddie was splashing and dashing with a half-dozen other kids in the humid heat after an evening rain. Beth and I and Julia and Ellen were yucking it up as Tony—with an eye for his boys—joined us sitting in the big pool. Ellen and Julia were in the *skimpiest* swimsuits…and Beth's…I've got *handkerchiefs* with more material.

I'd called my CO; she said not to bother coming in; make up the time later. Dead brothers are *real* good excuses, even for the Army.

All afternoon, Freddie sketched people around the pool. Her drawings included a *breathtaking* profile of Beth and me together; another of Julia and Tony; one of Ellen laughing at *something* or other; others of the boys in animated poses. What *she* could do with a #2 pencil and a pad… you *can't* catch *that* kind of character with a camera. We'd also watched Beth do cartwheels and walk on her hands for the kids. *Her* exercise was gymnastics.

"So, Tony," Beth stretched her back, "what do you *do* for the FAA?"

"Pilot reviews," he answered. "I look at suspended pilots and their licensing, see if they should be reinstated. Dull, really. What sort of work do *you* do for the IRS?"

"Payroll accounting," Beth grimaced, shifting closer to me. "*We* get paid the same way as everyone else." She made a face. "I was *wondering,* guys. I was talking to a guy from our *new* investigative audit department at lunch the other day. He says he's got funding to help *you* guys make *criminal* cases."

"*Heard* of that," Julia said. She nudged Tony with a knee, rippling the water slightly.

"Yeah," Beth answered, similarly nudging me.

"Huh," Ellen frowned. "What's this guy's name?"

"Thatcher," Beth said. "Art Thatcher. They call him *Bull* for whatever reason; he's just a little guy."

Tony nudged Julia back, stretching an arm behind her on the pool wall. Julia...call it a look of *pleasant* surprise. "Ellie," he asked breezily, "can you *watch* the boys while I have a *private chat* with Julia at *her* place?"

"Ah," Ellen gulped, glancing at a *more surprised* Julia, "OK. They *should* be in bed soon, yeah?"

"Yeah, I'll take 'em up." He looked sidelong at Julia. "Care to *chat*?"

"Lights *on* or lights *off*," she grinned through her...*bafflement*, I think.

"*Your* choice," he answered, standing up. "Meet you *there*?"

"*Fifteen* minutes, at least," she declared, getting up herself, shaking her head in mild disbelief. "Lock the door when you come *in*."

"Only if the lights are *off*."

"Do candles count?"

"We need *more* heat?"

Ellen shrugged, gave *me* a wink, and pulled herself out of the pool to help round up the boys.

"*We'll* call in the morning," Beth said, "have breakfast."

"O...K," Ellen answered, puzzled.

"Yeah," I asked, puzzled myself. "Breakfast?"

"Imagine how left out *she* feels right now: a default babysitter because *Dad's* got the hots for her *friend*."

"True," I admitted, watching Julia dry off the youngest boy. "But she *could* say...."

"No, she *couldn't*," Beth declared. "She loves Julia too much."

Beth had terrific insights; she'd have made a good FBI agent. I wonder what *her* CAQ score might have been?

✳✳✳

"*Long* week," Beth smiled, bussing my cheek like she always did as she marched into my apartment on Saturday afternoon before Labor Day. I'd *just* got back after two weeks on the road.

"I'm gonna get you a *key*," I announced. "Then I won't have to ring you in." She and I had been out with Frank and Joanne. Joanne was a nurse, younger than Frank—he called her his *child bride*. Joanne had the amusing tendency to laugh at even my worst jokes.

"OK by me," Beth said, setting her groceries down on my islet. "*You* look tired."

"Yeah," I admitted, "tired." *Not to mention guilty.* "I need to unpack, babe."

"I'll get dinner started. Are you coming to meet *my* family next weekend?"

"*Plan* to." *Maybe. Let's see how you handle…this.*

Beth had come to Michigan with me at the end of July. She slept in the *guest* room that had once been *mine,* and I got stuck on a cot in the basement. Beth spent two weeks playing with nieces and nephews I barely knew. She and Steve's wife Allison took charge of meal planning—and shopping—the whole time. She endeared herself to Dad by talking about her father's and brother's railroad layout that grew to take over her garage. She got in Mom's good graces by *wanting* to see my baby pictures. She taught Bridgit and the other kids how to cartwheel safely. Everybody came to town for the service; so did family members I hadn't seen in decades. Ernie found Dean's ex-wife and daughter in Colorado. Sherry declined to come to Michigan then but called and chatted with Mom and Dad, exchanging addresses and phone numbers.

We sat down to dinner—a small pork tenderloin—a couple hours later, after watching *Mad Max* on cable TV, holding hands and slurping wine…

She sliced the tenderloin expertly, doling out three slices for me and two for herself before she asked, "so, was it *Ellie* or *Ju-Ju* you had sex with?"

"Ellen," I answered blankly. Seven of us coordinated with law enforcement in four states. After *nine days* without a *break*, we *stopped* Eliot Steven Guzmanoff near Smith Lake, Alabama. Guzmanoff was a spree-offender—some call them *hurricanes*—who broke out of a county lockup in Tennessee, killing two guards, then robbed a dozen convenience stores and two banks, and killed fifteen people in the space of three weeks. "We just could *not* relax, and you *know* we don't drink much. It was *just*…"

"Cuddling naked?" Beth smiled sweetly; I nodded. "Ellen's *such* a good woman; *generous* to a fault. Can you pass the creamed spinach, babe? And you *got* that climax-rest *without* the climax? *We've* done that."

"You're *not*…?" Beth's attitudes took some getting used to.

"Of *course* not, babe. *How* can I object to *cuddling, naked* or not? But someday you won't *want* to do *that* with anyone but *me. Then* we'll talk about *our* future."

I reached *that* point then and there.

The Long Knives Society

Or, How the Truly Sick Keep Sticking Together

"*Another* election year, *another* administration." Ernie sighed. I had been surprised at how cold Virginia was in January, thinking like most Midwesterners that the Sunny South was *that* all the time. Sunny it *might* have been, but it snowed, too. Not a *lot*, but without snowplows, salt, or even sand, Northern Virginia went into a panic every time there were more than two inches of the white stuff.

"So, Dave," Ernie declared. "Something is *troubling* you this morning?" I'd probably closed a hundred Liberty Bell Files between the time I started in the SPD and that morning after Reagan's first inaugural while the confetti was still wafting in the corners. The celebrations over the return of the Teheran hostages were still ongoing…then *this* came to me. I read the summary:

> **File Number Ending: 69731-LIB**
> **Name: The Long Knives Society**
> **Date Identified: 14 December 1963**
> **Origin: Formed ca. 1962, Greenville, Michigan by Ernst Rohm, AKA Oliver Greene (b. 1946) and Rudolf Hess, AKA Solomon Axelrod (b. 1947?)**
> **Narrative: Organization claims roots in German Sturmabteilung (SA) of Nazi infamy. Begun either in or around Wolverine Military Academy in Greenville. Founders were said to have been students at Wolverine, but their age/grade level don't correlate. Group has goals and ideologies**

similar to the original SA but without the uniforms and speeches. **No distinctive uniforms, but a definite white supremacy goal.**
Updates: 1965: Organization has members outside of school.
1966: Two purported members arrested in Baltimore under suspicion of arson of a synagogue.
1968: Organization denied to exist at Wolverine; state police investigating possible related shootings in Flint and Detroit.
1972: Organization being investigated by Detroit area law firm Dietz O'Bannon & Associates. Principal investigator A. Block provided extensive information.

"*Wolverine* was that school that your *uncle* went to, Julia," I finished, and Julia started to laugh; we looked at her as if she'd fallen and hit her head.

"Oh, *yeah*," Ellen grinned, "and that guy in *Chicago* talked about it." We watched as Julia giggled. I looked at Ellen; she at me; we shrugged. *Something HAD happened in her head.* She'd found out the week before that Tony's first wife had been killed in a street robbery when the youngest boy was an infant.

"Ho, *shit*," Julia finally gasped. "This is bizarre. I *just* got a letter from JJ in Panama. He told me about a dream he had where he *blew* Wolverine to *smithereens*."

That was ringing in my head when Ernie asked me, "do you want to pass the file off? It might affect your cleanup record."

"No," I bravely answered. "The Founders was *my* file, too."

"Then, you *may* want to talk to Dusty and…*speak* of the Devil," Ernie declared as Dusty walked in.

"*You've* got Wolverine-related files," Dusty declared to Ernie, "from the *Lansing* agency." Not a *question*, a *statement*. That Monday's Wheel Game had yielded files from Michigan's capital.

"Yeah," I answered boldly. "Just *about* to…."

"*Bring* it," Dusty snapped. "*My* office. *Now*. Special Agent *Parkinson*: *you* have knowledge of Wolverine. *You* come, too."

We filed into Dusty's office, a crowded domain of Rolodexes, ledgers, computer monitors, trophies, and shelf after shelf of file boxes. It was headed by an oak and leather desk that *must* have been eight feet long and five wide. A wide oak table twenty feet long abutted the desk, with chairs of all descriptions around it. Three speakerphones dotted the table; Dusty's desk had two phones, both with headsets. The Oval Office wasn't as impressive as Dusty's, nor was it as *busy*.

"*Have* a seat," Dusty gestured. Dusty could be a scary guy; his small frame contained a great deal of energy driven by a powerful, analytical mind. "Close the door, SSA Packard," he murmured…which sounded like a death knell. *This* was *big*. The *only* time we used titles and last names was when we were in trouble *or* when something momentous was about to be said *or* done…*or both*. Dusty reached behind him to a tidy shelf, then casually flipped a file onto the table in my general direction. "Read the summary."

File Number Ending: 42234-LIB
Name: Wolverine Military Academy
Date Identified: 3 January 1971
Origin: Founded 1869, Greenville, Mich.
Narrative: An accredited private high school since 1890, institution was highly recommended for highly mobile professionals. However, anecdotal accounts of student abuse, suicides, drug use, and even murders have become common. Institution is said to teach American values but may have become a dumping ground for delinquents. Owners of the institution are unclear; series of shell corporations leading offshore. Death of one student, Jason Samson, called a suicide but circumstances suspicious (reports attached). Suicides said to top 20 in '68-'69 school year.
Updates: 1972: Witness statements from graduates (enclosed) and other attendees attest to brutality of student body, particularly as regards one J. Elrath.

"*I* created *this* file," Dusty declared. "Jason Samson was my stepson, killed at Wolverine Christmas Eve 1970. His mother was with State in Saigon trying to keep *that* waste of time going, and I was in California on the Manson mess. They *said* Jason killed himself; I *never* believed it. He wasn't *that* kind of kid." What we *heard* in his explanation was deep and abiding *guilt*. Dusty regarded Julia in a way no one could *ever* get used to. "J. Elrath is your *step-uncle*?"

"His mother married my grandfather when we were fourteen, yessir."

"Do you still *hear* from him?"

"*Just* got a letter…." Julia was hard to rattle, but Dusty was doing it.

Dusty nodded quietly, steepling his fingers in front of his face as he stared at the far wall, thirty feet away. I'd known the man for a little over half a year, and when he did *that*, momentous decisions were about to be made. He inhaled deeply, held it, then breathed out. "SSA Packard: form a *Working Group*," he glanced at his watch, "as of 1030 hours on 21 January 1981."

"Yessir," Ernie answered. "Cases?"

"Wolverine; Founders of the Fourth Reich; *anything else* that contains or may yield actionable information on Wolverine Military Academy. *All* SPD members are to search their indexes for files related to Wolverine or Greenville or anything else even *dimly* related by the end of the month. I'll put *The Call* out. Use Room 200. Add *Harry's* and *Win's* teams." *The Call* was a Request For Information (RFI) to anyone who *had* any or *knew of* any information on a subject, which could be as short as a single word or name or as long as an essay.*

We had no *clue* as to what we were in for, but it *felt like* we'd been told to storm a beach somewhere.

I wasn't *that* far off.

✳✳✳

---

* There was *no* National Criminal Information Center (NCIC) as we now know it, but it *was* under construction. The personal computer hadn't been invented yet, and the internet was nothing more than a party line between universities and the Defense Department. *Then*, there was just *The Call*.

One week later, reading a multi-page document, Ernie theatrically cleared his throat. "Wolverine Working Group is hereby established to forward a criminal referral or referrals against a person or persons having to do with Wolverine Military Academy shown to be responsible for felonious crimes falling under Federal jurisdiction..."

Over the next few minutes—except for occasional pauses to breathe—Ernie read the mind-*numbingly* dull whereas-therefore-heretofore-thereafter-once-upon-a-time legalese gobbledygook. Such a litany would bore the gentle reader to tears and makes *me* drowsy just writing *this* much down. And though it makes *editors* cringe, it pleases *lawyers* to no end. Such things *are*, after all, their bread and butter.

I am *sad* to say I understood *every word and clause.*

Forming an FBI Working Group is akin to declaring war on its object. It enables the Bureau to assign *any* federal employees and attach *any* law enforcement from anywhere. When confronted with the words 'FBI Working Group,' *Congress* gets nervous. An SPD Working Group makes the rest of the *FBI* shudder. It moves and acts as the *Voice of GOD* from *The Almighty Washington* and wields enough budgetary power to buy *New Jersey*…or a small country. The only entities with more juice are the better-known *Task Forces* or *film critics.*

We listened as Ernie finished with, "…by the authority of William French Smith, Attorney General of the United States."

At this time in DC, we were still in the legendary *first hundred days* of a new president. This is a period within which nothing substantive *ever* gets done—it's all flashy pomp for media consumption. But, former Marine Captain *Dusty* Harris called former Navy Lieutenant *Frenchy* Smith, and after talking about wives and kids, declared, "I need a Working Group, Frenchy."

"OK, everyone, get comfortable." Ernie set the papers down, gazing around at his group, Harry Benz's three and Edwin 'Win' Brock's three… and two women I didn't recognize. "You'll all *get* copies." Room 200 took up half the basement, with windows high on the north wall. It had a big U-shaped conference table in the middle and desks with telephones lining three walls except where the bulletin board-whiteboards stood. Room 200 had the floor area of my four-bedroom childhood home.

"*Any* of you been in a Working Group before?" Harry and Win raised their hands. "All right: The Working Group is where you will put your attention when it *needs* it. Initially, it will demand a *great deal* of attention. We have to interview a small *shit*-load of people, review as *much* material as we can find, and create a database specifically *for* the Working Group."

"*That* said," Harry added, "the difference between a Working Group and a Task Force is that the latter's a full-time job. After a while, the Working Group will demand less and *less* of your attention, *then* more, *then* less. It could be *years* before we close it up."

"Right," Win agreed. "The AG won't rescind our authority until he's convinced that there's nothing else for us to *do*." Win was younger than *most* SSAs in the SPD, but his glass eye and the missing fingers from his right hand excluded him from most field duty.

"We have *some* internal information," Ernie declared. "Special Agent Parkinson: please tell us what *you personally* know about Wolverine Military Academy."

"My step-uncle, John Elrath, went there 1970-'71. He told me about some things he *saw* first-hand." She went on to say *what* her uncle *told* her he'd been compelled to watch. She finished with, "he told the authorities *what* he'd seen, and for the rest of the school year, he was *tortured* to make him take it back. He *wouldn't*."

The room was silent; everyone looked away from Julia—except me. I watched her wipe some tears away. "A stand-up guy," I offered.

"No *shit*," Morgan agreed. "Show *me* to *him*."

I saw one of the new women shake her head gently, squinting dubiously.

Julia's description *did* seem both real *and* surreal. Her story *sounded* like a fantasy that some kid spun about military school abuse to keep from having to go. It *felt* like Jules was telling us she'd been abducted by aliens.

And like she was standing up for her *hero*.

I remembered that brochure…*At-Risk Young Men*…

We sat around looking at each other before Win cleared his throat and asked, "how did you *come by* this information?" A simple question, one that anyone should ask when presented with something *that* fantastic.

"He *sort of* volunteered it. We're *buddies*: movies, meals, the shooting range, just hanging out, *now* letters; I haven't *seen* him for *years*. In '71, we'd had *lots* of fun at his sister's wedding, but I could see *something* was bothering him, so I *asked*. And he *told* me *that*."

"Why would he *volunteer* such information to *you*," Frank asked. That was *another* excellent follow-up, entirely appropriate. "Why *you*?" He was asking *how close WERE/ARE you to your step-uncle*…politely, of course.

Julia glanced at me, then Ellen, then me again, as if asking for forgiveness before she answered. "We had—*have*—a mutual enemy: *my* grandfather; *his* step-father; Charlie Parkinson—my *father's* father. He's a letch and a drunk and a bully who *peeped* on me. JJ *caught* him the last time, and Grampa choked the *shit* out of him for it. Grampa tried to play the big hero and swore up and down that he caught us *doing it*. We denied it because it *wasn't so*. Nobody believed *Grampa*. That's why *I* think Grampa sent him to Wolverine: for telling the *truth*."

"Not much of an *explanation* for 'why *you*,' though," Christian Gruber grunted.

"I *said* I wouldn't go *out* with him anymore if he didn't spill…"

That raised a chuckle from almost everyone; even Ernie grinned. "OK," Ernie declared, "we'll consider Julia's account to be credible." Ernie looked around before he said, "We have two new members from other agencies: Deputy Marshal Nieuwpoort and DEA Agent Greely. They *also* have *some* knowledge of Wolverine. Introduce yourselves and tell us what you know."

"Yessir. I'm Grace Nieuwpoort, just *got* here last night from Miami." She was a stocky woman with dark hair and hazel eyes. "I went to college with a guy who went there: Adrian Newly. He was *different*."

"Different, *how*," Julia prompted. "Withdrawn; quiet; sullen?"

Grace started. "Yeah!"

"That was JJ's default mood for a long time."

Grace continued. "Adrian was a *sweet* guy, polite and respectful. Didn't fit *in* well with our campus crowd, though. We weren't *involved*, just friends. He was a guy I could be *with* to keep the *creeps* away. *He* told *me* some things, like Julia, but under *different* circumstances."

"You keep in touch?"

"No, but I know where his parents lived eight years ago: I went there with him one Thanksgiving." She was thoughtful again. "And he *could be scary* sometimes, especially with the *creeps*."

"OK; we'll want to *find* him," Ernie said. "Agent Greely?"

"Yes," she answered. She was slender and taller than Grace, "I'm Helen Greely from the Reno DEA office, got in *this morning*. My father was a teacher at Wolverine for ten years; we *lived* in Greenville."

"When?" Ernie's voice was even, but his eyes were penetrating.

"1963 to '74."

"Is your father still with us," I asked.

"Mom and Dad are living in Phoenix these days," Helen declared. "My brothers went there '72-'74." She cleared her throat. "As to *Julia's* account, I plan to send *my boys* there."

"All right," Ernie interrupted. "We can get first-hand testimony of activities from 1963 to at least '74. And there's this law firm: Dietz, O'Bannon in Detroit, *and* their investigator."

"If I *might* suggest," Julia glanced at me, "Dave and I hail from the Detroit area. We *might* be more efficient...."

"*And* it would give you a free ride home," Harry sniffed.

"Huh," Ernie grunted; his *you have a point that ain't on your head* grunt. "Someone needs to go to Panama to talk to this Elrath fella." He looked around. "Volunteers?"

"Yessir," I declared before I knew I'd done it. "I should take Helen with," I hastened to add, forming a plan as I went along. "Her father was there when Elrath was."

"Huh," Ernie declared, his *great idea; go ahead on,* huh.

"So *now*," Harry declared, "Lists of interviews, starting with Elrath. Add these guys from the Long Knives Society—hand *that* file over, Dave. Then we plan a strategy for conniving *possibly* confidential information out of an attorney."

"We can add *this* to the heap," Julia said, throwing a Wolverine brochure on the table. "It's…misleading."

"OK," Grace said, frowning, "but what Federal crimes do we believe have been committed?" It *was* an excellent question…

"If minors are being killed there and the perpetrators are fleeing across state lines, *that* falls under our jurisdiction. *Also*," Ernie said, "if the owners or the faculty or both are aware of these crimes and know they're housing fugitives from justice, *they* can be charged with harboring, aiding, and abetting interstate fugitives. So, we *also* have to find out who actually owns the joint *and* who runs it, if *that's* different. *Finally*, there's an inordinate number of Liberty Bell Files that mention this institution— *too many* coincidences to *be* coincidental. Clear?"

That's why some attorneys say that you can *indict* a ham sandwich, but *convicting* one may be challenging.

If it wasn't for J. Edgar's night terrors and his Liberty Bell Files, most of us would never have known about Wolverine and all those other outfits he was *so* afraid of.

And if I'd known *then* what I know *now* about that joint, I'd have saved everyone a *lot* of trouble and gone and blown it up myself.

✳✳✳

"I've got a *letter* for you," I told Sergeant John "JJ" Elrath when I met him. "From *Jules*." I handed him the sealed envelope; he took it, his hand trembling.

"*How's* my *first date* these days?" His blue eyes looked dull, his 6-foot-2 frame slightly stooped, favoring his right side. He was in solid green jungle fatigues, *long* out of the system but entirely appropriate for Fort Sherman, Canal Zone, at *any* time of year.

"She's *fine*, Sergeant," Helen replied, "and wants a *full report* on you." Where Helen could get away with a sleeveless blouse and light skirt, *I'd* look funny trying the same thing and had to settle for cotton drills.

"She *would*," JJ wheezed, sitting down across from us in the little CI office. "You'll *have* to forgive me if I *seem* a little spacy because I *am*. Had a biopsy in November that went a *little* wrong. Been on painkillers since; *trying* to get off them now." He turned Julia's letter in his hands absently.

"Not because of anything *major*, I hope," Helen asked.

"*Un*fortunately, no, but a condition they can neither *treat* nor *cure*; just alleviate symptoms. Nor does anyone *seem* to agree if it will ever go away." He looked sadly resigned. "Sarcoidosis *hurts*, makes it hard to breathe, has complications. It probably *won't* kill me, but it *might* see me dead."

"Well, then," I said, trying to get back on track. "The reason we're *here*...."

"Wolverine," JJ sighed, rolling his eyes slightly. "That's what Jules said." She'd called to give her buddy an unofficial/official *these guys are OK*.

"Yes," I answered. "We're looking *into* that place *and* some organizations that you may have *heard of* while you were there. You up for some questions?"

He pocketed Julia's letter. "What do you want to know?" For a big guy, he had a tranquil demeanor. Perhaps it was the drugs *or* the weight loss; I could see both in his face.

"First: Founders of the Fourth Reich," I asked. He stared blankly. "Anything?"

"Yeah. Just..." he trailed off. "Haven't *thought* of them. There were so *many* different little groups." He paused. "*Fourth* Reich...Bielefeld, like the railway viaduct in Germany that the RAF tried to wipe out in '45." I must have started or done something obvious; Helen gasped; JJ grinned like a cat with a canary. "It's how I remember stuff. Just gets filed with a handle. The dope's slowing me down today; I need *more* of it in this humidity."

"Handy kind of memory to have," Helen said brightly. "Anything about *them*?"

"Remembering *that's* a pain," JJ sighed. "Fourth Reich wasn't *visible*, really. Some of the faculty fought the Nazis, so they *didn't* want to rock that boat…not that it *mattered*."

"How's that," Helen asked. "My father—you *might* have known him—taught calculus, chemistry, and physics. Captain…"

"Captain Computer," JJ interrupted. "He subbed for our algebra teacher sometimes. He wrote formulas with his right hand while erasing them with his left."

"Captain *Marchand*," Helen said, slightly annoyed. "You were *saying* about the faculty?"

"Yes, I *knew* your father." There's a time in everyone's life when they see genuine contempt in another's face—a hatred *rarely* equaled. *I* saw it—briefly—in JJ's face then. "I *knew* him." His voice was even, flat, drained—*on purpose*. You get a sense of these things.

"*And*," Helen prompted.

"And *he*, like the other supposed grownups—except one—could *not* have cared *less* what happened to the *inmates* at that *asylum*. *I'd* go so far as to declare that your *father* was the *worst* of them."

Helen had spent ten years in the Drug Enforcement Agency and was pretty hard to phase. To her credit, she didn't blink. "Why do you say *that*?"

"He was the faculty member on the Disciplinary Committee. They had the final say on any disciplinary actions that called for more than three demerits." JJ struggled to keep his voice even; I could *see* it. "From October 1970 to May '71, I was given *eight* demerits nearly every

Friday for failure to obey orders. Your father *never* disapproved. To my knowledge, he never disapproved of a *single demerit slip* while I was there."

It seemed deathly still in that office; the cold air wafting down from the A/C vent seemed loud. "*What* orders were you *given?*"

JJ closed his eyes briefly, shook his head *just* a little. "I was ordered to *lie.*"

"About *what?*" Helen seemed relentless.

"I saw a guy get hurt bad and told the school *how* he was hurt after the kid collapsed in formation. Then I told the *cops,* and the guys that *did it* got thrown out. Their *friends* didn't *like* that, so they *ordered* me to *lie.*" He blinked. "*Your father said nothing.*"

"*That* sounds…" Helen started, then…"like a *personal* grudge."

"It was *battalion punishment,*" JJ declared. "Discipline at Wolverine was *not* interfered with by the faculty, even when guys *died.*"

I briefly drifted back to when Julia told us about Wolverine. Now, here, in front of us, was an eyewitness. "Guys *died?*"

JJ's eyes switched over to me. "*Twenty-one* the year *I* was there. *All* called suicides."

Helen cleared her throat. "If I *asked* my father about that, what would *he* say?"

"*I* couldn't care *less* what he'd say," JJ growled, glancing at her. "But if you *were* to ask him, look him *straight* in the eye. I guarantee you he'll look away before he says *anything*. I was deposed in '72 and '73 about what happened to Eddie. *That* number came from the school. Their lawyer tried to get me to say that what happened to him *might* have been a failed suicide attempt."

"Well? *Could* it…?"

I briefly thought there would be fisticuffs before he quietly answered, "lady, *what* manner of suicide would make *you* shit blood and pass out while standing up?"

"*We* need a break," I declared and hustled Helen out of the office. I cannot *imagine* what was running through *her* head. I'd heard a lot of bullshit stories in my time and would listen to *many* more. But some might *sound* like BS but were all too horribly real…and JJ's story sounded like it just *had* to be true because it was *so* bizarre, *so* unreal, and contained *so* many details. "Can you get ahold of your father…?"

"Not for *this*," she spat, shrugging my hand off her arm and dripping in the sudden heat and damp of the outside. "We would have *known*. My *brothers* would have known, would have *said* something. *They* went to that school, too. This guy's story's *pure* fiction."

"Why would he make *that* up," I asked.

"I don't *know*, attention?" She crossed her arms defiantly. "I *guarantee* you we can't believe *anything* that comes out of his mouth."

"One way to find out: I'll call Detroit, have *them* talk to that law firm."

✳✳✳

"So," I started, trying to sound solicitous, "you're making a career of the Army?" We were in the Visitor's Quarters lounge that night, sort of watching a basketball game on TV.

"Yup," JJ answered, tired. "Seven years in now. I'll re-up next year."

"You up for E-6?"

"Yeah. You?"

"*Just* made O-3 effective this month."

"*Thought* you were a *something* uniform." He leaned back, relaxed. "Where's your partner?"

"Her room. She didn't think much *of* your account this morning, but she came around." In my pocket, I had the Telex from the Detroit Division; it had been waiting when we got back from dinner. I showed it to Helen; she read it over and over again, shaking her head.

The message was short, simple…

EVANS VS WOLVERINE MILITARY ACADEMY ET AL. WITNESS TO ASSAULTS ON E EVANS OCTOBER 70 J ELRATH

GAVE DEPOSITIONS 72-73. NEGOTIATED SETTLEMENT 76. TOTAL PUNITIVE AND COMPENSATORY AWARDS FROM FIVE RESPONDENTS SAID TO HAVE BEEN OVER 20 M.

"Sometimes, I have to question it myself. *How* could all that *shit* have really happened?"

"She says she'd have *known* what went on in that school. She *lived* in Greenville; her father and brothers *went* to that school every day."

"It was the *nature* of that place." JJ stretched. "It was like there were two *different* worlds: inside, where the animals ran the zoo, and outside, where we were just watched by whoever had the fare. Her father and brothers just had the fare. When the lights went out at *night....*"

"I get it. The barracks are completely different places at night." I waited; he looked sleepy. "About the *Long Knives...*"

"Yeah. Maybe tomorrow, sir."

✳✳✳

"First, Sergeant," Helen began, "I want to say how *sorry* I am, doubting your account. But I *still* don't understand...."

"You ever been in the *building*," JJ asked quietly.

"No," Helen answered, knitted her brows. "No, we were *never invited.*"

"Your brothers were day students," JJ said. "Did they even *eat* there?" She looked blank. "No. *Dad* didn't either."

"And they participated in *no* athletic programs?"

"No. Said there was a problem with insurance."

"A *high school* without *sports*?" JJ smiled. "Insurance my *ass. They* didn't want to give those animals more weapons." His voice was *painfully* even. "Excuse me for *saying* this, but your father was a scene painter on a Potemkin village."

"I suppose you're right." Helen, to her credit, having cried through at least part of the night, didn't flinch. "Now, about the Long Knives..."

"They were very secretive but *not* as secretive as the No-names."

"No-Names," I repeated, "who were *they?*"

"*Good* question. They didn't wear nametags when all the rest of us did. *They* bunked in Patton Hall; five or six of 'em, I think."

"Patton Hall," Helen scribbled a note. "That was the *elite*…."

"You know *that* much," JJ smiled. "Yeah: the *elite* of the *elite*. *Best* of *everything* was expected of Patton Hall. *Always* the best inspections; the best *grades*; the *least* demerits. But *those* guys with no nametags…no matter *where* Patton Hall fell in chow order, *they* always went in when they *felt* like it, which was usually *first*. Didn't wait in line, either."

"Huh," I grunted. "Their shit didn't stink."

"Nossir," JJ nodded. "And they didn't *interact* with anyone, either. They came to formation; went to class but were *never* asked questions; they went to chow, but that was *it*. And they seemed *older*. *Most* high school guys had to shave maybe twice or three times a week. *Those* guys… *every* day. And they kept to themselves, didn't even come for the worm races. I tried to talk to one in the library once. He just stared at me and left."

"*Worm* races," I asked. "What's *that?*"

"They tied guy's hands and feet together, put 'em in a circle, and tell 'em to wiggle out. The winner *didn't* get a beating. The organizers placed bets."

"These held a lot," Helen asked timidly.

"Saturday nights."

There followed a silence, long and loud. "The Long Knives, JJ?"

"Yessir. I can tell you that Jay Pardon—my roommate—tried to join, and they wouldn't have him. But Chuck Wier…I think maybe *he* was a member. I *believe* Boehlke and Doyle were, too."

"*One* name at a time. Who was Jay Pardon?"

"Roommate after Eddie and Chuck left; prickly little asshole."

"And Chuck Wier?"

"He was a roommate, too, but he moved to Headquarters Company. *Big* asshole, Wier. They made him HQ Company Commander his senior year."

"And Boehlke?"

JJ sighed. "*Nestor* Boehlke. *Hulking* big guy; they must have fed him steroids or something. The Second Horseman…I ratted him out and never saw him again after the cops took him away."

"Second…horseman?"

"The *second* guy to have his turn with Eddie." JJ shook his head. "The Long Knives were *supposed* to be the enforcers. So *Jason* thought, anyway."

"Jason…?"

"Samson." JJ stopped, closed his eyes. "Buddy of mine. Near-as, in *that* place. He spoke Spanish better than the teacher, *he* thought. He got a *lot* of punishment tours like I did. He got handed demerits for insubordination because he kept winning the Spanish prize from Testa." He shrugged. "I found Jason Christmas morning, arms slashed open. *Maybe* he killed himself; it *was* pretty common around there."

I briefly thought I'd mention Dusty's connection but thought better of it.

"And, Doyle?" Helen maintained as much curious detachment as she could, but it was hard for her.

"Bruce Doyle, the Third Horseman. I ratted *him* out, and I ain't seen or heard from him since. But I talked to his *lawyer*. She tried to get me to say that Doyle *might* have been just *going through the motions*, not *really* reaming Eddie. *I* said that Eddie pissed himself while Doyle was *going through those motions*. Doyle was *still* laughing when he *finished* his *motions* all over Eddie's back and took the time to rub the *fruit* of his *motions* into Eddie's hair." JJ blinked, then stared at us in turn. "I *can't* make *that* shit up, ma'am; sir."

Of every statement I've *ever* taken from *anyone* in my career, *that* was the most convincing.

When Helen and I left the next day, JJ had a letter for Julia and a hug for Helen. He *grinned* as he hugged her, which made me think that she

190

was the first female he'd *had* in his arms maybe in a *long* time. But even tough guys like JJ Elrath need *some* tenderness, sometimes. He ended the embrace with his hands on her shoulders at arm's length, looking her straight in the eye with a slight smile as he whispered, "*Don't* hold it against him; he was as *trapped* as we were."

I could never imagine a stronger, more decent human being than he. After everything he *endured*, after everything Helen's father apparently *allowed*, he kept enough humanity to *not* hold it against *her* personally.

At *least* long enough to hold a pretty woman in his arms.

Beth dropped her purse on the table after we got to her place in my new '81 Chevy Blazer from Chevy Chase, Maryland. We had been car-shopping at a dealership that gave $2000 minimum for *any* trade—an "Inauguration Special Sale" that had lasted two months. My Buick's transmission was going south, making it worth more as scrap metal than transportation, but it could *never* be *two grand* worth of scrap. She'd traded her Karmann Ghia with its rotten heater boxes in at the same place a month before, got a '78 Volvo for a song. "Want a beer to celebrate your new indebtedness?" The Blazer *did* come with payments… *manageable* payments, but payments.

"Sure" She slid off the gold band she wore to keep guys from hitting on her. "Does it *work*?" Before I *knew* it, I added, "let's get married so you won't have to wear *that* anymore."

She turned, surprised. "Did you ever *ask* anyone *besides* Kim?"

"No, *never*." From about fifteen on, I "proposed" to Kim—often, loudly and publicly. Her laughing off my *serial wooing* was part of our banter and everyone *knew* it.* *Other* girls who laughed off my more *serious* yet clumsy advances were a *little* harder to take. But Beth saying *no*... I thought maybe I'd gone *too far*, but eight months *seemed* long enough,

---

* I asked *quietly* on my 17th birthday—she was just under 24—after my birthday kiss. She said "ask me *next year*" with a straight face. *That* was the last time I asked. I often wondered why.

even for the '80s.

I knew something *more* had to be said, something even *more* critical than a proposal of marriage, something like... "I *promise* I won't get killed on this job, Beth."

She handed me a beer and brushed my hairline. There's not a lot there since I crop it close, but it was the *gesture*, the gentle stroking of my forehead with *that* Cheshire smile. "You'll *try* not to, Davie, but let's *face* it: you're in a dangerous line of work...."

"I *promise*, Beth," I repeated.

"I *love* that you're committed to *that*, babe." She wrapped her arms around me and rested her head on my chest. "Your heart agrees." She looked up; her expression didn't change; no *surprise*, no *joy*, just her Cheshire smile on her sunny face as she asked, "when?"

"When we *know*. When *you* know."

"*Serious* business, sweetie. *Lifetime* commitment."

"I *know*."

"Live *here*..." She owned her place; Cindy was paying rent.

"I can give *my* place up in June."

She stared, smiling before she ever-so-slowly moved to lay her head on my chest again. "Move in in *June* so Cindy can find another place."

"Can *I* have more space here in the meantime?" I'd left a razor and a toothbrush in her downstairs bathroom and annexed part of her closet for some uniforms since her townhouse was closer to Anacostia. Hannibal withheld comment about me until my second night there when she deposited a generous, *un*-ladylike gastric rearrangement on my laundry bag.

"Sure."

"The Bureau is *not* so hot on cohabitation," I said, and they *weren't*. However, they couldn't *stop* it; enough *did* it to make J. Edgar's shade scream.

"The IRS doesn't care, but I want our friends *and* family to *see* us commit, but I don't *have* a church. Courthouse?"

"How about the Academy chapel?" There was an air of unreality: standing in her great room, discussing marriage, quaffing beer.

I wondered *what* we'd agreed to *if* we'd decided *anything*…really. Then she grinned, and said, "OK."

"You want a *ring*?" I tried my curious face.

"Your parents showed me your Gramma's ring." She squeezed me.

"*When?*"

"The day we left. *You* were still asleep. I think *they* were ready to give it to me." My father's mother died days after I was born; Grampa left her 1/2 carat diamond ring to me.

"So, they *want* you for a daughter-in-law. *Your* family doesn't seem to *mind* me." Jonas, Beth's father, seemed circumspect when I met him Labor Day but didn't reject me, either. I guessed that he trusted his daughter's judgment. At least, I *hoped* he did. Her mother and siblings seemed amiable enough.

"They *adore* you, babe. Does *this* mean we're engaged?" She giggled. "Stephen and Grace." Our Kid's Name Game *always* preceded…*you* get it. But usually, we were either in bed, or *close* to one.

"I *believe* so." I slid my hands around her hips. "George and Stephanie."

"Huh," she sniffed. "Thought there'd be fireworks, or whistles and bells or something."

"Do we *tell* everyone?"

"Why *not*?" I made a face. "Oh. *That*. Sure. Take out an announcement in the paper, say the bride will *not* be *expecting* until *after* the ceremony."

"That's the *bride's* family's thing, isn't it?"

"I suppose."

"You're the *least* enthusiastic bride I've ever *heard* of. The *least* you could do is *kiss* your new fiancée."

"Huh," she sniffed and grinned…before her *evil twin* took over and we *anointed* the living room couch a few minutes later to Hannibal's *stern* disapproval. We told *everyone* in the area that afternoon *and* called our families...*and* Kimmie.

And we smiled at *another* joke the three of us—me, Beth, and her evil twin—would play on the world.

✳✳✳

"Thanks for meeting us on such short notice," I began, smiling. Adam Block was a bullet-headed fire-hydrant of a man with a firm grip and a quiet voice.

"*No* trouble," Adam replied, smiling with everything but his eyes. He had the ever-wary demeanor of a store owner holding his sawed-off shotgun under the counter while facing the latest in a *long* string of gun-toting stick-up guys and was *moments* from making an example—*a red stain*—of *this* one.[*] Some people were eternally wary, ever-vigilant, ready at a moment's notice to act, often violently but *always* controlled.

"We've been studying the files you sent us," Julia smiled. We had since we received them a month before. Three of the new names JJ gave us weren't *in* them: Chuck Wier, Jay Pardon, and Herman Jimenez. But the Four Horsemen *were:* their families were the *et al.* in the lawsuit. We hadn't *found* Boehlke, Eyerdam, or Testa yet. Bruce Doyle, the figurehead mayor of a little village in upstate New York that his family owned, was hiding behind a wall of lawyers. Doyle's family was the *first* to settle, nearly a year before the others. "There's the question of ownership of Wolverine," Julia continued. "There's a *lot* of shell companies."

"*We* haven't found the cheese at the end of *that* maze, either," Adam nodded. "We get as far as either the Cayman Islands or Korea, then nothing."

"Any theories," I asked quietly. There are *ways* to answer questions that imply more than *I don't know.*

Adam, whose title was simply *consultant*, smiled, this time with his

---

[*] I *knew* the look. I interviewed "Hurricane" Guzmanoff's *last* stickup victim, who shot him in the legs with a sawed-off 12-gauge. Guzmanoff died in a shootout with the authorities in the vacant lot across the road.

eyes. "Greenville Investment Trust is the *public* face. Other firms have connections often enough to be of interest." He looked puzzled for a moment. "Once in a while, I think that there's *something* to do with Newhouse Properties."

"Who," I blurted. There was *nothing* in the files with that name.

"They're a big real estate and development firm in Southeastern Michigan. We started analyzing some of the shell companies. Some of them are quite old—dating from the 1930's—and *that* got us to thinking that since the Newhouse firm has been around *that* long, They might have something to do with it."

"We," Julia asked. "Who's *we?*"

"My *firm* was asked...."

"I thought you worked for Dietz, O'Bannon, and Associates."

"*My* firm, Block and Associates, *is* one of the *associates*. The *pattern* of the shell companies is *interesting*. They've been formed all over the Great Lakes, but most have PO boxes in Southeastern Michigan." He shifted in his chair. "Our *working* theory is that in '58, the then-owners of Wolverine were in an economic hole. Greenville Investment Trust came along like a white knight and offered them *30% above* market value. It was *thought* that they were just interested in the *land*. Then they obtained school accreditation from the state and kept going.

"According to our research, in the early '60s, *something* changed in the school. Before then, it was just a four-year high school in a military environment with an Army Junior ROTC program. In '62, they *officially* dropped out of the *Army's* JROTC—thought they kept *teaching* it—and started to take on boys who really *didn't* want to be there, some *violently*. I think they simply didn't want the outside observers."

"Abuses?"

"*Scores* of 'em; hundreds. Some boys died; some we *think* were murdered. No one's come forward saying 'I saw so-and-so kill so-and-so,' but Mr. Elrath has been the nearest we've come to a witness to a felonious crime."

"Ah," I said, "*Mr. Elrath*. JJ. The *only* one to report abuses like that?"

"The only one *on record*," Adam replied. "We've spoken to a couple dozen former students who'd been in that school from '49 to '80, and Mr. Elrath's the only one who was put under oath to make a statement."

"*Mr.* Elrath," Julia mused. "Funny; I've never *seen* him as a 'mister,' *anything*, but maybe I *know* him better."

"You know him *differently*, Ms. Parkinson. *We* know him by what he *endured*, and *we* know that grown men have *shattered* under less intense pressure." Adam had a way to shift his gaze so that you knew he was looking at *you*, but you also knew he saw *everything*. "*We* call him *Mr. Elrath* as a mark of respect. The Dietz firm sometimes called him *John-Zilla*."

"Where's *that* from," Julia asked.

Adam smiled oddly. "The tort law industry refers to tenacious and well-off clients as *gorilla* clients: they *won't* stop, and the Evans family had the resources and the determination to stay in the fight to the end. Mr. Elrath would *not* recant what he told the authorities about what *he* saw. Hence, Mr. Ben Dietz started referring to him as the Evans family's *Godzilla*, protecting his friend, the gorilla. Hence…"

"*John-Zilla*." I smiled. "Who *is* this Evans family with all the dough?" I hadn't been looking too deeply into the background of the Wolverine case, more interested in the Long Knives and the Founders of the Fourth Reich.*

"The Evans family are the majority owners of the firm of Evans, Shadsworth, Morgan, and Towne, a private banking and investment firm in Detroit."

Julia gasped, gulped; I was confused. "*Who?*"

"Aw, fer *Chrissakes*, Dave," Morgan groaned. "I'll *tell* ya *later*." She

---

* Ya *know*, the *Liberty Bell* stuff we were *supposed* to be cleaning up…and *my* cleanup rate was dropping faster than panties on prom night.

grinned wryly at Adam. "*Forgive* the *rube*."

"*No* matter," Adam nodded. "They have the resources to *buy* Wolverine if they desired…to buy *Greenville*. What we found intriguing was that, contrary to what the Evans family *wanted* and *expected*, the settlement did *not* bankrupt Wolverine's owners. Despite the loss of *tens* of *millions* of dollars, they're thriving."

"Didn't the state Department of Education…" Julia asked.

"No," Adam interrupted, "and I'm not *sure* why."

"*We* may have *that* answer," I sighed, reaching for one of *our* files: The Founders of the Fourth Reich. "Leonard Bielefeld. Familiar name?"

"Superintendent of Michigan Schools since 1968."

"And his *nephew*, Jefferson Knox Bielefeld, was at Wolverine from 1969 to 1971."

"So, the fix *was in*," Adam made a face. "I'll have to make a *note* of that."

"You said *what he endured after*. What, exactly, do you mean?" I knew what Julia said, but she cared more deeply for JJ than just as a *buddy* or a *step-uncle*, though *less* than…yeah, *less than that*, you *pervert!*

"He was beaten, frozen, compelled to march around in circles endlessly as punishment. He was pitched out a second-story window once. He was also clubbed in his sleep almost every night. According to *one* account, he once had castor oil poured down his throat."

"*Not* in the files you sent," I said, curious.

"That's what happened *after*," Adam replied patiently. "Your request was the background on the *lawsuit*. What Mr. Elrath endured was *after* Mr. Evans was assaulted."

"How much research material do you *have*, Mr. Block," Julia asked.

"*Twice* what we *sent* you," Adam replied: he'd sent perhaps twenty file boxes of material. "Most of it has to do with trying to find who *owns* the joint. I can't say what the Dietz law firm has; *that* would be confidential. For *that*, you'll have to consult Mr. Ben."

"We may do that," Julia said. "But now we'd like to arrange to make copies of *your other* Wolverine material and to arrange that you keep us updated *if* you find anything new."

"Very well," Adam nodded, rising from his chair. "I can have the material copied, but it'll take time."

"The Troy agency can help." There was an FBI Resident Agency just down the road from the Dietz offices.

"In the interest of *transparency*," Adam reached into his jacket and pulled out a small billfold and showed us a credential. "INTERPOL liaison. So you *know*."*

***

"You never *heard* of Evans and Towne," Morgan shook her head as we reached our car. Adam's office was in Birmingham, an attractive suburb outside Detroit, on the top floor of the well-appointed office building that housed Dietz, O'Bannon & Associates.

"Nope, never," I admitted. There was nothing to prepare me for the affluent suburbs around the Motor City—I'd only ever been to the zoo and the Cinerama theater downtown. The affluence on display in the apparently thriving suburbs around Detroit—considering the city's decay—surprised me. Most of what I saw of Birmingham was *stunning*: national chain grocery stores with elaborate storefronts that would make even Georgetown jealous.

"They're private bankers, only work with multi-*kazillion*-dollar investors. Some people think they *own* Wall Street. I need to touch base with them."

"Huh," I sighed, driving down a crowded street. "Wait: Evans and…"

"My great-great Uncle Erasmus was the *Towne* that founded the firm of Evans, Shadsworth, Morgan, and Towne."

"And the *Morgan*," Julia asked.

"My father's godfather." Morgan sighed. "Haven't seen Uncle Gam *or*

---

* We didn't *need* to know how Adam got INTERPOL credentials, but it did suggest he had once been in law enforcement, somewhere.

his family for a while. I *should* reach out."

The resident agents in the little FBI office in the industrial park down the road from Adam's office seemed more curious *about* than impressed *with* us from *The Almighty Washington,* who'd flown in for…*what, again?*

"It's an ongoing investigation," Morgan grinned brightly. "A matter that doesn't *concern* you." SRA* Paula Karris was in nominal charge of twenty other agents. She was a freckle-faced mild-mannered woman of 40 or so—it was hard to tell precisely.

"Anything *we* can do to help," Paula added, eyeballing us dubiously. "You're welcome to use what facilities we *have,* but if you need *manpower,* I'd need some notice."

"There *may* be," I said, trying *not* to be too demanding. "There's a bunch of files at Block and Associates that need copying and packing…" And here I was offering them a secretarial work bone. I felt terrible about it as soon as I opened my mouth.

"*Block and Associates* files," Paula asked, again looking at us askance. "What's the *case?*"

"You *know* the firm," Julia asked.

"Know it *well enough,*" Paula answered. "Wish *we* had *their* resources. They're legal investigators extraordinaire; they poached an agent from me. So, what's the *case?*"

"It's for an SPD Working Group…"

"*Oh,*" Paula said. Though everyone knew about Working Groups, no one *asked* about them or what they *did* unless they were included…and the Troy agency had *not* been. "We'll pitch in where you need us."

I looked at Morgan; she at me; we shrugged. "*I'll* make the call," Morgan said. A few minutes later, a fax came across:

Resident Agency Troy, Detroit FBI Division, is added to Wolverine Working Group…Harris.

"You'll get the paperwork by interoffice in a few days," Morgan

---

* Senior Resident Agent.

said. "In the meantime, can you spare someone to go over to the Dietz offices…?"

"I can spare *two* today," Paula declared, suddenly *inordinately* proud to be called upon. "We're not on anything *special*."

The Almighty Washington struck again…

✳✳✳

"*Huh*," Paula said, an almost-as-expressive *huh* as Ernie ever made. "So, Wolverine?" We were in the nearly deserted small dining room of the Sheraton Birmingham hotel; Morgan was dining with her family at The Roostertail. The Sheraton was a more posh establishment than we usually stayed at. I wondered if the taxpayers would appreciate paying for it.

"Yep. We've found them tied into several *possibly* subversive outfits… more than might be considered normal."

"*We* hear things, too," Paula said, twizzling her rye on the rocks. "My husband is in education. Sometimes he runs into a former student or a teacher from there. Few of them have anything *good* to say about it. But, there's *one*…" She reached into her huge purse—literally a saddlebag. "Here."

File Number Ending 90681-LIB
Name: Future Fascists of America
Date Identified: 19 September 70; Lansing, MI; avowed former member from Wolverine Military Academy traded knowledge of group for deal on Federal gun charges (BATF report attached), confirmed by anonymous informant inside Wolverine.
Origin: Founders unknown; probably started in and around Montcalm County, MI; possibly Greenville. If Greenville, almost certainly at Wolverine, which has many known members in student body. Known active members on attached list.
Narrative: Organization trains and organizes street brawlers. Ideological

bent not clear, but emphasizing organized violence. Wolverine faculty claims to be unaware of any such organized group.

Updates: 1971: Several known active members beaten in their bunks on the last night of school; one fatality. Regular event is called Last Night; thought to be either an initiation or a cleansing of undesirables.

1972: More members beaten in their bunks on Last Night.

"I *know* we were supposed to turn these in," Paula added quietly, "and I found this a few months ago in an old desk. Just never got *around* to it."

"Well, *now's* as good a time as any," Julia said. "Ah, *here's* my folks," she waved to catch the attention of her just-arrived parents. After introductions, Oakland County Sheriff's Captain Dorothy Parkinson asked, "how's *your* family doing, Dave?" Dorothy was a compact woman of middling height who contributed her titian-pale coloring—*and* her figure—to her daughter. I'd met them when Julia was in Michigan for Dean's memorial.

"Fine," I answered honestly. "Dean had been absent from our lives for so long." I shrugged. "I got engaged in last month, so it hasn't..."

"*Yeah*," Julia's father, Charlie, grinned. "Mighty Mouse?" *He* was where Julia got her *height*: he towered over everyone else at maybe six-foot-three. Her parents knew Beth from Julia's college days.

"Yeah. Eight months in, we knew each other well enough," I said.

"*He* didn't want her to get away," Julia added gratuitously.

"*Smart* guy," Dorothy grinned. "Congratulations, Dave."

Before we knocked off for the night, I asked Julia, "how did we get *this* hotel? Little high-end, even for us."

"My uncle is a part-owner," she said. "He gives us a rate."

So, we kept adding to our Working Group and to our files.

But that phrase *At-Risk Young Men* still bothered me, in part because we now had a list of known street brawlers who attended Wolverine.

✳✳✳

"*Hi*, Mom; Dad," I gushed, greeting them at the door. I still wasn't *quite* used to knocking on the front door of the house I grew up in, but it was getting *less* weird every time I did it. Since we were scheduled to leave Detroit on Friday, I'd decided to spend a few hours with my family Thursday.

"David," Dad offered his hand solemnly as Mom hugged me and Bridgit pecked my cheek.

"How's *Beth*, Dave, and *Washington*, how's *it*?" Mom *always* had her priorities straight. "I called Rose in Zanesville, had a *good* chin-wag. Did you know Beth's uncle is in Congress? I didn't *realize* that until I spoke with Rose…" Mom went on for a while about her future extended family, forgetting that I had told her about Uncle Max before.

"The Secret Service has told her uncle to clear the reception venue with *them*," Dad shrugged. "*I* spoke to Jonas; he's not *close* to the senator."

"OK, fine. Here, Mom." I handed her a proof of our invitation's cover—an inked version of Freddie's drawing of Beth and me from Fourth of July. "Do with this what you need. It's still only April, and we're talking *small* and four *months* away…" I started… a *big* mistake.

"Oh, that's nowhere *near* enough time to get everything *planned*," Bridgit cried. "Getting the *perfect* dress will take her at *least* that long. In fact, *next* August would be more *realistic*." My sixteen-going-on-thirty sister carried on in that vein. I didn't have the heart to tell Bridge that the bride had already rejected the idea of a *wedding dress* that she could only wear once. *This* came from my informant, Cindy, who *couldn't* shut up about it to save either her soul *or* her place in the bridal party. "I talked to Andy on the phone; he wrote to me last week. Seems nice. He's a grade ahead of me…" She rattled on about Beth's youngest brother, a handsome seventeen-year-old.

"OK," I told them as I left that evening, Gramma's ring in my pocket. "I'll put you in touch with Uncle Max, Dad: you two work out the reception with Jonas but leave *something* for Beth and me. Mom, whatever you and Rose work out for a shower will be *fine*. Just remember, everyone: August in Northern Virginia is *far* wetter than here, so be prepared for the heat *and* the damp." I winked at Bridgit. "Bridge: as the second-*youngest* member of the bridal party, we want *you* to take Beth's bouquet at the altar, OK?" Our bridal party consisted of Cindy as maid of honor, Beth's little sister Fiona, Bridge, and Julia as bridesmaids. Frank was my best man. Steve and Beth's brother Nate (two years older) and Andy were my ushers.

Bridgit pecked my cheek again with a smile. "*Anything* for my *favorite* big bro." She hardly knew Dean *or* Steve, so *that* wasn't saying much.

The fact was I barely *knew* my family anymore. I wasn't sure if I was supposed to be sad about that or not…or if growing out of your childhood home was *supposed* to be painful.

✳✳✳

"Do you *know* anything about *art*, Agent Clawson?" Adrian Newly led Grace and me around his Los Angeles gallery. "I know *Gracie* does from the art appreciation class we took together." He was about five-ten and affected a haughty, almost defiant manner, barely acknowledging us as Federal officers.

"*Not* much," I admitted. "I build models." It was temperate in LA that June, a *good* thing, I thought, because I was supposed to get my Advanced Officer's Course at Fort Irwin two weeks later.

"Ah! What *kind*?" Adrian had a long face and bright brown eyes on a slender-yet-strong frame.

"What strikes my fancy. Working on a *ship* right now." I'd worked on a USS *Constitution* model for months. I had just moved her to my hobby room/den in the townhouse, where Hannibal stared at the intricate rigging for *hours*. Beth's sewing/workout room was the *third* bedroom.

"I *see*." He stopped in front of a lithograph. "Do you see *this*?"

"I *do*." I waited, read the plaque: *Death for the Idea,* Paul Klee, 1915. The title reminded me of our first disagreement after moving into Beth's townhouse the weekend before: if the toilet paper should come off the *top* or the *bottom*. Bottom—*her* position—prevailed.

"Klee created this piece after some of his friends were killed in World War One." Adrian cocked his head to one side. "Stunning, isn't it? What do you *really* see?" We kept *all* my *new* furniture, giving much of *our* old stuff to Cindy…and the curb.

"I see a body; I see a city *perhaps* rising above it. Maybe the city is built *on* him; maybe it's *leaving* him, like a soul." I *kinda* did, but it took some work. So did my efforts to save my kitchen cutlery. They were in a box in the basement and *not* given to Goodwill—yet.

"That's *very* perceptive, Agent Clawson. Klee was spared most of the horrors of the war, spent *his* war camouflaging airplanes." Adrian paced slowly forward. "Klee painted *this* one as he was dying." The painting was bold, vivid, abstract, almost indescribable. "*Painfully* dying. *Death and Fire*, he called it." He slowly turned. "Have you ever *been* on fire, Agent Clawson?"

"I have *not*," I admitted. And, I *had* to admit that living in a townhouse with just one neighbor—a retired Navy commander and his wife—was quieter than an apartment building, especially on weekends. Hannibal still stared at me a great deal, though she was my best buddy when I *fed* her.

He turned again. "I *feel* that way, sometimes. Like these two Klee works: a city *leaving* me and being on *fire*." He looked down and studied the polished wooden floor of the gallery before looking up at the glaring patterns of *Ad Parnassum*. "And *that* was interpreted, like this painting has been so *often* interpreted, as *take care of it yourself*."

"I suppose," I offered, waiting.

Adrian turned away, then back to us, a serious look on his face as he stared behind us. "Wolverine's a *school*; *nothing* else. There are some *hijinks*, of course. But, it's just a bunch of *traditions*, that's all. You *misremembered* our conversations, Grace."

I stared at him until I *saw* the slight tremor in his cheek that spoke *volumes*: SOMEONE *scary got to me, and they may be watching now.* He pulled a card out of his pocket, scribbled on it, and dropped it on the floor. Grace stepped on it casually. "I don't know if I can *help* you," he said overloud. "I have *work* to do; if you'll *excuse* me…" and he stalked off.

"Got it," Grace whispered, tying her sandals.

The card read *Wild Onions, 10 tonight.*

✳✳✳

"Ever since I could remember, my parents said I would go to Wolverine. My *father* went there; my *grandfather*, my *great*-grandfather. A *fine* school, they said, *great* academic traditions."

I'd never been *in* a drag club before. Adrian's monolog got a good laugh from the house. "Ya *know, Scottish* drag queens wear *pants*…Say what you will about drag queens. but *they* get into more women's pants than *I* do… Remember *Achilles* from Greek mythology? *He* was a drag queen. *Yeah*, his *heels* were *killing* him…You *know why* drag queens love to *waltz*, right? A *lot* more *ball*room in *those* dresses…."

Adrian wasn't at *all* feminine—even in his wig and form-fitting cocktail dress—and his voice was a high baritone. With a bulge at the crotch, five o'clock shadow, and flat chest, he *was* convincing as a *guy* in a *dress*. But we *could* talk in the costume gallery backstage of Wild Onions, which was *why* the change of venue. "Gracie, dear; I'm *so* sorry."

"I *get* it, Adrian," Grace assured him. "Someone joined us in the gallery…."

"Someone I *couldn't* be sure of who's *been* hanging around." He lit and took a drag on a cigarette and glanced at me. "*Don't* worry, pal: getting gang-raped *doesn't* make you *gay*. My wife will tell you I'm as *straight* as *you* are."

"If you *say* so," I answered, watching a minor dispute between two convincing Marilyn Monroe's and a so-so Judy Garland in pigtails and gingham.

"We're a *straight drag* club," Adrian grinned. "Not *really* drag, not *really* straight. We're just entertaining a crowd." He high-fived Carol Channing as *she* sauntered by. "All *bullshit*, like what you *knew* was *bullshit* this morning."

"Ah," Grace said. "*Not* just hijinks?"

"Not *even*, honey." He shrugged. "*Bruce* called a few months ago; I hadn't heard from him in *years*. He said law enforcement was looking into Wolverine."

"Bruce *Doyle*," I repeated.

"Yeah. We *were sort-of* friends." He made a face: peculiar in itself. "*Grace*, honey: unzip me?" She obliged with some hesitation. He peeled the dress off his shoulders, made another face, and she turned around with an amused grin. He pushed the dress off his hips and pulled some shorts on. "*Thanks*, dear: we aren't *that* kind of friends, and I *can't* get into *that* dress with *anything* on. Now, where *was* I...we *were* friends once, but he got in with the Future Fascists, and I just *couldn't*...you know? He also fell in with Eyerdam and the rest of *those* losers."

"*Not* good guys?"

"Animals," Adrian sighed, lighting another cigarette. "Savage beasts, *worse* than the guys who did *me*."

"Let's back up," I said. "*When* were you...?"

"Delight Night, October 1968. There were *twelve* of us." He glanced at Grace; I did, too, noting a tear in her eye. Marlene Dietrich and Greta Garbo eyeballed us from across the room.

"It's *OK*; nobody's judging you."

"No," Adrian mumbled, "and perhaps *that's* the problem: *no one judges*. We were just *there*, and those beasts were just *there*, weren't they?"

"Did anyone...?" I asked, trying to imagine the kind of life he had *after* that in an all-boys school.

"Complain?" Adrian sneered. "To *who*? In our first *moments* there, we were told that punishment was a *battalion* matter. The school was *not* to be *bothered* with matters of discipline. So we wiped our asses, said nothing, and went about our schooling." He smiled wryly. "Until Last Night, when I clubbed *my* attacker a good one. Of course, in our *second* year, they didn't bother us. First-year, *regardless* of grade, you were fair game because you had no friends, no reputation."

"So, you graduated…."

"In 1972."

"But in '70, *something* happened on Delight Night…."

"The next *morning*," Adrian declared. "*It* happened the next morning."

"You *know* what I'm talking about?"

"That boy beshit himself and passed out in morning formation." Adrian shook his head softly, imperceptibly. "*Testa* didn't understand how *that* worked."

"That…*what*?"

"*How* we were assigned to Patton Hall. You see: those of us who came *back* to school the year *after* Delight Night—our initiation, if you will—were all assigned to Patton Hall." Adrian put on a wry face again. "When Testa reamed that boy with a broom handle …*he* didn't understand what it was he was *doing*. *That's* what made that boy do *that*. And that *other* one who *told* on *Cliff* and the rest…."

"Cliff…" I asked.

"Eyerdam. The senior class president who *should* have been battalion commander, but that pipsqueak *Luther* got the job with his Future Fascists of America…."

"Back up," I said. "Told on Cliff…*who* told *what*?"

"Elrath told on Eyerdam and Boehlke, Doyle and Testa, in *that* order. Told the *school*, told the *police*, told *everybody* what he saw. No Delight Nights after *that*."

At least JJ stopped that. "So, Future Fascists of America…"

"Yes, Luther and Boehlke *ran* that gang of strutting sloganeers."

"*Nestor* Boehlke," Grace asked.

"The one and only. *Nice* enough guy; if you didn't cross him, *then* you needed to be in the next *county*." He made a face. "Elrath: wonder what happened to *him*. He put *two* guys down on Last Night."

"I saw him in Panama in January. He's made a career of the Army."

"Huh," Adrian smiled, "I never thought he'd be caught *dead* in a uniform or marching *again*. They marched that poor bastard around in circles for *days*. He's OK, then?"

"*I* think so," I answered. "How about the No-Names?"

"The scary dudes who bunked at the far end of Patton Hall? I don't think I ever heard *one* of them talk to anyone outside their little circle."

"When did they start coming? Were they there before you?" Grace leaned against a clothes rack that moved unsteadily.

"There were three of them when I got there in '68. There were *nine* in '72. They were *older*."

"Anything else about them?" A *disturbingly* good Jackie Onassis grabbed a feather boa off a hangar behind Adrian and hustled off.

"They went to class; they stood for inspections—did *well*, too. But in Patton Hall, *that* was expected. *Nobody* messed with us; *nobody* came in, nobody used us for worm races. We just went to class and did our homework."

"*Who* do you think *got to* you earlier…and how?" I started to wonder if our witnesses would need protection.

"A Detroit lawyer came to the gallery in February, said he was with the Wolverine Alumni Association." Adrian shook his head swiftly. "I let him talk, tell me all about *my* life that he already *knew*. Then he asked me if anyone had been enquiring about Wolverine and my days there."

"And *you* said…" Grace prompted.

"I said *no* because no one *had*…not *then*. Then *Father* called a few days later, said *you* were *looking* for me, Gracie." He ground out his cigarette on a grimy jar lid. "A week later, that same lawyer came back, said the Alumni Association wanted to *invest* in the gallery."

"So…" I prompted. A *fat* Lana Turner reached behind me to pull out a gown.

"Since '72, I hadn't heard a peep from Wolverine and didn't *want* to. *Now* I smelled a rat—in the art business, you get to smell them a *lot*—took his card and said I'd get with the board. *He* didn't know that I could take money from *anyone*."

"You've *got* the card?" Grace asked, hopefully.

"For *you*, honey," he handed it to her: *Grover Fischer, Senior Partner, The Law Firm of Fischer and Ally, Bloomfield Hills, MI.*

"They put on a *great* spread," I declared at around 11 the night we got married, throwing the deadbolt.

"They *did*," Beth agreed, taking off her silk-floral headdress, a hand-made gift from Bridgit. "And it wasn't *that* spendy, either. But *now*," returning the headdress to its box, "my first order of business as *Mrs. Elizabeth Clawson*," she declared over Hannibal's cries for attention, "is to *feed* the *damn* cat." Her move toward the cat-food cabinet changed the cries to over-loud purrs.

"*Especially* not for the Arlington Country Club." Our parents got a *bargain* package for fifty-one guests; *Beth and I* covered the bar bill. Cindy *finally* got *inside* the Arlington. *Kimmie* and *her* Dave came, bearing a card from my old buddy Pete, who was still in Michigan. Mom and Dad could *scarcely* believe it was her; nor could Steve or Allison, only two years behind her in school. And I met Aunt Ruth, who was *not* bad to look at, but I could *not* picture her in a porn film. Maybe it was the grey hair…

"*Long* day," she sighed, slipping off her heels—the first shoes other than running shoes I'd seen her wear. Her dress was pale yellow chiffon, light and elegant on that 92-degree August day. "*Freddie* had fun."

"*Everyone* admired her work," I said, placing her drawing of us at the altar on the table. Freddie drew everyone and every*thing* she saw all day, giving her pictures away with a wide grin. Uncle Max, impressed with her talent, *paid* her as the official wedding *artist*. "She wore out *a box* of pencils today."

"I'd believe it," she sighed. "Know anything *about* Sam?"

"Never *met* him before," I said. "He *said* he's an auditor for the Department of the Interior." Ellen's date Sam Centerman *seemed* a nice enough guy. Ellen, for her own reasons, had kept him under wraps until then.

"Another number-head," she declared, reaching into the refrigerator for the water jug. "*Want* some?"

"Sure." We sat with our cold water on the sofa in the living room. Watching out our front window, we contemplated the rest of our lives with the lights out and our feet on the coffee table, Hannibal grooming between us. "Andy seems to like Bridgit."

"It's mutual." They seemed to *click* soon as they met on Wednesday, splashing in the hotel pool and chatting at meals…and Bridge *loved* the attention. "He's not *that* goofy all the time."

"If you *say* so." Andy let out a big whoop when the chaplain said: *ladies and gentlemen, introducing David and Elizabeth Clawson.* "I think Mom and Dad have gotten over Dean."

"*I* think so. Nice how the chaplain *did* that." She started the service with *we are gathered together in the sight of God, this company, and the departed Dean…* "Never heard *that* before."

"Me neither." We watched a car pass on the street, parking in front of the next building. "So, Elizabeth Ritter Clawson: is your *evil twin* as happy as *you* are?"

"She *has* to be," she groaned, stretching her back and legs simultaneously. "If not, *too* bad."

"You dismiss her that easily?"

"It's *gotten* easier. When's our flight?" We were going on a five-day honeymoon to Santa Catalina Island, courtesy of the SPD, the IRS, and the 511th, who all chipped in for it. I also got bumped from GS-10 to GS-11 that month…so I'd finished the training program. I *believe* Julia and Ellen got bumped, too.

"11:45."

"Good." She downed her water and stood up, pulling my hand and ignoring Hannibal, who looked up in alarm. "*Time enough* to ravish each other as husband and wife, sleep late, have breakfast, and get to the airport."

"One more thing," I asked. "What *did* you tell that guy at Hale Brothers when I got my furniture?"

She smiled, still pulling my hand. "Cindy *Hale*; her family *owns* that store."

✳✳✳

I sat at the edge of the chair, my elbows on my knees, my chin in my hands. Beth slept in the bed next to me, a cannula in her nose.

It was just before dawn, the Thursday before Christmas, 1982.

I tried to imagine what I was feeling. It wasn't like we were *trying*; just *do-de-DUNK* when the spirit moved us…often. By Beth's math, we conceived in mid-September…*plenty* of opportunities.

"Can I *get* you anything," a nurse asked, looking in from the door. I shook my head, uncertain of my voice.

Beth shifted. We'd got the *good news* three weeks before.

And last night…

Julia crept in the door, smiled. "How *is* she," she whispered.

"They knocked her out," I sighed. "She'll be down for hours."

"C'mon, Davie." She stood me up with little effort. "Get some coffee." We walked to a cafeteria, mostly empty.

We didn't *talk*; we didn't *glance*.

We drank coffee.

And I *still* didn't know what I *should* have been feeling. "What training do we get for *this*, Jules? Where do I *go* for a course?"*

"The same place you went for Dean, Davie," she smiled sadly. "Your heart."

"But I *knew* Dean; I *didn't know* the baby."

"Use *that*."

Later, I held Beth in my arms, and we cried for the child that we would never *know*, never *see*, never *hold*, never *feed*, and never *be proud of.*

Never ever.

---

* FBI agents were *on a course* of instruction about every third month. Most lasted a day; some a weekend; a few several weeks.

The DeVere/Wier Clan

Or, We Start to Get Somewhere

"**W**ell, *hell*," Julia sighed, "didn't expect *this*." What she *didn't* expect was champagne at the Friday dinner that Beth and I were hosting. Once a regular ritual for *three* in the same building, now for *six* scattered around town.

Tony had popped the proverbial question the cold January night before. The way *they* told it, Tony Junior—called TJ, then 12—asked Julia, "*when* are you gonna be our *real* mom?" They *had* lived together since school started.

Julia answered, "when your dad *asks* me."

Awkward moments ensued until Tony asked Kevin, a precocious ten-year-old, "do you *want* Julia for a *real* mom?"

He answered, "Sure; she *cooks way* better than *you*."

So...

"Congratulations," I grinned, hoisting my champagne glass. "Have you set a date yet?" Beth, bless her, hoisted *her* glass in celebration: *her* recovery was not *yet* complete. Christmas in Zanesville had been *quietly* joyous.

"No," Julia sighed. "I haven't got a *ring* yet."

"Well, don't *waste* any time," Ellen said. "Rope him in with a ring *yourself* if you *have* to, Jules."

"Are *you* trying to tell me something," Sam grumbled. "If you *want* to...."

"*What*," Ellen shot him a glance. "If I *want* to *what*?"

"OK," Sam declared, putting his glass down. "*Now* you've *done* it." He threw his napkin on the table, got down on bended knee, and… "*please* marry me, Ellen Constance Drew, and make me a *happy* man." Sam's sense of humor was as raucous as Julia's—easily greater than Ellen's.

"*What*," Ellen drew back in *mock* surprise, "*this* is so *sudden!*" We'd come to know Ellen's looks and dry humor; *this* was rehearsed.

"*Bullshit*," Sam grunted. "We've been dancing around *this* since Christmas. Now, say *yes, damnit*, and get me off my *bad knees*."

"You *must* ask *Father* for my hand," Ellen declared. She feigned a *haughty* impatience, complete with eyes closed, chin high, and her arms folded across her chest.

"I'll ask him for your whole *ass*, Ellie! Now say *yes!*"

Ellen genuinely laughed before she grabbed Sam's face, planted her lips on his, and declared… "*maybe*. Ask me *later*."

"How *much* later," Sam asked, a distressed look on his face.

"*Later*…later," Ellen declared with a grin.

"After *this*," Sam roared, scooping her up in his arms—Sam was a *huge* guy, bigger than Ernie—whisking Ellen into the living room.

Hannibal, alarmed, dashed upstairs.

There followed a *do-de-DUNK*-worthy soundtrack for our benefit before Ellen hollered, "*yes*, OK, *yes!* Now put me *down and give me back my underwear!*"

Catch bad guys we *didn't* often, but have fun we *did*. And for effect, occasionally like Yoda, we thought.

✳✳✳

"OK," Ernie declared, "*Julia* has an item to add." After Monday's Wheel Game, the Working Group gathered in Room 200 for the first time in a month. Ernie's prediction about the Working Group *was* accurate. A little more than a year into it, we spent *maybe* twenty hours a month on it instead of 120.

"I got a letter from JJ: he's at Fort Bragg. Anyway, he mentions something called the Second Century Fund that he heard about at Wolverine…"

"Yeah," Frank mused. "I ran into *that* in the material from Detroit." He scratched out a note. "Let me look." Frank and Julia were on the financial end of the investigation, looking into who *owned* the joint.

"That *brochure*," I said, "the one you got in Chicago…."

"*Yeah*." She perused the Xerox copy of the item and grinned slightly when she reached the line that haunted me:

Parents and Guardians of At-Risk Young Men: Ask About Our Second Century Fund.

"JJ says that the worst bullies at the school were somehow associated with the Second Century Fund," Julia said. "Lawyer Ben Dietz suggested that it was some kind of a slush fund."

"*Ah*," Ellen nodded, looking in her working ledger. "Something… Helen, *you* found something…" While she was on the Four Horsemen who raped Eddie Evans, she also sifted through new material like the rest of us.

"I *did*," Helen declared. Still technically with DEA, she was thinking about transferring to the Bureau. Her husband and kids liked our more-or-less 9-to-5, home-*most*-weekends environment more than the chaos of DEA fieldwork. She was almost *certainly* in the training program. Grace *had* transferred and moved her family to Manassas. "I saw a stack of those brochures at the county courthouse, right here in Virginia."

"*Yeah*," Julia asked. "How would they…?"

"I asked the clerk: she said they're put there by the courts; judges offer that place as an *alternative* to juvenile detention."

"Explains some of JJ's stories, fits with Bielefeld's account," Julia said.

"Yeah," I said. "And *SCF* shows up in association with FFA in a couple of files, like Future *Fascists* of America," I said, consulting my working ledger. "Wolverine's paying a *student group*?"

"Not necessarily *students*," Julia mused. "There are no names attached in the Liberty Bell File." She paged through her ledger. "Here's…*huh*," she grunted distinctively, as in *oops, ah-hah!* "*Here's* something I'd neglected:"

File Number Ending 31875-LIB
Name: New Falangists in America
Date Identified: 12 September 68
Origin: Montcalm County, MI, ca. 1965, associated with Greenville MI PD. Sylvanus Baker (b. 1947) (att.) and Junius Watson (b. 1946) (att.) thought to be founders.
Narrative: Identified as being in existence after the arrest of two members for blackmail and obtaining money by threat. Postal inspectors became involved when the mails were used to transmit threats. No known direct association with GPD, but heavily suspected as their denial of knowledge suspicious.
Updates: 1970: New member initiations discovered by county sheriffs in Greenville area. Two initiates thought to be from Francis Hartman School; returned there by sheriffs. Second Century Fund said to supplement their tuition.
1971: Members Luther and Boehlke (no details) associated with Future Fascists of America have similar ideological goals: social change by violence. Appear to be well funded.

"Mitgang's group got *this* from Lansing."

"Well, we can add to *Luther's* file," I grumbled, "*and* Boehlke's. When do we actually go to Greenville?"

"When we've got enough to know what to look for," Ernie replied patiently. "If the owner of Wolverine is as wired into that area as we *think* he is, going in too early could queer the whole case. Poking around the edges seems to be safe for the moment until we know more."

"Providing it's a *he*," Morgan added.

"Providing *that*, yes," Ernie added. "Now, let's get on these latest revelations, clear a few of your *other* files out for the week, and meet again next week."

When the Working Group wasn't taking precedence, our mandate remained the clearing of Liberty Bell Files.

✳✳✳

"Captain…um…" I stuttered. One of the names of former Wolverine students we got from Adam was Ramdas Brahmaputra-Reynolds, who, as fortune had it, was in the Army and stationed at Fort Belvoir at that time. I *couldn't* figure out how to pronounce his name.

"*Reynolds* is enough," he grinned and nodded pleasantly. "Call me *Ram*."

"OK, Ram. I got your name…."

"…from Adam Block's queries," he interrupted. "I *wondered* how long it would take law enforcement to get interested in *that* place."

"Well, *this* long," I sighed. "I grew up in Michigan, and I never *heard* of it till I joined the FBI." He had pale blue eyes and short-clipped hair; his uniform was immaculate, his voice clear. He spoke four languages and was said to be the *best* intel analyst in the business. So…*softly, softly catchy monkey.*

"Where?" *He is the very model of a Special Forces officer…*

"Hell." *With information vegetable, animal, and mineral…*and the rest of that silly song.

"Down by Pickney, yeah? I drove *through* there once."

"*Blink* and you miss it."

"Yep. So, what can I do for you?"

"Well, *you* were there…'69-70, yeah? Tell me about the place then."

He made a face. "Get *specific*, man. You *must* have read my statements." *Chit-chat phase over.* "I did. Tell me about *your* Delight Night."

"Nobody in *my* room got reamed. I knew *of* a dozen or so." There was a finality to his words that was both off-putting and reassuring. There are people who, with a few words and gestures, can make you feel at ease. Some people can make you absolutely certain that, after *one* false step, you *would* be *dead*. Ram could do *both* with a grin and a nod.

"Why do you imagine *that* was?"

"There was a black kid, an Asian kid, and me—black and Pakistani—in my room. That I know of, *no* black or Asian kids *ever* got it on Delight Night or got *most* of the *kind* of treatment that the white kids got." He shrugged. "They didn't want the attention of the brothers."

"The…brothers," I mumbled, scratching down a note.

He made an amused face. "*Black* brothers, man. Messing with brothers just *wasn't* done. Because I'm *half*-black, *I* was protected." He shrugged again. "Didn't keep me from getting cropped sometimes, just not as *often* as white guys and *not* so it showed. I got a kidney infection from getting hit when I was there, and they sent me home for a while…but I came back, and it was just…" He shook his head. "Wier and his gang just had a *great* time."

"Wier," I repeated. "JJ Elrath's roommate?"

"*Was* he? We *talked* about that place a little: we were at Brookfield junior and senior year. Didn't say any *names*, though. I saw him at Bragg a few years ago."

"I saw him in Panama last year."

"How's he *doing*?"

"He *seemed* well enough. But you were saying about Wier…."

"What *he* said, *went*. I don't think he ever *hit* anyone; he just *ordered* it done. Wier had a hand in that and all the other bad shit at Wolverine." He grimaced. "*With* exceptions. *You* should talk to Roman Caulfield."

"Fellow student?"

"Leader of the brothers when *I* was there. *Nasty* bastard, but under *his* control, *we* were protected." He looked thoughtful. "The way he put it was, 'we protect our own and whoever we get *paid* to protect.'"

"Any ideas as to where we can *find* this guy?"

"He wanted to be called *Romanus Africanus*; he was from Missouri. That's all I've got."

I pushed the list of Future Fascists at him. "Recognize anyone?"

"*All* of 'em," he sighed. "Stutz. Called him *The Hammer*; tall, dark, and stupid." He read for a while. "*Pale*. Good marksman; the only *sport* they had there." He read off a few more, their foibles and sins. "And Boehlke and Doyle and the rest of those assholes." He looked at me sideways. "This case of yours gonna *go* somewhere?"

"I think so," I said as casually as I could. "Got a lot of time in it now."

"If you can end that place, you'd be doing a lot of *future* guys a favor."

"No-Names?"

He made a face. "Those guys in Patton Hall? Couldn't tell you anything other than they had their *run* of the place: wherever they went, everybody just stopped and waited for them to leave. *Two* of 'em could stop a rumble with a glance. *Did*, too, once or twice." He looked thoughtful. "Couldn't swear to it, but I think Wier used to talk to them sometimes. *Maybe* Roman, too."

Well…maybe we should find Romanus Africanus…and Wier…

✳✳✳

We were at the Hampton Square Mall in Bay City in the spring of '83 to clean up *three* Liberty Bell Files: The Juvenal Society, the Believers of the Sun, and the Kabbalists of America. Bay City PD had files on all *three* outfits. "Hey: what's *that*," Julia asked, pointing at a dedication tablet. We were in the mall because they kept their Whack-Job Files in their mall annex. The mall was about half-empty, so they got the space cheap.

"What's *what*," I answered, looking.

"*That*," she said, pointing. The tablet read…

Construction and Development
by Newhouse Properties, Inc, of Bloomfield Hills
Made possible by a grant from the Second Century Fund
Parkinson Title and Trust, Facility Managers
Fischer and Ally, Attorneys At Law, Ferndale, MI,
Counsel for the Developers

"We can't get *that* lucky," I mumbled, scribbling the information down. "*Another* trip in Detroit."

"Yeah. I *should* try to talk to Grampa Charlie. He's giving *everyone* hell because I said our wedding's not to be *here*. 'Bride should be married where she's *from*,' he's screaming. '*Nothing* from me if it's not *here*.'"

"I didn't think you even *liked* the guy...."

"I *don't*," she sighed again, "but he raises holy hell with my dad and my uncles over it whenever it comes up. I'll *try* to shut him up."

"Want me to put the cuffs on him?"

"Now *there's* a thought."

***

"Agents Parkinson and Clawson, SPD, for SAIC Demeter." We were at the Detroit Division's new digs at the Patrick V. McNamara Federal Building. Though we'd actively used the Troy Agency, we'd never actually been to the Detroit Division, but they'd *finally* said they had some information of interest a year after *The Call*.

I suspect *their* tardiness was because we'd *been* in Michigan several times, talked to—and tasked—the Troy Agency, but *hadn't* come to kiss-the-ring, as *expected*. Some SAICs were like that: territorial. Bureaucracies—like families—have politics, and the FBI wasn't above them, even if SPD was. When *we* were involved, petty bureaucratic pissing contests were a definite *no-no*. *This* office would have to be educated, or reminded, of the power of *The Almighty Washington*.

On *this* pleasant spring Friday afternoon with the promise of a mild weekend, we waited...and waited...and waited. SAICs usually came-a-running...but not *this* one.

After *many* minutes of cooling our heels in reception, a middle-aged African-American woman came through a side door and *curtly* said, "*come* with *me*." She led us through the busy open-plan main office and past several open-door side offices to a conference room. "*Wait* here," she said...and left.

No offers of refreshments, no explanations, not even *please*…just *wait here*.

Maybe they knew our *guns* had more time in the Bureau than we did…

After *many more* minutes, a woman of Mediterranean extraction came. With a bored glance, she asked, "*what* can I do for you?"

"You're SAIC Demeter," Julia said, offering her hand. "I'm Special Agent Parkinson, Special…"

"I *know* who you are," Demeter declared, irritated and ignoring the offered hand, "and *you* know who *I* am, and I *know* what you came *for*. That *freak show* called Special Projects sent two *flunkies* to carry some *bullshit* files. They'll be ready in an *hour* or *tomorrow*. You can *wait here*, or you can *come back*. *Your* choice."

"Ms. Demeter," I said quietly, "we're from the Wolverine Working Group…."

"*Unless* you *came* from *The Ascended Christ*, as long as you've got the *stink* of *Harris* on your ass, you can *wait your Goddamn TURN*."

And she turned and stalked out.

"*Stink* of *Harris*," I whispered. "Someone doesn't like *Dusty*."

"Guess *not*," Julia sighed, picking up the phone, punching buttons. "Sir, SA Parkinson…*yessir*, we're there *now*. SAIC Demeter isn't *exactly* cooperative *or* congenial… *yessir*, we did…called us *flunkies* from a *freak show*, sir, and mentioned *the stink of Harris*…I *see*…I understand… yessir; we'll *wait*, sir." She hung up. "*Apparently*," she sighed, "Demeter was transferred out of SPD after a couple of months: *Dusty* was her SSA. Sued the Bureau afterward; got *this* job as a settlement." She grinned wryly and said, "sure glad I *didn't* get Detroit."

A line on the phone flashed a moment or two later. There was some indistinct shouting, then, about fifteen minutes later, *another* agent—an Asian-American woman—entered. "I'm Lorie Yang. I've *just* been made SAIC here. Your material will be ready shortly. Is there *anything* I can do for *you* in the meantime?"

"Do you have anything on Newhouse Properties or on the Fischer and Ally law firm?"

"I'll check." Lorie hesitated, then turned for the door.

"What *happened* to…?" I started.

"*SA* Demeter has been ordered to report to Anchorage *Monday*," Lorie said. "She's to be the Senior Resident at Point Barrow."

"*Point Barrow*," I muttered. "*That's* on the *Artic Ocean*…"

"Can't *go* any further north and still be in the US," Lorie answered, relieved that we *didn't* call for a whipping post.

Solely for the instruction of the others, you understand.

✳✳✳

"How can I help the FBI," Oscar Fischer smiled oleaginously. Long-term exposure to the denizens of the DC area was excellent training for dealing with lawyers like Fischer, who was about as genuine as a three-dollar bill *or* a typical Congressman. Uncle Max *was* a rare exception.

"You can start by telling us of your relationship to the Newhouse organization," I began. "How long have you represented them?"

"*Many*, many years," Oscar nodded. "*Good* clients; good *people*."

"Uh-huh." I hid my surprise because that question was *chum. Never thought he'd take that bait.* "Know anything about Wolverine Military Academy in Greenville?"

"No. Should I?"

"You *claimed* that you represented their Alumni Association."

"I don't know *who* would have…."

"Adrian Newly." He didn't flinch. "How about the Second Century Fund?"

"Now *that*," Oscar changed his expression slightly, "I *can* tell you about. It's the name that a private party uses to invest without too much muss or fuss. I happen to be a *trustee* for the Fund; we do a great deal of business developing malls and the like. I'm not *that* involved in operations; I just vote on…."

"As a trustee, according to the law, you *have* more than a *vote*." I drummed my fingers. "A *great* deal more. The Second Century Fund has some hooks in Wolverine," I declared quietly. "People pay *it* to take on boys that no other school will take." I didn't *know* that, but it was more chum…

"As I *said*…."

"As a trustee," I went on, "the IRS wants *very much* to speak with you; this afternoon, in fact."

Oscar's face changed, but *not* in a helpful direction…more like defiance. "*Bluff away*, young man," he huffed. "Now, *I* have work to do."

"Although your brother-in-law's in the IRS office downtown, I've arranged for someone *else* to come by. Great guy, if a *little* anal-retentive. He'll be here at *precisely* one this afternoon…unless you have something *constructive* to say in answer to my questions."

Oscar's face changed to something more *helpful*: resigned helplessness. "Wh…what do you want?"

"Wolverine: *who* owns it?"

"No *good* idea," Oscar breathed. "Mr. Newhouse *apparently* knows, but *I* don't."

"Second Century Fund: who's in charge?"

"Not sure. I just lend my name. I don't have *anything* else to do with it."

"Future Fascists of America?"

"Nobody wants *anything* to do with them. *Savage* brutes…"

"*Who's* in *charge*?"

"I don't know."

"Who *does*?"

"*Probably*, Mr. Newhouse."

I stared at him for several moments…a technique called *Silence*. It generally unnerves a source, especially one that's already scared. Julia, who hadn't said anything yet, opened her jacket with her genuine barracuda-grin, shifting to smooth her skirt. "Romanus Africanus. Roman Caulfield," I whispered. *More chum…*

"What *of* him," Oscar answered.

Huh? "What's your relationship to him?"

"He used to be a voice on the other end of the phone. He called *here* for several years."

"Called about *what?*"

"He gave me a name and a phone number. I called the number and passed the name on to whoever answered."

"*Local* numbers?"

"Just as often long-distance." We knew about the incoming calls for the past few months, but not their content. We had seen a *hectic* phone pattern at the offices of Fischer and Ally, one that didn't fit a two-partner law firm.

"Second Century Fund," Julia asked sweetly. "How does it work?"

"I get an envelope through the mail slot—*not* through the mail. I sign the forms and use the enclosed envelope to mail it."

"Sign what?" I tried to sound unconcerned.

"Forms authorizing disbursements."

"How *much?*" Julia crossed her legs.

"*Millions.*"

"How *often?*" I crossed mine.

"Once a month or so."

"*When* was the *last* time?" Julia bundled her hair.

"Two weeks ago."

"You *know* you're a patsy, right," I grinned.

"I know I get a fat envelope stuffed with used bills a week or so after I sign. More than *this* place pays *me* in half a year."

Julia placed our cards on his desk. "*Next* time, you'll let *us* know."

✳✳✳

"*Mr.* Wier," Morgan began pleasantly. "*Pleased* to meet you." We met with Edmund Wier at his once-prosperous farm machinery business, an establishment that was *now*—to be *fair*—dated. Most of their for-sale equipment was either used or rebuilt; the showroom a museum of old tractors. For planting season in corn country, he was suspiciously *un-busy.*

Chuck's family appeared in a Liberty Bell File that had been bouncing around the SPD for a few years…

File Number Ending 68904-LIB
Name: DeVere/Wier Clan Finance Network
Date Identified: June 16ᵗʰ, 1956
Origin: Thought to be from old Scottish money; apparent HQ in Greenville, MI. Connected individuals include Edmund Wier (b. 1921), McIntosh Wier (b. 1923) and Charles DeVere (b. 1920)
Narrative: A financial empire in numerous states associated with the financing of trafficking of all manner of goods throughout the Great Lakes. Several sources (depositions attached) claim that DeVere/Wier can finance anything.
Updates: 1960: Organization known as Second Century Fund said to have coordinated financing with DeVere to purchase property in NW Michigan.
1962: Greenville Investment Trust of Detroit, MI, said to have obtained financing from Wier/DeVere.
1968: Greenville Investment Trust audit shows no connection to DeVere/ Wier.
1970: Second Century Fund may have acquired Wier/DeVere Finance Network

"*My* pleasure," Edmund sighed, "but I don't know *what* I can tell you. I haven't *seen* my son in some years." Edmund either seldom needed to wear his newer, classic pinstripe suit, or he'd *just* bought it.

"*That's* what you said," Morgan smiled. "Any idea *where* he may be?"

Charles Fredrick "Chuck" Wier had been a Wolverine legacy—both his father and grandfather had graduated from there—attending from 7th Grade through 12th, and graduating in 1972. After graduating from Perdue, he went to work for his father and dropped out of sight in '77.

"*Not* a good one," Edmund nodded. "His *mother* misses him."

"Care to talk about your connection with Greenville Investment Trust?"

Edmund managed to *not* react to that question. "No, I'm afraid I *can't* help you with that."

"*Mr.* Wier," I sighed. "*This* isn't your sole source of income. You also own a big piece of Greenville Seat Belt, *don't* you?" The new factory on the southern edge of town employed hundreds…a new business that somehow materialized out of thin air and came to Greenville for no discernable reason.

"My family does, yes," Edmund agreed. "*That's* a matter of public record."

"Second Century Fund, Mr. Wier," Morgan leaned forward, her voice husky.

That, however, rattled him. "Where…where did you get *that* name…?"

"*Tell* us about it."

"It…it's a financial entity that we…used from time to time." Edmund genuinely began to sweat. "It's…I don't know *where* it came from. I knew enough *not* to ask. But we haven't communicated with *them* since '77."

Something in my head went *click.* "The same year that Chuck took off, and you broke ground on the factory," I said with a modest grin.

"Why…*yes.*" Edmund suddenly looked genuinely stunned that he, himself, had never made the connection.

"How did you contact them?"

"By telephone…"

✳✳✳

"OK," Ernie sighed expansively. "*Two* numbers were in Detroit; one was *never* used. No in, no out; disconnected a year ago. But we know who the *subscriber* was, and we know that the subscriber had several *other* numbers added when *these* were disconnected."

"So end the suspense, Ernie," Harry lamented. "*Who?*"

"A *very interesting* connection, my children: NP Investors, the last shell company in the Wolverine chain before it goes overseas. It has a PO box in Detroit, which has a physical address in…."

"Ferndale," I blurted. "Fischer and Ally."

"*Close*," Ernie smiled. "*Another* law firm: Rockland, Atkins, Terrance, and Schumpeter in Detroit."

"Who," nearly everyone in Room 200 asked at once.

"Who *indeed*," Ernie declared. "A *well*-set-up and a *well*-connected bunch of ambulance chasers disguised as a law firm. Former partners of that firm have been governors; some *are* governors; *some* have been disbarred. We shall have to tread *very* lightly when we look at *that* outfit."

"But," Harry grunted, "we *can* trap their lines."

Ernie nodded. "Can, will, and *have*."

"OK," Ellen asked, stretching her arms. "What about the other numbers?"

"One was used sparely and disconnected in '77…interesting timing. The same *day* ground was broken on the Greenville Seat Belt factory."

"There were *three* numbers," I asked, all innocent…

"Yeah," Ernie screwed his face up in a scowl that meant *this is confusing*. "The last number is in Berryville, Indiana." He stared around at us. "Anyone ever *heard* of it?"

"Yeah," Julia said, nodding. "It's where my Grampa grew up."

"On a farm south of town," Ernie said, "consisting of three quarter-sections on Route 9."

"Um…yes, I *think* I remember that. I can call Dad…."

"Currently owned by the Hayes family."

"My great aunt, but I never met *them*."

"*Good*. Because that last number is for a phone booth across the road from that farm."

"*Mr.* Caulfield," I started, speaking softly. Finding Roman Xavier Caulfield was as easy as following his social security number with the IRS. Three phone calls and we found him, aged 35.[*]

"*Brother Claudius*, if you don't mind," Roman Caulfield smiled. "I'm more used to *it.*"

"*Brother*, then," I nodded. There was a serenity to the small alcove off the grand square of the Missouri monastery, a *peace* I wasn't used to. Our office was seldom silent, with a teletype, phone, copier, or something else hammering away all the time. But the *townhouse*...I learned early that Beth liked music...*often.* "I spoke to Ram...."

"*Did* you," Brother Claudius grinned. "And *how's* my favorite Zoroastrian these days?"

"He's fine. A captain in the Army now."

"Ah. I *knew* he'd do well. What can I do for the FBI?"

"About Wolverine, and about the Second Century Fund."

Brother Claudius flushed briefly before recovering some composure. "*That's* why I became Brother Claudius," he managed after some moments.

"So you're no longer aspiring to be Romanus Africanus."

He nodded appreciatively. "*Good* research, Agent Clawson. No, I'm not. When I got *these*," he pointed to his nasty scar across his forehead and another on his right hand, incongruous on his otherwise smooth black skin, "I escaped from my captors and found refuge in a storefront church in St. Louis. The pastor hid me under his altar table; I stared at the cross for days while...."

"Who was after you?"

"Competitors," he smiled sadly. "A rival gang."

"Rivals to *who*?"

"You know, I never really knew *who* they were. I was just hustling the streets, but once in a while, this guy...."

"Gave you names and numbers to pass on?"

---

[*] The Church allowed him to call himself anything he liked, but the 1040 for his paltry stipend needed his *legal* name. The Church *ain't* the French Foreign Legion.

"*Yes.*"

"What were the names and numbers *for*?"

"No good idea, but I got a grand each time I called."

"How often and where?"

"About once a week; area codes all over. Called from payphones…."

"In Indiana?"

"Around St. Louis."

"So…Wolverine. Ram said you were paid, by *someone*, to protect certain people. Who paid you to protect John Elrath?"

"Wow," he chuckled. "Never thought I'd hear *that* name again." He looked out at the grand square. "My senior year. *After* he was pitched out the window, strung up by his wrists and beaten, I was given instructions that Elrath was not to *die*. I *was* to *allow* punishments, but *not* enough to cause permanent harm."

They didn't want the protection to be known. "How do you account for the *timing*? Someone *had* to have…."

"*Someone* got the word out. It was *possible*…"

"Who *told* you?"

"I took orders from different, ah, entities." He breathed deep, fiddled with the cord of his robe. "The orders on Elrath came from Wier."

"Huh," I said noncommittally. "Ever *talk* to a No-Name?"

"One, a couple times. He tried to outbid Wier. He never came *close*."

✱✱✱

"Clawson," I answered into the phone, wearily. Beth had been up and down all night, going to the bathroom and either throwing up or the *other*. I had no idea how *her* pregnancy would affect *me*.

"Agent Clawson," the voice answered, "Grover Fischer. I got an envelope."

"OK…" It took me a moment to make it register. "Oh! Did you contact the Troy office?"

"Yes. *They* said that the copies are on their way tonight, but you wanted me to call *you*."

"Yes…yes, OK. Did you *mail* the envelope already?"

"Yes, your colleagues *said* I should." Silence. "My partner may become suspicious, Agent Clawson. He's *not* involved in the Second Century Fund, I don't *think*, but he *is* involved with the Newhouse firm."

Cutouts; deniability. "We should minimize *our* contact, then," I sighed.

By then, we were trapping fifty-odd lines related to Wolverine, though not yet including lines to and from the school. Some lines made scores of calls every day, and some never made any. But *once* in a while, a quiet number would get an incoming call or make an outgoing, then get disconnected.

One number Fischer and Ally often contacted to an outfit called Parkinson Title and Trust, listed as defunct since '69. However, they still had four functioning phone lines. Two lines frequently called the law offices of Rockland, Atkins, Terrance, and Schumpeter; Two others called Fischer and Ally *and* the Newhouse firm *a lot*.

Defunct firms aren't *supposed* to have active phone lines.

A week later, the Great White Father in the White House made us work harder than we *ever* had before…and on *nothin'*.

Berryville, RFD

Or, Bearing Down HARD

The sun is burning in the sky
Strands of clouds go slowly drifting by…

"**W**hat are you *talking* about," I sighed into the phone. I discovered that *sleep* and *new baby in the house* were *not* compatible concepts. Dean was born the Sunday before Memorial Day, just before I got *that* call.

"I've got this bulletin that says to watch for anyone named *Neitelsmidt*," the voice repeated. "So I'm calling you *now*. We…"

"*Back* up, OK," I begged. I swallowed *more* bad coffee and hoped the voice on the other end didn't hear. Beth developed preeclampsia at 34 weeks, and we went through some harrowing days before she was induced at 36 weeks. "First: *who* are *you* and *where*?"

"Special Agent Rachel Cook at the South Bend Resident Agency." A week before *that* morning, Ernie's son had been injured in a shootout in Philadelphia, and Ernie was still there.

"South Bend…*Indiana*," I repeated, the clouds clearing. On top of *that*, we were seconded to the Counterintelligence Division* that March after Reagan announced the Strategic Defense Initiative—the *nothin'* I mentioned earlier. "OK, *got* you fixed in my head. Forgive me: new baby at home."

---

* Abbreviated CI within the Bureau, just as *Special Projects* usually dropped the *Division*.

"*Ah*," Rachel said with *tremendous* empathy. The SDI might have been derided in the press as *Star Wars*, but the Reds went after that stuff like baby poop to diapers. "My *husband* sympathizes. I *just* had my *second* three months ago."

"I'm sure," I said, "but, OK, *what* now?" To be frank, my attention to work had been *obliterated*, SDI aside. This was my *second* day back to work, and I hadn't even *thought* about Wolverine *or* Neitelsmidt all *month…*

"Three nights ago, we *arrested* a Ned Neitelsmidt…."

"*Hold him until we get there*," I told Rachel…loudly.

"But…" I didn't *hear* the rest; I was too busy getting Ellen and Morgan moving. Our teams had been shifted around; Julia was working with CI then.

In retrospect, it would have saved a great deal of time and trouble if I'd *heard* the rest of what Rachel had to say. But I was only triggering on certain things just then, and *that name* was one of 'em. The other was my need for rest, and *that* was *not* about to happen.

∗∗∗

Now the sun is in the west
Little kids go home to take their rest…

"He's *where*," I asked, not *quite* believing what she said. The flight from DC to Indianapolis was short, but at least I could get some rest. We'd landed at nearly 10 at night, drove up to South Bend, and got a *bit* more shuteye on a bed-of-nails in a little Motel 6.

"Out on *bail*," Rachel repeated patiently, glancing at me, Ellen and Morgan in turn. I've never been able to sleep well on airplanes, but at least I wasn't awakened every hour, *on* the hour by a needy little voice who, despite being my beloved first-born son named for my late brother, was beginning to *irritate* like a politician on the stump.

I blinked at Rachel, glanced at my companions. "But you *said…*" I'm not sure just *how* childless women regard new fathers: exhausted, frustrated, frightened, and not sure *what* we're doing with the squalling little bundles of fussy/messy joy who were *supposed* to be the center of our attention for *part* of every day for the rest of our lives. I believe they look upon us with either empathy or contempt. Or both.

"*…just* enough for you to hang up," Rachel interjected. "If you'd stayed on the line, you'd have *heard* he was released yesterday morning." Women *with* children regard us as either useless appendages who *contemptuously* sleep through the hourly feedings[*] or as willing helpmates just as deserving of credit/empathy as moms. Or both.

"OK," I sighed. "Where *was* he?"

"Elkhart County Jail," Rachel said, "just down I-90."

"Let's go."

Deputy Davis presented the paperwork with alacrity at the jail, apparently impressed that *The Almighty Washington* wanted something *from* him. Either that or the young man was trying to hit on Rachel, in *terrific* shape after two kids. Beth was struggling to get back down to 110, let alone her wedding weight of 95.

We studied the paperwork on Ned Neitelsmidt:

Born 1956, Tempe, AZ; no wants, no warrants. Arrested 17 June 1983 for…

"No *wants*, no *warrants*," I said. "We've had an alert out on *that name* since '81." I may have been sleep-deprived, but I remembered *that* much.

"Yessir," Deputy Davis answered patiently, "on *George*, not *Ned*. Our system isn't tied to the Federal database yet."[**]

"So, how did *you* get the flag," Morgan asked patiently. Her Jerry was back from overseas but was not feeling well, and no one knew why, so *she* was a little frayed around the edges, too.

---

[*] Beth *tried* to nurse, but neither Dean nor she took to it, so *I* was up every *other* hour.

[**] This would be a persistent problem for another few years.

"Backwards, ma'am," Deputy Davis answered. "We arrested seven men and three women at the I-90 toll road oasis in Berryville on suspicion of trafficking in untaxed cigarettes and methamphetamines. Ned Neitelsmidt had *four* ID's on him." He showed us a xerox with images of four driver's licenses with four *names* from four *states* using one *picture*. "Then we got a *local* hit on his prints." He showed us *that* ID: a current Indiana driver's license with the same picture. "He did *not* have any contraband and didn't resist, so the judge set a $10,000 cash bond, and his wife posted it yesterday morning. I contacted the FBI because…well, *something* wasn't adding up. *One* picture, *five* IDs, and he got *bailed?*"

"Where's the bond paperwork," Ellen asked, and was handed a separate file. It contained a copy of the driver's license of the woman who provided the bail…in cash…

"Not far off *her* range," Morgan smiled, looking over Ellen's shoulder.

"Nope," Morgan said. "And *still* on the game."

"Yep," I said. "Holly's *Molly* Neitelsmidt now. And a *redhead*. Address in Berryville."

Now the sun is sinking low
Children playing know it's time to go…

"Who do we *expect* to find," Rachel asked. We were in a utility service truck parked near a small substation, watching the Berryville address just across the road. We'd knocked on the door, but there was no answer. It was nearing midnight, and the crickets were out in force after a dry day.

"*I* suspect…no one," I sighed, waiting for any sign of habitation in the little saltbox house. It was on a quiet street a hundred yards from its nearest neighbor, just two minutes from I-90, the county line, and the Michigan border. The nearest street light was two hundred yards off. A *perfect* place to hide out again and again. "They *may* be using the address for a dead drop."

"Yeah. Rachel says you guys are from Washington," Deputy Davis asked. We brought him with us as a reward: not every sheriff's deputy would have put *that* together.

"Yep," Ellen drawled. "Sodom-on-the-Potomac. You're from *here*?"

"Next town over," he answered. He was about 25, with short, dark hair and a tough beard. "Only time I've left Indiana was two weeks at Interlochen in '74."

"That music camp," I asked.

"*That's* the one," Deputy Davis answered. "Two weeks of playing scales." He sounded disappointed. "*Almost* got laid, though."

Morgan and Ellen choked; Rachel batted at him. "*Ignore* him," Rachel sighed. "He's just a brother-in-law with an imagination."

"*I'd* like to hear it, though," I snickered. "What *else* we got to do?" On a stakeout/surveillance, it's easy to get bored…and sleepy. You avoid getting *either* by telling stories…true or not.

"Yeah," "Sure," my partners said.

"Not much to *tell*," he declared. "Rachel and I went to Interlochen after 11th Grade."

"*Had* to *say* that, *didn't* you, Red," Rachel sneered. I couldn't tell if it was good-natured or not. "*OK*. We were an *item* then; his *brother*—my husband—is a year older. I played violin; Red played…."

"That's your *name*?" Ellen tried to settle on her stool.

"No: *Ethelred's* my *first* name. Folks call me either *Davis* or *Red* or *Hey-You*. Anyway, we practiced twice a day, had a concert every *other* day. The rest of the time, it was just a camp by a lake."

"Yeah," Rachel sighed. "One night after lights-out, we snuck out with a bunch of other kids down to the lake. Well, I *wasn't*…."

"*Willing*," Davis added, "I sorta *pushed*…we were a little ways away from the rest…."

"And here *I* was with this cute boy, so we *started*… in a *kid's* way…."

"Until the counselors started flashing their lights on us," Red chuckled. "We never *got* any closer than *that*."

"I got interested in his *brother* after that," Rachel declared.

"That's the way it goes sometimes," Ellen said, "but you *both* went into law enforcement."

"Yup," Rachel said, shifting on her milk crate. "We kept *that* in common."

"And your parents didn't *like* you, Red," Morgan asked, "hanging *that* name on you?"

"*Family* name," Red said. "Been in the family for…*hello*."

"*Hah*," I said, watching an old Ford Galaxy pull into the driveway. It stopped in front of the dilapidated garage, shut off the lights…then nothing.

"Watching *us*," Ellen suggested.

"*Could* be," Morgan agreed. "Let's…door opening…" A man got out of the driver's side, big and broad-shouldered. He stuck his head back in the car.

"If they're *watching* us," Ellen asked, "should we *oblige*?"

"Wait," Red suggested. "Not *us*: the *house*." It was a long few minutes before we saw a bare light flicker in a window.

All four doors opened. Three men and two women walked up to the house. The front door of the house opened silently; no light came out. The door closed; no lights were shown in the place.

"*Huh*," I said, my *what-the-hell huh*. "Could be a tunnel entrance," I suggested.

"Or a time portal," Morgan sniffed. "Something *else* is going on."

"Let me try *this*." Red pulled a big gun-like thing out of his kit bag. "At least *seven* people inside," he said, looking through it. "Here."

It was my very first look through a real-time thermal imaging device sensitive enough to see body heat through walls. I saw science-fiction-looking shapes moving around, flares of cigarettes, and hot spots—lights and hot water pipes. I could distinguish between men and women in profile, but no more. "Wow," I said, handing it to Morgan. "Sees through clothing."

"And *one*, I think, is pregnant," Ellen sniffed.

"Yep," Rachel agreed. "We *should* object to the child being exposed to second-hand smoke."

"If we need a reason to knock on that door, *that's* as good as any," I declared. "But, let's go do a *bond address check* instead."

"A *what*," Red asked.

"*You're* going to perform a *routine bond address check*," I said. "Since *you're* the local *gendarme*, *you* get to do it."

"Never *heard* of it," Red said. "Never…"

"*Not* so *loud*," Rachel told him. "You'll *wake* the *neighbors*."

So Red knocked on the front door…and nothing. Knocked *again*, louder. Still nothing. While we waited, I looked through a window: painted over on the inside except for a tiny sliver, covered by a curtain. Light was escaping only on command. "Sherriff's deputy," Davis called loudly. "Bond address check. If you *don't* open up and identify yourselves, your bond will be forfeited, and I'll have to force entry."

Moments later, the door opened—*this* time, light shot out like a beacon—and a pregnant Holly/Molly appeared, silhouetted and in a half-open shirt and underpants. "What's *this*, now," she moaned, her belly swelling out from under her shirt.

"Bond address check, ma'am," Red declared. "We check newly-bonded person's address to ensure the accuracy of the bonding agent's information. Now, ma'am, if you'll show us your identification."

We were standing away from the door—I doubt if she saw us—but I *knew* she could *sense* us. "Just…*just* a minute; let me get my wallet." She appeared again: what was left of her modesty was guarded by a single *too-low* button. "Here," she leaned over, proffering her driver's license.

Now, *most* young men would have been distracted by the display. But Red flashed his light on the license, checked it against something he'd had, and handed it back, ignoring what Holly was displaying. "Thank you, ma'am. Is *Ned* Neitelsmidt at home? I need to see him *at* this residence *with* the ID he produced for his bond."

We didn't *prompt* that…good thinking on his part.

"He…he's *here*, but he got drunk, and he's sleeping it off. I don't want to…he gets mean if I try to wake him up."

"I'll restrain him if it comes to that, ma'am," Red continued. "With your permission, *I'll* wake him…."

"No," Holly said quickly. "No: *I'll* do it." She started to close the door.

"*Please* leave the door open, ma'am, or I'll *have* to come in." Red covered his weapon swiftly. The rest of us in the shadows did the same.

"What…oh," Holly sighed. "Yeah. Come on, or you'll let the bugs in."

This was a crucial moment. *We* had no *lawful* reason to go inside that house. But, there were at least seven people inside, enough to easily overwhelm a single deputy entering on a bogus pretext at our behest. Red mounted the two concrete steps and stepped across the threshold…

"*Go*," Morgan declared: she was technically in command, so the decision *was* hers. I was right after Red—it just *happened* that way.

"Say hello to the FBI," Holly yawned to those inside the house. There were three men in a tiny living room to the right, a man and two women in a little dining room on the left. All were surprised to see *us*.

And Holly, in a little hallway under a small chandelier…her enigmatic grifter face and her belly covered in stretch marks…

The most surprised was a face in the living room we knew only from his photograph, Ned Neitelsmidt. "*Mr.* Neitelsmidt," I loudly declared, "*stand up* and identify yourself, please."

"*Who* the *hell* are…?" was as far as *he* got.

"Special Agent Clawson, FBI," I declared.

"Just…*get up*," Morgan said. "The rest of you, *please* stay where you are and leave your hands where we can see them."

"Lady feds," an older man in the kitchen said. "*That's* one for the books."

Ned—or whoever he was—stood slowly, his hands about waist-high. "What's the *Fed* want with *me*," he asked quietly.

"Just…slowly…get your ID, please," Morgan asked. "Just don't move *anything* faster than you are right now."

He reached into a front pocket and pulled out a money clip. He peeled his license out of the back, holding it out. "Here…" he reached for his waistband…I stepped left and reached for my weapon…

> *Now the sun has come to Earth*
> *Shrouded in a mushroom cloud of death…*

There are times in your life when everything seems *crystal* clear. Dean's birth and Beth's laughter afterward…are clear to this day.

> *Death comes in a blinding flash*
> *Of hellish heat and leaves a smear of ash.*
> *And the sun has come to Earth…*

The next few moments in that little house will always be frozen in my mind…I *never* heard anything *so loud*…or *felt* anything *so…I'm sorry, Beth; I didn't mean for us to end like this…I know I promised…I'm sorry, babe…*

> *Now the sun has disappeared*
> *All is darkness, anger, pain, and fear…*

Booming; yelling; flashing lights; *screaming* sirens … a kaleidoscope of sight and sound…

Simon and Garfunkel ended, and David Clayton-Thomas started…

> *And when I die*
> *And when I'm dead, dead and gone,*
> *There'll be one child born*
> *And a world to carry on…to carry on*

Funny, the stuff that goes through your head when you die. Dean, two *days* old, grasping my thumb…Pulse-ox 90 percent…he's in *defib*…we're *losing* him….Three Dog Night lip-synching…

Before the breathing air is gone
Before the sun is just a bright spot in the night-time
Out where the rivers like to run
I stand alone and take back something worth remembering…

Something worth remembering…only my dying will tell…one child born…I told Beth I wouldn't get killed on this job…AGAIN! CLEAR!…Amp bicarb, NOW!…CHARGE to 200…NO! WE'RE not gonna end THIS way, babe…I need a different size thread for the working rigging on Constitution…

*IN…out…*But I hadn't *worked* on *her* since we had to consolidate Beth's sewing/workout room with my hobby room to make the nursery. *That hobby shop in Mechanicsville with high prices has that thread….*

ONCE more…IN…out…

But there was no light, no images of loved ones gone before…

Just a monumental effort to breathe…

✳✳✳

Soft…soft…breathe…what the hell is standing on my chest…breathe…so tired…breathe…what's that I hear…lights…what…breathe…what…?

I glimpsed a stack of IVs hanging above me; heard a steady *beep…beep…*

Where the hell am I? Breathe…

A rough-faced *somebody* in white flashed a light in my face. "He's *awake*," the face loudly declared.

Breathe…

There was Beth, smiling, her lips touching my cheek. "*Hi*, sweetie," she whispered. "*Hi*."

"Hah" was the best I could do, with the respirator and all.

Breathe…

"You're OK, sweetie," she added. "Don't *try* to talk."

Breathe…gotta think about it…breathe…why…

"Dave: you're in Notre Dame University Hospital," the face shouted. "*Don't* try to speak; just *blink*. Understand? *Once* for *yes*."

I blinked.

Breathe…

"*We love you, sweetie*," the face said…I *think*…

   To her Cheshire smile, I'll stand on file…

***

Breathe…

A white and fuzzy world. I didn't feel *anything* but the *weight* on my chest.

"*Haack*," I said, *unnaturally* loud thought I, "*Water*," I complained.

Breathe…

Suddenly there was ice in my mouth. It was hard to focus, but I sensed Beth and someone *else* at my side…and a small *shitload* of others within earshot.

"*Hey*, sweetie," Beth declared. "I *knew* you weren't going *anywhere*."

"*You'd* be *pissed* if I *did*," I grumbled hoarsely, raising a hand, painfully, breathing gratefully. She laughed and repeated it louder before the room was filled with laughter.

The doctor did that thing with his flashlight again and asked, "how do you *feel*, Dave?"

"Like something *landed* on me," I groaned.…*breathe…*

"You were shot twice in the chest…" *breathe…* "but your chest plate* stopped *both* bullets."

"Yeah," Beth added, "two .44 Magnums at *about* eight feet."

---

* Did I mention that we were wearing those new vests with the quarter-inch-thick cold-rolled steel plates in the front? Those monstrosities that no one wanted to wear because the plate weighed as much as the rest of the vest and was hell on your shoulders? Yeah, we were.

241

Morgan appeared. "You had us *going* there for a while, Davie." She squeezed my hand. "*You* went down like a redwood tree: slow-motion."

"Shit," I sighed....*breathe*... "Anyone *else?*"

"Me," she pointed to a bandage. "Creased my cheek. Rachel caught a through-and-through in the shoulder."

"The *rest?*"

"*Four* dead; two wounded." She seemed indifferent. "*You* hit one."

"Oh." I felt weary. "How *long ago?*"

"Almost *two* weeks," Beth said. "The vest saved you, but it broke your breastbone. Your heart *stopped* for a while."

And when I die... "Neitelsmidt?"

"*Holly's* OK; Ned's *not*," Morgan added. "Red's gun at *that* range..." The Elkhart County sheriffs were *over-armed*. At household ranges, their Colt .45 automatics or less *could* blow a hole through *two* people *and* a plaster-and-lath wall...his *did*.

Morgan stepped back, a hand on her shoulder, and Dusty appeared with a concerned face. I never saw him other than either *concerned, jovial,* or *pissed*, but every mood started with *concerned*. "Dave: the *Director* has expressed *concern* about you..." ANY agent injured in the line of duty is worthy of the Director's *concern*. "So has the AG *and* the President..." *Whoa: Reagan's moved to concern himself with a humble SA?* "...because of your *extreme* heroism. It's not *every* Agent who will step in front of a gun to save a pregnant woman."

I did? Really? When? Breathe... "Thanks, sir," I wheezed, "I appreciate...."

"Time *you* called me *Dusty*, son," he said. "They're trying to decide whether to give you a Shield of Bravery or a Medal of Valor."

I managed to *remember* to ask, "*Dean?*"

"At the hotel. Today's *my* mom's day; tomorrow, *your* mom."

In between sleeping cycles ver the next week, I touched hands with Red, Rachel—arm in a sling—Ellen, my family, Beth's family, and a LOT of people I did *not* know. I got more business cards than I could remember faces.

Finally, Holly came. "If it's OK, I named him David." She had a pretty smile; so did her baby. "I'll *tell* your people what I know. But first: the *name's* pronounced *Smith* when you *know* that's *not* the right name."

It was the key to the mystery of the Neitelsmidt moniker: a way into *that* world.

Two .44 Magnums In the Vest is *not* an approach *I'd* recommend.

✳✳✳

"We got more in *three days* in that house than we have in *two years*," Morgan sighed, "yielded a *ton* of information and *millions* in cash."

"So did *Holly*," Ellen agreed. "Information, *not* the cash."

By July, I no longer had to *think* about breathing and checked in at the office once or twice a week. I was off the painkillers, *finally*, but I'd always set off metal detectors because of the hardware that mended my sternum. My summer off was punctuated by Mom, Rose, Bridgit, and Fiona, who took weekly turns helping Beth with Dean *and* me. Hannibal took to purring in my ear when I napped on the couch, so I figured she'd accepted me.

That summer, Beth and I reached a *not*-difficult decision. After her two *failed* and one *nearly fatal* pregnancy, my vasectomy would be in August. Family members who *didn't* get a kid's name would have to just suck it up. "So, what *did* we find?"

"It was a transit stop," Morgan declared. "One stop on a *long* circuit. Holly was a *minder* and a *cover*."

"Right," Ellen said, pushing a sheaf of xerox copies in front of me. "At that house, people would drop one identity, get *another* somewhere else, or vice versa. For the most part, *never* both in the same place…with *one* exception, we *think*. *This* one," she pushed three IDs at me, "is the *only* one with *three* pieces here."

I studied the IDs, all showing more or less the same picture. One was a Michigan driver's license issued in 1962 to a Robert Kevin Newman, born in '46. The second was an Indiana ID issued in '70 to an Edward Foster Forsythe, born in '52. The *third* was an Illinois driver's license issued in '75 to a Timothy Norman Whalen, born in '46.

"They'd handled *hundreds* of people, as far as we can tell," Ellen said.

"And Wolverine," I asked.

"A common destination for *younger* guys," Morgan said. "At least a hundred in the past decade."

"How'd they connect?"

"*That* we don't know," Ellen answered. "We know the names of *some* who took on new IDs, and we know *some* of the new IDs that were adopted. Other than this Newman/Forsythe/Whalen character, we've got *zip* to connect to. We're running *all* those names, but *Newman* dropped off the edge of the *Earth* in '70."

"And there's *this*," Julia added, pushing a file at me. "Leigh Elizabeth Taylor was married to Randy Newhouse in '73. They were separated and annulled before the ink was dry on the license, and she joined the Army. Now, here's the kicker: the Newhouse clan—using Fischer and Ally—has been trying to get her to come back to Randy since '74, claiming that they had a child together in '71."

"What's *that* to do with...?"

"Look who *else* makes a *lot* of calls to Fischer and Ally."

"Wier Equipment; Greenville Seat Belt; Wolverine...Francis Hartmann School for Girls? Who are *they*?"

"A school in Greenville. It seems that there are more *adoptions* out of there than there have been graduates of the school."

"School for wayward girls?"

"Something like that. Fischer and Ally appears to be handling most of those adoptions." Julia sighed. "*Why* would a little two-man shop in Ferndale have so many clients in Greenville? And look at *this*...."

The Fischer and Ally phone logs showed steady traffic with Rockland, Atkins, Terrance, and Schumpeter, at *least* as far back as the technology of the time could go. "Fischer and Ally is a front."

And this Taylor woman and Randy's kid? Leverage, maybe?

✳✳✳

"Like I said in the class," Bob Bell declared, "when you're writing reports of surveys, you need to *avoid* coincidence." Bob was a Reservist from the Detroit area, aspiring to be a HUMINT warrant officer. He was *teaching* the reports-of-surveys part of the company officer's supply administration course I was in. "Coincidence is a sure-fire way to get a survey kicked back or audited."

"So, how do you avoid it?" I was well enough to fulfill my annual training requirement at Fort Belvoir later that summer. I *should* have taken it *before* since I'd been the 511th's executive officer for a year. I'd invited Bob to our place—with advanced notice to SWMBO,* of course—for a relaxed dinner. He was an intelligent guy about the same age, blonde and blue like JJ Elrath, but not as beefy. "I mean, it just happens sometimes."

"Yeah," Bob replied, "but write *around* it."

"What do you do in real life?"

"Tech writer; I contract to the auto companies." *Then* he said, "Deb just got a letter from her friend Ann in Japan. They had been wondering where their high school swim-teammate, Leigh Taylor, had gotten to, so we were looking *her* up. She's in the *Army*, we think."

"Leigh *Taylor*," I repeated. "Swim team…*when*?" I whipped out my credentials. "*Kinda* official. Deb's your…?" With my Medal of Valor hanging on the dining room wall, it would have been hard to miss the fact that I was in the Bureau, but I hadn't drawn attention to it before.

"Girlfriend. We *might* get married sooner or later, " Bob answered. "But *that* was before I knew them. They won the state championship for the medley relay in '70. Why?"

"If I was to get you a current address for Leigh Taylor, can you get your girlfriend to talk to us *about* her?"

"Probably." Bob regarded me with suspicion. "About *what*? And *who*

---

* She Who Must Be Obeyed, of course.

is *us?*"

"Nothing *you'd* be *involved* in, nothing *dangerous*. *Us* is the Bureau."

"Her *marriage*, maybe?"

"You *know* about that?"

"I know it didn't survive the wedding night, but *that's* second-hand from Deb. I went to a *different* school, so I don't *know* anyone involved."

"OK. I'll see what I can do about an address." *I could have it with a phone call...*

Sometimes we find ourselves having to decide if and how to deal with a *friend* as an *informant* if the information is worth the risk to the friendship.

***

"*Sir*," the officer said with a nervous lilt to her voice, her hand *politely* hovering over her pistol. "*Please* stand still and *keep* your hands visible."

Though the Greenville Public Library was nearly deserted, I was in my shirtsleeves on that warm October day. The librarian *probably* became alarmed at the sight of my pistol on my hip. We were in Greenville because a public library invariably has a collection of local school yearbooks. Hence, I was being braced by a Greenville Police officer named Diggs. Another officer, ten feet away, held *his* weapon at a safe angle.

OK, I screwed up. Just don't shoot me again! "Officer," I answered calmly, "I'm with the FBI, My credentials are in my right chest jacket pocket." I nodded toward a chair on the other side of her partner. "Your partner can reach in there."

Diggs seemed to relax; her partner, wary, glanced back and forth at me and the path he took toward my jacket until he pulled out my badge. "Got it, Melissa: *he's* good."

Visibly relieved, Melissa seemed to deflate slightly. "Can *I* see, Bill," she asked, still eyeballing me. She glanced at them before she passed them to me. "*Thank* you, Agent Clawson. Is there anything *we* can do for the FBI?"

"*Behind* you are Special Agents Drew and Towne," I said, nodding at Ellen and Morgan between the shelves behind the officers and lowering my hands *slowly*. Every law enforcement professional knows that *this instant* is *the* most dangerous: *relieve* tension only to *add* to it.

So I kept my hands visible.

"*Always* check your danger zones, officers," Morgan said. "We had you dead-to-rights *before* you braced Dave."

Embarrassed, both officers grinned. "Good thing we're all on the same side," Bill answered.

"We're just doing some research," I said, "Looking for some background on fugitives who went to *school* here."

"Which school," Melissa asked. "I've lived here all my life, went to Francis Hartman…."

"We're interested in Wolverine," I said. "Know anything about *that*?"

Melissa and Bill once again eyeballed us with suspicion. "No," she replied, putting a card down on the table. "If we can *help* the Bureau in any way, let us know," she said, turned and left.

"Have we let *another* cat out of the proverbial bag," Morgan grimaced, watching them leave.

"Oh, *yeah*," I replied. "If the owners of Wolverine are as wired into this town as we *think* they are, we're *blown*."

✳✳✳

"Are there *any* real estate records that *aren't* in big, dusty books," I asked the next day. The booming metropolis of Stanton, Michigan, was but twenty minutes and change from the *slightly* boomier metropolis of Greenville. Stanton *was* the county seat, so *that's* where the real estate records were.

Morgan sneezed, wiped her nose, and answered, "wish there *was*; my dust allergy's *killing* me."

"Someday, they'll *all* be computerized," Ellen said, coughing slightly as she pulled out *another* volume.

"Huh," the clerk sniffed haughtily. "*That* would take *some* doing."

"*Here*," I declared. "County Section 33, Tracts 8504 through 9201 with improvements, sold to Greenville Investment Trust, May 1959." Which *was* Wolverine. Out of the corner of my eye, I watched the clerk pick up her phone while holding a piece of paper. I mumbled, "mark the time."

"Check," Ellen answered. There was something *not right* about the clerk's demeanor, particularly her occasional furtive glances in our direction. Sometimes, you just get a *feeling*...

"And *here*," Morgan inhaled deeply just before she sneezed again. "County Section 43, Tracts 9302 through 10,252 with improvements, sold to Greenville Investment Trust December 1962." *That* was Francis Hartmann School for Girls.

"Same owners," I declared, closing up my notebook and cocking my head as the matronly clerk chattered on. "*Let's* get back to Lansing." Of course, Lansing was *not* where we went, but the Michigan Bell Central Office outside Greenville. *You* know, where we'd already set the traps.

Twenty minutes later, we were standing in front of the clerk's desk, smiling broadly. "*Mrs.* Gustafson," I asked, *ever*-so-cheerily, "*who* do you know at the Law Offices of Fischer and Ally in Ferndale?"

"Why, I..." I flashed my credentials, which she *hadn't* yet seen. Real estate records being a matter of public record, we didn't *have* to let everyone know *who* was looking at *what*...until now. "I don't *understand*," Mrs. Gustafson sputtered, "I *merely*...."

"Called Fischer and Ally as *soon* as you heard Dave talk about that first property," Ellen added smoothly, smiling. "I *saw* you, ma'am." Ellen was good at that: adding *just* enough torque to the thumbscrews to loosen most tongues. "Now, *who* wants you to call when you hear *what* names?"

"I didn't ask *who* he was," Mrs. Gustafson sighed. "He walked in here in a suit worth more than my mortgage payment, handed me ten hundred-dollar bills, and gave me a list of names…."

"What *kind* of names?"

"*Names*. Said, 'call this number if *anyone* asks or *mentions* these names.' He handed me another stack of hundreds and said, 'have *all* your friends do the same.'"

"When was *this*," Ellen asked.

"A year or so ago, I think."

"*Try* again," Ellen sneered. "We have you calling *that* number as far back as 1970." It was a bluff; there was no way to trace phone records that old, nor much older than a few months. Not *then*, anyway.

But it worked. "All *right*, all *right*. I've been here since '58, and the *first* guy came in here the *first* time in 1960 or so."

"*First* guy, *first* time," I asked. "How many guys; how many times?"

"That I know of, three men; the first one twice a year since *then*; the others two or three times, when the first guy *didn't* come. No names, just lists and bundles of cash."

"When was the *last* list?"

She eyed us suspiciously. "Why?"

"*When* was the *last*," Ellen pressed.

"Two months ago." She handed over her paper.

> *Greenville Investment Trust*
> *Wolverine Military Academy*
> *Francis Hartmann School for Girls*
> *Newhouse Properties, Inc.*

✳✳✳

We needed help watching Greenville, and the nearest FBI office was the Lansing Resident Agency, an hour away. The Lansing Federal building was surprisingly unimposing for one in a state capitol; sort of squat and dull, really. Then again, I thought *Lansing* was rather squat and dull.

We got there mid-morning that Wednesday. Morgan enquired of

the receptionist, a slight Hispanic woman, who called in back. After a few minutes, a tall man emerged with a genial grin...just a *little* greasy. "Good morning," he announced. "Eric Winter, SRA. What can I do for Washington today?"

"We've got a logistical problem," I said, shaking his hand and introducing us. "Need your help."

"Come on back," Eric nodded. He led us past maybe thirty cubicles, of which twenty were occupied. "We're a *small* shop," he explained, "but we'll do what we can."

"Our working group is running phone surveillance up in Greenville," Ellen declared. "We need someone to collect phone logs."

"Huh," Eric grunted, gesturing to chairs in a small conference room. "*I'm* not sure I've got the manpower. How *often?*"

"Weekly," I said. "Not more than that."

Eric fiddled with his overwide tie. "Where?"

"Central office is outside Greenville."

"*Huh,*" Eric sighed. "So, an hour each way, and then we'd need to inter-office the printouts to you?"

"That's about the size of it," I said.

Eric, distracted, seemed not to hear, studying something on his jacket sleeve. "Not sure I've got the *manpower* for that. We're a small office, but we're busy. If you could get us maybe two more agents..."

"Might be possible," Morgan smiled, her winning *I can do anything you want, Sugar*, smile. She'd talked *me* into a lot of things with *that* smile. "Maybe some *loans* from..."

"No, *not* loans. Until I get two more *permanent* agents, not sure I can help you." Eric studiously avoided looking at us directly. "Now, if you'll *excuse* me..."

"Looks like he's found a more artful way to say drop dead," I said softly in a few minutes later.

"Yep," Morgan sniffed. "Used my best hook on him, too..."

"Short of stripping," Ellen murmured. "*That* might be too demonstrative."

"Not to mention desperate," I said. "Wonder how short he really *is* that he can't spare somebody three hours a week?"

"Let's find out," Morgan said, stepping into the elevator.

The marshal's office was just a few floors down. The chief deputy—a small woman named Pat Henry—said, "Winter doesn't put himself out any further than he *has* to."

"Is he *that* overworked," I asked.

"I'll put it this way: I get more requests for assistance from every other agency *in* this *state* than I get from the FBI in Lansing."

SRA Winter played office politics—bartering for manpower—by brushing off a request for assistance like so much lint from a new suit. *Not* a great career move—not exactly *Point Barrow* material, but certainly *Omaha*.

Still, we came away from that Michigan trip with a *whole* lot more to work with. The yearbook pages we'd copied at the Greenville Library had photos of the teenage versions of *everyone* we were looking for…*very* handy.

***

I hadn't been part of many bridal parties before that late September of '83—Steve's and my own—but I was in Julia's. They'd waited this long because Tony's mother—one of the boy's sitters—had been ill, and JJ had been in Colorado and out of leave…and Jules *wanted* him there.

Tony's boys were ushers. Jules called me her *Man* of Honor and Ellen her *Lady* of Honor. JJ had been *suddenly* called to Grenada the Tuesday before, winning a Silver Star and getting promoted to E-6.

Some people just have *different* priorities.

There were only a dozen guests at the wedding, including Julia's parents. The *reception* was a pretty big blowout. Freddie—TJ's guest— drew everyone at least once. Jules and Tony went to Bermuda for a week afterward.

That was fun, but there were about a gazillion different things we had to follow up on that fall and winter. In the way of the SPD, we worked methodically, painstakingly. We gathered evidence and built criminal referrals that were so air-tight nothing could escape, and no one would question our methods or sources. It would have been easier if we knew who was in charge of Wolverine, the Second Century Fund, and all those other outfits we were chasing. And *if* we could get close enough to find out.

Judges sent *At-Risk Young Men* to Wolverine. I was coming to believe—but I couldn't *prove*—that the Second Century Fund was *how* they *bought* their way in.

✳✳✳

We subdivided the work—no one person could be an expert on all of it. Morgan, Ellen, Frank, and I were the team's experts on the guys who *went to* Wolverine. These included the Four Horsemen and the Three Assholes—JJ's roommates Herman Jimenez, Chuck Wier, and Jay Pardon. Collectively, they were The Knuckleheads. Julia, Ed, and Tom led the financial end, looking for the owners and financiers of a network created, it seemed, for hiding people.

We found Lucas Luther early. He had joined the Marines and was killed in May of '75 off Koh Tang Island, rescuing the crew of *Mayaguez*. At least he *died* with *some* honor.

We *found* Testa...*sort* of. We had a visit from a DEA buddy of Helen's and a CIA *handler* of defectors named Larry Phelps a few days after we put out *The Call* on Testa. Estavo Roberto Testa Cruz was in *Luz de Guía*—Shining Light—a mad-dog pack in Latin America. Estavo was *last known* to be working for the Medellin cartel of Columbia. He was known to have killed at least fifty people in ten countries and was wanted all over the hemisphere.

The trail on Boehlke went cold after '71 when he graduated from a private high school in Chicago. There's no record of him using his social security number after that, and he never filed an income tax return. Eyerdam went back to his native Oklahoma, got a diploma from a school in Tulsa in '71, and went to a trade school. Then *he* vanished, like Boehlke, having never used *his* SSAN again. There was no record of either of them applying for another.

That made *them*, in our trade's vernacular, *in the wind*. And it was *too* coincidental to *be* a coincidence since they went cold within *weeks* of each other. That left us with Jimenez and Wier.

Herman Jimenez Ortiz had been a *hit-scout* for drug lords in Miami. But he scouted a *wrong* shot and spent the next two years *hiding* at Wolverine, working first as muscle and then as a shot-caller. By '84, the Miami Division had him working in a sweatshop on the edge of the Tamiami Trail, *suspected* to be involved in human trafficking.

Wier was *in the wind*, too.

We had tentatively tied the Newhouse organization to Wolverine and the defunct real estate outfit that Julia's grandfather had owned. From there, it went to shells…and shell games are *not* fun.

More mazes, more cheese. But we *knew* where *one* of The Assholes *was…*

❊❊❊

"*You're* a new one," Jay Pardon said when he glimpsed me in the spring of '84. He was in a red jumpsuit with leg irons chained to handcuffs, shuffling around in paper slippers on the cold linoleum floor. "What do *you* want?"

"*Chat* about things, Jay," I replied. Jay was domiciled in the United States Prison at Marion under tight scrutiny because he'd shanked a guard there just a few months before. He was initially imprisoned for drug trafficking on federal property in Korea. "Just…chat."

Jay regarded me as if I were a lump of meat. "*Chat* away." He had a sharp face, an angular, pointed nose, and a chin that seemed to project beyond it. As his hands were chained to the table between us, I could see that they were powerfully delicate, like the burglar we knew him to be.

"Want to tell you a *story*, Jay. A story about *you*." He didn't twitch. "Your family had money, but you wanted your *own*. So, you developed an ability to jimmy locks and doors, and you found buyers for the jewelry you made off with. In February of '70, you burgled the home of the Flint GM plant manager and ran off, on instructions from your fence, headed for Berryville, Indiana."

We'd spent the past year culling information from multiple places, putting just enough of *this* and *that* together to come up with *this* part of Jay's story. The house in Berryville helped to put *most* of the pieces together.

"But at fourteen, you were *not* ready for life on the run. Berryville told you that Wolverine Military Academy was an option you *might* have... so you should *volunteer* to go there. *That* would preempt that juvie hall you *knew* you'd go to when you got home. So, you went to Wolverine in September of '70."

Jay yawned...nervously. We'd guessed at how he landed in Berryville that winter, but he *was* there: Holly had pictures of *several* guys who ended up there. She also *overheard* things.

"You were told to tell *someone* that you were willing to do what *certain people* told you to do to get by."

He blinked...and started to sweat.

"You knew *who* to talk to, who to say *what* to, *and* you knew about those guys *without* name tags."

He swallowed hard.

"Then came Delight Night—your *first* test. You and Herman Jimenez held Eddie Evans down while Eyerdam, Boehlke, Doyle, and Testa raped him, for which you have *never* been held to account. How am I doing so far?"

He shifted in his folding chair uncomfortably.

"So *those* four guys got thrown out because Elrath—the guy on the top bunk that saw the whole thing—spilled his guts. You and Jimenez got orders from Chuck Wier: get Elrath to take it back."

I waited while he stared first at the door, then craned his neck. "Don't know *what* you're talking about."

"The brothers told you not to hurt him *too* badly?" *Turned to stone, Jay?* "You stayed at Wolverine for another two years. Then you graduated and went to work for the outfit that backed your play while you were there. And they *were*…?"

"I don't.…"

"Yeah. OK. You learned a *special* skill: combining high-level alkaloids into *very* potent combinations. Then you got a job in Korea as a maintenance welder. Here's the catch: you've never welded *anything* in your *life* but one kind of dope to another one. In '83, your luck ran out, and you were sent *here*."

He just stared.

"*Second Century Fund* begat Chosin Exports, the container company you were contracted to work for in Korea. *Second Century Fund* was your protection at Wolverine. *Chosin Exports* sent you to Korea to make and pedal drugs, *not* weld containers."

This was a wild leap of logic, but we figured it was worth the risk. Julia had guessed at it only a week before. Jay was a cog in the machine, and *not* a critical one, at that.

We *thought*…

He closed his eyes slowly. "What…"

"What did *Forsythe* promise you to shank the guard? The *Forsythe* who you *knew* at Wolverine, who you led *into* Wolverine?" *That* tidbit, to *us*, was four *days* old.

"Shit," he said, *quite* involuntarily, shaking his head. "I thought… what do I get for the answers?"

Cons never *give* anything away. "Maybe a reduction to life…for a plea."

"But *that bastard* walked away! He…if I *ever*…."

"If my *uncle* had *tits,* he'd be my *aunt. What* did *he* promise?"

"Ten grand."

"Think he was good for that?"

"Based on what he *told* me, on what he knew about *who* and *how* he knew, yeah."

"Which was…?"

"*I* knew him first as a No-Name called *Forsythe.* That *screw* knew him someplace else as *Newman* and *here* as *Whalen.* The *fact* that *Forsythe* was *alive,* he said, was *dangerous* to a whole *lot* of connected people. *Me,* he could pay off. The *screw*…not as easily."

"So he turned to *you* for help, and…?"

"So he and I did the CO. Then *Forsythe* ratted *me* out and…" He looked at me suspiciously. "He's in The *Rat House,* yeah?"

"Can't *say.* You can't get him there."

"It's not *impossible,* but…" he stopped. "*Impractical.*"

"You know something about getting *that* done?"

"I *might,*" he was suddenly wary. "Get me out of lockdown, and I *might* know *something.*"

"Tall order, in *your* case. Killing a guard in a Federal lockup's serious shit." Pardon was a model prisoner except for shanking that CO, so the penal authorities were puzzled. "Second Century. Speak."

"My family had to pay into it."

"How *much?*"

"Can't *say,* really. A *lot* the first year; less after. That's the impression I got from my old man."

"And you graduated and went to work for Chosin Exports."

"They sent me to junior college for basic chemistry, then I got *specialized* training: combining opiates with cannabis products."

"Then…"

Jay might have been a cog, but he could connect Second Century Fund—which protected *at-risk young men*—to Chosin Exports, Limited. And whoever the *hell* owned *them* probably owned Wolverine. All we had to do was find where they *started*, other than a PO box rented by a succession of shell companies.

We'd filled *ten filing cabinets* tracing Wolverine-related shell-within-shell companies, like those Russian dolls. There simply weren't enough whiteboards to hold them all.

Jay connected *two* of the most persistently *unconnectable* dots. Dots that we *thought* connected Wolverine to Newhouse and the Second Century Fund…but not *firmly enough* for a criminal referral.

Future Fascists of America

Or, Getting to the Heart of the Matter

"**M**ayor Doyle, thanks for meeting with us," I began lightly. We were in his office in Bloomington, NY, a pleasant though *lackluster* little borough. Getting to that remote town in January of '85 was a picturesque reminder of my youth's snowy Great Lakes winters.

Aside from Wolverine work, we had *other* assignments. One of *my* side gigs had me in Boston interviewing Barbara Walker, ex-wife of John Anthony Walker. I thought her story had too much detail to be dismissed as drunken rantings. Based *partly* on my interviews, FBI Counterintelligence prepared criminal referrals for Walker—who turned out to be America's most devastating spy—that winter.

"You're welcome," Bruce answered. "The State's Attorney made it clear that I *should* talk to you. Those photos you found would be embarrassing if they became public without *context*."

"*Indeed*," Julia added. "We have some questions about Wolverine."

"Well, I'm an *alumnus* of that august institution, like my father *and* my grandfather…" Bruce began. Like many politicians, he was somewhat pallid and thin of face, accustomed to being made up and in front of hot lights. He hosted a weekly local-origination cable show, "Talks with the Mayor," with a regular audience of at *least* three households. "Sir," I smiled, "you *were* expelled in October of 1970…."

"A *clerical* error," Bruce answered smoothly, pointing to his framed diploma on the wall, one of many. "See? Graduated."

"And your family *did* settle the lawsuit with the Evans family in '74," Julia said.

That rattled him. "I...*that* was *sealed*. *How* did you even *know* about...?"

"John Elrath is my uncle," Julia declared. "*And* we *spoke* to Adrian Newly."

"*That's* enough," Bruce declared dismissively, reaching for a file on his desk. "Agent Addison, I *know* about you *and* your mother in the Oakland County Sheriff's Department. Don't think I can't just make a *call*...."

"I wouldn't *threaten*, Mayor Doyle," Julia grinned widely. "It *is* a crime...."

"To *discuss* making phone calls? *Don't* make me laugh." He looked at me with a snide grin, reaching for another file. "*You*, on the other hand, Agent Clawson, are an *easier* target. Your wife at the IRS? Think she's still a good fit there after *all* that sick leave? And your *father's* business? You know *that* can vanish, too, yes? All *I* need do is spread a *little* manure."

Then I understood why his lawyers stalled for so long. They spent that time on a respectable counterintelligence job, getting whatever they could on *us*. "All further questions will be directed to my attorneys." He stood. "*Use* those pictures at your *peril*, you bureaucratic *puppets*. Now, *get out of here* before I have you *thrown* out."

"OK," I sighed, getting up. "*Thanks* for speaking with us. But *now*..." I added, opening his door, "*these* friends of ours want to know *how* a town of less than a thousand souls pays half a million a year to a *full-time* mayor."

"*What*...?" Bruce gulped, starting to genuinely shake.

"*We* ask the questions, *Mr.* Doyle," Bull Thatcher declared as he walked in the door, flashing his credentials. " IRS. And *we've* got a *lot* of ground to cover, so please, have a seat, and let's get started, *shall* we?"

"*Well*, Agents Clawson and Addison," Bruce said quickly, loudly as we left, "we'll talk again soon. I *know* things you *need*...."

Whatever these boys don't get, Brucie-boy, we will.

***

"My attorney assures me that anything *I* know is long past the statute of limitations, so fire away." Two days later, we were back for a *chat* with a chastened but still defiant Bruce.

"*We* want to know about the Future Fascists of America," I smiled, "*and* the Long Knives."

An instant before, he looked like we'd just asked him for the time. Now, he looked like he was on Death Row, and *I* was the preacher. "What *about* them?"

"You were one of the founders," I said.

"Leaders *lead*; followers *follow*," he shrugged. "*Point* and say: '*sic 'em.*' We just gave 'em a name."

"I see," I said. "So, who's *we*?"

"Eyerdam and Boehlke, Testa and Luther, and me. We sat around one night, dreaming up what to do with our little army of slave-bullies, then I think it was Eyerdam who asked, 'what would we have them do after we all leave *here*?' *I* said, 'they might be the core of *fascism* in America,' and Future Fascists of America was born out of boredom." There was a *sneer*, a *lilt* to his voice that said *who the hell cares about them?*

"And the Long Knives?" I tried to keep from sounding like I wanted to beat his smug face in.

"Ah, *them*," he shook his head. "Strutting assholes. I never understood how perfectly reasonable people could be so *ugly*."

"You were one of them," Julia said.

"I joined any outfit that would protect me."

"But you couldn't join the brothers.." I started.

"Wrong skin color, but I *did* pay them for protection, as well."

"So, tell us about Last Night at Wolverine. How did *that* work?"

He looked puzzled. "*Last* Night? Nothing to do with the FFA *or* the Long Knives, not directly. We didn't form FFA until '68, and Last Night had been going on for years *before* that."

"Tell us, anyway."

"Well, like it says, it's the last night at the school, and things get a little crazy, as you might imagine…."

"Guys died," Julia said.

"I don't know *anything* about *that*," he answered coolly. "There was a lot of shaving cream, a lot of TP and water, but…."

"People were clubbed," Julia pressed, "it was revenge-time."

"I suppose it *could* have come to that."

"Tell us about Pills."

"*Who*," Bruce squeaked before he cleared his throat. "*Oh*, yes. Our Provost-Marshal. *What* a joke. Pushed *him* out of the way whenever he *interfered* with punishments."

"Because *that* was a *battalion* matter," I said, trying sarcasm.

"In*deed*. Discipline was for the *student body*, *not* for the school."

For the inmates, not the guards. "So, you didn't *allow* interference."

"No, and the FFA was supposed to help *enforce* that…for all the good they did *me*, obviously."

"So, *your organization* failed you?"

"That *rat* Elrath spilled his guts to the cops, and the Greenville Police came for *us*. That *Evans* kid…nobody *told* us his family had *that* kind of money and influence." He looked wistful. "But, the district prosecutor came to *understand* that *me* and a *criminal record* were *not* a good match. My family paid the Second Century Fund *good money* for that diploma." He gave us a derisive smile. "*And* because of Elrath, they learned they needed a better *handle* on the police."

"Who's *they?*"

"The Second Century Fund. *They* greased the necessary palms."

"The No-Names?"

"I didn't *want* to know about them."

✳✳✳

Leigh Elizabeth TAYLOR Petitions for Annulment of Marriage to Randall Fred NEWHOUSE IV on the Grounds of Non-Consummation…

Marylyn's last name was Taylor; her sister called herself Lizzie, but her name WAS Leigh. There weren't THAT many girls around there.

In Detroit in March, we risked the *only* six hours we were granted to view the Dietz, O'Bannon files—unable to *copy* anything—*without* a subpoena or a warrant. "Hey, Ellen, what do *you* know about *state* annulments?"

"They're just as much work as divorce, just different *grounds*. What are you looking at?" I showed her the petition:

Petitioner TAYLOR declares that on 9 June 73, Respondent NEWHOUSE told her of a minor child he fathered before their marriage. NEWHOUSE declared his intention to adopt said child in due course. Marriage NOT consummated (statements attached).

"It's not the *petitioner* that's interesting, it's…*this*:"

Respondent NEWHOUSE declares TAYLOR declaration false. Further claims that their child was delivered of Leigh Elizabeth TAYLOR 15 May 71 in Greenville, MI, said the child resides with a caretaker (statements attached).

"Newhouse; Greenville…"

"Too many coincidences to be coincidental," Ellen agreed.

"Yeah," I mumbled, "and I might have *known* this girl."

"May I ask *how* you knew her," Adam, who had been watching us, asked.

"Junior high in Hell," I blurted, surprised. "Pickney, really…"

"I *know*," Adam declared quickly…then hesitated. "*Different* young woman. The person you *knew*: *how* well?"

"She was in foster care with her older sister just down the street. The sister, Marylin, and Leigh left at the same time in '69. *Leigh* called herself Lizzie."

Adam stared blankly. "Please…the person you *knew*, she…" and fell silent, like a curtain fell on his whole body. "There's *no way*…" he muttered before he left the room. We kept rifling carefully through the files, knowing they contained confidential matters that had *nothing* to do with Wolverine, and suddenly we're confronted by *this*…

A few minutes later, Adam returned with a large man in an immaculate suit. "I'm Attorney Ben Dietz. If you will all give me your attention for a moment? Thank you." He had a commanding voice, like a quiet drill sergeant. "Mr. Block has made me aware of some of the information in these files that may be misinterpreted. I can *assure* you that Miss Taylor—the one *in* the files, is *not* yours, Agent Clawson. However, we believe *yours has* been the target of some *interests*. Agent Clawson, what you've just told us adds *considerably* to what *little* we've known of the *other* Leigh Taylor, the mother of Randy Newhouse IV's child. We know *her* name from the child's birth certificate that Randy produced *more* than once, but not much more. I found it *more* than coincidental that the mother's name and date of birth were the same as *our* Leigh Taylor."

Too many coincidences to be coincidental…

✱✱✱

While we were up in Detroit, we did a routine search of newspaper archives in the area, discovering, among other things:

- Leigh Taylor, Ann Mueller, Debbie Ford, and Marcie Guinan winning a state swimming championship in November '70;

- A baptismal announcement for *Renée* and *Randy* Newhouse V in Bay City in June '71;
- A story on Leigh Taylor and other female MPs in Grenada mentioned her meeting a *childhood friend*…accompanied by a photo of her *and* that *friend*…Staff Sergeant JJ Elrath.

I studied that photo for a while. Those two stood close together, and they looked…*animated* is one way to put it; *familiar's* the other. They were *more* than *friends*. Unless she was an Amazon, *this* Leigh was *unlikely* to have given birth in the spring of '71 if she was swimming like *that* in the fall of '70.

While we were at it, we did some more research in the Bloomfield Hills Public Library. There was some fascinating *other* information there, too, if you knew where to look…and for *what*. I needed to talk to *both* Leigh Taylors. The one in the Army was easy to find. The *other* one…

I had the Troy office find an address for the guardian of Randall F. Newhouse V, age about 14…just to see if it came up as Lizzie or Leigh.

It came up as *neither*.

✳✳✳

"Mrs. Parkinson," Stella Elrath Parkinson was a handsome woman, a female, older prototype of JJ Elrath, "*thanks* for meeting with me." While I was in Detroit, looking up JJ's mom *wasn't* hard. We met at the Troy Agency, a location I thought best because of a *possible* Newhouse connection with her husband's allegedly defunct business.

"You're very welcome," she smiled brightly, with a dash of suspicion in her eyes. "You said this had something to do with my son?"

"Yes, ma'am; indirectly. Do you remember a young woman named Leigh Taylor, a friend of your son's?"

"Certainly," Stella said quickly. "They met in the church youth group. She went to a different school than Johnny. Her mother, Cathy Taylor, *was* divorced, but they got back together. Johnny says she's in the Army, in the Military Police."

"Yes, ma'am. Now, ah. On a *slightly* different subject, do you remember a neighbor on Franklin Road named Newman?"

"Newman? Well, *yes…*"

JJ's mom had a *phenomenal* memory.

✳✳✳

"What can I do for the FBI," Leigh Taylor sighed, fingering her nightstick. When I met her in June, she was stationed at Fort Gordon, a clearing in the red-clay-and-pine-trees of northeastern Georgia.

"Just some routine inquiries, Sarge," I answered. I'd had her called in from patrol, which was unexpected since she was an Army detective. "You're *not* in CID* anymore?"

"I *am*," she nodded, sipping from her water bottle, "but we've had a *nasty* flu bug here, so we're filling in every third day. As an E-6, I *should* be a shift commander, but I'm out on patrol since we're *so* short. *Wait* one," she stood up. I waited while she took off her patrol kit. Without all the encumbrances, she had a nice figure.

I shifted in my blown-plastic chair, my pants sticking to me in the damp heat. "Tell me about…this *may* be a sore subject, but…."

"Randy?" She looked like a horrible old harridan with light brown hair and haunting green eyes for a moment. *But, those eyes; she ain't MY Lizzie.*

"Well, *about* Randy's child. *We're* convinced he wasn't yours…."

"*Thanks*," she smiled brightly. "There was *no way*…."

"We believe you. Why do *you* think they keep insisting that he's *yours*?"

"I gave up trying to figure *that* out years ago," she shook her head. "Never made any sense to me."

---

* Because the old and extinct Counter-Intelligence Corps was known as the *CIC*, the Army's Criminal Investigations *Command* was still known as a *Division* in its acronym—CID. When the old soldiers die off, *maybe* they'll change it.

"Have you heard from John Elrath lately?"

"*Yeah*," she smiled, a gleam in her eyes. "He just got orders for Florida; might meet up with him before he gets there. Why?"

"I saw his name in your file." I shrugged, trying to make it seem trivial. "Just wondered if you're still in touch."

"Yeah, *have* been since '74." Her face changed again. "*Why?*"

"*Just* making a connection is all." Interviewing civilians is easy. Interviewing criminals is a little trickier because they're so guarded. Interviewing other *cops* can be perilous because they know how interviews *work*; no question is *ever* an impromptu, 'oh, by the way,' like on TV.

And I just gave Leigh Taylor—a good interrogator by all accounts—a heads-up that the FBI was interested in JJ's *and* her life.

That didn't concern me *near* as much then as what was going on with Ellen. She'd got a dose of viral pneumonia and was fighting for her life.

✳✳✳

"So, Timothy Whalen…who isn't *Timothy Whalen*, but Robert Kevin Newman: *pleased* to meet you." He was a bulky man of middling height, with a nasty scar along his jaw. We were in an interview room, a dull and hollow space without windows that smelled like it had been recently painted. The hot and humid July weather that I'd suffered to *get* here… think hot, *hotter*…and a *sauna*.

This was The Rat House, located…OK, I *can't* tell you *that*. I <u>can</u> tell you its *official* name is the Department of Agriculture's Fertilizer Evaluation Establishment, run by the Bureau of Prisons. It's surrounded by corn and soybean fields, accessible only by a long, unpaved-but-carefully-watched road or helicopter. Its location is a better-kept secret than what's *really* in Area 51.

The Rat House is the destination for snitches who've talked about too many dangerous people, for whom even witness protection wouldn't be safe. Unlike most prisons, the Rat House is virtually silent, like a mausoleum. *Nobody* talks to *anyone*. Hell, that's what *got* them here. *Honor among thieves* was never a thing for *these* guys.

"I don't know *what* you're talking about," Tim/Rob answered, looking vaguely puzzled. "*I'm* Tim Whalen…"

"No, sorry," I sighed, opening his file. "Newman, Robert Kevin, born in April 1948, Detroit, Michigan. Moved to Bloomfield Hills as a child, you and your brother and sister. Your father *is*—or rather *was*—VP of marketing at American Motors."

"Listen," he shook his head, "I don't know *what*…."

"Oh, but *I* do. You went to Bloomfield Hills Central High, competed in their state-champion swimming squad. You and…" I pushed a picture across the table, "Brenda and Lois *Elrath*, your neighbors down Franklin Road in Bloomfield Hills. You used to bring them home after swim practice. Remember now?"

"No, I don't…this *isn't* me."

"Oh, *yes,* you *do*, and *yes*, it *is*," I smiled, armed now with… "Here's *you*, and Lois, and *Brenda*, and *little Johnny* Elrath in front of *their* house." I pushed the copy of the faded picture that I got from Stella across the table. He looked at it like it was a scorpion about to strike. "*His mom* says you taught Johnny the backstroke."

He sat, blank. "*What* are…?"

"You graduated from Central in '66, but your mother divorced your father. You moved out of posh Bloomfield Hills to a *different* neighborhood, and there was suddenly *no* money for college. You went to work, but *that* was dull, so you stole a car and were arrested at the end of '66…the *first* time. In '68, you were busted for pandering, spent six months in Wayne County Jail, where a corrections officer named Otto Meisner worked. Then you went into the big time because the drug war in the after-riot chaos of Detroit was just *too* tempting for an enterprising young man such as yourself. In '69, you were in on a drug rip-off that went sideways, and you blasted an off-duty cop and the brother of the biggest dope kingpin south of Schoenherr Avenue.

"One of the guys you were *with* on the run in the Motor City was a young burglar named Jay Pardon. The *cops* wanted you; the *drug lords* wanted you. You *had* to disappear. So, in 1970, at age 20, you enrolled in Wolverine Military Academy as Edward Forsythe, and you spent four years as a teenager again, avoiding everyone who *wasn't* in Patton Hall," I went on, "but then…here's *little Johnny Elrath trying* to talk to you. You didn't say a *word* to him. How am I doing so far?"

"*What* do you *want?*" Tim/Rob had stopped smiling.

"And there was *Jay*, too, but *he* wasn't gonna say anything. You left Wolverine in '74. A *year* later, you became Timothy Whalen and went into gunrunning; you got busted in North Carolina in '82 and were sent to Marion. And *there* were *Jay* and *Otto*."

Rob had the look of a guy who just glimpsed his own gallows. "*What…?*"

"Not *done* yet." I gazed at him steadily. "You paid Jay to *help you* kill Otto. Then you ratted out *Jay* and got moved here. So now we've got at least three homicides plus Gods-knows-what-else on you. Your parole officer's great-grandparents haven't even been *born*."

"Just tell me *what* you want and what it's *worth* to you."

The value of the *We Know All* approach is that it doesn't allow the source *any* wiggle room at all when you *do* know it all. "What *I* want to know is: who got you into Wolverine as a No-Name?"

"What's it worth?"

"Ten grand in your prison account."

Rob shifted uncomfortably. "*Twenty*." I nodded. "I'll give you what I've got, but it ain't much. I was given a phone number. On the other end, this *ADS* guy told me that the Second Century Fund could make me disappear, but it took *four years*. The guy said, 'do this one little job *and* come up with $20,000.'"

"What was the job?"

"They had me burn a draft office in Ann Arbor, told me to make sure to do it when there was somebody *there*."

"What did ADS stand for…?"

"Americans for a Democratic Society. I didn't know *much*, but *their* kind of *democracy* didn't have anything to do with elections. They were deep into some *real* subversive shit…"

"Subversive, like…"

"The ADS made the Weather Underground look like Quakers."

We *knew* about the ADS because it was the link we needed to tie Rob to…*well…*

File Number Ending 66902-LIB

Name: Americans for a Democratic Society (ADS)

Date Identified: 19 October 1969

Origin: ca. 1966, Bloomfield Hills, MI. Probable originator Randall F. Newhouse IV (b. 1955), but probably taken over by George Neitelsmidt AKA either Nestor Boehlke (b. 1953), Estavo Testa (b. 1953), or Charles Wier (b. 1954).

Narrative: Another SDS. Phony anti-war marches with little participation took place in Bloomfield Hills and Greenville, MI, handing out literature calling for "the overthrow of the money-controlled world."

Updates: 1970: ADS claimed responsibility for destroying draft records in Washtenaw County; Robert Newman (b. 1948), thought responsible, disappeared September '70.

1971: ADS statement: "We declare war on all fascist/Zionist/capitalist institutions in pig-dominated America, and call for all Americans under 30 to end one pig life a day until a true democracy based on love and peace is restored."

Perfectly fashionable claptrap for the '60s…you *had* to have been there. But Rob was still talking… "They said that if I was willing to cool my heels for four years and do what they said when and where they said, they *guaranteed* a cold trail. By *that* time, I'm ready for anything, so I say OK."

"You did the job?"

"Yeah…and they had a *picture* of me doing it. Then they set up a meet at an oasis in Berryville. This kid named Randy picked me up in a limo, took the money, drove me up to Greenville, and I walked in with a footlocker over my shoulder."

"And all *you* had to do was…."

"Talk to no one outside Patton Hall except this Wier kid."

"Describe this *Randy*."

"Maybe fifteen or so. Red hair, chapped skin, and freckles."

"Who was *with* him?"

"The driver…Randy called him Dave. There was *another* guy…Sid."

"OK. Then…"

"Then, one day, *Johnny Elrath* tries to talk to me in the library. Something in his eyes…*should* have been mean, *dead* even for what they were doing to him, but *not* him. I *thought* he recognized me. I told *Wier*…and he said, just shut the *Hell* up, keep my head down. So I tried to get this Parsons guy—ran a protection racket there—to take Elrath out. But he said *my price* wasn't *high* enough."

"OK, so, you came out in '74, but you changed your ID again in a little over a year. Why?"

"*That* answer's gonna cost you a *lot* more than twenty grand."

"How *much* more?" Twenty thousand dollars in *their* account was like two *million* on the outside.

"Two *hundred grand*."

"Give me a *taste*." I'd have to have something *really* good to justify *that*….

"In the summer of '75, I was the wheelman on a *real* quiet job. I picked up a big package and two guys in this house in Bloomfield Hills and went to a chroming shop in Warren. The guy who *got* me the job gave me my Whalen ID, told me to *vanish*…like a ghost, never to be seen again."

"Who?"

"Tony DeVere." Tony DeVere, a boss in the Wier/DeVere organization, was one of many names attached to the disappearance of James Riddle Hoffa in the summer of '75.

No self-respecting Motor City gangster would leave *that* important a body lying around; even *buried* it was too risky. So Hoffa would *have* to vanish. The chroming shops that *every* major Detroit villain has available to them have *huge* acid tanks where, after a few hours of immersion, the *biggest* pieces of a body left are memories.

"Got any way to *prove* this?" Rarely do you catch a mere *glimpse* of the brass ring of your profession. *I* saw that golden prize, *right* there, *right* then.

"Addresses for both the pickup *and* the drop-off. Truck rental receipt from the 30th of July to the 1st of August, '75 under the name of Ed Forsythe. I attached the gas receipt for the Gulf station at Telegraph and Maple. My lawyer has it all."

It all checked out. He got his money.

Because Tony DeVere had been killed in '77, there was nothing to do *legally* with this morsel. Because the chroming shop in Warren closed in '83—and its giant acid vats safely disposed of—there was forensically nowhere to go with *it*, either.

But…I found out what *probably* happened to poor Jimmy Hoffa.

If JJ recognized his old neighbor under a *different* name, the whole operation might have been in jeopardy. A good enough reason to *want* to kill him at Wolverine. Then, *somebody* said *don't* and was counter-bidding.

Who…and why?

***

"Well, it was *edible*," I declared, pulling into the little Greenville motel parking lot that September. The choice of eateries there was small: two local restaurants—we'd just had dinner at one—and a Pizza Hut, besides the Dairy Queen and a McDonald's out on the highway. Melissa had called *me* in Washington just two days before, told us where to stay. The library was well and truly intact, telling us that Melissa and her partner *weren't* in the Greenville mob, nor was the librarian.

"It was *that*," Morgan declared. "Ellen's on limited duty now?"

"Twelve-hour weeks." She'd left the hospital at the end of July, half a lung and forty pounds lighter. I'd seen her in the hospital a few times. Her spirits *never* flagged, *never* wavered, and Sam was almost always there. While she was rehabbing, she started to teach Dean how to swim, much to Hannibal's disapproval and Beth's amusement.

"Nightcap? C'mon, Dave: I took my meds *hours* ago."

"I'll be *right* there." I stepped into my room to see the message light on the phone. I heard Melissa's voice, with a *husky* tone to it: "Meet me tonight at the truck stop on County 14 & Lincoln after 10," in a manner that *seemed* to be saying: *for a good time, come to....*

We went to the truck stop at about 9:15, gave the place a good once-over...and again practiced our waiting skills. The sixteen-pump truck stop was busy. On our side of the building, the twelve car pumps serviced about a car a minute.

It was 10:20 when Melissa pulled into the parking lot in a beat-up Chevy—alone—to a spot under a streetlight. She was in thigh-high boots, a short leather skirt, and a jean jacket, with a skimpy halter under it: all she lacked for a hooker getup was the fishnets. "Been working tonight," Morgan guessed.

"Probably," I sighed, flashing our lights. She looked around carefully-yet-casually, waved without looking at us, and strolled unconcernedly to the travel store. Whoever Melissa *was*, she knew tradecraft. "That's our cue."

We made our way to the travel store, where she waited near the ladies' room. With a glance and a slight nod, Morgan followed her in. "Clean," Morgan declared, emerging a few minutes later. "If she's *wired*, they've got CIA-level equipment."

"Thanks for meeting us," I said when Melissa came out moments later.

"No problem," she said, leading us into the little snack bar, peopled only by a couple of truckers munching hot dogs and a pimply-faced clerk, who nodded at Melissa.

"Know *him*," I asked.

"Sheriff's deputy doing me a favor," she answered. "I've been in Wolverine as an officer *fifteen* times in *six* years, always for suicides that *don't* look very suicidal."

"Staged," Morgan asked.

"Almost like there's a *textbook* for it." Melissa lit a cigarette and took a drag, shivering. "I was an Army MP—still in the Reserves—so I've *seen* some things, *know* some things, and *that* place *ain't good.* They tell *us not* to talk about it."

"What were you *told?*" Morgan's question was valid, even if unexpected.

"To fill out the reports a certain way. Not *lying*, exactly, just not leaving *anything* to chance."

"When was the last time you were there," I asked, watching a guy squeegee his car windows.

"Last June. My *report* said a guy fell and hit his head; my *training* said he was clubbed…a *lot*."

"Uh-huh," I said, watching out the window. "But *why* are you meeting us now?"

"Because the Chief *has* to be in the owner's pocket…whoever *they* are." She shivered again. "Just *fed up* with it."

"You *take* payoffs," Morgan asked.

"I've been handed envelopes with cash every time I went there." She hugged herself. "The chief calls himself *Nestor* on the phone sometimes."

And…how many guys named Nestor are there in this world? "What happened to the *old* chief?"

"He retired in '78; he *was* getting on in years, but he still *had* some years left in a ten-person department that had on average five *calls* a week; three of 'em from *one place….*"

"Wolverine?"

"Yup. Bill Simmons—my partner—*was* senior, *griped* when he was superseded. *We* didn't understand."

"I think *we* do," I said. "But we can't fill *you* in just yet. You about to quit?"

"Got a reason why I shouldn't?"

"One." And we told her who we *thought* her chief was.

"OK," she nodded, "I'll give it another year."

"Well, we *had* to know," Julia sighed. She'd *just* knocked on my Holiday Inn door in Key West, Florida; the night was clammy-wet but annoyingly warm for October. I'd just gotten off the phone with Beth: Dean had recovered from chickenpox and gone back to pre-school. Hannibal purred into the phone for me.

"Yeah, I guess," I agreed. She'd just been to see JJ at his barracks. We flipped a coin as to who would talk to him; decided it would be better if it was *her* when I won.

"He's *certain* that the Taylor girl didn't have any kids. In fact, the idea surprised him," Julia said, shrugging off her jacket. "He couldn't imagine why the Newhouse family would say different." She looked out to the Gulf through my porch windows. "And he found his Cloud."

"You said that before, yeah. She's *who*, again?"

"Claudia Mueller…goes by Ann. A childhood friend he lost track of years ago. As a teenager, he was always looking for *her*." She shook her head slightly. "I haven't seen him *so* peaceful…*ever*."

"We still need to…." I started.

"*Yeah*, I know," she sighed. "Dot *all* the I's and cross *all* the T's."

***

"*Miss* Mueller," I smiled a week later, "*glad* you could talk to us." To call Ann Mueller *statuesque* would put every statue *ever* to shame. Even in dungarees, I never *saw* such a *perfect* figure on any *other* woman, even in *comic books...*

I'd hid out in Key West after Julia left, avoiding public places so I wouldn't run into either JJ or Ann. We just weren't ready to *officially* let them know we were *sort of* watching him.

"*Call* me Ann. I'm just a *little* confused," she answered. "*This* is about my brother George?" I struggled *not* to get lost in her eyes. There's *pretty,* and then there's *brown-eyed pretty...* and Ann *was* the latter.

"Yeah, just a minor thing about your brother that the Defense Investigative Service wants us to follow up on. You know, the *Johnny Walker* effect."

"Yeah, I *get* it," she sighed. Walker's security investigations had been a joke. Since his arrest, *everyone's* periodic security investigations had uncovered minor issues that would have been forgotten before. Now they were yanking clearances left and right for trivial reasons, *just* to be sure. "*What* can I tell you?"

"George's wife, Holly: how *well* did you know her? Did you *know* members of her father's family lived in East Germany?"

"No. I barely *know* her family." She went on for a while. I didn't ignore her, but I was wondering how JJ got so *lucky.* This was a link we wanted to make sure wasn't coincidental in a case that had so *many* coincidences... and Julia *was* his family... and ours, professionally. She finished with "... but Holly's family's had very little to *do* with mine. I think her parents moved to Gross Isle."

"Yes, *that's* right. When you were in Sicily in '79, you had contact with Dimitra Liguria. Any *more* contact with her?" Dimitra Liguria was the world's *third* naval diver—Ann was the *first*. "Did you *know* she had been in the Italian Communist Party?"

"We were together for an hour or so. We didn't even *dive*." She made a face. "*They* just wanted to take pictures of us chest-deep in the drink with gear on. *She* was as disgusted with it as *I* was."

"Ah. You've been in touch with Leigh Taylor, your old swim teammate?"

"Lately, yeah. I got a letter from her a couple weeks ago." She looked at me askance.

"Just one more thing. John Elrath: any contact with him?" I *had* to look ignorant…just in case.

She grinned as if I'd said something amusingly naughty. "*You* need to talk to *your own* organization. We ran into each other in September. I met his niece—one of *your* people—*with* him just last week. Why?"

"Just cleaning up files. He's quite the phenom himself."

"Johnny's lucky to be *alive*, Mr. Clawson," she smiled warmly…with *that* glint in her eye, the same one Leigh had when *she* talked about JJ.

✳✳✳

"Wish there was a better way to *do* this," I sighed, stretching my crampy back in the telephone service van. We were parked down the street from the home of Mary Newhouse, a two-story Colonial Revival on a comfortable lot in Essexville, an enclave of Bay City. She worked for Parkinson Title and Trust in the Hampton Center Mall.

"Me, too," Morgan agreed. "Wish it was *warmer*, too." She cracked her gloved knuckles against the roof. "You guys gonna come to Thanksgiving?"

"I'll check," I answered. "How *is* Jerry these days?" Her fiancée had been diagnosed with and treated for leukemia.

"He's got it beat," Morgan answered quietly…which meant maybe *yes* and maybe *no*. Either way, she didn't wear it on her sleeve.

"Sam wants to go by *his* family in Louisville," Ellen said. *Their* marriage had *yet* to take place. "*Heads* up," she announced. "School bus." At the bus stop two houses away from our vantage point, we watched five kids get off. "Three girls and two boys at this stop…one boy and one girl are headed towards the…wait; the *girl's* turning around."

Carrot-tops, both of them. "Randy's boy." *Gotta be…we know from the pictures.* "This would be one helluva lot quicker if we could just knock on the Goddamn door," I complained.

"On *what* pretext," Ellen asked…and she was right. Despite our charter as the Fourth Department, we couldn't misrepresent ourselves in interviews without a criminal referral—direct or indirect—on the subject. As far as we *knew*, the boy and girl who lived in *this* house—*whoever* they were to each other—were just potential leverage. Against *whom*…we weren't *sure*, it would be impossible to use it until we *did*.

So we waited. The boy went into the house; the girl went down the street with *another* boy. An hour later, the girl came back down to the house.

"What about the girl," Morgan asked. "Sister?"

"Only thing we *know* is that they are *both* in the custody of Mary Newhouse," Ellen declared. "IRS says she's their aunt."

"*Not* adopted," Morgan sighed. "We only know who their mother *isn't*. What do we know about this aunt?"

"Not a lot," I said. "Moved here with a sister in '69. She was nineteen, and her sister was fourteen. Sister's in the wind.." I blinked…*can't be.*

"They live *alone*," Morgan asked dubiously.

"Yeah." *Nice neighborhood, too; no sidewalks, no alleys.* "Where's the *money* coming from?" Based on her tax returns, Mary couldn't afford *this* neighborhood.

"*Good* question," Ellen said.

"Yeah." I glanced at my colleagues. "Let's say that the *Lizzie* Taylor *I* knew in Hell was the *mother* of this kid like the Dietz firm believes and that other *Leigh* Taylor was to be a *proxy* with a *close-enough* name…."

"When *nothing* makes sense, start making shit up," Morgan grunted.

"Yeah," Ellen sighed. "Kids *aside*, if *Leigh* Taylor is JJ's friend—or *more*—he'd be interested in *her* welfare, yes?"

"Yeah," I added, "but he's *got Ann.*"

"That *Leigh* knew, too," Ellen declared. "A *rival?*"

"More like a teammate." I glanced at them. "Ann is JJ's childhood friend, pre-teen, I understand."

"Yeah, OK," Morgan said. "JJ *knew* Leigh from church." She sighed. "JJ's kind of a hero, yeah?"

"Yeah." It hit me. "What if *Newhouse* is using Leigh to get back at *him* for ratting those guys out and costing him—*his* organization and *maybe owners* of Wolverine—a fortune?" All our fantastic speculation just *clarified*. "Follow the money. Whoever's pulling the strings owns the joint, lost money in that lawsuit."

"Yeah," Ellen asked, "and if all this blue-sky fantasizing we just did makes *any* sense, and we're *right*…what's the issue with this *kid*?"

"No father in the picture that we've seen," Morgan mumbled. "Someone's dirty little secret?"

"Randy's?" Ellen shook her head. "*Wouldn't* make sense. Teenager fathers kid, so *what*? Even in the *'60s*…."

We all looked at each other and simultaneously made *another* wild leap of speculation: "RF?"

"*They* look like *him*, too," I declared. *Marilyn? Could have been…* "And the sister?"

"Missing. *Dead*, maybe." Morgan sighed. "Important?"

"*Can't* say." I blinked in the darkness, rubbing my cold hands together. "If Newhouse owns Wolverine—and we made a *fair* case—*he* may be the leverage we need on RF."

"Yeah, but if he's *Randy's* kid," Ellen asked. "Why would *Dad* care?"

"If Randy's paying *these* bills now," I said. "*Dad might* have paid them earlier. But we just explained why Newhouse keeps insisting that *Leigh's* that kid's mother."

"*Dossier*." Morgan sighed. "JJ Elrath was one of her references on her Form 86."

"*Really*," Ellen said.

"*Interesting*," I added, with some feeling. Standard Form 86 was the Questionnaire for National Security that anyone wanting/needing a security clearance had to fill out.

"Yeah," Morgan said. "Because you want your references to say *nothing but* good stuff about you, not just 'yeah, I knew him at church.'"

"Think they *knew* each other *well*, then?" Ellen leaned back in the little folding chair.

"Maybe *not*...but I think *better* than just *church*."

Ellen nodded. "So's Michael Dietz." We knew *of* him—Julia had met him in Florida. He and Leigh were *pledged* to each other, and he was in the Army, in Counterintelligence. So far, that was his only connection to anything. Like Ann Mueller, he was connected-without-connections.

Ellen sighed as darkness loomed. "Yet the Newhouse family has been suing to get Leigh back here for this boy who she could *not* have borne." She sighed again. "Just to get *at Elrath*? *That's* a stretch."

"And *where's* this Mary's sister? *Which* Randy is this boy's father? *Who* was and *is* paying the bills? And what's all *this* got to do with Wolverine, except as leverage against Newhouse?" They stared at me. "Well?"

I consulted my pocket pad. "Two names we never talked to from the Adam Block files: Joe Dryden and Sid Jackwell. Dryden works for Newhouse—may not want to go *there* yet. Jackwell's in a business similar to Block, but he *also* worked for Newhouse at one time."

Silence for several minutes. "If we miss our *flight*," Morgan declared, "Jerry's gonna *cream* me."

"Yeah, so will Beth," I agreed. "We'd better...who's...?"

A car pulled into the house's driveway, and a tall guy stepped out. We watched him walk unconcernedly up to the front door. Even at that distance, standing in the porch light, we could recognize Sid Jackwell from his high school yearbook picture.

Now that's interesting...

We'd never met him, but now we *needed* to.

We *also* had to do some fast shuffling to get to Metro Airport to make our flight. Else our respective mates would have been *quite* unhappy... and just before the holidays...*not* good.

∗∗∗

"That's *him*," Ellen smiled at me just after New Year's in '86, looking over my shoulder. We were doing a *performing seal act*, frolicking in the pool of *another* Detroit-area hotel.

"Jimenez," I murmured, gazing at a beefy guy in a busboy's uniform. We'd been alerted about his *possible* whereabouts just three days before—six weeks *after* the fact. He'd landed in Detroit under his own name just before Thanksgiving. At least Detroit's airport security kept up on their bulletins.

I was already *here* because Dad had had a mild heart attack. Ellen was on *her* way to Detroit an hour after Detroit called DC, carrying the relevant files and a few things from home since my stay would be *longer*. She'd also brought a note from Beth *and* one from Dean: *Dean luv Daddy*.

"The *very* one. And I *think* that's *Wier*," she smiled broadly.

I ventured a glance; the two were chatting just outside the pool enclosure. "Yup."

"Think this suit's *risqué* enough to get *them* to…who's *that*?" The tank suit she wore hung on her like a sack after losing *all* that weight.

"Who?" I dared a glance at a reflection in the glass enclosure.

"That *woman*." I saw Ann in a dark two-piece suit covering everything from neck to knees to elbows. She did a funny dive-that-she-wasn't-supposed-to-do into the deep end.

"Ann Mueller," I mumbled, smiling. "Prepare to *turn*," I started to spin around hugging Ellen in the shoulder-deep water just as Ann did a flip turn about two feet from us. *Beth understands…* "oh, *shit*! *Prepare* to *make out*," I whispered as JJ Elrath entered the pool enclosure.

"What, *n…*" was as far as Ellen got before I put her in a lip lock and pressed her against the pool wall, giving her a wink. *NEED to hide.* It was *too soon* to break our cover within sight of Jimenez and Weir *or* Ann *or* JJ.

She winked back. *Follow MY lead, Davie.*

This was *supposed* to be all *show* and no *go…*

Gentle reader, I *hope* you understand that *this* was an emergency. Both Ellen and I were and still *are* happily—*blissfully*—joined and would *never* have done *anything* to hurt our respective spouses or relationships under *normal* circumstances. But JJ stood maybe ten feet away, and Ellen and I just *had* to *keep my face hidden…convincingly. And* make it *look* good, ya know? Sure, we'd had *some* training at the Academy on making *it* look good that was some of the most amusing and *useless* of our *entire* course of instruction.

We made *it* look *so* good…she *wrapped her legs around me* and *pressed, grinning…*

And JJ just STOOD THERE *as we both…*

I swear I was gonna *collapse*; I got *so* weak in the knees as *I…*. Ellen was a vibrating-if-limp rag for several moments.

Then the *oddest* thing happened…

"*Spectacular*, isn't it," Ann quietly murmured, *standing next to us*. I *never* figured out *when* she got *there*…or *when* JJ *left*.

"*Ah yeah*," Ellen panted, holding my cheek against hers. "You've *done it* in water before?"

"At *five fathoms*," Ann murmured. "Word of advice, though: water pressure makes it more *intense*, but the water carries away *your* lubricating fluids, can cause problems. Maybe we'll see you at breakfast. I'm Ann."

"I'm Nancy, and he's *Dave*; he's *shy*."

Ann pulled out of the pool and walked away.

We crawled into *separate* beds in our double queen room.

I had my *best* C-Sleep since Dean was born, babe. Sorry, but after *all* these years, I *had* to tell ya…

If it's *any* consolation, Beth—and I hope to *God* it is—it *was loudly* interrupted by a fire alarm at around 11. We hustled into the atrium—the hollow core of the hotel—where we spotted Jimenez on the second tier, his pants smoking…

I gave my card to a passing police officer while we milled around, and the fire department did *its* thing. After a few minutes, a detective discretely questioned us. When we got back to our suite around midnight, we managed to relax and sleep without any *do-de-DUNK…*

Really, we *did*.

✳✳✳

"Go down *without* me," I told Ellen, looking into the atrium where the breakfast buffet was ongoing. I looked over where the police department had blocked off the burned-door suite with yellow tape.

She went back into the suite, emerging with a towel around her neck after splashing her face with water. "Camouflage," she explained. "*You're* still in bed, you *slug*." I watched her go down to the buffet from a spot on the third tier where I could see *enough…*

Ellen took her time, getting breakfast for the two of us on a tray. She stopped by her new friend Ann, nodded at JJ, and sat briefly, acting solicitous. She made her way back up after maybe fifteen minutes—an *expert* job.

"*Helluva* alarm clock," Ellen said as we sat at the little table. "Did you know JJ's *brother* owned this place?"

"He's Julia's uncle, so…yeah: *step*-brother."

"Yeah. The fire caught the door and the carpet inside; more *smoke* than anything." She munched toast. "*We're* invited to dinner tonight." She smiled beatifically. "We're on our *honeymoon*, darling."

"We'll *have* to beg off, *darling*, but you *had* to make up *something*. Where are we *from*?"

"Virginia."

"At least *that's* true. We don't want to say what we're *doing* here yet, and we *can't* lie. I really *should* go down there today." Dad was in no danger—they said—but Mom was nervous.

"I'll go with. *They're* engaged as of two days ago. They're headed back in five days." She sipped coffee. "*Ann's* not buying my story."

"You know *this*...how?"

"*Trust* me; I *know*. If JJ recognizes you, *you're* just in town to see your family."

✳✳✳

The next day, JJ paused and turned to gaze back at us in a dark and hard-to-see (we *thought*) corner of the Oakland County Sherriff's observation room. He'd *just* picked Herman out of a lineup, identifying him as both his tormentor and as a busboy in the hotel. "*Work* for you?"

"Just *fine*, Sergeant Elrath," I said.

"I *know* you," JJ declared. "FBI?"

"Yes, *we've* met," I answered. I waited for a few beats before I added, "don't worry about Herman anymore."

"How about Chuck Wier," he asked. "I thought I saw *him* at the hotel the other night."

"Yeah," Ellen asked, trying to sound surprised. "Thanks for the tip."

"Let's *go*, JJ," Dorothy said, taking JJ by the arm. "*They've* got stuff to do."

Two days later, we were back in the observation room with Dorothy and one of her detectives, this time watching Mike Dietz ask Leigh Taylor, "*who* called you, again?" Mike had no *lawful* business talking to Herman.

"*That* guy," Leigh hitched her thumb over her shoulder at Ellen and me. Mike glanced at us. She had as much *lawful* business talking to Herman as Mike did. "I met him last spring. He wants us to take a crack at him."

The truth was *our* boss called *her* boss, who called *me* before *I called her*. This is a *very* grey, *very* tricky kind of thing in law enforcement. Though *we* had certain protections, Leigh and Mike did *not* unless we filled them in and got them on Working Group orders…which we could *not* do yet.

"Remind me why," Mike grumbled. "We've gotta catch flights this afternoon." The file I'd given them on Herman was not thick but thick enough. Their advantage was *they* knew stuff about what Herman had done to JJ that *wasn't* in the file.

"*He's* Herman…JJ's Herman Jimenez," Leigh explained. "*This* will be a brief, information-only interview requested by *Someone Else*."

Mike fell silent, staring at Herman through the observation glass. He'd been in the racket long enough to know what *Someone Else* meant: *stop asking questions and do the job*. They chatted quietly, planning their *roast* of Herman.

We watched a *perfectly* orchestrated interview that started with a two-person *Silence*—challenging enough for *one*—blend *seamlessly* into a *We Know All* approach.

"*They're* pretty good," I mumbled.

"Yeah," Ellen said. "*Got* him," she whispered, grabbing my hand when Herman spilled Joe, Randy Newhouse III, and somebody named Dave.

"Yep," I smiled, squeezing it. *Wish they were in the Bureau.*

A few minutes later, Leigh and Mike joined us in the observation room. As she buttoned up her blouse, Leigh asked Dorothy and the detective, "Got that?"

"Got *enough*," Dorothy said. "We can continue to talk to him based on that, ah, interview-that-*didn't*-happen. You're *good*, I'll say that." Again, Dorothy pretended *not* to know *me*.

"Army gives me plenty of opportunities to play the *femme fatale*," Leigh sighed. "*Always* works on the dense ones."

"But Joe *who*," the detective asked.

"Joe *Dryden; Dave* is Dave Harriman," Mike answered. "Two Newhouse goons. RF would be Randal Fred Newhouse III. Herman has a *personal* grudge to settle with JJ, and so does Joe Dryden."

Leigh squinted. "But *how* would my ex-father-in-law *or* Dryden *or* Harriman *know about* Jimenez?" She glanced at me. "Any ideas?"

"Not that we can talk about," I answered. "Thanks for the help."

"*Who* are *you*, again," Mike asked.

"Special Agent Clawson, Sergeant Dietz."

He let it go at that. He was no stooge, but Mike knew which questions would *get* answered and which *wouldn't*.

We believed the Second Century Fund was the connection...but we had to be transparent for the moment. We had more on the Newhouse organization than we had before...but *still* not enough.

✳✳✳

"*Thanks* for meeting me, Mr. Jackwell," I said, offering my hand. This *frigi*d day was three months *after* we'd froze in Essexville and a month after we'd seen Jimenez and Wier. I wasn't *used* to Great Lakes cold anymore.

"*My* pleasure," Sid intoned. He was about six-one, maybe 160 pounds, with dark eyes and long arms that ended in overlarge hands. Sid was a *lot* like JJ Elrath and Adam Block. You picked up on the sense that, given the right reason and circumstances, he'd just as soon kill you as look at you. "What can *I* do for the FBI? And you may call me Sid." We were in a barren office in a big, *empty* department store building that he used for an office and a residence. "From what Mr. Block tells me of your inquiries, there are some things I *cannot* or *will not* discuss."

"Well..." I began, leaning forward for my coffee. "*What* do you *understand* from Mr. Block?"

"You're looking into Newhouse Properties, Randy and Leigh's relationship, and Wolverine."

"All right," I felt a little deflated...and on my guard. "What *can* you tell me about your time with Newhouse Properties?"

"*Almost* anything you want to know. I *didn't* leave them on good terms."

"I see. Why *did* you leave them?"

He blinked several times. "I saved Leigh Taylor from harm."

"And they didn't like that?"

"*They* would have harmed her."

"*You'd* better back up," I said, trying not to look as baffled as I felt. "Why?"

"She had just broken Randy's jaw on their wedding night."

"I see…" I said, quickly going back through everything I knew about Leigh. "*Because…*"

"Randy told her about his son in their nuptial bed."

"OK. *That* was in her annulment petition."

"I never *saw* that; none of *my* business."

"What was your role *before* that?"

"I worked for Newhouse Properties, but my duties were to do what Joe or Randy wanted or *needed*. Sometimes, for RF himself."

"Which meant…?"

"Running errands, going here and there. Often, we'd deliver someone up to Greenville. Sometimes, just people from *there* to *there*."

"Someone…?"

"Men, mostly. Youngish men we took to Wolverine; young women to Francis Hartmann."

"How often?"

"Every few months."

"From where?"

"Different places. Mostly around southern Michigan, sometimes Indiana or Chicago. Cleveland once."

"Berryville?"

"Yes." He blinked for a few moments. "I made *several* trips to Berryville, and not *just* to pick guys up."

"For what?"

"I never really knew, though I *suspect* some of it was for Joe's angle."

"Joe *Dryden?* You worked with him. So did Dave Harriman."

"Yes. Should you talk to Joe, believe *little* of what he says. He lies because he's awake. Too crooked to sign his own name. Dave, on the other hand, is too stupid to lie."

"Thanks for the tip. So, how *long*...?"

"You talked to Claudia Ann Mueller, too, yes?"

How...? "Yes. In the course of investigation...."

"Of course." He smiled benignly. "And the woman you were *with* at the hotel *isn't* your wife. *That* was Special Agent Ellen Drew. She has lost weight recently."

"How...?"

"Don't worry, Agent Clawson. I have contacts everywhere. Claudia Ann has been my friend since 1st Grade. She's *still* my friend; I keep tabs on my friends. So you have nothing to fear from my organization *or* me."

"I'm with Special Projects," I said.

"I *see.*" For the first time, he looked impressed. "*Please*, let's go on. I worked for Randy and Newhouse Properties through high school. My father is a construction contractor, so I was a part of that, ah, *community* in school." He sighed. "Complicated."

"I'll bet." I took a deep breath. "Ever thought about working in law enforcement? You'd have a future there."

He smiled, a complicated look on a hard-to-forget face. "I *have* a future," he laid a business card on the table between us. It read *S. Jackwell, Organizational Readiness.*

"What's *organizational readiness* mean here?"

"I help organizations prepare for the worst."

"I see. I understand that *your* business is a *lot* like Mr. Block's."

"I worked *for* him for some time." He looked around. "I bought this building for my business and my hobbies. I live in another part of it. My business is a *little* different."

"I *see*." I waited for a pace. "What do you know about Francis Hartmann?"

"Not *much* more than what's outside the front gate. Many of the young women I took there were, um, in a *family* way."

"Home for wayward girls?"

"Yes, but some, I believe, were just troubled." He paused. "The Wolverine runs…*those* guys were not in high school."

"I got *that* sense, too. Any ideas?"

"Not good ones. They were *running from* something. The young women we took to Hartmann…*they* were school-age, *that's* certain."

"When did you start these *runs*, as you call them?"

He thought for a moment. "1970: January. The first was from Detroit Metro Airport to Wolverine. Joe was driving."

"The last?"

"*My* last was June '73, up to Francis Hartmann. They're still being made to *both* schools, but with greater *frequency* to Wolverine."

"About forty a year," I made the leap… *About the bunk capacity for Patton Hall.*

"Why, yes," he answered, surprised.

"Just a guess. Do you know *anything* about Mary Newhouse in Essexville?" I thought about saying *I saw you there in November*…but held that…for now.

He hadn't registered a great deal of emotion for most of the interview, but he did *then*. "I *can* tell you *some*. Ask specific questions."

"Where's her sister?" He shook his head slightly. "Who's those kid's father?" Nope. "Who's their *mother*?"

"What will you do with *that* information?"

He knows. "*Nothing* to do with a criminal referral. Just…*who*?"

"Please *stop* your recording if you have one." I shook my head. "Write *none* of this down." I nodded. "I made a *personal* promise to that family. They *deserved* better than they were *going* to *get*."

"I understand."

And he told me what he *knew, and* what he *suspected*…and what he had *done* and *for whom*…and *why* he was there in November. *As we were coming to believe…a pattern was forming…but still unbelievable.*

Then, he seemed to make a decision. "Agent Clawson, I have a source who has spent a *lifetime* inside the Newhouse organization. I will share information *from* that source with the FBI if you exceed to *one* demand."

"Yes?"

"You must *not* contact my source directly. Agree to this as a gentleman, and I will share what my source has *just* told me."

Handling a deep-cover informant was not in my brief, but the potential here was too great to pass up. "Agreed." We shook hands.

"My source has just told me that the Newhouse organization knows where Leigh Taylor and Michael Dietz have been assigned and that they are planning to compromise* them."

That information was *technically* classified—For Official Use Only, or FOUO. Both Taylor and Dietz had jobs that depended on no one *knowing* what they were doing. This was *huge*; a federal crime—*minor* espionage—in itself. "Why?"

"My source thinks they want to neutralize them; end their careers; destroy them professionally." He hesitated. "*We* think because of their relationship with John Elrath."

Holy…we were right… "Anything *else*?"

"How long have you *got*?"

And for the next few hours, Sid filled in *many* blanks —and some gaps we didn't *know* about.

✳✳✳

One of the advantages of being in the 511th was that it gave me access to a great deal of gossip within the intelligence community. That grapevine told me that Mike Dietz was being awarded the Defense Superior Service Medal at the end of February '86. Such prestigious awards are

---

* *Blown*, in the vernacular. In the secret world it means exposed as to their true identity.

usually presented in front of the awardees' units. In *this* case, he was being honored at the same time as Emily Naris, his partner in his award-worthy work. Hence, the Department of Defense moved the ceremony to a Washington Beltway convention hotel, flying the awardees' families (and Leigh Taylor) in to witness the ceremony.

That's what everyone was *told*. The *truth* was SPD wanted to lay eyes on Taylor, Dietz, and Naris. We needed to satisfy ourselves that they were not chimeras, that they had the kind of think-on-your-feet talents that we needed for the future…because we *were* thinking of *their* future. At the ceremony, Larry Phelps (whose *work* name was Brown) spoke a few words about how those in his secret world are usually honored only after death…and *then* often anonymously.

The orders for both awards bumped both up a stripe (accidentally on purpose). The after-the-speeches appetizers and drinks were consumed by a mixture of Army and Congressional hangers-on joined by a healthy dose of SPD agents. We listened, laughed, ate, drank, and generally had a great time. I stayed away from Leigh and Mike, not wanting to give them any ideas about what was going on…but Mike saw me, anyway.

Think of it as informal vetting. Mike and Leigh passed; Emily did well but not well *enough* for SPD. Both Mike and Leigh had put in for warrant officer; both would get it. We'd make sure of that.

Based on Sid's information, I wrote a Memoranda for Record—my first as a military officer *and* FBI agent—that Taylor and Dietz *would* be blown. When Taylor and Dietz *were* blown, I got an *atta-boy* from the Chief of Army Counterintelligence and an Army Commendation Medal.

TJ and Freddie went to their middle school spring frolic…no, not a *date*, just *together*.

And all that summer, we worked on Sid's information. And Dean grew and grew and chattered and got into everything…but that's what toddlers do.

In August, I wrote a memo about an idea I had to break the Wolverine case.

And *somebody* paid attention.…

Operation TURNABOUT

Or, Me and My Bright Ideas

"**E**ver *been* here," I asked Ernie as the Metro rail car doors opened. "*Years* ago." We followed Dusty and a brace of full colonels onto the Pentagon Station platform. "Had a meeting with the British and Canadian Special Branch and Army CID, and they only *had* so much time..."

"I never felt so compelled to salute," I sighed, passing three admirals waiting on the platform. "This place is *way* above my pay grade."

"*Not* today," Dusty said as we got to the escalator as we hung our badges around our necks, trying to *look* like we *belonged*. "Today, you're one with *these* guys."

The Pentagon Metro station is a transit hub; a big, imposing, and busy place with busses, trains, shuttles, tour busses, limos, and other ground transportation coming and going constantly. We followed the colonels to a cab/limousine stand, where we met a Lincoln limousine that took us to The Building. For those of you who've never been to the Pentagon, to call it *imposing* doesn't *begin* to do it justice. *That* place is no less than *awe-inspiring*. Every entrance is numbered and lettered. Metal detectors are everywhere; *everyone's* in uniform...

Actually...no, *not* really. I was surprised by how humdrum it really *was*. Yes, every door is numbered, and everything *seems* overbuilt. And yes, there is a *sea* of uniforms from all services and several other nations, but we saw just as many civilian suits and more than a few blue jeans.

We *beeped* through a metal detector and received ID badges. Then, we followed a better-than-average map to Room 1-5-171: Corridor 1, Wedge 5, Room 171, also known as Conference Suite Five, about a quarter-mile walk from the north entrance.

The suite had two rooms, where valence lights illuminated fake trees in each corner, giving it a *funeral home* feel. There was also coffee and tea and water and sweets on two round tables. The seating was remarkably comfortable and lacked a *trace* of Naugahyde.

Our tax dollars at work...

We were just getting acclimated when The Director and an aide entered the room. He was followed by Paula Kerris of the Troy Agency. Then came two generals and *their* aides—the Provost Marshal of the Army and the Chief of Army Counterintelligence. Joining them were Colonel Ivan Thomas of the National Intelligence Support Command detachment in Detroit, and Warrant Officer Third Class Amy Armor, commanding the CID Detachment in Troy.

All of them were *there* because I wrote a couple of memos.

After availing themselves of the refreshments laid out in the anteroom, everyone made their way into the conference room. The principals* took seats around the large oval table; everyone else took theirs along the wall. That's where *I* was until Dusty *directed* me to the podium at the *head* of the table. It was then I thought: *I'm surrounded by people who not only outrank me but who've been in this racket since before I was thought of...and now they want to hear what I've got to say. How did I get so...*

"Special Agent Clawson," the Director nodded. "*The floor is yours.*"

"Yessir," I croaked, my throat suddenly Sahara-like. "Our Working Group..." and I went through how *it* came to be—too fast—Ernie waved his hand down slightly. "What we're *seeing* is too many coincidences to be coincidental." I swallowed hard before I went through the evidence we'd amassed. "*We* think the Newhouse organization has a *significant* financial interest in Wolverine *and* wants to see John Elrath destroyed.

---

* The *big* guns; the *highest-ranking* guys; the ones with *aides* hanging on their every word.

I believe they want to use Taylor—and *possibly* Dietz—as bait to get Elrath to Detroit or are *ready* to. We also think that *both* organizations are heavily involved in changing identities for huge profits.

"Last month, Elrath and his fiancée were put on orders for Alaska. By current DOD policy, they need to get married by December to take advantage of the DOD's stay-together policy. *I* think they intend to marry while on leave in November in Detroit. It seems to be a perfect opportunity for whoever's been *after* him to execute a plan to get Elrath. If Taylor and Dietz just *happen* to be in town, so much the better."

"So, *how* do you think you'd *know*," Amy asked. "By the way, I *served* with Leigh Taylor in Korea." I think Paula and Amy both looked at me with some sympathy...or maybe I looked like I could *use* some.

"Elrath contacted his family about his orders last month. According to my *source*, there have been several large cash movements in the Newhouse organization since that time, including some overseas. So, we *think* they're getting ready for *something*."

The room was quiet; everyone seemed to be thinking, not looking at me. I made to sit until the Provost Marshal spoke up. "Agent Clawson, your proposal to transfer these military members on short notice is *radical*..."

"It's *meant* to be, sir," I answered. "Five days to clear post, especially over a weekend. *No* time to get a letter home so we can eliminate the Postal Service as a Newhouse source. It will surprise them *maybe* into making a mistake or an overt move."

"They *were* both blown this summer, Harry," the Chief of Counterintelligence said to the Provost Marshal...who nodded. "Agent Clawson predicted *that*. That's why I'm *here*."

An aide came forward, whispered in the Provost Marshal's ear. "Captain Clawson: I'm informed you're up for major next year. Put in for the Command and General Staff School and *Harry* and I will put in a good word."

The Chief of Counterintelligence shrugged noncommittally. "What will their *roles* be, Taylor and Dietz," he asked. Suddenly, I saw on many faces what every public speaker wants to see: acceptance.

"Dangles. That, and Taylor knows intimate details about the Newhouses. We need to get *someone* to make an overt act, bring them out in the open." I was proposing that the Army *potentially* sacrifice two of its best mid-career senior NCOs at the altar of law enforcement.

"They will have to be *told*, of course," Ivan mused. "Even as bait, we'll still need them for their knowledge of the Newhouse family, yes?"

"True," the Provost Marshal agreed. "They won't have arrest authority, but if there's a threat, they shall *have* to be armed for their own protection."

I have to admit I was surprised. I was surprised that my proposal was being taken seriously, that I'd convinced this bunch that my ramblings had any merit at all. I *had* my *doubts*...

"And they're good soldiers," the Provost Marshal mused, steepling his fingers. "They're engaged themselves. *May* want to tie the knot *then*. More *opportunities*, yes?"

"Yes," I heard myself say. "Whoever it is supplying the money—*and* who wants Elrath punished—will almost *certainly* make a move before Thanksgiving this year." *That's a guess I JUST made...*

I sat down slowly. Ernie nodded benignly; Dusty cocked his head in acknowledgment. "Ladies, gents," the Director cleared his throat. "It sounds just *damn-fool* enough to *work*. We'll swear Taylor and Dietz into Special Projects when they get to Detroit. Dusty, where'd you *find* this kid?"

"*Hell*, Michigan, sir," Dusty smiled. "That's where he's *from*, anyway. *We* got him straight out of the Academy."

"That tourist trap in Pickney," the Provost Marshal exclaimed. "Wow! Small-town Michigan strikes again! I'm from Keego Harbor, myself."

"It's *small*, all right," Amy agreed. "Everyone knows *where* it is, but it's not on *any* maps."

"Like Cinnamon Grove, Tennessee," Ivan sighed, "where *I* came from. *It's* not on the maps, either."

"We're decided," the Director made to stand up. "Agent Clawson, my compliments. This operation will be called...ah..."

"Operation TURNABOUT, sir," Ernie declared. "That's what we were given for planning purposes."

"So it will be," the Provost Marshal sighed. "Lunch on the Fourth Floor?"

And so it was that day that a Reserve MI Captain/GS-11 Special Agent was privileged to break bread in the same room as *eleven* generals and *five* admirals.

Also, on that day, I altered the lives of Leigh Taylor and Mike Dietz by making them live bait for a trap that, I was coming to believe, was being laid for JJ Elrath…though I had little *idea* by whom.

✳✳✳

"There's been a development," I announced a month and a half later. "Detroit's gone hot." We'd been planning a couple weeks in Detroit— bringing families to make it *look like* a home visit.

"*How*," Ellen asked. "We're supposed to meet with Taylor and Dietz *next week*..."

"Charlie Parkinson had a stroke last night. It's triggered a *lot* of activity in the Newhouse camp."

"Who," Morgan asked. *That* name seldom came up, and then mostly in our attempts to connect the dots…somehow.

"Grampa," Julia frowned. "I gotta call *Dad*...."

"Hmm." Ernie wasn't often at a loss for words, but *this* time…even his shrug said *I don't know.* "Yes, go ahead," he told Julia. "Dietz and Taylor will be in Detroit tomorrow night. But *this* may be a connection between Parkinson and Newhouse."

I nodded. "*Now*, there's..." I pushed a picture of a slight, redheaded woman in an Army uniform across the table. "Know who *this* is?"

"No," Morgan answered. "Pretty girl...who *is* she?

"Name's Wendy Corey. She's Elrath's neighbor in Florida. She and Elrath *met* last September; Newhouse has been aware of Elrath's movements for *years*. She's been *corresponding* with the Newhouse's for *months*. Our information on *her* comes from Sid's source."

"Yes." Ernie looked out a window idly, which he *rarely* did.

"The source also thinks that something very, *very* bad is in the offing," I added.

"*We* should speak with that source," Ellen said, toying with a pencil.

"No." Ernie sighed deeply. "*Dave* made the agreement." My colleagues knew *of* my agreement with Sid; Ernie and the Bureau knew more. What surprised me was that my superiors merely nodded and said *run with it* when I told *them*. That's the nature of *our* business: information depends on trust between provider and consumer. "Dave: how have *you* been feeling lately?"

Talk about coming out of left field! "Um...OK." I waited for a beat. "You?"

"*Tired*, frankly. I forgot how *wearing* the cloak-and-dagger business can be."

"How's your boy, Ernie?" Ellen sounded solicitous.

"One hundred percent disability pension," Ernie answered, still gazing out the window. "*Won't* be cleared for field duty again. His left knee's OK now, but the *right*...just too much bone destroyed. But the Commonwealth of Pennsylvania hired him for the crime lab."

"How's his *family*," I asked. Ernie had pictures of his son's wife and two kids on his desk.

"His youngest is in school now." Ernie turned, looked at us all. "And *thank you* for asking. Kinda makes *me* wonder why I'm still doing *this* job. I could take my pension and leave tomorrow, but..." He smiled. "But I *like* this job, as messy and as wearing as it gets. And I feel that *you guys* aren't ready for me to give it up just yet. Surprisingly, my *stepson* wants to go into law enforcement."

"Dennis," Ellen asked, surprised.

"Yes, and it's confusing Farrah no end." Ernie grinned conspiratorially. "I'm not sure if he's doing it for himself or just to burn his sister." Three years younger than Dennis, Farrah still didn't *like* her stepfather, Ernie, though she *had* become *civil* about it. "No matter. The trouble with using a source like Sid's is that it's *so* easy to blow them. If I send you down to Key West to talk to the Corey woman, she'd wonder how we *knew* she was in communication with the Newhouse's. That could *easily* blow a deep asset." He looked around. "Well, children? On the matter of Wendy Corey...?"

"Watch and wait," I said.

He nodded, Buddha-like. "Detroit Thursday."

❋❋❋

I hustled Julia, her family, Beth, and Dean into the hotel elevator as Jules waved at JJ Thursday afternoon. JJ's eyes were *bright* blue...and mystified at seeing us.

"He's a nice enough guy," I told Beth in our room. "Jules is introducing *her* family first. Come down with Ellen and Morgan." Sam and Jerry would be joining us in the next few days.

Jules and I shared a wink on the elevator, trying not to think about JJ's potential rage/questions about what *we* were doing there. "Hey, Jules," Julia and JJ shared a hug before she said, "JJ, this is..."

He extended his hand. "Clawson. Sorry, but your *first* name...."

"*Dave*," I added, trying warmth on. "We met in Panama in '81 and *here* in January."

"We *did*," he nodded. "Talked about Wolverine. How's all that going, anyway?"

"That's one thing we're here for," Julia answered. "We're both official and *un*official this trip. Mom said you were headed for Alaska?"

"Yeah," JJ said as Tony and his boys joined us. Julia introduced them; the boys were fascinated by the hero-uncle *and* the concrete terraces and structural glass, scanning around.

Barely had we shook hands when Beth—carrying Dean—with Ellen and Morgan came down. "*This* one's my wife, Beth," I declared, putting my arm around her, "and my *other* partner Ellen Drew," I added.

"Ignore him," Morgan rolled her eyes punishingly, "like he just did me. Morgan Towne," she offered her hand. "I'm with *them*."

"*Pushy* as usual," I sighed. "Yeah, she's with us. Busman's holiday."

"Well, glad to meet you all," JJ sighed. "Chow's over there," he pointed.

"Let's put on the feed bag," Tony announced, leading most of us away. I figured Jules and JJ needed a minute to talk about her grandfather, and Beth's presence wouldn't interfere—besides, I was hungry. Beth has that talent: to fade into the background when needed.

By the time I got back with plates for the three of us, JJ had left. "Seems...nervous," Beth observed to Julia. "Is he like that a lot?"

"More haunted as a teenager," Julia said. "No; this is different."

That night, with Dean safely asleep in the junior bed—with rails— Beth snuggled up to me. The beds were newer, so the snuggling wasn't *required* to get out of any grooves in the mattress. "He's scared of something, of *failing* at something."

"Another of your feelings?"

"Same *kind* of thing I've seen in you, sometimes, when something isn't going well."

"Are all guys like that?"

"Most. But JJ...feels like he keeps to himself a lot."

"That's what Jules says, yeah. He's getting married between now and Thanksgiving..."

"There's *nervous groom* worried like you were, and there's *can I do this* worried. JJ's *that* kind."

***

"Ladies and gents, I'm Senior Special Agent Ernest Packard—call me Ernie—and I head the FBI's Special Projects Division Wolverine Working Group...."

That's how we started that Monday morning in the Troy Agency, a stone's throw from the CID office.

And *then*, everyone *knew*. The SPD is not a mystery to law enforcement; neither are Working Groups. After Mike and Leigh got over their surprise, Ernie went on. "Now, *most* of us are strangers to each other, so let's start with the *round-the-table* game. Julia: *go*."

"Julia Addison; SPD;" "Dorothy Parkinson, Oakland County Sheriffs—*her* mother;" "Ellen Drew, SPD;" "Dave Clawson, SPD;" "Morgan Towne, SPD;" "Frank Hitchcock, SPD;" "Tom Greenowitz, SPD;" "Ivan Thomas, Army Counterintelligence;" "Amy Armor, Army CID;" "Leigh Taylor, Army CID;" "Mike Dietz, Army Counterintelligence." "Paula Karris, this is *my* office."

Leigh nodded in my direction with a little grin. Her green eyes were enchanting...Mike just nodded slightly.

I half-listened to what I knew already for the next few minutes until Ernie said, "Now, Special Agent Clawson?"

I cleared my throat. "For some time, Sergeants Dietz and Taylor's duty stations, movements, and even relationships have been known to the Newhouse organization soon after they happen; in some cases, *before* they arrived at their stations. The simplest explanation for this is that someone's reading their mail." I glanced at them; they stared back. "You're here on such short notice because the Chief of Counterintelligence and the Provost Marshal thought my cock-eyed theory had merit."

"Five days to clear post," Mike nodded, "not enough time for a letter to get from either Belgium or Korea. But how would *you* have known that the *Newhouse's* know...?"

"Mr. Jackwell's organization has a source," I said.

"*Sid*," Leigh asked. I just nodded curtly. She got the message: *shut up*.

Ernie talked about what we'd been doing for five years, the leads, the restrictions on what everyone could do, and Mike and Leigh's roles. When asked, Leigh described her wedding night. "We were in bed— our *first* time—and he (being Randy) said *something* like, 'even if I *could* screw you *now*'...*you* get it."

*Beth would have broken more than my jaw...*Even so, it *was* entertaining even though *I* knew Sid's more detailed version.

I had to add, "whoever owns Wolverine *may* be using you as bait for John Elrath. You two are the common threads running through this case."

"Right," Julia said, "and NOTHING about that leaves this room." Julia glared at Leigh and Mike. "Nothing."

"Elrath cost Wolverine's owners millions," Frank added. "Dave's theory makes sense from that perspective. The maternity, though, confuses the matter. Those kids up in Essexville...."

"Those...*those* kids," Leigh asked, puzzled.

"Yeah: two of 'em," I said. "Both named Newhouse, both living with a woman claiming to be their aunt. We saw them on surveillance a year ago, been trying to figure out what they are to each other ever since. One is named Randy; the other, Renée, according to their guardian's tax returns."

Leigh said, "Randy has four sisters. One of *them*...?"

"No," I answered. "Only two of his sisters have had children. None of them are named Mary."

Then there was the *fire*. The Taylor's townhouse complex had been attacked by arsonists the Tuesday before; they were smoked out and staying with the Dietz's for the moment. What troubled me was we had no intel on that at *all*. And, *at least* one Newhouse hireling was involved, according to what Leigh had found out on her own.

And the phone book. Leigh found a little phone book among some boxes that Randy may or may *not* have packed before their wedding. It yielded more phone numbers, but to help break the tedium of the meeting, Mike called a number labeled *Mary*…and I heard a bit of *that* voice from my past: *Marilyn.* She called herself *Mary* Newhouse and said she worked for Parkinson Title and Trust in Essexville. He got an answering machine for a residential number on the second and no answer on a third.

"But," Dorothy squinted, "Parkinson Title and Trust is defunct."

"We've been aware of *that* for a while," I said. "That one little office in the Hampton Center Mall…can't find it in any business registry."

We were told to build up domestic legends—cover stories—for Leigh and Mike because they *could* misrepresent themselves. Then Ernie administered The Oath to everyone *not* in SPD. I think *they* thought it was a joke, but of course, it wasn't. Not to *us*, anyway. It pulled them into the Working Group, giving them cover for whatever happened later.

This is a great place…and a happy hour, too…

"*Hi*," the voice said Tuesday afternoon. "Dave *Clawson*?"

I turned and looked…*up* and *up*…to see Ann Mueller with a plate full of appetizers standing next to the next table. "Right. Just *Dave's* fine. This is my wife, Beth," I pointed to an empty chair next to her. "Come *on*; join us."

"Well," Ann hesitated.

"C'mon, *sit* with us," Beth smiled. "Keep Dave from *boring me* to *death* with FBI-talk on vacation." I'd left her and Dean alone until noon when Jerry arrived. Sam and Joanne would be in that night, though Frank was staying at a different hotel.

"If you are *sure* we're not intruding," JJ added, coming up behind Ann. We'd left Dean with Bridgit…who was expressing *matronly* feelings. *Fine; deal with a toddler for a while. See how many kids you want in a few days.*

"No, *have* a seat," I said. "I heard you set a date for the wedding?"

"Saturday," JJ said. "Gotta pull it all together in *four days*."

"*Piece* of cake," Ann declared. "Found a dress this morning...."

"Oh, *I* took about an hour," Beth gushed...and *they* were off in wedding-talk land. JJ and I looked at each other, shrugged, and just listened.

After a while, JJ muttered, "got the catering *here*; need to look at flowers *tomorrow*."

"We didn't have that much to do with ours," I said. "Beth's uncle's President Pro Tempore of the Senate; security and all that...."

"Need *that* for us, too," JJ sighed.

"*That* so," I said, all innocent-like.

"Yeah," JJ grunted. Ann glanced over at us, gave JJ a knowing *tic*; he *ticed* back. *They know more than they are saying.* "Join us down here tonight; we'll *hoist* one for the regiment and for absent friends."

"If you don't mind a *Reservist*...."

I sat between JJ's step-brothers Will and Kurt and across from Mike's father and uncle, and with a *lot* of other guys *and* gals talking about their service from WWII and Korea through Vietnam and Grenada. Though I had as much time in as JJ, I *felt* somewhat left out. "I just put in my fifty-odd days a year as a captain in the Army Reserves."

"You're *part* of the *force structure*," JJ declared. "The Russkies look at the total force, not just the Active. So *you're* doing *your* bit, too."

That from *him* made me feel a *little* better.

✳✳✳

"Ann *seems* nice," Beth smiled and stretched when I got back to our suite that night; only the valence lights were on. "*Big* women often are."

"*Big*, as in..." She wore a translucent *something*.

"*Big* as in, she's near twice my weight and a third again my *height*. She was probably a Big Girl." She handed me a glass of wine calmly.

"*Big* Girl," I repeated. "Sounds like a title." The wine was warm and sweet.

"Remember that *one* girl in 3rd Grade as tall as the teacher who needed a bra? Yeah, well, *Ann*..." She strolled *slowly* into the bedroom. *Mine was Zakie something*..."and by 9th or 10th Grade, *most* kids had caught up. Not *me*, of course. *Ann* and the other *Big* Girls just *kept growing*." Diffuse light through the sheer curtains making her diaphanous whatever-it-was *vanish* as she gazed out the window.

"Yeah," I agreed. "If I was to *ask* you to..." I set my wine down.

"Spy?" She pulled the tie on her halter; gravity did *its* thing.

I caught my breath...barely. "No: watch and listen. They're *family*, babe; *Julia's* family, so by extension..."

"Uh-huh." She turned around...

To her Cheshire smile, I'll stand on file...

Battle of Baroque Circle

Or, Cue the Wedding March

"**H**ey." She nudged me out of a dream about balls of string and cans of paint.

"Huh?" *We slept THIS late?*

"Door," she sighed.

Then I heard a furious pounding on the door. "*Yeah*," I shouted from the sitting room, making my way to the suite door.

"*Dave*, come *on*," Morgan yelled as I cracked the door open. "there's been *shooting. Lots* of it. Julia and Ellen already left."

"OK; give me *five*...."

"You've *got two*...."

***

I'd never been *that* close to a battlefield before I got to Baroque Circle. I'd never *seen* a crime scene before either—not a *real* one—although I had been *in* one. What struck me first was the *smell*. Michigan in mid-November smells of fallen leaves, of brisk air out of Canada.

When I stepped out of the car a half-mile from the scene and hung my badge around my neck, I smelled *death*; sickly-sweet blood and guts and acrid smoke, whiffs of the vomit and the piss and shit that dying people often pass...

Without the smoke and blood, a *lot* like the home of a baby.

And I flashed—briefly—back to Berryville. PTSD does that, some-times.

Our FBI credentials got us past the state troopers at the first roadblock on Telegraph and 14 Mile Road, and I could tell that our presence piqued the *hell* out of the curiosity of the troopers, reporters, and camera crews—*what are the Feds doing here?* "*That* much shooting," I shrugged, "*everyone* wants a look."

The second roadblock—manned by deputy US marshals—was more circumspect. We had to use the *big* gun on them. "SPD Working Group," Morgan explained, and we walked onto the Baroque Circle service drive.

We passed Ellen in coveralls searching in the ditch alongside the road; we saw Ernie by a big map board, talking to various agencies and uniforms, pointing on the map. We chatted with Frank and Tom at the ID van, where we got IDs that showed we *belonged* there, unlike the reporters who were being escorted away by the proverbial scruffs of their necks. As we reached Baroque Circle itself an ambulance roared by, siren screaming. Two coroner's vans followed.

Then, we reached the battle scene…and I flashed again, frozen until Morgan nudged me.

Two cars were shot to pieces, outlines of seven people in and near them. *Oceans* of brass and shotgun shells; two houses shot up; ambulances on the grass, flashing lights. Uniforms and plain-clothes and coveralls hustling around, taking pictures and statements, measuring angles, recording, writing, chasing reporters and other interlopers away, and shaking their heads while helicopters noisily hovered overhead.

This was one of the most affluent neighborhoods in the world…and *seven people* were *killed* here in less than a minute, most by armed civilians.

A two-story Colonial was our destination—Kurt Parkinson's house. The upstairs windows had been shot out. The plate-glass windows on the downstairs around the door had been holed in several places. Pillars had bullet scars; the garage door was holed. An old Crown Victoria was halfway up the driveway, surrounded by brass, shotgun shells, and four tape silhouettes.

JJ and Ann were already there; so was Dorothy. A young woman was being treated for shock in the living room, sitting with a deputy and a paramedic. Another paramedic was standing by. Kurt and his wife were talking to Dorothy; Julia was chatting with JJ, Ann, and two Bloomfield Hills policemen. Dorothy was on her radio about every three minutes. Then, finally, she picked up the ringing phone.

It was, according to the timeline, about two *hours* after the shooting stopped. When she hung up, she called out. "Kurt; Mary. All four men out of that second car were killed."

"Yeah, *then* what," Kurt coughed. "Those guys were shooting at *us*."

"Do we know *who* they were; *why* they were shooting," Mary—his wife—asked, bundling her hair.

"The driver's ID was for Estavo Testa…."

"*Bullshit*," JJ shouted from across the room. I looked at Morgan; she was wide-eyed. *YEAH, bullshit. No WAY…*

"That's the name on his license. Familiar to you," Dorothy asked.

JJ chuckled. "Sure, like a wart on the back of my hand. A guy with that name was at Wolverine with me. I had him thrown out, along with Cliff Eyerdam, Nestor Boehlke, and Bruce Doyle."

"Tell me *why*," Dorothy pressed.

"Not…not *here*." There were still a half-dozen strangers in the house; technicians, police, and paramedics. "Back yard." Dorothy, Julia, and I joined JJ out back. "The Four Horsemen—Eyerdam, Boehlke, Doyle, and Testa—attacked a little guy named Evans one night. I ratted them out, and they were expelled."

"OK: attacked *how*? *What* was…" Dorothy asked. Part of me cringed.

"*Mom*," Julia interrupted with a *tic* at JJ: he *ticed* back. "*Attacked-attacked*, OK?"

Recognition slowly crossed Dorothy's face. "*Oh*." She sighed. "So, then, when I say that Eyerdam was in the *first* car—he's dead—and Boehlke and Doyle were in the second, *that* won't surprise you."

"No, Dot, it would *relieve* me. Let's go back in."

"Whoever they *are*," I added, "*two* of them are *not* Doyle *or* Boehlke. Take my *word* for it." *And I DON'T think it's Testa, either...*

"All right, then," Dorothy resumed her narrative. "*We* aren't sure why they were doing this, but I don't think it occurred to them that *anyone* would shoot back. We may *never* figure out *who* shot *who*."

"So, are *they* in trouble over there," JJ asked, distractedly looking out a living room window.

"With three handguns in the first car, and a shotgun, and four submachine guns in the second?" Julia sighed. "Don't *think* so."

"Dot; Jules: come look at *this*," JJ said.

Dorothy stood next to him. "What are we *looking* at?"

"Somebody in that hedge there, in that little park in the circle."

"We've *been over* it...."

"Steak dinner says there's *somebody* in there."

Dorothy spoke into her radio as I went to look. "Sierra Two to all Sierra units: unknowns in Baroque Circle Park."

"Sierra Two." Moments later, two cars arrived, and five deputies emerged. One shouted into the hedge as two others went around to the park benches by the little pond. Geese honked and flapped. Moments later, there was an exchange of gunshots before three deputies rushed the hedge. Then, more shots, some shouting, and deputies emerged with two prisoners.

"I owe *you* dinner," Dorothy smiled.

"Uh-huh." JJ took a good look at the handcuffed men. "I'll be *damned*," he grunted, "Pale Face and The Hammer."

"You *know* them?"

"Yeah. The big one's Rick Stutz: we called him The Hammer because he's about as *bright* as a *bag* of hammers. The other one's Boniface Pale: called *him* Pale Face. He was the top marksman for four years running. When I beat him in '70, I got eight demerits for insubordination."

"Oh, *shit*, I just lost *another* dinner," I grumbled.

"Why?"

"I *bet* that Stutz was still in *Oregon*." JJ stared at me. "We've *been* tracking him."

It was dark before SPD met as a group that day. "Only an *amateur* could screw up *this* bad," Ernie declared.

"That *firepower*, though," I added, "suggests *pros*."

"Seems *likely*," Morgan added. "*Planned* by amateurs and *executed* by a few professionals who did *not* expect to meet armed civilians because the amateurs didn't *know* to *look*."

"Let's start with *that* presumption and move on," Ernie nodded. "Julia: stay with your family. Frank and Ed: stick with the perimeter as long as there *is* one. Morgan and Dave: go to the morgue to ID the bodies if you can. Ellen and I will go to the crime lab to oversee the processing."

✳✳✳

"*Jesus*," Morgan gasped as the medical examiner lifted the sheet. Testa had been hit by 10-gauge magnum shells loaded with #3 buckshot, 12-gauge shells with 00 buckshot, and the glass of the shattering driver's door window. The combination had shredded his left side and destroyed most of his head.

"*That's* who he's *with* now; Him or the Devil." I glanced at his left foot: three toes missing. He'd lost them in a duel with a rival.

"Look for the tattoo on his back," Morgan said. The ME rolled the corpse up gingerly—with that much damage, he was literally coming apart. A tattoo of an angel fighting a demon covered his back from neck to buttocks. "Uh-huh. That fits *our* information."

"So, what's *he* doing *here*?" I glanced at Morgan; she shrugged. "Keep this out of the papers, if you *can*," I asked the ME. "*This* guy's wanted in about half the world."

"What about *him*?" He pointed to the next table, where Boehlke supposedly lay.

"Print all of them and run them through the system. Whoever *those* two are, they *are not* Boehlke *or* Doyle. *That...*"

"*Could* be Eyerdam," Morgan nodded. "Hard to tell." Victim #4"s head was mostly *not there*, and we had no information on Eyerdam's other identifying marks.

"The other three?"

"Just run their prints and check their IDs." Most had been hit with multiple shotgun pellets or buckshot; three by 9 mm pistol bullets; two by .30 caliber carbine slugs. All had been hit by flying glass or splintering metal. Two had had their faces smashed by flying trash cans coming through their windshield.

I struggled *not* to flashback to *my* shoot-out while I tried *not* to imagine what their last thoughts might have been.

They didn't see it coming, either.

At about midnight, we watched Roger Harriman identify his son Dave on the slab. Harriman's company was a frequent contractor with the Newhouse organization, but the *last* thing I wanted to do was interrogate *this* poor guy whose son was, by all accounts, no more than a stooge.

What a *waste...*

✳✳✳

It was 3AM before we were done filling out all the requests for information at the ME's office. Finally, we found an all-night eatery where we got some breakfast and enough *good* coffee to make it back to the hotel 20 minutes down Telegraph Road.

I called up to JJ and Ann's suite just after 6, thinking he was probably up already. He stumbled down in sweats and a field jacket.

"JJ," I said; Morgan nodded.

"What ya got?"

"*One* of 'em's Testa," I said. "No *doubt* of it. Another's a local guy, Dave Harriman. The others we haven't ID'd yet."

"How'd you *know* it was Testa?"

"We've *been* looking for *him*," Morgan sighed, relating Testa's colored post-Wolverine career and identifying marks. "Doyle's in New York; Boehlke's *elsewhere*."

"The only one of those IDs whose whereabouts we *don't* know is Eyerdam," I said. "Just so's you *know*. Now," I glanced at Morgan, "*we* have waiting bed partners and some *sleep* to catch up on."

"Your *little* one," JJ asked.

"With his aunt and grandparents," I sighed.

I trudged up to our suite, washed up some to get the stink of death and disinfectant off me, and bussed Beth on the cheek.

She woke up, smiling. "I *saw* the *news*, sweetie," she purred, raising the covers. "Flashbacks?"

"Some," I admitted. I'd never *had* many, but *that* day…

"You *need this*."

Beth *always* knew what I needed and generously provided it.

✳✳✳

"Now hear *this*," Ann announced in the atrium Thursday afternoon. "*These* guys," she pointed to Mike and Leigh, "are old friends. *He's* one of my oldest friends," she glanced at Sid. "*Those* two," she gestured to Morgan and me, "are with the FBI, and collectively, *we've* got a problem."

"Ladies and gents," Sid smiled. "We're going to need your eyes and ears for the next few days. The simple truth is…."

They addressed a diverse group that had just arrived from Florida: two men, six women, and a toddler. But the *simple truth* that Sid spoke of wasn't simple at all.

The crowd didn't seem to flinch when they heard about it. Three women were Navy divers; the men were Army Rangers; two women were *assigned* to the Rangers; one woman was a Ranger wife. They acted like that sort of thing happened all the time.

Then…Wendy Corey walked into the atrium. We'd *heard* that name only a few weeks before, and we'd never *seen* her…but here she was, hugging and chatting away with friends.

And Morgan and I just *stared*…

Ann sidled up to me and whispered, "what?" as JJ chatted with Wendy.

"*They've* visited both the Newhouse home *and* offices this last week."

We had to make a snap decision. After a silent conversation, we put the *Wendy* issue on the back burner…again.

That night was the stag smoker for JJ and the bachelorette party for Ann. I worked the smoker; Morgan and Ellen both worked the ladies' party. I chatted up Mike Dietz briefly, who remarked, "Special Projects. No one knows just *what* they are…."

"We work on *lots* of cases," I said. "*Arcane* cases; *old* things; *cold* cases and some *not*-so-cold. But we came *here* because *Jules wanted* us here."

"I don't *know* Julia."

"Ellen and I graduated from the Academy with her. We've worked *with* her for the past five years in SPD. We'll do a favor for her favorite uncle."

"Uh-huh." He knew *that last* bit was bullshit. "*I've* known JJ since '71."

"Uh-huh," I said. "Jules filled us in on you and your girlfriend. I *should* be going: supposed to see my family tonight…" *That* was true; I was to spend Thursday *and* Friday in Pickney because I was working the weekend.

But *then*, as I was grabbing my bag…

"Who's *whose what*, now?" Morgan's voice on the phone sounded unreal.

"Wendy Corey is Leigh Taylor's *cousin*. They were just chatting at the party and…."

"*Wait* a minute," I said. "How…*what* kind of documentation…?"

"Wendy's family Bible. The way I *got* it, there was just a *mention* that Leigh had the same name as Wendy's long-dead aunt; her *father's mother* died in childbirth in 1930."

Too coincidental to be coincidence…but we *had* to *know*. I woke Paula up and drove to the Troy office to make a *bunch* of phone calls to get *those* gears turning. At nearly midnight, I made a *lot* of people unhappy.

The way the story unfolded over the next couple of days, I half-expected Rod Serling to appear and tell me I'd just crossed over into…*The Twilight Zone*…it sure as Hell *felt* like it. Wendy's mother's maiden name *was* Taylor; her sister died in rural New York in 1930, at age fifteen.

That's why I had to work those two days, Beth. Sorry, but I figured you'd *never* believe the whole story if I'd told you then. But you got to spend some *quality* time with *my* family…didn't you?

✳✳✳

Morgan and I, Ellen, and Ernie watched JJ and Ann's ceremony from the wings behind the sanctuary. We heard the most *beautiful* rendition of "Ave Maria" I think I'll *ever* hear, as Ann floated down the aisle on the arm of her father.

After the pastor said the magic words, "you may kiss the bride," *we* had to be outside. My job was shotgun in the bridal limo.

Yeah, *we* were supposed to be *working* the reception, too, but Adam's people took all the *good* spots. We heard Ann's siblings and friends sing an *a Capella* verse of "Bridge Over Troubled Water" that brought the house down. We danced to standards, including "Up Where We Belong." The Florida women *vamped* a saucy rendition of "Rangers in the Night" at the end…that *was* something. I was surprised, pleasantly, to see Major Ramdas Reynolds at the party. He nodded benignly when he saw me, didn't make anything more of it. I *did* wonder how he got wind of it.

Even Dean had a great time. We took advantage of Mike's sisters' free babysitting service. Dean played with Gabrielle—the toddler from Florida who was just a year old and not yet steady on her feet.

As the party was breaking up, we knew that there would be a risk of infiltration as everyone's guard went down. I watched Mike, Sid, and

Ram eyeballing a replacement bartender who was busy setting up for happy hour.

That replacement was Chuck Wier…JJ confirmed it as he and Ann left. Tipped off by Ram, Mike and Leigh were about to sweep in before I waved them off.

"Guys," I said quietly. "Wier's over there. We need to talk to him."

Morgan and Ellen put their drinks down, hunched their shoulders, and moved in.

***

"*What* can I talk the FBI out of," Chuck said lightly. We'd managed to ask him for a non-custodial interview in a quiet corner of the atrium, out of the way of the clean-up crew. He hadn't resisted; he even acted like he'd expected us. "Make this quick, OK? I gotta get back to work."

"Just a chat about where you've *been* for the past decade or so," I started. "We've been *looking* for you."

"Haven't been *hiding*," Chuck shrugged. "Been moving around a lot."

"Your parents have missed you," Morgan said. "They…"

"You've *talked* to them," Chuck frowned. "*When?* I was at their anniversary party last month. Why would they *say* such a thing? Huh."

"It's *been* a while since we did," I admitted, "but you *haven't* been easy to find. The IRS…"

"*They* haven't caught up to me," Chuck sneered. "I work a lot of under-the-table jobs. I got tired of the rat race, decided to spend some time traveling, see the world." He made to inspect his fingernails. "Honest work, if untaxed. Maybe I *should* settle down."

"OK, I'll bite," Morgan smiled. "Where have you *been*?"

"Oh, around, here and there, everywhere."

"How did you *get* there? You haven't had a driver's license since yours expired in '80."

"Oh, bus; train; ferry; airplane. I hitched a ride on a salmon boat from Nome to Seattle last spring. I like sleeping under the stars in open country." His answers were glib, plausible, practiced. Using public transportation, working for cash from day to day, week to week. Don't need ID for that…

"Living rough, eh?"

"Yeah."

"You were here in Detroit, in *this hotel*, last January."

"Was I? You can *prove* that?"

"I saw you…."

"*Did* you, now? You can *prove* that?"

"Employment records…"

"Under *what* name," he interrupted. "Go on and *look*."

"You're using your *own* name now."

"Since when?"

That response, coupled with his dead stare, told us *who* he was *and what*. He was Tony DeVere's replacement, a top shot-caller for the Wier/DeVere Organization who took over—and went off the grid—when Tony was killed. It was likely that he'd never taken public transportation or slept in the open in his life. If we looked hard enough, if we knew his identities or had a crystal ball, we'd probably find a string of bodies in his wake.

There are two kinds of grifters that law enforcement has to deal with regularly. Holly's was the most common: she grifted strictly for the money, living for the long and the short cons, moving on to another angle and identity when the heat got wise. She could function on her own, get in and out of bad situations by guile and cunning. Sometimes, she had to go to jail for a while. *But* her kind of grifter was rarely violent.

Chuck was the other kind, and somewhat rare: he lied to stay alive, to keep operating, to keep law enforcement guessing, to keep running whatever operation he had going—*always* illegal and *always* for big money. All he *had* was the long con that was his life. Chuck's kind of grifter needed a supporting organization for him to work, to cover his tracks, to create the next opportunity. But Chuck *couldn't* go to jail; he could *barely* afford to be arrested. And *his* rackets often involved violence of the sudden, fatal kind.

There was also no further point in talking to him. He wouldn't give us a straight answer no matter *what* we asked.

"OK," Morgan said. "*Thanks* for talking to us."

Chuck silently got up and left, farting loudly as he departed. "Later, *feebs*." The ability to flatulate at will *was* Chuck's defining trait.

"He'll stick around for a while," I said, "just to prove that we've got nothing to hold him on."

"He's waving his prior employment here in our faces," Morgan nodded. "Maybe we should look into *this* place."

"Maybe we *should*."

Finding the Cheese

Or, Snap Go the Traps

"**Y**ou *have* something for the class," Ernie asked Mike in the Troy agency early Monday morning.

"Yessir," Mike answered. "JJ called me, said these two young women here found the current offices of Parkinson Title and Trust."

We all turned to look. "I see," Ernie said, interested. "If you would *introduce* yourselves, ladies?"

"My name is Josephine Parkinson," the first woman announced. She was a small woman with bright eyes, only a little bigger than Beth, and was the woman treated for shock at Kurt's house. "Just *Jo* is fine. *She's* my cousin," she nodded at Julia.

"I'm Roberta—*Bobbi*—Eldon," a dark-haired woman with glasses, bigger than Jo, said somewhat less confidently; she'd been at the reception. "We form the Bobbi/Jo Partnership. We provide forensic financial services and have been contracted by Mrs. Parkinson to look into her husband's finances."

"I see," Ernie said. "And what skills do *you* bring to the party?"

"I have a business intelligence degree from Wayne State University," Bobbi answered, "and I have a private investigator's license from the state. Jo is an attorney and a CPA, and *also* has a PI license."

"*Huh*," Ernie declared with a nod that meant *very interesting*. "*How* did you come to even be *looking* for this?"

"Because Gramma Stella needs money," Jo said.

"JJ's mother," I asked.

"Yes," Jo answered. "Her financial arrangements with Grampa Charlie are out of the 19th Century: she gets enough for groceries and not much more. We were given permission to search Grampa Charlie's financial records." She pulled a contract out of a folder. "Under Michigan law, because Grampa never incorporated, Gramma Stella is his sole heir and has authority. We found traces of the trust firm in his truck dealership and followed the bread crumbs to Telegraph and Fenkell."

"Very well, Jo," Ernie said. "I *have* to make you aware that what we are doing may uncover important, *life-threatening* information. Do you understand?"

Jo didn't seem phased. "I *get* it."

"We could *hire* them," I shrugged. "That would make them legally liable. That or, when we're *done*, cut off their heads and stick them in a safe."

"The latter is *melodramatic*," Ernie grunted, with a crick in his neck. "Jules…"

"Jo," Julia squinted, grinning, "let's make a *contract*. *You guys* are joining the FBI."

"*Ladies,*" Ernie announced an hour later. "Hold up your right hand and repeat after me: I—state your name—solemnly swear that I shall never divulge anything of what I learn having to do with the Wolverine Working Group or the Special Projects Division, so *help* me, *Hanna.*"

They kept a *semi*-straight face doing it. I doubt they knew how deep they were in.

"Now, we need to get inside that building," Ernie declared, "but without a criminal referral, we can't get a subpoena or a warrant. So, therefore, we need the owner's permission."

"First, we need to *verify* ownership," I said. "Mike, that's *your* cue."

✳✳✳

"OK," Mike explained a few hours later. His smooth, convincing sales pitch for free marketing services got the office manager, Ingrid Torgerson, to lower her guard *just* enough. "Charlie Parkinson is the *owner* of the business. He's in the office about once a week or so but hasn't been *seen* for three."

"The timing fits," I nodded. "What do *they* do? What does *she* do?"

"She's like a caretaker."

"He's *got* several real estate investment trusts," Bobbi said. "Saw traces of them at his dealership."

"Huh," I grunted and glanced at Mike. "*JJ* has more business going in there with his mom."

"Yeah, but when I was there, she got a phone call, said she had to leave for the rest of the day."

"Why?"

"All *she* knows is she gets paid for the day for *not* being there *after* she gets that call."

"Let's watch tonight and see why. Mike: *take* the night off."

The smartest thing I'd said all *month…*

✳✳✳

"I *hate* stakeouts," I mumbled honestly. "Wait for something to *happen*, not knowing if it even *will*." Ellen and I were in a used van in a parking lot across the street from Parkinson Title as a light, cold rain started late that afternoon. I had *hoped*, since it was *my* brilliant idea, that I'd be spared the *honor* of having to sit out here, *but…*

A plain white van pulled into the parking lot, rolling up to the door. "At *last…*" I sighed as Joe stepped out of the driver's side, joined by...

"Herman Jimenez," Ellen mused, "bailed by Dryden last February; in the wind since." We watched Joe and Herman wheel stacks of file boxes from the van into the building on a handcart before the lights came on in Parkinson Title and Trust. "Coincidence?"

"*No* way in *hell*," I declared. We watched as the pair moved stacks of boxes like they were *supposed* to be there. After a dozen such trips, the two got back into the van and drove off. "*Heads* up." Another truck pulled up, *this* one with a Newhouse Properties logo on the side. A different crew unloaded this truck, not *file* boxes but smaller ones. "Cancelled check boxes. What *else* is in this building?"

"A marketing firm; some sales something; an architectural firm and a computer outfit," Ellen said. Barely ten minutes had passed when Joe and Herman's van returned. It was followed by a Lincoln Mark V. Joe and Herman unloaded their van again while an older man exited the Lincoln and went around to help someone else out the other side. They entered the building, one clutching the other's arm. "That's RF *and* Randy," Ellen mumbled. After a few minutes, an office window lit up.

"Hiding material under a *different name*," I sighed.

Half an hour later, back in the Troy agency, Ernie declared, "we *need* to get in there…" he glanced at Julia… "*un*obtrusively."

There followed a *brief* non-verbal exchange between them before Julia sighed, dialed the phone, and turned the speaker on.

"Elrath," JJ answered.

"Hey, JJ," Julia *said* brightly; her *eyes* were sad. "Listen, buddy: Mike *had* to tell us what Jo told *you* about Gramp's trust office."

Too quiet. "*OK,* I suppose. *Why*?"

"We…have our reasons."

"To do with Wolverine?"

"*Maybe*." She paused, swallowed hard. "John, *trust* me, OK?" I'd seen her under stress before, but *this* was different. "If there was *any* other way, buddy…I'm *sorry* to…" This *felt* like a betrayal; she looked miserable.

"Always, Jules."

"We need to get *in*, buddy. We need you and Gramma Stella to go down there and…."

"We…the FBI?" In Julia's eyes, I could see two teenagers sharing a secret on a hot summer night…

"Yeah."

"Sergeant Elrath, Ernie Packard. We've seen too many coincidences to be coincidental, but not enough to get an indictment or a warrant." He inhaled deeply. "We may find something to cause trouble for Wolverine."

"Yessir," JJ answered. "*What* do you suspect he's into?

"Human trafficking."

There followed a deep and dark silence. "What do you want *us* to do?" *That* voice was hollow, almost unfeeling. Julia wiped a tear.

"Just...open the door."

Another silent pause. "Does it *affect* my mother?"

"*NO*." Ernie declared swiftly, glaring around.

A pause, *not* as long. "Tomorrow? Be advised, Mom doesn't get *up* before 9."

"Fine." Ernie hung up. He picked up the phone again, glanced at a note, and dialed. "Ms. Parkinson; Ernie Packard. Your grandmother and your uncle are going down to that office tomorrow morning. *We* will be there *perhaps* an hour afterward. If *you* were to get there ahead of us and *happen* to find financial information there...You *understand*, then... coordinate with *them* as to time, but it will *probably* be late morning. Good *evening*, Ms. Parkinson."

"Um," Ellen grimaced when he hung up, "under RICO, the proceeds of a corrupt enterprise...."

"Will *NOT affect that woman*," Ernie declared, glaring. "Am I *clear*?"

"*Crystal*, sir."

✳✳✳

We arrived at the building on Fenkell* the next morning, about an hour after JJ, his mom, and her lawyer. The '50s-style steel-and-glass building was fully occupied; the parking lot ¾ full and aging, but recently topped

---

* Also known as Five Mile Road. Many of the Detroit area's thoroughfares have multiple names to confuse visitors and other invaders.

and lined. Morgan and I walked in just as JJ's mom, Jo and Bobbi, and their big bear of a lawyer were leaving. Ernie nodded at Jo. "Any luck?"

"*Yes,*" Jo grinned.

"Then, please," Ernie smiled, "we'll take *this* from here." I'd got used to the Liberty Bell Files in their zillion or so cabinets…but *this*…it looked a great deal like my apartment right after moving in: too much *stuff,* not enough *place*.

"We'll have to move this," Ernie grunted, "can't secure it here."

"May I ask *where,*" JJ asked.

"Just don't expect an answer," Ernie smiled. "The fewer people who know, the better."

"I get it," JJ answered. "I appreciate you letting Jo…."

"My dad was killed on the job when I was fifteen," Ernie said quietly. "Small, rural sheriff's department; no pension. My brothers and I had to scramble just to keep a roof over Mom's head. I won't *allow* another family to suffer like that if I can help it."

I'd never *heard* that before; I doubt I was *supposed* to have heard it *then*. I moved off to try to catalog the…*stuff*. JJ left not long after.

We were still cataloging the sheer volume of cabinets, boxes, envelopes, loose folders, and whatever-else-have-you mid-afternoon when Julia loudly declared, "*Ho..ly…SHIT*! *Guys*: come *see* this."

So we came.

The big closet lit only by a single bare bulb contained a half-dozen duffel bags stacked on the floor; an open one was stuffed with cash. There were also pallets with crates; an open one was full of gold disks.

"*Ho*-boy," I gasped. "*How…*"

"*Stop what you are doing,*" a voice called from the front of the office.

"Says *who,*" Ernie snarled.

A man of middling age and thinning hair who looked like a well-dressed Jacob Marley*was just inside the front door. He declared, "I have

---

* The first ghost in Dickens' *A Christmas Carol,* but regrettably without the rag to hold his jaw shut.

a restraining order from the 47ᵗʰ District Court, enjoining *anyone* from accessing this property."

"Let me see *that*," Ernie declared, reaching for the papers the apparition was waving like a flag.

The Marley look-alike managed to hold them back. "And *who* do *you* think *you* are? I am Lewis Rockland of Rockland, Atkins, Terrance, and Schumpeter, Attorneys at Law. *You* have *NO* business on this property. I *demand* that *you*…."

"*I* am Senior Special Agent Ernest Packard of the Federal Bureau of Investigation, here on the business of the Wolverine Working Group of the Special Projects Division. Just who are *you* representing, *Mr.* Rockland?"

Rockland winced. "I am representing Mr. *Charles* Parkinson. There are *personal* papers and records that are none of *anyone's* business."

"They *are* the business of the Wolverine Working Group," Ernie declared, nodding at me. "Give Mr. Rockland a copy of the Working Group's charter and escort him out."

"You *cannot* do *that*," Rockland sputtered, exchanging the charter for his court order. "The court order *stands* until vacated, and the court *won't* be in session again until tomorrow. I *demand* that you leave, leaving *everything*…."

I passed the court order to Morgan, then whispered into Ernie's ear: "we lock the place up; set up on it tonight; see who comes."

Ernie nodded. "We'll *go*," he announced loudly. "WE will ALL go."

"And you shall *leave* the *keys* with *me*," Rockland shouted.

"Show us where *that* is required in this injunction," Morgan asked sweetly.

"It is *implied*," he declared. "*All* access…"

"But not the *means* of access," Ernie grinned. "*We* shall *keep* the keys until a *judge* orders that we surrender them."

Ya *gotta* love that kind of thinking.

We ushered everyone out to the glass-enclosed building lobby, piquing the interest of a woman standing at the architect's office door before abruptly turning away.

Rockland stared dumbly at the office door as Ernie locked it. Marley/Rockland seemed to spin like a jewelry box ballerina before returning to his car and picking up his phone.

"Wonder who tipped *him* off," Ellen asked.

"*Prime* candidate is Ingrid," I said. "I'll check the traps later, but *right now*, I've got another interview that I'm already *late* for."

As we watched Rockland drive away, Ernie cocked his head and sighed, "now, *tonight*, we get a peek at some *more* players…*maybe*."

✳✳✳

"This is Dave Clawson, with the FBI," Mike said. "He's here…different reason." Matt Corey—Wendy's father—nodded in my direction. He resembled Wendy; coloring, height, and face shape. "Well, we'll start simple: how often do you have *any* contact with the Newhouse family?"

They described their *very*-little direct contact with the Newhouse family, a branch we didn't even *know* about until Wendy told Leigh about it. I listened vaguely until I heard Matt, talking about two girls named Newhouse, say…"they were taken in by a lovely foster family. Ran a grocery store in Pickney..."

"My *neighbors*, I *think*," I said.

"Indeed? When Charity died in '69, RF moved them," Matt said.

"And that's the last we knew of *them*," Faith, Matt's wife, said.

"What are the girl's names," Leigh asked.

"You know, we *don't* really know," Matt declared. "I never *saw* their birth certificates—couldn't *find* them anywhere—so, they went into the system *without* them. The older one called herself Marylin—bleached her hair like Marylin Monroe and wouldn't *give* another name. The younger one was either Lettie or Lizzie. When I filled out the paperwork for their foster care, Charity *wanted* them to be 'Taylor,' so they became Marylin and Elizabeth *Taylor*."

"They were Mary and Lizzie when I knew them," I added. "Mary *called* herself Marylin; Elizabeth was Lizzie's *middle* name; I heard *that* in school."

"And that was the last *we* saw or heard of *any* Newhouse's," Faith—Wendy's mother—said, "except for the annual ham."

After that, there wasn't really anything for *me* to add. Then I heard the story about a rural family and a young girl who got *in trouble* by a beguiling stranger. The girl died in childbirth; the infant—Leigh's father—went into foster care himself, the family too proud to keep an illegitimate child.

I'd heard sad tales before, but this was the first time I'd heard one about someone I knew *of* personally. Of course, *that* moved it closer to home.

✳✳✳

"Wish these guys weren't so predictable," one of the marshals grinned as the pickup *slowly* passed us a second time. "Right about when we'd expect them. Detroit police shift changes around 8." I'd *just* got there myself. It hadn't been sunny, so the asphalt hadn't absorbed any heat: my feet felt frozen.

"*He'll* be around again," another one declared.

"*Has* to…" I added for no particular reason.

A big van pulled directly into the parking lot, and Paula and three other people stepped out. "Here to relieve the shift," she declared. There's *no*…."

The pickup noisily roared down Fenkell and into the parking lot, coming close to us. It sped across the small sidewalk to the building's front door before someone stood up in the box and heaved a cinder block at the door as the truck roared off again. The block cracked but did not shatter the heavy plate glass door.

"Let's call the local gendarmes," I calmly said.

"On it," Paula replied, reaching into her truck. "You guys got that new low-light imagery camera?"

"Yep," a marshal declared. "We'll see who it was in a few hours."

***

"She seems to be actually believing what she's saying," Mike sighed that Tuesday evening. "But *no* contact from the Newhouse family."

We were finally debriefing Mike. He had gone up to the Hampton Center Mall that day to *chat* with Mary Newhouse about a non-existent insurance policy on Randy V.

Mary's version of her relation to the kids was consistently *aunt*. She said that her *sister* was their mother, which contradicted the version Randy IV gave Leigh on their wedding night.

"Nope," Julia declared. "Not that surprising if she's who Dave *thinks* she is...."

"Too coincidental to be a coincidence," Morgan said. "But Mary mentioned 'kids,' plural?"

"Yes," Mike said. "No names, no mention of a relationship...just 'kids.'"

"Huh," Leigh sighed. "A look at a birth certificate might help. Might confirm..."

"All we know for sure about that is that both parent's names are not on the boy's," Dorothy nodded. "That locks it down by Michigan law, so we can't see it without a court order unless a parent or the child consents."

"But we know...." Mike started.

"No: we've been *told*," Leigh corrected, raising a finger. "Randy said Mary was the kid's mom. Now *she's* saying it was *her sister's* kid and that she—Mary—was married to Randy in '72, a year later. He turned seventeen that May. Without parental consent...?"

Mike frowned. "I *should* have asked what her sister's name was, but there

was no reason to ask that; nothing to do with the policy if Mary's the legal guardian."

"How common is the Newhouse name in Michigan," Julia asked.

"There are two residences listed in Oakland County," Ellen said, "and one in Bay County, which includes Essexville."

"Mortgage on that house: did she declare it on her taxes," Amy asked.

"Nope," I said. "Her tax return says 'owned by a family member.'"

I admit I had to tune out for a while, thinking about how this might play out, who Mary Newhouse might be, who those kid's mother might be. For me, the answers kept coming up the same, especially when Leigh said that her five-second exchange with her new husband was never verified.

I listened to everyone talk about those trapped numbers that kept coming back to the same place: Newhouses and their lawyers. We knew they were moving people to Wolverine; we knew they were using the place to hide young men. But we didn't know *for whom*.

✳✳✳

We finished moving the contents of the Parkinson Title and Trust office to Sid's store Wednesday. We stood around the edges of the collection of filing cabinets, bulletin boards, tables, desks, and other office furniture that filled eighteen 16-foot-square bays, agape. We recreated the overall *layout* of the office—but more spread out—leaving incongruous stacks of file boxes isolated from tables piled with envelopes. Lines of banker's boxes we'd found lying on the floor sat apart from envelopes that had been, too. Tables, screen panels, and whiteboards surrounded the mass. Table and floor lamps offset the glare of the overhead fluorescent ceiling lights.

For convenience, everything had been cataloged by location and description. Each was given a unique location number in a ledger—*and* cataloged using any external labels. Some of our ledger entries read:

- Table A31, folder 22, "Oakland Properties LTD 1974 Annual Report;"
- Cabinet B66 "Titles 1962," folder 91, "Hanover Title, March 1962;"
- Desk C5, RH middle drawer, envelope 546, "Stella Christmas '69;"
- Floor box D237, "Destroy January 1987;"
- Credenza E3, Hanging file 2710, "The Rat;"
- Envelope F6242, "Disbursement, 1976."

Off to the side, the heap of duffel bags and skids of boxes sat alone.

Before we'd finished getting our morning coffee, Morgan appeared with a clean-cut guy in a *Saville Row* suit worth more than my *car*. "Everyone," she announced, "my cousin, Felix Towne, of *Evans* and Towne."

"Ladies," Felix nodded, "gents. Cousin Morgan asked about the Second Century Fund? The firm has authorized me to, ah, *speak* of it."

"*Have* they," Ernie said broadly, in his sarcastic way. "*What* can you tell us, *on* the record, of *course*."

"Naturally," Felix smiled. He looked more like a genial librarian than a banker. "Understand that my firm has a *considerable* reach and *wide-ranging* interests." He paused as if for effect. "We *have had* dealings with the Second Century Fund and the Wier/DeVere Organization. *Both* deal in dark money—the source of which *no one* wants to know."

"We *got* that sense," Ernie said patiently.

"Private banking often works in the shadows. At Evans and Towne, we *do not* tolerate shady dealings, but some of our clients *have* been so engaged *before* they became our clients. When we find that they still *are*, we disassociate ourselves."

"*Admirable*," Ernie replied.

"When Eddie Evans was hurt at Wolverine, we began to look into the school. We found that Second Century was getting money for *keeping* students there; Wier/DeVere was providing the customers."

"Ah," Ernie nodded. "Your *sources*…?"

"*That* would be difficult," Felix answered, "and beyond my brief. We learned that the sole cooperating witness to Eddie's assault was in danger at the school. We informed the Wier/DeVere organization that their access to resources would be, um, *interfered with* if that witness were to be badly hurt."

That's what kept JJ alive. "So, *you* outbid…" I started.

"I don't *know* the details," Felix replied. "It was before I started working there. Father *personally* told me to inform you of this."

"How would your firm have *interfered*," Ellen asked.

Felix looked benignly at her. "By blocking their access to anything *but* Second Century and the like. *That* would make them subservient to dark sources, and *no half*-legitimate financial organization wants *that*."

"You have *that kind* of clout," Grace asked innocently.

"We have the *kind of clout* that can and *has* disrupted *national* economies, madam," Felix smiled. "When other banks are in trouble, they come to *us*."

"Can you tell us who *owns* Wolverine?" Ernie's question sounded benign.

"I can't because we don't *know*. Nor do we have a *vague* idea who's behind Second Century. We stopped inquiring when Eddie's lawsuit was settled. Wier/DeVere, however, is *well known* to us."

"I see," Ernie sighed. "*That* confirms what we *suspected*. Thank you for that. *Now*," Ernie led us to the heap of duffel bags and skids of boxes. "This *luggage* was found at the Parkinson Title office and *now* belongs to…."

"Mrs. Stella Parkinson," Felix nodded. "A *new* client."

"In*deed*," Ernie said. "We would appreciate it if you could get *that* luggage where it *belongs*."

"*A-hem*," Grace noisily cleared her throat. "Sir; a *word*?"

"Once this *luggage* is removed, certainly." Ernie glared at Grace, then the rest of us. "We'll *help*." *That* glare distinctly and loudly announced *argue with me and spend the rest of YOUR career in Point Barrow.*

So we hauled *about* $1.9 million in cash and gold into a waiting armored truck, driven by an armed guard, with Felix and two more guards in the back. After the armored truck left, Ernie said, "now, children, we must get *to* work." He smiled at Jo and Bobbi and loudly announced, "*we'd* like it very much if you ladies could remove any *strictly* personal material. Get it out of *our* way, as it were."

"Sir, *that* would be..." Grace sighed.

"*Perfectly* acceptable, as long as you work *with* my agents," Ernie finished, glaring again.

Bobbi set up a folding table away from the rest of the furniture. As we began our painstaking and *somewhat* painful research, they simply looked over our shoulders, taking folders and envelopes away that we handed off.

It was Thursday afternoon that Julia found the smoking gun. Charlie Parkinson had kept meticulous cash-out records in enormous leather-bound ledgers that he stored in big vaults. And...

"Holy shit," I shook my head, looking over her shoulder.

"Yeah," Julia sighed. "Holy *and* shit." She paged back and forth. "Gramps *bought* Wolverine in '59."

"*Damn*," Morgan moaned. "Who's gonna tell *JJ*?"

"Agent Addison will transmit *that* information," Ernie declared. "Better from a friend than from a stranger."

"There's more," Julia said, opening another ledger. "He *still* owned it when the Evans lawsuit was settled. JJ got *his* share from Gramps via the Evans family."

"Barrel of dollars to a bucket of shit Parkinson knew *of* it," Morgan said softly. "It's *him* behind all this."

"*Can't* be *just* him," Ernie said. "He didn't have the *reach* to get Testa here. There's someone *else*." He moved to a blank whiteboard, picking up a marker. He drew a circle in the middle. "*This* is Wolverine." He drew three smaller circles touching the big one. "Parkinson Title—*defunct* but still operating; Newhouse Properties—*trafficking* in IDs; Second Century Fund—*dark money* and hooked into the Wier/DeVere outfit. We know they all *touch* Wolverine. What we *don't* know is their relationship to each other."

"Parkinson and Newhouse are in-laws," Jo said. "Gramma Ellie—Gramps' first wife—was a Newhouse."

"*Huh*," Ernie grunted with an appreciative nod. "You know this *how*?"

"*Her* birth certificate; *their* marriage license." Jo showed us the documents.

"*Copy* those, if you would," Ernie said, drawing arrows to connect those two bubbles. "So...Second Century..."

"Hampton Center Mall, where Mary Newhouse works, was *built* with Second Century financing, and Newhouse Properties manages it." Julia drew another arrow to join Newhouse...then another dashed arrow to join the Parkinson bubble.

"But we still *don't* know who *owns* the Second Century Fund," Ellen sighed.

"I *might*," Frank said, plopping a file box on a table and pulling out a carbon so old the type had gone from blue to gray. "Articles of Incorporation, Second Century Fund. Chairman..."

"Charlie Parkinson..." I started.

"Nope: Randal Fred Newhouse, *Junior*."

"RF's *father*," I blurted.

"Yep. The *President was* Charlie Parkinson in 1955." Frank held out a more recent document: an annual statement to the Chairman of the Board—Randal Fred Newhouse IV—and the President of the Second Century Fund—Randal Fred Newhouse III—*from* the Chairman of the Board of Trustees of the Second Century Fund: Charlie Parkinson.

Finally...

✳✳✳

"Well," I declared, sitting in the Dietz's living room Thursday, "we've got a problem."

"What," Mike asked, sitting across from me.

"We've got IDs on everyone from that shootout last week." I pushed file folders across the glass table. "Two are who their IDs *say* they are: Testa and Harriman. The rest...one's a *local* thug; another's a hitter from LA; three others are associated with Testa's cartel protection racket. What's *more* interesting is *this*." I pushed another folder. "*Three* images of Cliff Eyerdam: one driving a truck that attacked the Parkinson's office Monday night. The second, last night in Beaumont Hospital with Randy Newhouse. Then, *this morning*, right outside here, driving a Newhouse limo. And we've been *looking* for Eyerdam for *five years*."

Randy's visit to the Dietz home was surprising. So was his appearance—standing next to Ann Mueller-Elrath while waiting for an elevator—at the hospital Wednesday night. Adam had helpfully provided his surveillance videos of the Dietz home as soon as he got them. Ann had told Sid about her chance encounter with an old classmate; Sid contacted us; we called the hospital...

"And he surfaces *now*," Mike frowned. "What do *you* think?"

I nodded. "*I* think we need to talk to him. Tomorrow morning, Leigh and I will *ask* Randy Newhouse—*politely*, of course—just *where* Cliff is."

✳✳✳

"What can *I* do for the FBI," Randy asked expansively on Friday morning. "My business is all above-board." The small, somewhat barren office was lit by valence lights along the walls, casting the room in a diffused glow.

"I'm sure it *is*," I said. "Mr. Newhouse, is there *something* wrong with your vision?" I was using a *softly, softly catchy monkey* approach because Randy just wasn't *right*. And going at him hard...no, I was putting Beth and Dean on a plane home this afternoon. *No* time for hard-ass.

"I suffer from a degenerative eye disease," Randy said lightly. "I can see *you* around jagged little cracks and holes." He side-glanced at Leigh, winked slowly.

"*What*, exactly, is it that you *do*, Mr. Newhouse," I asked. It was a small office; he was the only one there. The Newhouse Properties sign out front was a fig leaf. There was a reception desk near the door, but it was unused.

"I'm a gopher, Agent Clawson. *Please* call me Randy: it would save time."

"Very well, Randy. For whom do you *gopher?*"

"For my father's business."

"I see. Gophering…*what?*"

"As an attorney, I handle legal chores. I'm *also* a notary."

"Really, Randy," Leigh interjected. "Can you *see* well enough?"

"I *can* read, Leigh," Randy answered patiently without looking at her.

"Uh-huh," I nodded. "How often do you *gopher* between Berryville and Greenville?"

He was impassive. "Where…"

"We've *talked* to a few people, Randy," I said. "Where can we find Cliff Eyerdam?"

"Who?" He managed a puzzled look.

"The guy driving you around yesterday, Randy," Leigh interjected. "We have him on videotape."

Randy turned his head. "Mr. *Block's* cameras, honey?" *His* version of *et tu, Brute* was convincing.

"*Yes*, Randy. It's…"

"I *get* it, honey. I won't *live* long enough to hold a grudge." He turned back towards me. "I don't *know* where he lives *or* hangs out."

"How long's he been driving you?"

"Um…maybe three months? Joe's had *other* things for Dave to do, and now, *poor* Dave…." He fiddled with his tie. "I don't get to pick who works for me; haven't for some years."

335

When you see a crack in a source's façade… "Who *does?*"

"I don't know for sure, but I think Joe Dryden."

Place your wedge… "Americans for a Democratic Society, Randy: ever *heard* of them?"

Randy blinked furiously. "No."

And…tap-tap-tap… "We have a Greenville parade permit with your signature on it from 1972," I handed him a copy. "Americans for a Democratic Society; Randal F. Newhouse IV, Secretary."

He switched on a high-intensity light, putting the paper under it and covering one eye. "Ah, *that,*" he smiled. "Yeah, I made *that* up, got a permit to counter the *rah-rah* Fourth of July parade."

Tap-tap-tap… "*I* see." I pushed a picture of Wier across the table. "Familiar?"

"No," Randy said at length after peering at it under his light, "don't recognize him."

Tap-tap-tap… "Funny. He recognized *you* from when you *led* that parade. Said you were screaming about how the capitalists were destroying civilization. Kinda funny for a *rich* kid," I pushed *another* picture across the desk. "Remember *him?*"

Randy looked carefully. "No."

TAP-tap-TAP… "*He* remembers when *you* and Sid and Dave took him to Wolverine in September of '70." I leaned forward. "*Try* again. ADS."

CRACK! Randy's eyes seemed to dart around like moths on a candle. He swallowed hard before he spoke. "ADS was one of my *great* schemes to get away from Dad. Too bad it *couldn't* work the way I needed it to; you know, get under the old man's skin, make him disown me, then wait till Mom dragged me back into the fold." He blew out his cheeks. "No, *not* after the *baby* was born."

"Yeah, *about* him," Leigh leaned forward and smiled like a mongoose to a cobra. "*I'm not* that kid's mom, Randy: you and I both know that."

"*Yeah,*" he smiled. "Look." He reached into a drawer and pulled out…

Certificate of Live Birth

Child's Name: Randall Fred Newhouse V Born: 15 May 1971
Mother: Leigh Elizabeth Taylor, DOB 12 April 1955
Father:

"The *father's* blank," I said. "Why?"

"That's the way *you* wanted it, *darling. Don't you remember? I* do. Until we got *married*, you said, and we made it *all....*"

"The medical authorities *all* say I've never *given* birth, Randy," Leigh said, barely audible. "And there are tons of people who *saw* me in '70-'71 who say...."

"They are all *lying*," Randy declared, snatching the birth certificate back. "*All* lying." He sighed heavily. "Look, I have a *lot* of important work to do, so unless you have something *urgent,* you'll *have* to excuse me."

As we left, we met Mike and Morgan outside, huddling against a blustery wind as Ellen listened to a radiophone. "*C'mon,* c'mon," she mumbled, "*make* the call...."

"Who's this ADS outfit," Leigh asked.

"Bunch of mad dogs from the '60s," I said. "Blew up a draft office in '70, according to one account."

"And *Randy* started it," Leigh asked, incredulous.

"We *don't* think so," Morgan said. "But we *think* whoever's calling Randy's shots *did*...or knows *who* did."

"*There,*" Ellen smiled. After several minutes, she said, "yeah...good." She hung up. "Newhouse Properties in Bloomfield Hills; three and a half minutes."

I keyed my radio. "Fed Four: *trap* on *one.*"

"Sierra Two: affirm," came the answer.

Now, we wait. "Let's hope these people are just *that* stupid...."

"Sierra Two," the radio announced ten minutes later. "Eyerdam in custody."

"Yep," Ellen sighed, "they *are*."

"Let's wait for Randy to figure out who to call *next*. Let Cliff stew for a few hours. You guys can go by Sid's place if you want, but *I* have to go to Bay City, see if it *is* Marilyn."

"Sid's," Mike asked.

"An empty department store in Southfield," I said. "It's where we moved the contents of the Parkinson Title office. SPD's leasing it."

Leigh murmured, "Randy as much as admitted that his role in the business is minimal Thursday morning. This façade is just busy-work."

"Not entirely," I said. "His name's on some very damning paperwork."

✳✳✳

"Mary Newhouse," I said casually, walking in the door of the little office in Hampton Center Mall. "FBI. Care to answer some questions?"

"Ah," she said, almost as if expecting someone. "Sure. *Have* a seat. What can I do for you?"

When I knew her in the '60s, *Marilyn* had a glint of violet in her right eye. She also had a *tiny* mole on the edge of her left ear that I found *fascinating* as a teenager, for whatever reason. "Remember *me*, Marilyn? Dave Clawson."

"Dave," she blinked, her face switching from weary to wary to recognition to alarm to surprised delight almost simultaneously. "Dave *Clawson! My God.* What are *you* doing here?"

"Just *talk*, Mary," I said in my most reassuring voice. "*Just* talk."

"Well, *wow*, I mean…you took the time to *find* me. *Can't* be *that* simple."

"Kimmie's in public relations in a firm near Pittsburgh," I said casually, *trying* to keep it light. "Pete lives in Roseville; works at Willow Run."

"*Kim* was great fun. How are your *brothers* these days?" They did hang out together from time to time.

I told her about Steve and Dean, adding Bridgit. "Where's *Lizzie?*"

"*I* don't know," she looked away. "I haven't seen her since her kids were born." The whole atmosphere had changed as if an iceberg had moved in...*and I don't think this is 'legend.'*

"OK," I said, jumping out of *friend* mode and back to *FBI agent* mode, if briefly. "When was *that*?"

And she told me a *version* of what Sid said, *without* what happened *after*.

But few knew *that; she* certainly didn't. "I know *where* she is," I mumbled. In truth, I *knew* someone who *knew*...

"I take it you *can't* tell me," she declared flatly.

"For *everyone's* safety...no." I glanced around her desk, where pictures of the kids were prominently framed. "What if I was to take some pictures *to* her?"

She eyed me suspiciously. "Why?"

You didn't ask how? "She's interested enough to send cards. She *might* want to know...."

I hadn't finished before she was taking pictures out of their frames. There was a school portrait of each and one of both kids *and* Mary at a lake. "I have *more*," she said, handing them over. "If you *talk* to her, *tell* her I *think* I understand."

"I will," I nodded. "Ah, Mary. *That* day, in the basement. *Pete* said you two really *did it*."

She wore a puckish grin. "Did you *do it* with Kim? If *I* have to tell, *you* have to."

I smiled. "Tell me about that afternoon *and* who you work *for now,* and *I'll* tell *you* about that afternoon...*and* some more."

Some secrets are kept better than others...but we shared *those*.

✷✷✷

"So, Cliff, didn't *know* you were dead, *did* you?" Mike flashed his credentials; Ellen, Morgan, and I were in the observation booth, watching *that* impresario play Cliff like a grand piano. Step by step, Cliff said what we were thinking and much of what we already knew...

Then... "What am I buying myself?" Cliff became adamant.

"You're only facing conspiracy charges so far, so, *maybe* a walk." Mike had no such power, of course, but *Cliff* didn't know that.

"I get it in writing, or we're done." Cliff crossed his arms. "Nothing else until I talk to the state's attorney...*and* a lawyer."

The US Attorney for Eastern Michigan had already created the paperwork for Cliff's deal with a court-appointed attorney...but we let them wait.

"Let's *hear* it," I said a couple hours later. "Who got you *here?*"

"Like I said, a couple of guys came to my club," Cliff sighed, "said wait to be contacted. Then I got a call from a guy at the end of July who says I can have a hundred grand for six month's work."

"Who's the *guy?*" Ellen studied her nails.

"I only know him as Neitelsmidt."

BING—GO! "Where *were* you when this call came?"

"El Paso."

"OK: *what* work?" Ellen shifted in her chair.

"I didn't ask. The next day I got an envelope with ten grand and an address."

"*Then* what?" I sighed with *great* effort.

"Then I went up to this little house just off the tollway a spit from the Michigan border...Berryville, and I met *another* guy who gave me *another* ten grand. I drove a guy to Wolverine the next morning."

"*What* guy?" Ellen shifted.

"*Can't* say."

"Just him?" I leaned back, taking the excited tension out of my legs.

"No. Joe Dryden and Randy Newhouse were with him."

AHA!!! "*Then* what?" I scribbled a meaningless note.

"Then we came down here."

"OK." I yawned ostentatiously; Ellen stretched. "So, you're up... when? September? *Then* what?"

"So, I drove to *another* wide spot in the road in Minnesota, just short of the Canadian line, where I met Testa and *his* guys. Then, I start driving people around back here."

"Ever drive Randy Newhouse around here?" Ellen *tried* to look bored.

"Yeah, couple times a week."

"OK," I glanced at Ellen, her eyes glowing. *Time to spring this trap.* I pulled another file out of a valise. "We *ran* your prints; came back this morning." *Actually, a week ago…*

Suddenly, Cliff's entire demeanor changed. "*Shit.*"

"Uh-huh," Ellen sighed. "Your deal's *gone*. Want to make *another*?"

"Bring the lawyer back." His court-appointed lawyer *and* the state's attorney were back in the room minutes later. "Cliff" signed without hesitation.

"So, *Mario*," Ellen started. "Let's start. Born in 1946, you were twenty-two when you got to Wolverine…." And she laid out the story of Mario Constantine Kosta—Cliff's *birth name*—wanted in connection with a car bomb in Pittsburgh that killed seven people, including two children, in 1967. "What *we* want to know is *who* set up your new identity? *Who* sent you to Wolverine?"

"I wish I *knew*," Cliff answered. "My Uncle Feodor just told me to go to a house and wait. I got picked up after a couple of days."

"By *who*?"

"Some guys in a Lincoln limo like the one I drove around. They gave me a driver's permit and a Social Security card, told me I was fourteen again, and to keep my head down at Wolverine for four years. I'd be shacked up on long holidays and in the summer."

"Shacked up…where?"

"I went to a cabin in Minnesota in the summer, a trailer park in Florida in the winter. They provided everything; food, money, transportation, broads. All I *had* to do was *not* draw any attention, or they'd turn me over to the Pittsburgh PD."

"Then *you* screwed up."

"Yeah. They didn't know *how* to turn me in without exposing themselves. So they sent me to Texas, handed me a high school diploma and a thousand in cash, and said get lost and *not* to go back to Pennsylvania."

Can't take this anymore. "*We* need a break: been a *long* night. *Want* anything?" We strolled out of the interview room, quietly closed the door, and Nancy wrapped herself around me like she was drowning.

"*We got the bastards*, Nancy," I grinned after a *too*-long kiss, "we *got* 'em!"

"Davie, we *finally* did it," Ellen whispered, swooping in once more.

Morgan surprised Mike in the booth with a soft smooch before I heard him say, "I'm getting married in a few weeks."

"Me, too,"* Morgan smiled sweetly, "but we've been *five years* trying to get *this* much on the Newhouse bunch *and* verify what they're doing."

"Yeah," I said, squeezing Ellen before letting her go. "*Now*, we sort the evidence to burn them down and hopefully figure out who they're doing it *for*."

"Doing *what*," Mike frowned.

"Enabling interstate flight. Now, *maybe* illegal entry. *Wish* we could talk to the uncle," Ellen sighed, sweeping her hair back. "He was gunned down in '79."

Morgan stared at Cliff through the observation mirror. "Mike: how about *you* and *me* take a run at him, try for some *straight* answers about last Wednesday?"

Mike was *more* than willing…and Morgan in *that* skirt…

"Your fingerprints are all over two cars at a crime scene where people died last week, Cliff…or do you prefer Mario?" Morgan started…

And Cliff was most talkative. As we thought, JJ's friends and family were bait, and Testa was in nominal charge right up until he got shredded by a *shotgun* intended to stop *trucks*. Joe thought it was *funny*; JJ's execution *had* to take place in Detroit. But *then*…

---

* She and Jerry *had* set a date in January, finally.

"The fire at California Circle…." Mike asked.

"*That* gang-bang." Cliff sniffed. They got the wrong building; the Taylor's *were* the target.

"What was all *that* for?"

"The way *I* got it, week before last, a phone rang at the Newhouse office that was un*published*, un*listed*, un*distributed*, un-*everything* and was never *supposed* to ring unless…I *dunno*. But they started looking all over for a phone book that *somebody* lost *years* ago, saying, 'if Randy left it in *her* shit and *they* put *that* together, *we're* dead. Last week it rang *again*, and everybody's *freaked*.'"

"The phone book," I mumbled. "When *Mike* called…."

"The *first* call, though," Ellen asked.

"From the logs, it was one of those new robot-dialing telemarketers." Yep: they burned the place down in part because of a *robocall*.

"Then, somebody went into the hospital…."

"Charlie Parkinson," I said. "It was *him* in charge all along."

"…and Dryden tells me to burn the place down. Testa didn't know *anything* about it, got pissed because it drew unneeded attention. Joe *tried* to tell him it was part of *his* plan. *Somebody* called the office a couple hours later, and Joe shut up."

"Dollars to doughnuts it was Newhouse," Ellen declared.

"So, what do *you* think the Newhouse game plan is *now?*" Morgan asked, doing a *femme fatale* stretch.

"Dunno about Newhouse, but *Dryden's* got *something* cooking."

"What's *his* game?" Mike asked.

"All *I* know is…Elrath."

✳✳✳

"All of *that* was to bait JJ here," Leigh gasped when Mike explained it. We were back in the Troy agency Saturday afternoon, digesting Cliff's revelations, debriefing Leigh after her road trip to Essexville, and still trying to figure out *those kids*. *Why were they important to Newhouse?*

"*Looks* like it," Morgan shook her head. "And the fire was because they wanted to burn that phone book. So, they *are* twins?"

"Yeah," Leigh mumbled. "Randy has no idea."

"I think, *oytzer*, we showed that that family hasn't seen a Newhouse in a long time."

Leigh shook her head. "Randy said he expected to adopt his son... *why?* He's in Mary's custody, his wife. It's a *custody* matter, *not* a matter for adoption."

"A whole *lot* of things aren't adding up here," Ellen said.

"Our ONE source on *all* of *that* was my five-second verbal exchange with Randy, which I can *barely* remember," Leigh declared.

"Are you suggesting, my dear, that you could have got *any* element of *that* story *wrong*," Mike asked.

"Even if I only got the *basics* right, we never *verified any* of it."

Just as I thought... "We've got something *else* to think about," I said. "You left their house at 11:10. At 11:15, the unpublished voice line at *that* residence—one you called the other day, Mike—called Ingrid Torgensen. The call lasted 49 minutes."

"They both work for Parkinson Title and Trust." Mike looked cross. "What...?"

"Give Julia and her team a few more days; they'll figure it out," Ellen declared.

Morgan winked at Mike, then smiled at Leigh. "I kissed your Mike." Mike nodded, looked guilty.

Leigh looked back and forth at them, then at Ellen and me. Mike nodded, looked guilty. "Kiss her *back*, Sandy?" He looked even *more* sheepish. "*Yeah*, you *did*." She glared at Morgan. "Do that *often* on your job?"

"*Some*times," Ellen grinned. "We don't *actually arrest that* often, so..."

"This *was*..." Morgan smiled.

"*Very, very special*," I agreed.

Leigh glared mildly at all of us. "You guys owe *me*."

"Collect *now* if you want," I shrugged…not thinking that she would collect…like…*that*.

You *met* her, Beth. You *liked* her. *All* we *did* was *one unforgettable kiss*.

✳✳✳

"*So*, Mr. DeVere," Morgan started, "*thanks* for taking time out of your schedule on a Saturday evening."

"*Always* ready to help law enforcement," Max said expansively. His office behind the front desk of the Northwestern Hotel and Suites was only slightly cluttered, with no photographs, plaques, or anything *personal* in sight. "*What* can I do for you?"

"You're a part-*owner* of this place *and* the general manager," Julia smiled. Of course, it *was* public record, but her Uncle Kurt was *accommodating*.

"Yes." Max was one of those people you never notice because he just looked like everyone else. Creepy in a way.

"I *see*." Julia looked around at me; I was just observing this interview. "You *hired* Herman Jimenez last December. He was terminated for cause in January."

"If you *say* so," Max answered. "I don't keep all my employees in my head."

"I understand," Julia nodded. "And Chuck Wier? You employ *him* as well?"

"I'd *have* to look, but the name's *not* familiar."

"Huh," Julia said. "You *don't* know Chuck Wier?"

"Not *familiar*." Max did a ceiling search. "What makes *you* think…."

"He goes by Chuck *Wilson* here, but that's *not* his name," Morgan said, her voice even. "He's been identified as Charles Fredrick Wier; lived in Greenville as a kid, where *you're* from. His family's associated with the DeVere Organization." She paused, letting *that* sink in. "*Ring* any bells?"

"DeVere *Organization*," Max shook his head. "What's…"

"Your family's financial *network*," Morgan answered. "We *know* about it *and* its use of the Second Century Fund."

Max tried a deadpan, but his eyes became frightened. "I don't know *anything*...."

"*Yes*, you do," Morgan replied, her eyes burning onto his. "You know *enough* about Second Century to be *uncomfortable* with law enforcement's interest. Now: *about* Wier and Jimenez..."

"Well, now..." Max said, trying to break free of her stare, "I'd *have* to look...."

"*No*, you *don't*," Morgan declared. "You *know* who we're talking about. You *know* who they are. Who *told* you to *hire* them?"

"*No* one! *I'm* the general manager...."

"*Wrong* answer," Morgan whispered. "*Try* again."

And...*sproing*! Morgan had worked her particular magic on Max, but instead of *release*, she had instilled in him *unease; disquiet*. Not only were Max's *eyes* frightened, but so was the *rest* of him. He broke out in a sweat, blinking furiously but unable to look away from Morgan. "I got a phone call right after we opened, said 'hire Herman when he gets there.' I got an envelope with $20,000 dropped off at the desk the next day. In January, and again two weeks ago, a voice on the phone said hire Chuck under whatever name he's using." Max swallowed hard. "*Another* $20,000."

"Didn't strike you as *odd*," Julia asked.

"In my business, I've learned to *not* ask questions," Max croaked.

"*What* business is *that*?" Morgan's eyes didn't leave Max's.

"I...I manage businesses for the family." For twenty-odd years Max had managed seven hotels from Cleveland to Minneapolis, all of which had the DeVere Organization as shareholders. "*This* one, I used my *own* money...but I *couldn't* say no."

"And *now*," Morgan leaned forward slightly.

"Now..." Max croaked querulously.

"*Uncle* Kurt and his partners want to *talk* to you *now*." Julia gave her *most* disarming, cult-leader smile.

"We'll leave them *to* you," Morgan nodded, rising.

As we left, I glanced at Max behind his desk, having been reduced to gelatin in a shirt and tie. The *curious part* of me wanted to know how Morgan *did* that; the *smarter* part *didn't.*

✳✳✳

"Blessed morning. Who *is* this, please," the Mother Superior asked over the phone. Sid and I flew up to Copper Harbor *very* late Sunday.

"Claudia Ann Mueller-Elrath. I'm putting you on speaker. Who is *this*, please?"

"Blessed morning, Ms. Mueller-Elrath: you too are on the speaker. I am the Reverend Mother Pauline Maria of the St. Perpetua Sisters of the Blessed Oubliette. Who *else* is listening, please?"

"Leigh Elizabeth Taylor, ma'am."

"Michael Ethan Dietz, ma'am."

"John Jacob Elrath, ma'am."

"And Special Agent Clawson and Mr. Jackwell are *here,* on the other side of the screen." Because the St. Perpetua Order was cloistered, Sid and I were separated from the Reverend Mother by a heavy mosaic screen, through which we could only make out basic shapes. But her *voice* was loud and clear.

"*Dave*," Mike and Leigh asked.

"Yep," I answered. "Official *and* personal." It *was* official: we needed to know what hold this woman had on the Newhouse clan that they would try to replace her. The *personal* part…harder to describe.

Sid and I stayed quiet while the Reverend Mother verified who was on the other end of the phone, using the information I'd provided. St. Perpetua *was* a women's shelter, after all. Not everyone knew that they even *existed*; they *had* to be careful.

Then…"Very good. Sister Evangeline Marie is here."

"Hello." Lizzie cleared her throat. "I'm under instructions to tell you about my circumstances and why I came *here*. My name before *was* Lizzie Newhouse *or* Lizzie *Taylor*."

This was where Lizzie had lived since three days after she gave birth to her twins in 1971.

"Sister, *who* were your parents?" Leigh asked.

"Charity Taylor and Edward Newhouse. Mom's *sister* was your *grandmother*, Leigh."

Until a week before, Leigh's family—that she knew of—consisted of her parents and herself. Then came Wendy Corey… "Sister, where *is* your family?"

As Lizzie described her journey, I tried to imagine what having no family beyond your house might be like. It wasn't easy, 'cause it felt… hollow. Mine was neither big nor close, but at least I knew it was *there*.

"Pleased to *meet* you, cousin," Leigh answered. "But, as a military cop, I have to know: *why* are you talking to us *now?*"

"Call *me* Lizzie, please; it's what my family called me. Dad *hated* the name Leigh." I could hear Lizzie struggling. "The Church has grown weary of the *Newhouse's* irritation."

"Just where did you go *first*, Lizzie," I asked.

"Chicago. We saw the moon landing on a hotel room TV. That fall, Uncle RF put us in a big house in Essexville and came by every week. A man named Charlie Parkinson came by maybe twice a month—usually during the week. Some boys—Joe, *Sid* here, and Dave somebody—came around sometimes, usually with my cousin Randy. I *tried* to dodge *them*, but, as Charlie said *all the time*, they *were* paying the bills. Mary's part-time job didn't come *close*, and they *were* paying for her school…"

"That's Charlie, all right," JJ muttered. "He's my stepfather, Lizzie."

"My condolences to his wife…and you, JJ. I thought he was an awful man."

"A view many people share, Lizzie," Ann said. "What were these visits for?"

"They brought groceries *or* cash, or *both*." There was a whispered conversation on the other side of the screen before Lizzie came back quieter. "My friends, the Church is *ordering* me to tell you this."

"*Tell* them, Sister," Reverend Mother ordered quietly, a hand over the phone speaker.

"Reverend *Mother*…"

"*Sister*…"

"Very *well*, Reverend Mother, I'll *say it*. My sister and I were little more than *prostitutes*. New Year's Eve 1969 was the first *night I* slept with Randy." Silence. "But *he* was frustrated, and so was *I*."

"He *couldn't*…?" Leigh asked quietly.

"*No*." Lizzie struggled behind the screen. "*RF* and *Randy* traded beds the next morning. I can *still* smell Mary's perfume on him."

For the love of… Violation of the Mann Act. Human trafficking of the worst possible kind. RF took his nieces for his own pleasures and shared them with his brother-in-law. I can't remember being *so* pissed at *anyone* in my life as I was at that instant.

"Go on, Lizzie," Mike prodded.

No! Stop this NOW! I prayed Lizzie would get a sudden attack of laryngitis. She and I didn't hang out growing up, but I knew when a shy young woman was in deep pain, even behind a screen. "*Charlie* only wanted to *watch*."

"Watch *what*," JJ asked. *For GOD'S sake, man…*

"*Me* while I ate, watched TV, slept, studied, what*ever* as long as I had *nothing on*. He *paid* a hundred for an *hour* or a thousand for a *day*; what he called *shows*."

"Lizzie, would you like to pause; collect yourself?" Ann asked. *Capital idea; let's stop this and…*

"Thank you, Ann. I *would like* some refreshment. Reverend Mother brought tea." We couldn't see much, but I saw a flask pouring into teacups…Lizzie *choked* on it. "*That's not tea*, Reverend Mother!"

"Medicinal *whiskey*, my dear. We can *both* use some bracing this morning." The Reverend Mother pushed teacups under the screen. Neither Sid nor I was in the mood.

"A week of novenas for us both," Lizzie laughed. "In the summer of '70, RF staked *me* out as *his*, said Mary was *Randy's* because she *said she* could get him *done*. She *lied*, but we both felt sorry for poor Randy because RF demanded that *he*…and he was *so* frustrated *every* time. I was fifteen when I became pregnant and went to a school in Greenville…."

"Francis Hartmann," JJ said.

"*Yes.*"

"Lizzie," Leigh interrupted, "*when* did you get to Hartmann?"

"Sid drove me from Bay City to Greenville on the Saturday before Christmas in 1970; I was twelve weeks pregnant."

"You *might* have tried to meet me at the Spring Fling at Wolverine in April," JJ added.

"That's *possible*, JJ; I *was* there." Even through the screen, we could see her smile. "Have *any* of you *seen* my children? I *think* of them *constantly*, but I *never speak* of them as an act of obedience."

"I saw them Saturday, Lizzie," Leigh declared.

"How *are* they? Is Renée a *good girl*? I'm looking at pictures here… *my*, they are…."

"The twins are well, strong," Leigh added. "Randy is a scholar; Renée is his best friend. She *seems* like a fine young woman. Her brother said *she* was born first?"

"Yes. When Dr. Best delivered her, Mary took *her* away; I was devastated that I couldn't *see* her, but I could *hear* her. I named her Renée the moment the doctor said, 'it's a girl,' but RF *demanded* a son.

"Then came Randy, and a girl my age I didn't know took *him* to RF in the waiting room. *His* name—Randall Fred Newhouse, the Fifth—*I* didn't choose. RF was excited, but *I* could only cry. Excuse me." Lizzie sobbed for a moment and took another slug of whiskey. "*Two* weeks of novenas."

"You were *still* at Hartmann, Lizzie," Leigh asked.

"Yes, their maternity clinic." She cleared her throat. "Oh, I'll do a *month* of novenas." She knocked another slug back. "Now I'm tipsy for the first time since I was fifteen—*whew*. The next day was a *perfect* spring day, and Sid came: I was no longer pregnant, but I had *no* babies, and I wanted to *die*. He handed me an envelope containing a one-way bus ticket to San Francisco and $100. Then, he drove me *here*. We prayed the Rosary all the way from Greenville. Sid never *touched* us though he had many opportunities. I even offered, but he wasn't—*isn't*—like the others." She put her hand under the screen next to our neglected teacups. "I still *have* that bus ticket."

Sid had his little grin on his face. He didn't move.

"Lizzie; are *you* OK," Ann asked.

"I'm *fine*, Ann. I haven't spoken of *any* of this since I was preparing for my vows. When I turned eighteen, I decided to stay here to help other women in this little place of forgetting."

"Did you ever *see* their birth certificates, Lizzie," Leigh asked.

"Sid filched Renée's. Leigh Elizabeth *Taylor* is recorded as their mother—even *though* that *wasn't* my legal name; the father is blank."

"*Randy* has the other one," I added.

Ann asked, "Lizzie: how would the *Newhouses* have known *you* were *there*?"

"I believe I can answer that," the Reverend Mother interjected. "Several women left between the time Lizzie came to us and when she took her new name. Our charges all live together, go to school together, pray together. Any one of them might have told *someone* about Lizzie; *they* are under no obligation of silence, though we *ask* for it."

"The kids say they write to you, but you *don't* write back. Why?" Leigh asked.

"I never know what to *say*. My order sends cards, but responding *personally*…I just…."

351

"Just answer *their* letters, Lizzie," JJ murmured. "*Any answer* is better than *no answer…*" I listened to JJ talk about the emptiness and the pain of *alone*. Other than a few days—*hours* in comparison—when I first arrived in the dorms and when I first moved to Virginia, I'd never felt as *alone* as *he* had. I don't know that *anyone* there had.

And when he was done, I could sense that Lizzie felt it too. "I believe you are right, JJ. I sense that you *know* what *that* feels like. May God bless you for your *patience* with my sex."

"Lizzie," Ann sighed. "Did you seek shelter because of *what* their father is?"

"Because of my *mortal sins*, Ann. I can't *say* enough novenas for those."

"You were a *girl*, Lizzie," Mike answered, "barely fourteen and, from what you've *said*, a sex slave. You had no *choice*. You and Mary were *each other's* support; even if it were *possible*, you *couldn't* just walk away. RF should have been *protecting* you, *not* exploiting you."

"I *thank* you for saying that, Mike," Lizzie replied. "And…Dave's given me pictures of my children. Oh, *how* I would…" She stretched her hand under the screen; I did the same, *without* touching.

"You *may*, dear," Mother Superior interrupted. "You *may leave* the cloister, transfer to Bay City. It's *possible*."

"*May I*," Lizzie gasped. "*Oh*…oh, *how I*…."

"We'll discuss it with the bishop, dear."

"I should *go*…."

"Lizzie, please," Leigh added. "Our cousin Wendy Corey has a family Bible that has generations of Taylors recorded in it; it's how I knew *you* even existed. Can *she*…"

"I would be pleased to *hear from* Cousin Wendy. Have her write." Silence before she added, "may God bless you all. Perhaps we shall *meet*, cousin?"

"Yes," Leigh answered before the Reverend Mother hung up.

Through the screen, I could see her dabbing at her eyes as the call ended. "Want me to come back, Lizzie," I asked quietly.

"I'll be all right, Dave." She folded her hands in her lap, gazing at the photos. "They look *happy*."

"Mary *says* they are," I replied. "I *think* Renée has a boy down the street."

"Oh, *my*," Lizzie said brightly. "I *do* hope she's a *good* girl."

"They've been raised in the Church, Sister," Sid added. "I have First Communion and Confirmation photos if you'd like them."

"*Lizzie* to *you*, Sid. You've been keeping track? You *said* you would."

"I *keep* my promises, Lizzie. You said you wanted to know only significant events." He shrugged. "I was waiting for a graduation, a wedding, or a child."

"Yes, that *is* what I asked." Lizzie sighed heavily. "Mother Superior: what you said about transferring…is that *possible?*"

"It *is*," the older woman answered. "In fact, the Sisters in Bay City are looking for nurses. Unfortunately, you would have to leave our cloister, but you could remain in our *Order*."

"*If* I leave, I *can't* come back?"

"*Not* necessarily," Mother Superior answered. "If you don't give up your vows, there's no reason to think you *couldn't* come back here."

"How many nuns have children," I wondered…like any *non*-Catholic.

"You'd be surprised," Lizzie, Sid, and the Mother Superior all answered at once before the Mother Superior continued. "Unwed, like Lizzie; widows like myself. So *many* laypeople forget that we *are women* who *became* nuns." She chuckled. "You may even acquire a taste for whiskey, Sister. Drinking in moderation *is* permitted outside our cloister."

Lizzie giggled brightly, "*without* the novenas, Mother?"

"*Without* the novenas, my dear."

I like to think Lizzie grinned at that. "Lizzie: Mary wanted me to tell you she *thinks* she understands."

"I *think* she understands a great deal more than she lets on, Dave," Lizzie said. "If you see her before *I* do, tell her…thank you for raising my children."

"Of course."

Everything that Lizzie said made sense; it filled in blanks that we thought were unfillable. The Mann Act *had* no statute of limitations since Lizzie became pregnant when she was fourteen. We *could* nail all of 'em to a federal wall. I wondered if anyone would mind if I handcuffed Charlie to his bed.

I flashed back to my hot afternoon in Kimmie's cool basement, learning about sex from a generous young woman. It made me sad that Lizzie's introduction to *that* joy had been *so* sullied and brutal as to be *criminal.*

✳✳✳

"I thought I should let you know," Leigh said on the phone Tuesday night. "I met Sid's source this afternoon."

"Ah," I said, attentive. I wouldn't know his source from Adam unless he banged me upside the head and *told* me who he was, but I *tried* to sound nonchalant.

"She told me there's a joint Greenville Investment Trust account with Parkinson Title…closed out now, she said. *Should* I…?"

She? "Put it in your after-action; we'll figure it out. Did she give you *any* idea as to what her *position* is?"

"Bookkeeper and Randy's girlfriend. She was in school with me."

She'd be in a position to know many, many secrets. "You *know* her?"

"Not *personally*; it was a big school with lots of cliques. Her name's Megan Cornwell. She talked about some other stuff, *probably* not germane to the investigation."

"*Any* idea as to what drove her to…?"

"My wedding night: it was *her* and *Sid* that got me away from Randy because they knew Joe and the others would *do* to me. *They* decided *she'd* work both sides of the fence."

"Brave woman." *Untrained double-agent for thirteen years AND sleeping with a principal? Brave AND smart. Maybe WE could hire her…*

"Joe has something planned for tomorrow."

"We'd expect that." I waited. "Nervous about tomorrow?" Her wedding with Mike had been abruptly moved up from the first week in December to the Wednesday before Thanksgiving.

"Some." Silence. "Dave: we don't *know* each other, but what you *did* for Lizzie…."

"Just what a former neighbor would do, Leigh."

"Sell *that* load to someone who might *buy* it, Dave. 'Night."

How much *could* I do to honor a *most* generous first lover *and* her friend's sister?

✳✳✳

"Congratulations," I smiled at Leigh and Mike as they entered the atrium after their wedding. That afternoon, I was to be on a *chartered* flight to DC as soon as the reception was over. The night before, each of us had a note slipped under our doors from an outfit called CloudWays. It said our transportation would be available at the Pontiac International Airport that afternoon. We would have the *option*, if desired or required, of returning the following Monday using the same accommodations.

How this was arranged and by whom was a mystery…until I did a little research, finding that JJ was on the board of CloudWays. He was almost certainly the wealthiest Sergeant First Class in *anyone's* army.

It wasn't five minutes later that Randy made an appearance. A young woman held him by the arm; his father lingered in the lobby. "All I want is to say a good word to Leigh," Randy said. The young woman nodded.

I let them through and Randy, true to his word, exchanged a few words and a hug with Leigh before being led away and seated by his companion. The woman came back to where I was just as the brunch began. "Megan Cornwell," she sighed. "I've been with the Newhouse firm as…"

"You're *talking* to the FBI, you know," I said lightly. "You've *been* talking to the FBI."

"*I know*. And I *may* be looking for a job after I give you the books I've got in my car." She shifted around, looked back at Randy. "Randy...*poor* Randy. His *father*...asshole...has been using everyone for *ages*."

"Thought about law enforcement?"

"From time to time."

We started background checks on Megan *and* Mary when we got back to Washington. Maybe we *could* use another bookkeeper...or two...

✳✳✳

"*Restful* holiday," Ernie asked Mike and Leigh. We'd gotten back to Detroit the Monday after Thanksgiving and got the news that Charlie Parkinson had died that morning.

"Yeah, sort of," Leigh sighed. "Thanksgiving is always a big party for the Dietz family. When we got back *here*, RF was waiting for us in the lobby. He told us that he brought the kids down to see Phyllis before she passed—coincidentally just down the hall from Charlie. *She* died a few hours later. *Then* he told us that last October Charlie declared 'that rat bastard'—JJ—was going to be dead at his feet...and that his *mom* would *know* who ordered it."

"Confirms what we thought," I said. "How one man could hate *so* much...."

"Yeah, but," Mike said, "on the *brighter* side, RF gave us *this*." He placed a thick envelope on the table between us. "There's $70,000 in there for property taxes and insurance. He *also* paid off their mortgage and created a trust for both of them."

"He *also* admitted to being in bed with the DeVere/Wier Organization," Leigh continued, "and that he knows the state's attorney is coming for him."

"We'll *persuade* the state's attorney *not* to seize *those* assets," Ernie intoned. "The sins of *this* father will *not* visit *these* children, either."

"Gramma," Julia smiled, "we need to talk. *This* is my partner, Dave Clawson, and my boss, Ernie Packard." We met in Stella's living room the day after Charlie's funeral.

"Pleased to *meet* you, Mr. Packard," Stella smiled. "Mr. Clawson and I *have* met. You want to talk about what Charlie was into?"

"Yes, Mrs. Parkinson," I nodded. "I don't know what your son has shared with you already…."

"Just some vague details," JJ said. "She knows he owned Wolverine, was into some shady business."

We ran down the essence of the Parkinson/Newhouse operation, leaving out details they simply didn't need to know. Then Ernie said, "then your son stumbled onto an early benefactor of the operation."

"I did," JJ looked surprised.

I pushed a picture at him. "Remember seeing *him* at Wolverine? In the library…he had no nametag."

JJ looked, squinted, pulled out his glasses. "Um…no. I don't remember him. Who *is* he, other than a No-Name?"

"Well, he's *one* reason for all that shooting a couple weeks ago." Julia smiled brightly. "To bait you back to Detroit…so you can be *killed* here."

"Because Charlie wanted *me* dead here," JJ blurted.

"So did others, but that was *part* of it, yes," Ernie said. Then he got into how Newman/Forsythe/Whalen was involved in the disappearance of Jimmy Hoffa.

Although Stella appeared to be listening passively, I could see she was getting angrier by the moment. "Is he still in danger?" `

"Unlikely. We *know* who's been paying all the money. but…."

"How much," Stella asked. It wasn't greed in her eyes; it was *rage*.

"Your husband had been getting as much as $10,000,000 a year for his cooperation since 1967." Ernie folded his hands. "An organization called the Second Century Fund was collecting *four times* that."

Then Julia said, "Grampa's been giving them copies of your letters home. *That's* how they knew where you and Mike and Leigh were all the time," looking at JJ.

"Why Detroit," Stella growled. *NOW* there was *fury*, a fury like I'd never seen in a 60-something woman.

"*That* was Mr. Parkinson's condition for his participation," I said. "Simple as that, we think. He wanted *you*, ma'am, to know that *he* was responsible for your son's death."

Sometimes, you get treated to seeing a human being *so* in control of their faculties that they can choose *not* to act on them regardless of impulses. *That* was Stella that afternoon, who went from raging-fury-in-a-chair to ever-so-polite-hostess in a matter of moments. She nodded graciously as we left, but JJ followed us. "How clean *is* Mom, really, Jules?"

"Clean *enough*, Sergeant Elrath," Ernie said. "We shall make *certain* of it."

Julia winked, *not our first rodeo, buddy.*

✳✳✳

"*Chief* Mueller-Elrath, this is Dave Clawson. May I speak to your husband, please?"

"Yessir," JJ answered. I called him Sunday afternoon. Finally, we had enough on enough people to have the state's attorney sign off on our referrals on Saturday. We spent twelve hours coordinating the arrests. Hence...

"JJ, we're serving warrants in Greenville tomorrow morning. It might be a *great* deal less *trouble* to gain access to the Wolverine grounds if a representative of the *owner* were present. We know that Joe Dryden and Chuck Weir are holed up there; we think *Herman's* there too. Want in on the kill?"

Like I *had* to ask...

The Battle of Greenville

Or, Getting the Rats Out Of the Traps

"**J**esus…" I moaned, watching the Air Force plane unload. Most of the Special Projects Division marched across the Grand Rapids airport hardstand before dawn that Monday morning…

"And *Mary*," Morgan agreed. The sun wasn't up yet; it was cold, but Morgan was in a flimsy, loose blouse and skirt. She made *me* cold just *looking* at her…but she was unaffected.

"*And* Joseph," Frank added. We were part of the advanced party, sent to arrange ground transportation and coordinate with the other federal and local agencies for the raids. There would be over a hundred federal officers from as far away as Cincinnati and nearly twice as many state and county badges.

Greenville had a police force of *ten*. We could bury *them* in nylon jackets.

We expected to meet the rest of the federal officers, the district commander of the state troopers, and the county sheriff at the truck stop west of town. But, much to our surprise…*they* were there ahead of *us*. We also met *most* of the Greenville PD there.

We had four targets in Greenville—Wolverine, Francis Hartmann, police headquarters, and Greenville Seat Belt. State troopers were *also* going to be at the county records office in Stanton to stop any *sudden* fires.

We were also hitting three dozen *other* targets simultaneously, from the Newhouse lawyer's offices in Detroit to the private residences of *both* Randy's *and* their executive offices *and* their construction sites in five counties. It was one of the most extensive federal raids in Michigan history. The trigger would be when the Greenville police chief arrived at headquarters.

Ellen and I pulled the trigger just after 9 that morning.

"James Franklin Best," I loudly announced, standing in front of the chief's desk. "*You* are under arrest for the subornation of perjury, for violation of the Mann Act, and for aiding and abetting the escape of fugitives from justice."

"*You* gotta be kidding," the chief laughed. "You even got my *name* wrong."

"Nope," Melissa grinned. "You *ain't* Wayne Rudder, cause Wayne Rudder with *your* supposed record died in 1976; a *very* suspicious car accident a week before *you* showed up here. Wayne Rudder's prints belonged to a John Doe in the Ingham County morgue who was cremated in '77 after nobody claimed him."

"But we *found* him in our new database: you know, the one we *just* put together," I said. "We were *finally* able to check your prints against it. *Yours* turned up as belonging to James Franklin Best, part-time loan shark, part-time pimp, and blackmailer in Chicago."

"*I* supplied the exemplars, *asshole*," Melissa sneered. "When you visited my *apartment* that time."

"You disappeared in '67 at age 25," Ellen added. "Your picture in the Wolverine yearbook for 1968 said you were a tender lad in high school. JJ Elrath picked you out, named *you* as Nestor Boehlke, the name the Second Century Fund used to *hide* your sorry ass at Wolverine."

Boehlke/Best no longer laughed. "When Wolverine tossed you out," I said, "somebody said, 'we've got an idea.' And *you* stepped into Wayne Rudder's shoes after *you* killed him...but we can't prove *that*."

"And then it got *worse*," Ellen went on. "Wolverine started taking on more refugees for more money every year. Like you, they stayed for four years then moved on with new names and a *big* hole where those *other* lives had been. Not a bad racket. But unlike you, *they* paid attention to their instructions."

"But the murders continued," I added, "with the delinquents killing the snitches and the stubborn. JJ Elrath—remember *him*—he still remembered enough to frighten you *and* the other Four Horsemen… and that *other* guy."

"That No-Name who JJ *tried* to talk to," Ellen said. "The one who told *your* mob to *get* Elrath."

"I want a *deal*," Boehlke/Best grumbled.

"Stand up," I said, "I'm gonna lock you in your own jail." I motioned to Mellissa. "And I don't think a *single one* of your officers is going to help you."

"If they *do*, there are a dozen state troopers outside," Ellen said. "Now, we have to…" She stopped at the sounds of distant gunfire. "C'mon Davie."

***

"*Sonofabitch*," Dusty growled. "I'll be a *sonofabitch*." He pointed at forty guys in handcuffs, corralled by the marshals along one wall of the drill floor. "Been looking for *some* of these guys for a decade."

"No-Names," I said. "*All* No-Names."

"At a hundred grand apiece a year," Julia sighed. "Newhouse *and* Grampa invested about half of *their* end on the various expenses to keep the operation—and the beasts here—from attracting attention."

"Like the police chief," I said, "who is now sitting in his own jail."

"And *this* guy," Dusty pointed at a dumpy guy wearing a major's rank, "their provost marshal, *saw* all the shit go down here…but nobody ever *asked him*."

"We'll ask *him* plenty," the county sheriff declared.

Across the big drill floor, JJ and Leigh were answering questions from two Greenville PD officers. JJ nursed a bruised shoulder from a Mini-14 that he wielded. He shot Boniface Pale off a light tower at two hundred yards, plus four foot-long loudspeakers at up to *three* hundred.

I listened, flicking back and forth between the officers and their sources. This wasn't a custodial interrogation but a series of questions about *stuff* that happened. Leigh had apparently beat the *crap* out of Rick Stutz outside the gate (she was a black belt in karate), but hadn't *killed* anyone with her weapon. However Joe's face was severely cut from some pictures that she shot up while missing him. The large stain on *both* sides of his pants was Joe's *worst* injury.

"So, let me get this straight," one officer said at last. "*You* knew the dimensions of this building from fifteen years ago and told *her*," he pointed at Leigh, "*how far* and *at what angle* to run to get to the commandant's office."

"Yeah. I marched around this damn place most of the weekends I was here," JJ sighed.

"Then *you*," he pointed at Leigh, "what, just took his word for it and dashed over *there?*"

"While *he* shot the door open, yeah," Leigh smiled at JJ...then gave him a wink, like Julia and Ellen and Beth and I had *been* sharing...

That wink.

They might be married to *other* people, but *this* was a silent declaration of trust.

Unmistakable.

Epilogue

Or, A Journey into Sequel-Land

S o.

Now you know how I got to the SPD; how we generated a paper database to close files nobody cared about, created because of Hoover's paranoia. And, how we found the truth about how Dusty's stepson died so tragically…using those files nobody gave a *damn* about.

And what happened to Jimmy Hoffa's body.

And my very first arrest, after six years in the Bureau. About average, I'm told.

We closed 295 Liberty Bell Files related to Wolverine, the Wier/DeVere Organization, and the Second Century Fund in the first quarter of 1987.

Harry retired within a year; Grace was shipped out to San Francisco to be Senior Resident; Helen was sent to Albany.

In March '87, three 60-foot containers full of Liberty Bell Files arrived in Quantico. The concept of a *death march* was *not* lost on us.

Ernie retired in '88; his stepson Dennis would join the marshal's; his stepdaughter Farrah would go into to the *Secret Service*, of all things.

The Packard System had gone the way of disco and Rubik's Cube by then.

Winifred Marjorie Malone—Freddie—was sponsored into art school by Senator Max Ellington. Not *all* politicians are wastes of space.

But there was *still* Neitelsmidt, the name that *still* kept popping up all over.

Of course, those are stories I'll tell *later* while we're closing *more* Liberty Bell Files.

BUT...

They didn't exist...nope, *never. They* would have been illegal. And so, too, would the SPD...be unlawful, that is. It *could* not—and thus, *did not—even exist.*

And that Fourth Department? Utter nonsense! Forget I said *anything* about *that. Pure* fiction...

So help me Hanna...

Lightning Source UK Ltd.
Milton Keynes UK
UKHW021059050821
388368UK00012B/716